Exquisite Justice

A Marc Kadella Legal Mystery

by

Dennis L. Carstens

Previous Marc Kadella Legal Mysteries

The Key to Justice

Desperate Justice

Media Justice

Certain Justice

Personal Justice

Delayed Justice

Political Justice

Insider Justice

email me at: dcarstens514@gmail.com

ONE

Damone Watson, his ever-present Bible tucked securely under his left arm, stood in the doorway and surveilled the scene. Damone was in the entryway of the Minneapolis City Council meeting room. He was half an hour early for the meeting, and the room was already full. About two-thirds of the faces were black, and the rest were a combination of white and Hispanic. Almost every one of them was here to pay homage to Damone. He was here to receive a plaque of appreciation from the city council and a key to the city from the mayor.

Damone stood in the doorway for less than thirty seconds waiting for it to happen. Someone in the audience noticed him and a buzz went through the room. As it did, he went inside and began to humbly work the crowd. By this point, everyone was on their feet, applauding as he strolled around smiling, shaking hands, and acknowledging the adulation while making his way to the front row. Of course, three seats in the middle of the front row had been reserved for the evening's man of the hour and his two aides/bodyguards. Before taking his seat, Damone, holding the Bible in his left hand, pleasantly waved with his right.

Damone Watson was born forty-three years ago on the South side of Chicago. His father, Victor Watson, was a part-time construction worker and a full-time drunk. Victor's brother, Albert, was a business manager for a local union which allowed him to get no-show jobs for Victor which kept the family afloat. That is until Victor got into an argument with a man in a bar over some minor transgression. Within seconds, a push and a shove escalated into a one-sided gunfight that left Victor on the floor with a third eye in his forehead.

Damone, all of eleven years old at the time, was now the man of the house. His younger brother, Jeron, age nine, and two younger sisters, Jamella and Elesha, six-year-old twins, all looked up to their big-brother for support.

Their mother, Danielle, had barely an eighth-grade education. Minimal job skills and experience made her almost unemployable, except for the most menial of jobs; minimum wage in the hotels downtown doing maid and laundry service.

Uncle Albert did what he could until he was caught up in a union shakedown scam six months after Victor's death. Because all of his co-

conspirators sang like canaries to the prosecution, Albert ended up the patsy. A ten-year sentence he would not survive in a federal prison ended his contributions to his nieces and nephews.

Before his twelfth birthday, Damone was a first-class dope slinger for a local street gang. The Parker Boy Crips, named for a local park, were a small collection of wannabe tough guys with a one-block turf to call their own. Little did they know that the young Damone was the best thing to happen to them.

By the time he was fourteen, helped by a borderline genius IQ, Damone had become the de facto gang leader. By the time he was twenty, his little gang had grown to over two hundred members and Damone Watson's income was in excess of a hundred thousand dollars a month. It would have been considerably more except Damone knew how to buy loyalty. He had also ruthlessly eliminated the real competition for the top spot. Damone had personally put seven people in the cemetery. It all changed shortly after his twenty-second birthday.

His eighth personal homicide became his undoing. The leader of a rival gang became a little too bold intruding on Damone's turf. Damone knew the young man, and he believed the two of them had a turf understanding. Instead, the rival decided to test Damone with a minor incursion across the border. Damone knew an example had to be made. Except, this time, there were witnesses including an undercover cop. To compound his carelessness—some would say arrogance—he failed to dispose of the gun. When he was arrested, the gun was found in the wall safe of Damone's luxury apartment.

During the trial, after pleading self-defense, his lawyer managed to convince the jury that his fear of the rival had some merit but not much. Instead of premeditated first-degree murder and a life sentence, Damone received a break. The jury came back with a second-degree verdict instead.

The judge, an older black man, thoroughly fed up with the South Chicago chaos, was clearly displeased with the verdict. During Damone's sentencing hearing, the judge spent a half-hour verbally hammering him. Unable to give Damone the life sentence the judge believed he so richly deserved, he gave him the maximum twenty years. The judge also put a lengthy letter in the file to let the parole board know how he felt. He wanted Damone to serve every minute of it. The letter worked. Despite the parole board having been convinced of Damone's conversion to Christianity while in prison, he did the full twenty.

Upon his release, he went back to Chicago for a short while before moving to Minneapolis. In the nine months Damone had lived there, the city had come to embrace him as a gifted community organizer and role model. Gang violence was down, two new first-class community centers were being built, school attendance in the black neighborhoods was up, and cocaine sales had practically dried up. Damone, while outwardly humble, inwardly was delighted to take full credit for all of it.

At precisely 7:00 P.M., the thirteen members of the city council and the mayor came into the room. As they filed in, every one of them looked at Damone, smiled and nodded their head at him. The thirteen city council members were made up of six whites; four women, two men and seven blacks; five women, two men. There were no Asians, Hispanics or Muslims. The council president was one of the white women, Patti Chenault. The mayor was a white man, Dexter Fogel.

For the next hour plus, each of the fourteen in turn, including the mayor who went last, took four to five minutes for a brief speech to lay accolades on the man of the hour. In reality, the show was for the cameras. There were local TV news cameras in back getting film for the 10:00 P.M. broadcasts. The politicians, being politicians, used the opportunity to make sure the city's residents knew they were all on the Damone Watson bank wagon.

And why not? Damone was their success story. A tall, attractive, intelligent, articulate black man, who was sacrificing his own life for social justice; a troubled young man from a broken home. A murdered father, a struggling mother trying her best to keep her family together on the mean streets of Chicago. What choice—the media loved to point out—did the young Damone have but to be drawn into a street gang?

Then, a near tragedy for him. A gunfight—many said it was self-defense—and another young black man was railroaded by the criminal justice system into an undeserved prison term. But instead of turning him even more bitter, angrier, more anti-social, Damone Watson found Jesus and has now dedicated himself to helping others. To lift children out of the grip of generational poverty was a wonderful story of redemption. The media and political class ate it up with a spoon.

There were only a few minor matters on the council's agenda following the paean to Damone. By 8:30, the assemblage was starting to thin out and by 9:15, the meeting was adjourned.

Damone and his bodyguards, along with a small group of admirers, took the tunnel under Fifth Street to go back to their car. They were parked in the ramp below the government center. Ever mindful of his image, Damone's transportation was a modest five-year-old Chevy Tahoe. Not the shiny, new Cadillac Escalade he would have preferred.

The two aides/bodyguards—Lewis Freeh and Monroe Ervin—were each six-foot-four and a solid two fifty to two sixty. And well-armed. When they reached the Tahoe, Lewis got in the driver's seat while Monroe opened the passenger side back door for Damone. Monroe quickly joined Lewis up front and a minute later they drove out onto Fourth Avenue. Monroe shifted around to look at his boss.

"I got a text during the meeting from one of Jalen's people," Monroe said. He was referring to Councilman Jalen Bryant. The text message came from his campaign manager, Kordell Glover.

"Now what?" an obviously irritated Damone replied.

"Same thing," Monroe said. "When can we meet?"

"You gonna endorse him?" Lewis asked while looking at Damone in the mirror.

"We'll see," Damone answered.

"You think he's serious about his big crusade?"

Damone heartily laughed and said, "Of course, he's a politician. They're all serious when running for office." Then Damone turned serious and said, "That's what I need to find out."

Damone had converted a small, run-down office building on Plymouth Avenue in North Minneapolis. It was a three story. On the first floor, it was converted into a place where neighborhood kids could hang out. There were two pool tables, three rooms with TV's and a hoops court next door.

The second floor was a set of offices for Damone's business. His office was twenty feet deep and the entire width of the building. It was in the very back of the building with eight windows. The glass in all eight of them had been replaced with one-way glass. Damone could see out, but no one could see in. The office was paneled and furnished expensively enough to make most Fortune 500 CEOs envious.

To maintain his humble, modest image, he never met outsiders in his office. He had a conference room to use for that. It held an oval conference table with squared off ends on each end. There were eight comfortable yet relatively inexpensive leather and chrome armchairs around it. The only windows were the tinted exteriors and the interior walls were paneled with modest, walnut paneling. Nice, but hardly ostentatious. It served well his "man of the people" image.

The third floor was his home. The entire five thousand square feet had been remodeled into a two-bedroom and three-bath luxury apartment, always secured by alarms and armed guards; mostly Lewis and Monroe.

For an hour and a half after arriving back at his office, Damone was on today's burner phone making calls. He never used a phone for more than one day. It was a touch inconvenient, but he was not paranoid, he was careful.

Shortly after 11:00, while he was sipping his Cognac, there was a knock on the door. Before he could respond, Lewis opened it and stepped aside for Damone's late-night guest.

Lewis closed the door behind her and took up his position guarding it again. Damone casually sipped his drink while the woman walked toward him. She reached the left-hand side of his huge, antique mahogany desk and stopped. So far, neither had spoken a word.

While he watched, the city council president, Mrs. Patti Chenault, pulled the zipper in the back of her dress down and let the dress fall to the floor. She stood before Damone dressed in a white lace, see-through bra, a white lace garter belt holding up mid-thigh, white silk stockings and high heeled spikes. For a woman pushing fifty, she pulled it off quite well. A twenty-year-old would get horned up as quickly as Damone did looking at her.

"Well, what do you think?" she asked with her best sultry voice.

"It's okay," Damone said with a shrug.

"Asshole," she said with a soft laugh.

She moved to him, and as he sat in the chair, she straddled his knees. While he ran his hands over her, she unbuckled his belt and opened his pants. She reached inside his underwear, smiled and said, "It's okay. Junior is ready to go."

"He's always like that," Damone bragged.

Patti stood up and pulled his pants and underwear down to his ankles. She moved up and this time, straddled his lap.

"Ahhh! Oh yeah," she purred. "That will do just fine."

TWO

"Are you sure you want to do this?" Maddy Rivers asked Marc Kadella.

They were in Marc's townhouse getting ready to start their day. Marc was becoming a successful criminal defense lawyer. He was in his early forties, a once divorced father of two young adult children. Eric, his twenty-year-old son, and Jessica, his eighteen-year-old daughter, were both in college.

Marc was also a solo practitioner and rented office space from another lawyer, Connie Mickelson. It was in the Reardon Building on Lake and Charles ten minutes from downtown Minneapolis. There was a total of four lawyers, including Connie, who shared the expense of three staff members. The third lawyer was Barry Cline, a litigator trying to do only business litigation. The fourth was another man several years older than Marc and Barry. His name was Chris Grafton and had a thriving corporate practice primarily for small to mid-size businesses.

Their staff consisted of two legal assistants—Sandy Compton and Carolyn Lucas, whose husband was a St. Paul police detective, John. The final member of the merry little band was an outstanding paralegal, Jeff Modell.

Even though none of them were formally in business together, they were all good friends and helped each other without question. It was Carolyn, like a good top-sergeant, who ran the place and kept the wheels turning.

Maddy Rivers was a private investigator who originally came to work on cases for Marc with the recommendation of a PI friend of both of them, Tony Carvelli.

Before moving to Minnesota, Maddy had been a police officer with the Chicago P.D. A tall, statuesque beauty, on a foolish whim had posed for Playboy magazine. The immaturity of most of the CPD had driven her out of Chicago.

Over the years, without even realizing it was happening, Marc and Maddy had grown close. Recently each of them had almost died. Marc was the target of a hit and run "accident." Maddy had been shot while they pursued that case and broke open a serious conspiracy involving stock manipulation, insider trading, political corruption and murder.

Almost losing each other had caused the two of them to realize how much they meant to each other. Because of it, Marc and Maddy finally admitted how much they loved each other, and a deep romance had resulted.

"Yes," Marc replied to her question. "I need to do this," he continued while Maddy adjusted the knot in his tie.

"Why are you wearing a tie?" she asked.

"I don't know. A habit, I guess. Besides, it's always good to look like a lawyer if you're going to prison. I think it gives you a better chance to get out."

"Why? Because they don't want you contaminating the inmates?"

Marc paused then said, "That's a good point. I hadn't thought of that, but it could be the reason."

"Be careful," she said as she kissed him. Being almost as tall as Marc, she did not have to look up to him when she did this.

"Yes, Mom," he sullenly said.

"Hey, Bub," she said poking him in the chest with an index finger. "You started this…"

"Am I ever going to hear the end of that?"

"No! I'm going to enjoy holding it over your head. And I'm going to worry about you. Get used to it. Don't you worry about me?"

Marc silently thought about the question. The honest answer was to say no because she was far more capable of taking care of herself than him. Plus, she carried a gun.

"Well?"

"Of course, I worry about you," he said.

"But you had to think about it?"

"No. But you can take care of… wait. I didn't mean…oh god, I'm in trouble again."

"You're in a hole, babe. Stop digging," she laughed. "I have to go meet a new client. A business guy Tony tossed to me. And I need to stop at my place first."

She kissed him again and said, "I'll see you later. Give me a call and let me know how it went. This is a little weird."

Maddy turned to walk toward the front door. She looked back and said, "Love you. See you later."

Marc said, "Love you too. I'll call." Then under his breath, he said, "What did I get myself into?"

"I heard that!" she yelled as she opened the door.

When the door closed behind her, Marc quietly said to himself, "Great! That will give me something to look forward to tonight."

Marc turned onto the frontage road and drove past the sign that read Columbia Correctional Institution. He was arriving at a maximum-security prison in Portage, WI. Stopping for lunch at a Wendy's in Wisconsin Dells had pushed the drive time to a little more than four hours, perfectly timed for his one o'clock meeting.

He found a spot in the parking lot marked for visitors. As he walked toward the imposing structure, even though it was warm, early-summer weather, Marc felt a slight chill. Despite what certain big-mouth politicians liked to spread, even a so-called country club prison was still a prison. And a max-security was a scary place.

Marc was meeting a former client who had been transferred to this facility. He was here at the client's request, and Marc had made arrangements with the warden himself. Despite the presence of the warden to greet him—Marc had called ahead—he still had to go through the entire security screening process. At 1:10 the warden led Marc into the secured visitor's area.

As he entered, he immediately saw to his left, a row of booths. Each one was equipped with a telephone to talk to the inmate. There was bulletproof Plexiglas all the way to the ceiling. On the far end was an observation room with a corrections officer inside to observe and monitor.

"Take whatever one you want," the warden said indicating the empty booths.

"How is he?" Marc asked.

"Health-wise he's fine. He's only been here a couple of months. According to the staff he seems to have settled right in. I let them know you're here. He'll be brought in any minute."

"Thanks, Warden," Marc replied.

"You're a lawyer. Legally, you can see him whenever you want." The warden shrugged. He pointed at the observation booth and continued, "Obviously, we can't monitor your conversation. But he'll be watching. When you're done just wave to him to let him know, and someone will come and get you."

As the two men shook hands, the secured door in the inmates' area opened. A man Marc would not have recognized came in wearing blue

8

prison dungarees. Despite the fact he was barely in his sixties, his hair and beard were snow white. He was sporting a full beard, and his hair was at least six inches longer, slicked back and three inches over his collar. He had also aged ten years, even though it was less than three years since Marc had last seen him.

Marc sat down in the booth he was standing next to and picked up the phone. The inmate did the same.

"Hello, Judge," Marc said. The gaunt, white-haired man he saw through the Plexiglas was former Hennepin County District Court Judge J. Gordon Prentiss III.

At one time Prentiss was an almost aristocratic member of Minnesota society. The son of an extremely well-connected lawyer, Gordon, the name he preferred, was the governor's selection to the U.S. Senate. A Minnesota senator had suddenly died, and Prentiss III was headed toward the big time. Unfortunately, his wife was found lying on her bedroom floor with a knife in her chest. Almost on top of her, unconscious with his hand on the knife handle, was the would-be U.S. Senator. The cops took several photos before they brought him around. The photos, along with documented spousal abuse, cooked Prentiss' goose. Marc was his lawyer.

"I haven't heard anyone call me that for quite some time."

Marc and Judge Prentiss, while Prentiss was on the bench, had a long, acrimonious relationship. Most of the defense lawyers in Hennepin County also had a difficult time with then-Judge Prentiss. His attitude toward criminals was barely enough to let them have a trial before execution. At the time, to say Marc was stunned when Prentiss asked him to represent him would be putting it very mildly.

"What can I do for you, Gordon?"

"I just wanted to apologize to you, in person. And to tell you how terribly sorry I am about your friend," Prentiss said.

While doing his time in a prison in Indiana—it would be too risky to let a judge do prison time in his own state—Prentiss had become angry with Marc. After exhausting his state court appeals procedures, he hired a pair of thugs to murder Marc. This was done through a fellow inmate.

The two hitmen followed Marc to a small town in Minnesota. Marc and his friend, a client by the name of Zach Evans, were leaving the courthouse. The hit was attempted by running Marc down as he crossed the street. The driver of the van that tried it, no one's idea of a genius, hit

9

and killed Zach instead. He did manage to hit Marc as well, but he survived.

A couple of months later, Prentiss and his inmate co-conspirator had a falling out over the money Prentiss paid. The argument led to Prentiss being stabbed—a slight wound—that resulted in the entire story coming out. Additional time for Zach Evans' death was tacked onto both men's sentence. Enough extra time to ensure Gordon Prentiss was going to die in prison. They were also transferred to different prisons.

Marc sat silently for almost thirty seconds staring at the old man. Finally, he said, "What the hell got into you? Did you really think killing me would accomplish anything? And now my friend is dead…"

"I don't expect you to understand or forgive me. I was angry. I was innocent of my wife's death, and I needed to blame someone. I know it's not rational. I know it's not right, but these places can do things to you. That's not an excuse. It's just a fact.

"I admitted what I did, and I'll die in here. Or, maybe get out when I'm in my nineties. I just needed to say I'm sorry."

"Are you finding Jesus?" Marc asked.

Prentiss laughed a little and said, "You won't believe it, but I am. At least a little. It gives me a little solace. Not that it matters now, but I believe you know I was innocent of Catherine's death."

"You're right; it doesn't matter," Marc replied. "But you know what? I guess I do forgive you. Hanging onto that anger accomplishes nothing. And it won't bring my friend back."

"Thank you," Prentiss quietly said.

"You should know, I had occasion to meet one of the jurors. She told me it was the photo of you lying on the floor with the knife sticking out of Catherine's chest and your hand on it that did you in. She told me they couldn't get past it," Marc said.

"It was too prejudicial. It should have never been allowed into evidence," Prentiss said with obvious bitterness.

"Stop it. There isn't a judge out there, including you, that would not have allowed the jury to see it."

"Yes, I guess you're right," Prentiss agreed.

"Take care of yourself, Gordon."

While Marc was walking back toward his car, he thought about Catherine Prentiss' death. Gordon was absolutely, one hundred percent correct. He did not murder his wife. But he did drive her to suicide, and she brilliantly set him to take the fall for it.

THREE

Minnesota State Senator Jamal Halane, a very light-skinned, second-generation Somali, was having breakfast at his usual restaurant, the Guriga. Guriga in Somali means home. The Guriga is located on Washington Avenue near the Cedar/Riverside area of Minneapolis. It is in the heart of the largest Somali community and is a popular meeting place. This, of course, was very dear to the hearts of most Somalis. Being driven from their homeland by terrorists and landing in this country of promiscuity, drugs, and crime made many yearn for a return. The good senator was not one of them. He was quite at home with the American dream, especially the promiscuity part.

Halane had a reserved booth that he used daily whether or not the legislature was in session. Today, during the summer, it was not. He had been on the premises since 8:00 A.M., and it was now almost 10:00. Having finished his usual breakfast of Malawah—a sweet Somali pancake—he had stayed to greet constituents.

Every morning the restaurant would fill with those who would respectfully approach him. Halane had developed a politician's memory and amazed himself at the number of names he remembered. This would invariably impress the supplicants who would pass it on to friends and family. In the coming election, Halane would receive ninety percent of their votes. A solid constituency.

Halane looked toward the door and saw a small man come in. He was about Halane's age—fortyish—and dressed in traditional Muslim clerical garb. Halane checked his watch and smiled at the man's punctuality.

It took the man almost ten minutes to make his way to Halane's booth. The customers crowded around him to give and receive traditional Muslim greetings. His name was Imam Abdullah Sadia and he was the most respected Imam of the main Minneapolis Mosque.

"As-salamu alaykum," the Imam politely said to Halane as he sat down across from him. The standard 'peace be upon you' greeting among Muslims.

"Wa aykumn as-salam," Halane replied. 'And upon you, peace' was the reply.

A waiter appeared—no woman could wait on the Imam—with a cup of his favorite coffee. The Imam nodded and gave the man the same greeting then sipped the spiced French press brew.

While this took place, the booths in front and back of them emptied as did the nearby tables. It was well understood that these two community leaders demanded privacy.

"Are you meeting with our friend?" the Imam asked.

"Yes," Halane replied. "He will be here in about a half-hour."

"And?"

"All is proceeding on schedule."

"I have heard from our friends," the Imam said. "They are impatient. Grateful, but impatient."

Halane smiled and replied, "Allah's plans are long-range plans…"

"You are aware of how long Allah's plans are for?" the Imam chastised the senator. "Do not speak blasphemy."

"I meant no disrespect, Imam. I only meant these things will proceed as Allah wills them," Halane quickly, nervously replied.

"Of course."

"The young ones are doing their duty, even though they don't know it," Halane said.

"This accursed country fills the heads of our children with many temptations. Too many are lured by the trivialities of greed and luxury they believe they can have. They throw away Paradise for foolish pleasures here in the land of Satan."

Halane had no response to the Imams rant. If he said anything at all, he feared the Imam would throw it in his face. Halane had no idea how much this man, whom he considered a fanatic, knew about the senator's own wanderings from the path to Paradise.

Halane had heard this man's tirades about the land of Satan many times. The last thing he wanted was to trigger another one. Halane knew what really galled the Imam was a loss of control over people's lives. And their money. Fortunately, he saw the man he was meeting pull up at the curb in front of the restaurant early.

"He's here," Halane quietly said.

"Go and bring back good news."

"Insha Allah," Halane replied. God willing.

Senator Halane hurried out of the restaurant. He left no money for the bill, believing quite incorrectly the owner would be insulted. The owner of the Guriga Restaurant was not a particularly devout Muslim. He was simply adept at portraying himself as one. As to the good senator, he was glad he brought in customers willing to kiss the politician's ass but despised Halane for being a cheap, petty phony.

When he reached the sidewalk, Halane ran, or at least moved with what passed for running for him, toward the vehicle. Years of soft living on other people's money had left the politician a chubby candidate for an early heart attack. He went around to the street-side backseat passenger door. His ego expected someone to open the door for him. Instead, when no one got out to open it, he opened it himself and climbed into the backseat of the Chevy Tahoe.

Halane closed the door behind himself and said, "As-salamu alaykum," while buckling his seatbelt.

"And peace be unto you, brother," Damone Watson replied in English. "How is the Imam this morning?"

"Impatient," Halane said as Lewis drove the Tahoe through the light traffic.

"Unfortunate, but that is your problem. These things take time," Damone said. "He will have his representative back in the State Senate this fall," Damone confidentially said referring to Halane.

"Insha Allah," Halane said.

Damone laughed and said, "You can stop pretending you are a devout Muslim. We both know better."

"Are you sure we can speak freely in here?" Halane asked.

"Yes, it is checked for listening devices at least daily. And GPS location devices. Is your phone off?" Damone asked.

"I do not have it with me. I left it in my car."

For the next forty minutes, Lewis, with Monroe literally riding shotgun, drove around while the two men talked. The fall elections were only a few months off and campaigning was already in full swing. Halane was being challenged by a well-known black woman and his re-election was anything but certain. He was counting on Damone's support. Damone quietly put out the word through the black community. For solid business reasons and his attitude toward women, Damone was going to help the groveling fool sitting next to him.

"What do you think of Jalen Bryant? What do you think of the woman who is running, Carpenter?" Damone asked referring to the mayoral race in Minneapolis.

14

The fact that Damone was asking Halane his opinion about anything was a boost to Halane's ego. He threw his shoulders back, sat up straight and paused as if considering the question. After a few seconds, he said, "Jalen Bryant is a crusader, or at least claims to be. Carpenter is a lightweight fool. But she's a very appealing liberal which plays well with white, Minneapolis liberals."

"You don't think a black man such as Jalen would appeal to white liberals?" Damone asked.

"In Minneapolis, certainly. Jalen could defeat Carpenter," Halane replied.

"I agree," Damone said. "This will do, Lewis," Damone said to his driver.

Lewis pulled the Tahoe to the curb and stopped. Lewis watched the senator in his mirror, Monroe turned his head to look at him as did Damone.

"Thank you for your time, Senator. I will be in touch."

Halane nervously looked about the interior of the vehicle and said, "You want me to get out here? How will I get back?"

"I'm sure you'll find a way," Damone replied.

This time Lewis exited the car and opened Halane's door for him. Lewis stood patiently in the street waiting while the bought and paid for senator fumbled with his seatbelt before getting out. Lewis shut the door with a solid thump and without a word climbed back in, took his seat and drove off.

"I don't know which is worse," Halane muttered as he walked to the sidewalk. "Dealing with the fanatic Muslims or the arrogant blacks."

He reached inside his coat to retrieve his phone to call Uber. The empty pocket reminded him he had left it in his car. He cursed loudly drawing attention from a passerby, then started walking.

"He is an insufferable little man," Monroe said to Damone after Lewis started driving away.

"Yes," Damone said with a sigh, "but useful. I have it on good authority that his Senate colleagues hold him in high regard. They're terrified of being labeled a racist, so he is eagerly accepted.

"Now," Damone continued, "Lewis, I want you to contact Jalen's campaign manager, Kordell Glover. Set up a meeting in our office for this evening. Helping elect a black mayor will offset our support of this dog, Halane."

15

"Yes, sir," Lewis replied.

"The more I think about it, the more ambivalent I become about getting his endorsement," Jalen Bryant said. He was in the passenger seat of his campaign manager's car on his way to meet Damone Watson. "What does he want, and can we really trust him?"

Kordell Glover was driving and laughed at his client's statement. "What, you mean that maybe all of this 'man of the people, rehabilitated gangbanger, drug dealing murderer' might not be as it seems?"

"I don't know," Jalen said. "I'm not sure what to make of him."

"We'll use him, get you in office and then we can decide whether or not to keep him around."

Jalen Bryant was a thirty-seven-year-old married father of two children, an eight-year-old and a five-year-old, both boys. Unknown to everyone except his wife and Kordell was Jalen's true political philosophy. He was a closet law and order candidate who, unlike previous mayors and city council members leaned toward the police. Criminals needed to be taken off the streets and locked up. He was secretly in favor of school choice. Children of all races, especially inner-city black children, deserved better schools and the opportunity to go to the same schools as the children of the white politicians. As bad as these beliefs were, his worst sin was the abortion statistics that showed the black community was being decimated by careless sexual behavior and irresponsibility.

"Come in," Damone said to his guests. Monroe had greeted Jalen and Kordell in the office parking lot and escorted them to Damone's second-floor conference room.

"Please," he continued after handshakes, "have a seat."

The three of them each took a chair at the table, and Damone started off.

"I'm sorry this took so long. I guess you're looking for an endorsement," he politely said with a pleasant smile while looking at Jalen.

"Well, yes," Jalen replied. "You seem to have a good deal of influence around the city. I believe your endorsement would be a big help."

"Absolutely! I'll do whatever I can to help you get elected. This city needs a strong, capable black man as its mayor."

The three of them continued for another hour. They discussed events Damone could help with and he promised fund-raising and other contributions he would make. When they finished, as Jalen and Kordell were leaving, Damone assured them his election was a foregone conclusion.

Kordell had driven less than a block from the meeting place when he said, "That was easy."

"A little too easy," Jalen replied. "We haven't received the real bill, yet."

"What, you mean you don't believe he is only interested in civic improvements?" Kordell asked with a touch of obvious sarcasm included.

"I don't know what to believe, but all this 'brother this and brother that' talk seems a little phony," Jalen said.

"It does, indeed," Kordell agreed.

FOUR

Philo Anson sipped his Wild Turkey on the rocks while standing at the end of the bar. Philo hated bourbon. He would rather be sipping a quality Cognac than suffering through what he considered hillbilly piss. But if he was going to be the star reporter he knew he was, he believed he had to act like one. The hard-drinking, tough guy reporter seeking the truth. In public, especially in this bar a block from the Star Tribune building, bourbon it had to be.

Philo was a twenty-eight-year-old reporter with the Minneapolis Star Tribune. Fresh out of UW-Madison, he had scored a decent job with the Wisconsin State Journal, a very good paper. Philo had stayed for three years. His writing was a little better than excellent and he knew it. In fact, his ultimate dream was to be a Pulitzer winning novelist. Pretty much the same as every other print reporter. Most of whom would try to write a novel, realize how hard it is after fifty or sixty pages, then give it up. When the three years were up, still twenty-five, he scored a job at the Star Tribune, another step closer to the New York Times. He had two more years to go to meet his goal of the Times by age thirty.

"Hello, Philo," he heard a familiar female voice say.

He turned his head as a woman slid onto the bar stool next to him. Her name was Raina Harris. Raina was an on-scene reporter for a local TV station. She was also someone Philo had been trying to bed for a couple of months,

Philo preferred black women. As a card-carrying, progressive liberal, it showed the world how hip, open-minded, and progressive he truly was. Contrarily, he also believed treating black women like whores was what they wanted. Philo had heard this from a friend. Another card-carrying, progressive liberal. Raina, far above Philo's reach, knew Philo was more than hot for her. Raina had been playing her own game for a couple of months.

"Courvoisier," Raina told the bartender. "And yes, on his tab."

"So, when are you going to let me give you the time of your life?" Philo asked while the bartender fetched her drink.

"Are you sending me and my girlfriend to Paris?"

"Very funny," Philo smiled. "I know you're not gay…"

"How do you know I don't like a little variety in my life?"

"Anytime you want to do a threesome, I'm available," Philo said.

"I'll keep it in mind. Don't wait for me."

"Hey, Philo," a man said behind him and slapped him a little too hard on the back. The man took the stool on the opposite side of Philo and held up his glass to signal the bartender.

"Hellooo, Raina," he suggestively said.

"Hello, Wayne. How are the wife and kids?"

"Who?" he asked trying to look confused.

Raina laughed as Philo said, "What do you want, Wayne?" Like most of his colleagues, Wayne, a Star Trib reporter himself, did not like Philo and the feeling was mutual. Mostly because Philo would backstab his own mother to get ahead. Philo justified every bit by reminding himself he owed it to the profession. The world needed Philo to escape the backwater of flyover country. For the benefit of civilization, whatever he did was not only allowed, but moral, ethically correct and virtuous.

"Steal any stories lately?" Wayne asked.

"You don't need to worry about it, Wayne. Proctor will never assign anything to you that anyone else would want," Philo replied. Proctor was Vince Proctor, their boss and city editor.

"Oooooh," Wayne purred trying to feign being insulted. "Please stop, Mr. Pulitzer. You'll hurt my feelings."

Raina, who had been listening with a smile openly laughed at this. "Be nice, Wayne. Someday you'll be working for him."

"Seriously, Philo," Wayne said. "I actually want to congratulate you on your story about police brutality. It was good. Well-written."

Philo turned his head to look at the man and saw a sincere expression on Wayne's face.

"I mean it," Wayne said. "It was good."

"It was good, Philo," Raina chimed in. "I thought it was well done. How much of it was true?"

Philo looked at her with a mischievous look and a twinkle in his eyes. "Why, all of it, every word, of course."

Raina poured down the remnant of her brandy and stood. She draped the strap of her purse over her shoulder and said, "You lie well, Philo. I know for a fact that story was ridiculously embellished." She bent down and whispered in his ear, "I've been sleeping with one of the cops you trashed, you lying asshole." Raina stepped back and said, "Bye, Wayne. Thanks for the drink, Philo."

As she walked off, Philo sipped his drink with a stunned look on his face.

"What did she say?" Wayne asked.

"She said she was hot for my ass and wanted to do a threesome with another girl, a friend of hers," Philo replied.

Wayne laughed then finished his drink. He set the glass on the bar and said, "You do have quite the imagination, Philo. Thanks for the drink."

Two hours and four snifters of Cognac later—he could not take any more hillbilly piss—Philo tossed a hundred-dollar bill on the bar. Thanks to very successful dairy farming parents who kept him on an allowance, money was not a problem for Philo. More than a little buzzed, Philo went out to his car, a two-year-old Jag and headed for home. Again, thanks to mom and dad, the Jag and his luxury Edina condo allowed Philo to maintain a certain style.

Philo drove West on Fifth Street alongside the light-rail tracks. He took a left on Fourth Avenue, running a red light to do it, for the run south to the freeway entrance. As he passed by the big government center building that straddled Sixth Street, the light on Sixth and Fourth Avenue began to change. Instead of stopping the way he should have, he punched the gas, and the Jag jumped to fifty as he blew through another red light. Except for this time, he did it right in front of an MPD squad car heading East on Sixth waiting for the light.

"Nice ride, Em," Officer Mike Pascal said to the squad car's driver.

"No, kidding," Sergeant Emily Logen replied. "Hit 'em," she said to her junior partner. "Let's go have a chat with him."

Logen hit both the lights and siren as Pascal roared down Fourth. They caught up with Philo on Tenth, before the freeway ramp. Even with the roof bar lighting up the night and the siren shrieking, Philo did not notice them until he was a mile down the freeway past the Lake Street exit.

Most city cops hate pulling someone over on the freeway, especially at night. Too many drunks out and the shoulder of a freeway can be a dangerous place. Fortunately, being a weekday and fairly late, traffic was relatively light.

While Mike Pascal stood at the back of the car, his hand on his gun, Em Logen went to the driver's window. She held her flashlight in her left hand, her right on her gun. She shined the light on Philo's face who stared at her through the window.

Logen tapped the flashlight on the glass and politely said, "Shut off the car and put the window down, please, sir."

Philo shut off the engine and buzzed down the window without realizing her body cam was on. The smell of alcohol hit Logen in the face as Philo arrogantly said, "Do you realize who I am? I'll have your ass for this. This is retaliation pure and simple. You'll be sorry you ever met me."

Logen calmly said, "Yes, sir. I'm sure that's true. Now, I'll need to see your license and insurance verification."

"Bitch," Philo snarled just loud enough for the camera to pick up.

He stumbled and fumbled around getting his license and insurance certificate. While he did this, Logen motioned for Pascal to join her.

"Sir, have you been drinking?" Logen asked. Philo had handed her the license and insurance certificate. She gave them to Pascal.

"I had a drink with dinner," Philo admitted.

This made Pascal smile and Logen opened the car door, stepped back and ordered Philo to get out. The officers led him onto the grass. He was stumbling, muttering and slurring his words. All the while, both cops' body cams were recording and also the one on the dashboard of the squad car.

"You run the field tests," Logan told Pascal. "I'll check for warrants and order a tow truck."

"Do you know who I am?" Philo asked Pascal several times while miserably failing each field sobriety test. He was putting on quite a show for the cameras.

After the third or fourth time Philo asked the question, Pascal finally said, "No sir, I don't know who you are, and I don't care. Now, be quiet for a moment, please. I am placing you under arrest for driving while intoxicated. You have the right to remain silent…"

Philo awoke in the morning to the sound of cell doors being banged open and closed. His head felt like a small bomb going off and his mouth tasted like loon shit filled swamp water.

"What was his score?" Assistant City Attorney Aleisha Cotton asked.

"Point one three," Emily Logen replied.

21

"And you want to do what, now?" Aleisha asked.

The two women, along with Mike Pascal, were seated in a conference room in the courtroom where afternoon arraignments were being held. Along with a dozen or so others picked up the night before, Philo Anson was about to be arraigned. Unlike most of the defendants, Philo had a private attorney standing by waiting to talk to Aleisha.

"We got the okay for this from our captain as long as it is okay with you," Logen said. "This Anson guy is the asshole reporter who wrote that trash piece for the Star Tribune about police brutality."

"Oh, really? You want me to press for the death penalty?" Aleisha asked only half-jokingly.

"It's an idea," Pascal replied.

"His record is clean. We want you to offer him a deferred prosecution for a year if he agrees to go on a ride-along with cops, at night, four nights a week for two weeks," Logen said.

"The arrest is perfect. We got it all on film," Pascal added.

Aleisha took out her phone and said, "Let me check."

Two minutes later, having been given the okay, Aleisha Cotton left the conference room to talk to Philo's lawyer. By 1:30 they had put the deal on the record for the judge and Philo Anson had set up several dates to find out what cops have to put up with every hour of every day.

FIVE

Sgt. Jason Moore turned his squad car left off Plymouth Avenue at the Fourth Precinct station house. Moore, a black man with twenty-four years on the job, was finishing his evening tour. In the passenger seat was the reporter, Philo Anson. This was Philo's last night doing ride-alongs, his second with Sgt. Moore. Outwardly, Philo appeared to be chastened about his attitude toward cops. Inwardly, he was delighted to be done with this. Philo believed he was being subjected to cruel and unusual punishment for an article he wrote and because he had a couple of drinks.

Philo had learned that the cops, especially on the two-night shifts, evenings and midnight to morning, dealt with a lot of domestic disputes. What he had not learned was that a large number of police homicides occurred during these encounters. Philo had also had his prejudice about inner-city black people solidly affirmed. To Philo, they were children, unable to control their most base instincts. This also confirmed his belief that because they were children, they were not really responsible for themselves, should never be held accountable and needed the government to take care of them. If Sgt. Moore had any inkling that his passenger was, like most elitists, a hard-core, liberal racist, Moore's head would have exploded. Jason Moore grew up on these very same streets.

Moore parked the squad car in the lot behind the precinct building. He turned in his seat and said, "Well, here we are. I hope you got an objective look at what we deal with."

"Oh, for sure, Sergeant," Philo replied. "Who do you think killed those two young men?"

There had been a shooting tonight and two black men in their late teens or early twenties were dead. They had been found in an alley barely a mile from where Moore was now parked. It was obviously an execution type slaying. Both victims were found face down in an alley with two small-caliber bullet holes in the back of their heads.

"Hard to say," Moore replied as he removed his seatbelt. "Gang violence has been down, which is what this looks like. Odds are pretty good we'll never find out since no one ever sees anything when it comes to these things."

"That's quite an assumption, isn't it?" Philo asked. "To automatically assume they were in a gang."

By now the two of them were walking toward Philo's car and the precinct house.

"How do you know it wasn't a white supremacist out hunting down young black men?"

Moore stopped and looked at Philo with an incredulous look on his face. He shook his head and continued walking.

"Well?" Philo asked again.

"They were wearing gang colors."

"So, it could still be a white supremacist," Philo insisted.

Moore laughed, looked at Philo, smiled and said, "I guess it could be, anything's possible." He then shook his head at the absurdity of it.

It was almost midnight when Philo drove away from the Fourth Precinct. He was desperate to stop for a drink but too keyed up. It would have to wait until he got home. Instead, he drove downtown and straight to the Star Tribune building.

For the past week, during his ride-along punishment, he had been working on a story about it. His editor was hot to get it and because of its length was making it a three-part series. The first part would run in two days, Sunday's edition. Then the two-part follow-ups would run Monday and Tuesday. Philo had about another three thousand words to add to finish up. More importantly, he had a front page, above the fold headline story for Sunday to kick it off.

Damone Watson was normally a late morning riser. His activities required odd hours, especially late-night hours. Sunday morning at a quarter past ten, Damone came out of his third-floor bedroom, cinching the belt of his silk robe around his waist. The woman who had kept him company during the night was gone.

"Good morning, Lewis, Monroe," Damone greeted his aides.

Both Lewis Freeh and Monroe Ervin were standing by the dining room table. By itself, this was a bit unusual. While Monroe poured his boss a cup of coffee, Damone looked at both men.

"Okay, what's up?" he asked as he took his seat at the head of the table.

"The paper," Lewis said pointing at the morning edition of the Star Tribune.

Damone picked up his cup while reading the headline blazing across the entire front page.

WHITE SUPREMACISTS SUSPECTED IN SLAYINGS

Damone set down the cup, picked up the A section and began to read the story. The first two paragraphs were brief reviews of the execution-style murders on the Northside of two young black men Friday evening. The bodies of Kolby Simmons, age 19, and Ja'von King, age 18, were found in an alley off of North 18th Street. Both were executed by shots to the back of the head.

The reporter claimed a police source confirmed that it could be the work of a white supremacist, possibly more than one, stalking young black men. Caution is advised in the...

Damone started laughing as he continued to read. When he finished the story, he folded the paper back to its original form and set it on the table.

"Okay, who is this source that this reporter is quoting?" Damone asked, barely containing his laughter.

"Who knows?" Lewis shrugged. "There's another big article with it. This reporter, Philo what's-his-name, did a court-ordered ride-along with the cops and he wrote up a story about it."

"What does he have to say?"

Monroe replied, "He was ordered to ride-along to get a look at what the cops have to deal with. This reporter is some hanky-wringing liberal who hates cops."

"According to what he wrote, he still hates cops," Lewis added.

"Really?" Damone said. He then took a moment to stare past the two men in thought. He then said, "We'll have to keep that in mind. A reporter like that could be useful."

That evening a crowd of about two hundred people—about half black, half white—were marching through the streets of downtown Minneapolis. Ten or twelve of them were up front holding a large 'Black Lives Matter' sign. Every local TV station had been informed of the march ahead of time. There were camera crews from each of them filming the small, but raucous protest.

The next day, Monday morning, every network and nationwide cable news show was leading their broadcast with the film. The crowd size estimates they gave ranged from a thousand to five thousand participants.

At 7:00 A.M. on Monday morning, police Captain Jody Wells was at her desk sipping her coffee. She was scanning the Star Tribune front page when she heard a knock on her door.

"Come in," she said loudly without looking up.

Sgt. Jason Moore hesitantly came in and quietly greeted his precinct Captain.

"Have a seat," Wells said. "What are you doing here so early?"

"I have to tell you something, Captain," Moore said.

"Okay, what?" she asked.

"Um, I, ah, think, I might be the source this reporter used for the white supremacist story," Moore said.

"What? How?"

In less than a minute Moore told her about the brief conversation he had with Philo Anson and his off-hand comment about white supremacists.

"You were joking?" she asked when he finished.

"Of course," Moore said shaking his head in disbelief. "I even told this arrogant little shit it was a gang killing. They were wearing gang colors. I didn't even know who they were until their names were released. And now that I know their names, I know they were both drug dealers and gangbangers."

"I'm gonna send this up the line so the higher ups can get it out to the media. I think they'll do it without using your name, but we'll see. In the meantime, keep this to yourself."

"Sorry, Captain. It was a joke. I didn't think he'd use it," Moore said.

"You've been around long enough to know you can't trust these people," Wells said, annoyance in her tone.

By nine o'clock that Monday morning, traffic around the Hennepin County Government Center and the Old City Hall building across Fifth Street was at a standstill. The only things moving were the light rail trains on Fifth. A crowd of three thousand people had taken over the streets.

On the steps of City Hall, at the Fifth Street entrance, Damone Watson was standing with a dozen civic leaders. There were microphones set up and each was taking a turn demanding to know what was being done to protect the black community. There were even references to the Ku Klux Klan being involved.

At 10:30 those leaders, including Damone, were allowed into the building to attend a press conference. The police also selected another thirty members of the crowd to come in and watch. When everyone was settled in and reasonably quiet, Mayor Fogel, City Council President Patti Chenault, the Chief of Police, half dozen council members, Captain Wells and Sgt. Moore appeared.

Mayor Fogel gave a brief statement then turned the lectern over to the Chief. Chief Marvin Brown, with homicide Lieutenant Owen Jefferson at his side, assured everyone there was no Klan presence in Minnesota. The murders were clearly gang-related. To which, after being introduced, Lt. Jefferson of the Homicide Division fully agreed.

Finally, having been pressed into duty, Sgt. Jason Moore stepped up and told his story. Seated in the front row, almost dead center, was Philo Anson. Before Moore finished, he was staring down right at Philo.

"I laughed and smiled when I jokingly agreed with what was a silly comment by you. You knew I was joking, and you used it anyway. Look at what your irresponsible behavior has caused."

Moore looked over the crowd and said for at least the fourth time, "It was a gang killing and he knew it. And I have known Lt. Jefferson for almost twenty years. He will make sure these killings will be thoroughly investigated."

As Moore stepped away from the microphone, every media member started shouting questions. The mayor's press secretary held up his arms until they had quieted enough to tell them no questions would be taken.

"I have another meeting with Bryant," Damone reminded Lewis.

They were in the Tahoe, Lewis driving as usual, leaving downtown.

"Yes, boss," Lewis replied. "We're fine for time."

"How was the press conference?" Monroe asked Damone.

"Amusing," Damone answered. "But it did remind me to always be very careful what you say to the media."

SIX

"So, what's your excuse this time?" Jerry Krain, the Hennepin County Assistant Attorney, asked Marc.

"Excuse me, Mr. Krain," Judge Philip Moran said. "Please allow me to take the lead in my chambers," Moran added sarcastically.

"Sorry, your Honor," Krain insincerely apologized. "I just thought I'd cut to the chase."

While this exchange took place, Marc was looking at Krain with a slight, smartass smirk on his face.

Jerry Krain was a thirty-year lifer with the county attorney's office. He was a solid, methodical prosecutor with an excellent win/loss record. Of course, like most prosecutors who like to brag about their wins and losses, Krain only tried cases that he had a 100% chance of winning. Defense lawyers did not have that luxury.

Jerry Krain, because of a Gibraltar-size chip on his shoulder, had managed to make enemies of just about everyone. Defense lawyers despised him and called him the Nazi even to his face. Krain actually enjoyed the appellation. Bad enough that every defense lawyer loathed the man, his compatriots in the county attorney's office felt the same way.

"What about it, Mr. Kadella?" Judge Moran asked. "This is our third attempt at a pretrial and no report from your psychiatrist yet. What's going on?"

"Well, your Honor…" Marc began.

"This should be good," Krain snidely said interrupting him.

Marc looked at Krain, narrowed his eyes and used his thumb and index finger to make a key turning gesture at his own lips. The universal signal to lock your mouth shut.

Krain's face reddened and he gave Marc a dirty look which did not go unnoticed by Judge Moran.

"All right you two," Moran said. "Put an end to it."

"As I was saying, your Honor," Marc continued, "Dr. Butler is, um, how shall I put this? Finding the Kullen family to be, without violating privilege, an interesting challenge."

"I'll bet she is," Krain said.

"But she assures me she will have a report with a treatment recommendation by the end of the week," Marc finished while ignoring Krain.

"Your Honor, these psychos don't need treatment, they need prison time," Krain said.

"So, you admit my clients have psychological problems?" Marc quickly asked Krain. "If so, then obviously they need therapy which they won't get in prison."

"That's not what I meant, and you know it. Besides, this fiasco has gone on long enough. He's obviously using defense tactic number one; stall, stall and stall some more. We need a speedy trial date," Krain said.

"It's my client that has the right to a speedy trial, not you. Is there a clock running somewhere? Are we in a hurry, your Honor? My clients are not going anywhere."

"Is there a reason we can't set a trial date today?" Judge Moran asked. "Will you need more discovery time?"

"I may want to amend my plea, your Honor," Marc said referring to a possible insanity defense.

"And if he does, we'll have to have him court-ordered examined," Moran said looking at Krain.

"Okay," Moran continued while pulling up his schedule on his laptop. "How does next Wednesday look for you two? I have a short trial starting Monday morning and a long weekend starting Thursday."

"Judge," Krain said, "I'm booked full until Friday."

Perfect, Marc thought.

"Wednesday is fine with me, Judge," Marc quickly said. Let Krain be the problem.

"What time, Marc?" Moran asked.

"Whatever time works for you, your Honor," Marc said.

"Ten o'clock," Moran said.

"Your Honor, I can't…" Krain tried to say.

"Have somebody sit in for you. It's a pretrial," Moran said cutting him off. "I've got a fishing trip to Canada scheduled and I'm not rescheduling to accommodate you."

"Yes, your Honor," Krain sullenly agreed. "I'll have somebody sit in if I can't make it."

"We can only hope," Marc said under his breath, loud enough to be heard.

"Let's have that report no later than noon on Monday, Mr. Kadella," Moran said.

"Yes, your Honor. I'll deliver it myself if I have to," Marc said.

"Email will be fine," Krain said.

"I meant to Judge Moran," Marc said.

"Are we done? Thank you, your Honor," Krain said then stood and walked off and out of Moran's chambers without waiting for a reply.

"Marc," Moran said while Marc was preparing to leave, "this bickering between you two has to stop."

"He's pissed off at me, Judge, because I handed him his ass at an evidentiary hearing a few months ago. He and his detective did a sloppy job and he paid for it."

"I know, I heard. But…"

"I don't see this going to trial. If someone reasonable from the prosecutor's office shows up next week, we can probably work something out. I have a pretty good idea what the shrink's report will look like. Thanks, Judge," Marc said then turned to leave.

When Marc went into the back hallway, Jerry Krain was coming back.

"What did you tell the judge?"

"I told him that you were really a sweet guy. Just a little misunderstood."

"If I find out you had an ex parte discussion…"

"The next time you won't leave early," Marc said finishing for him. "Jerry, seriously, you need to lighten up. You're really not carrying the burden of the world on your shoulders. Relax."

Krain glared at him then snarled, "I owe you one."

"Or, maybe you can send someone to Auschwitz. That should make you feel better."

Krain's face and bald head turned beet red. He pursed his lips, turned and stomped off. As he walked away, Marc clicked his heels together then silently raised his arm in a Nazi salute.

Marc got off the elevator on level two, then hurried into the courtyard. When he took the right turn away from the elevators, he was stopped by the crowd milling about on the second floor. He saw a lawyer he knew and muscled through the crowd toward her.

"Hey, Beth," he said.

"Hi, Marc," she replied.

"What's going on?"

"It's the protest across the street at City Hall. The one about the report that it was a white supremacist group who killed those two black kids Friday night," Beth answered.

"It was the Klan," a black teen who looked to be about fifteen turned to them and said.

"The Klan?" Beth incredulously asked. "In Minnesota? I doubt it."

"That's what they're sayin'," the kid said.

"My car's downstairs," Marc said. "I need to get out of here."

A sheriff's deputy Marc recognized strolled over to them. Marc asked the man if they could get out. "They're not letting anyone out the North exit," the deputy said.

"My car's downstairs," Marc said.

"Mine too," Beth added.

"You can get out that way. The cops have Fourth open. I'll guide you to the elevator," the deputy said.

With the deputy in the lead, the three of them made their way toward the corner where the parking ramp elevators were. As they were about to break through the crowd, Marc heard a very familiar voice call out his name. Marc turned and saw Gabriella Shriqui waving at him.

"That's Gabriella Shriqui waving at you," Beth said. "I'm impressed. Tell her I'm available to do her show anytime."

"Divorces don't generate a lot of ratings unless you get a juicy one with rich people and a lot of infidelity," Marc said.

"I'll see what I can do," Beth replied.

"Give me your card. If she wants someone, I'll recommend you," Marc said.

"No shit? You can't buy that kind of publicity. Do I owe you a blow job or something?"

Marc laughed and said, "I'll keep it in mind."

A minute later, Marc was being led by Gabriella to the building's exit door.

There was a reporter who works for Gabriella and a cameraman waiting. While they made their way through the crowd, he handed Gabriella his friend's business card.

"If you need a lawyer for your show to do a divorce segment, give her a call. She's really good and could use the publicity," Marc said.

Gabriella looked at the card, flicked it with her index finger, and then said, "That's not a bad idea. I think I'll look into it. What did she offer you for this?"

Marc told her what Beth had said and Gabriella heartily laughed.

"I can't wait to tell Maddy about this," she said.

Marc hung his head, shook it, looked at Gabriella and said, "I didn't even do anything and I'm in trouble."

"Relax, big boy. I'm kidding. Although I think I will tell her. She'll laugh too."

When they reached the front of the crowd, they found sheriff's deputies blocking the exits. No one was coming in or getting out that way.

"What's going on?" Marc asked.

They were looking through the glass doors across the plaza and Fifth Street. On the steps of City Hall, in front of a bank of microphones using a bullhorn to be heard was a black man making a statement. Unfortunately, they could not hear what he was saying. In fact, he was the only one of the speakers who was trying to calm down the crowd.

"Everybody's all wound up because they think there's some Neo-Nazi, Klan, white supremacist group hunting down black men. The word I got from the cops was that it's bullshit. Those two that were shot Friday evening were executed, likely by a rival gang. The mayor's having a press conference in a few minutes," Gabriella explained.

"Why aren't you in there?"

"Because I got stuck in here. We have a camera and reporter in there," she said referring to the TV station she worked for, Channel 8.

"You know that guy with the bullhorn?" Marc asked.

"Yep," Gabriella replied. "That's Damone Watson. He's the latest hot thing in Minneapolis. Reformed drug dealer, gangbanger from Chicago. Now he's bringing Jesus and light to Minneapolis."

"You sound pretty skeptical. I like your cynical side. Very sexy."

"Speaking of sexy, how are things with you and Maddy?"

"Good. Truth be told, I'm head over heels," Marc admitted.

"I was wondering when that was going to happen," Gabriella said.

"Everybody says that. Why didn't we know?"

"Maddy did. She was waiting for you to figure it out. If she ever kicks you to the curb, let me know."

"Why?" Marc asked.

32

"Seriously? You don't know why? Maddy has nice things to say about you. Plus, you have a job. Okay, you're a lawyer, but still, those men are rare."

"Oh, so, it isn't my overpowering sex appeal?"

"Well, um, yeah, that too," Gabriella said and laughed. "Hey, got anything juicy going?"

Marc thought it over and said, "Well, yeah. Not juicy, but bizarre and interesting. Different."

"That's right," Gabriella snapped, remembering the case. "You have that Kullen family thing. The one where the son went after the father with an axe. Is it true that he tried to chop his way through the bedroom door like Jack Nicholson in The Shining? Is it true the old man took a shot at him? What can you tell me?"

"Nothing. I have to go," Marc said.

"Thanks a lot," Gabriella said.

"Maybe when it's over," Marc said. He kissed her on the cheek, she gave him a hug and Marc went to his car wondering about Damone Watson.

SEVEN

The object of Marc's attention was in the back seat of the Tahoe being driven back to his office. Before Lewis reached Washington Avenue, he asked his boss, "Do you believe the cop who said he was joking about the white supremacist killing Simmons and King?"

"Of course," Damone replied.

As he said this, Monroe took a call on his phone. He listened for a minute, thanked the caller, and hung up.

"That was Saadaq," Monroe turned around and told Damone. "They have the answer."

"Good," Damone replied.

"Do you want me to…?" Lewis started to ask.

"Yes," Damone said knowing Lewis was going to ask if he should change their destination.

Monroe told Lewis where to go. Instead of turning left on Washington to go to the office, Lewis turned right. Ten minutes later, he parked the Tahoe in a residential garage near Cedar/Riverside.

A young Somali man was waiting and opened the garage door. When Lewis shut off the engine, the man closed it.

Damone, still carrying his Bible, got out of the Tahoe and said, "As-salamu alaykum," to the young man.

The Somali bowed his head reverently and returned the greeting. He then led the three men into the house and down the creaky, wooden stairs to the basement.

The house itself was built shortly after World War II. Unlike most of the ones in this neighborhood, this one had a semi-finished basement. The concrete floor had a fresh coat of gray paint. The cinder block walls were a bright white and the ground-level windows were painted black. The entire area was well lit with several bare lightbulbs attached to the ceiling.

Waiting for Damone were six Muslim men. Three were standing nervously on a large, plastic sheet in the middle of the room. A fourth man stood next to the three on the plastic. This man was casually holding the universal firearm of choice for revolutionaries and radicals: a knockoff AK-47. A fifth man was seated in a comfortable chair along the wall to Damone's right. He was a much more light-skinned man wearing Ray-Ban wraparounds and sporting a very stylish three-day beard.

The sixth man was Saadaq Khalid. He was the one who had called Monroe a few minutes ago. Saadaq was a 27-year-old Middle Eastern Muslim and Damone's liaison in the Somali community. Being Damone's man was well known among the Somalis which made Saadaq both highly respected and feared.

Saadaq bowed his head and greeted Damone in English. Damone returned the greeting, respectfully in Arabic. Saadaq then led Damone to the men on the plastic.

"These are the two fools," Saadaq said, indicating the two of the three. The three were lined up left-to-right. The ones Saadaq pointed to were the one in the middle and the one to Damone's right.

"Have they confessed?" Damone asked.

"Yes," Saadaq replied.

Damone looked at the two young men—both looked to be no older than eighteen—and asked, "What do you have to say for yourselves?"

The one in the middle, noticeably less frightened than the other, replied, "They offended our women. They said hateful things to us about all Muslim women."

"What did they say?" Damone asked.

"I cannot and will not repeat it," the man said. "It was too offensive. They deserved to die."

"What should you have done instead of seeking justice yourself?" Damone asked.

"We should have gone to Hanad Rahim, who would go to you for justice. I know that now," the same one replied. He was referring to the third man standing on the plastic. Hanad Rahim was the Somali selected by Damone to oversee the Somali gangs, get them to work together and keep the peace.

"You were ignorant of this before you acted so foolishly?" Damone asked.

"Yes, sir," both of the killers replied.

Damone looked to his left at Hanad and said, "Did you fail to inform them that there are procedures in place to deal with trouble such as this? To maintain the peace?"

Hanad started to say something but was abruptly cut off by Damone.

"Do not lie to me."

35

Hanad stood up straight, shoulders back and stared straight ahead. "Perhaps," he said.

Damone turned around and took one step forward. He was less than a foot from Monroe who handed him an object that no one else could see. Damone held it for two seconds then quickly turned around and pointed it. The .40 caliber semi-auto sounded like a cannon being fired in the confines of the small basement. From barely three feet away, the bullet made a neat, round hole in Hanad's forehead when it entered. It exited the back of his skull and blew a spray of bone, brains and blood all over the plastic sheet.

While Hanad lay lifeless on the plastic-covered floor, the blood from his head spreading beneath him, Damone turned back to the two young Muslims. Pointing the handgun back and forth at their foreheads, he quietly asked, "Are you prepared to die for Allah?"

"Yes," both answered, each expecting to be lying next to Hanad at any moment.

Instead, Damone lowered his hand with the gun and looked at both of them.

"Good," he said. He reached behind himself and handed the gun to Monroe.

"You will go with this man and do what he tells you," Damone said nodding his head toward the man wearing sunglasses. "You belong to him now," Damone continued. "If you disobey him in any way, he has the right to punish you however he sees fit. Including death. Do you understand?"

"Yes."

"Do you object?"

"No, sir," they both said.

The man with the sunglasses stood up and addressed his two new slaves.

"You are giving your lives to Allah. You should be proud. There is no greater purpose in this life."

"Find a more capable replacement for this dog," Damone told Saadaq referring to Hanad. "We cannot have these things happening. I have had to spend too much time the last three days keeping the peace. Choose someone this poorly again and I will beat you like a woman. Understood?"

"Of course," Saadaq nervously replied.

36

As the three of them were leaving, Lewis handed Damone his Bible. Damone tucked it under his arm and went up the stairs behind Monroe.

The ride toward Damone's office was done in silence for the first five or six minutes. Damone had agreed to meet with Jalen Bryant again. Lewis and Monroe, knowing their boss' moods, did not want to interrupt him. He was likely thinking about what the mayoral candidate wanted this time.

"Lewis, I want you to get ahold of that political researcher, what's-his-name…"

"Addison Farmen," Lewis answered.

"Yes, that sleazy little man. Anyway, have him research Bryant's opponent, Betsy Carpenter. Let's see if we can help him."

"Yes, sir," Lewis replied. "Consider it done. I'll do it through a cutout, so he won't know it's you."

"Very good."

That morning's Star Tribune was still lying on the backseat next to Damone. He picked it up and read the article about white supremacists again. When he finished, he read the byline with the reporter's name.

"Philo Anson," Damone said. "What kind of name is Philo Anson?"

"I have no idea," Lewis replied.

"Who is Philo Anson?" Monroe asked.

"The reporter who wrote this story," Damone said. "Let's do a background check on him, too. Anyone who hates cops as much as he does might prove to be useful. Get that computer kid on it."

"You mean Delmar?" Monroe asked.

"Yes, have him dig up what he can. We may want to hire a private investigator at some point, but have the kid check him out first."

"Councilman, what can I do for you?" Damone asked Jalen Bryant.

Bryant had been escorted to the second-floor conference room by Lewis. When he was shown in, Damone put on a friendly display to welcome him.

"No Kordell Glover with you?" Damone asked as the two men shook hands.

"No, I would like to meet with you alone," Bryant replied. He was referring to Lewis and Monroe.

37

"I'm sorry," Damone said with a smile. "That's not possible. I never meet anyone without my two closest advisors. Please, have a seat."

"Well, all right," Bryant said as he sat down at the conference table. "I'm going to speak bluntly, and you might not want them to hear this."

"Go ahead. Speak bluntly." Damone was sitting on the table top, one foot on the floor, three seats from Bryant looking down at him. A position of power.

"Okay. I know who you are, I know what you're up to and if you want to continue, I want a million dollars wired into an offshore account."

"I have no idea what you're talking about," Damone said. He gestured with a flip of his hand to Monroe and Lewis. The two of them went to Bryant and literally lifted him out of his chair.

"Hey! What the hell…" Bryant tried to protest. He looked at Damone who smiled and held an index finger to his lips.

"I will not be quiet…what do you think you're doing?" he yelled.

While Lewis held the much smaller man in a grip like a vise, Monroe started undressing him.

"Relax and you won't get hurt," Lewis whispered in his ear.

In less than a minute the councilman was stripped completely naked. Monroe did a quick visual search which included looking in his ears. Satisfied, the two bodyguards returned to where they had been standing.

"You thought I was wired?"

"Please get dressed," Damone said.

"This is outrageous," Bryant protested as he pulled up his underwear and pants. "I won't…"

"You come here demanding a million-dollar bribe and you're upset if we suspect foul play? Please, spare me your indignation.

"Of course, I'm not going to give you a million dollars. Where would I get a million dollars? You should be ashamed of yourself."

Bryant looked nervously around the room as he finished dressing.

"How do I know you don't have this room wired?" he asked.

"You don't," Damone replied. "You should have thought of that before coming here and insulting me like this. But, to show you there are no hard feelings, I'm still going to work for you.

"Was there anything else, Mr. Bryant?" Damone asked.

"Ah, no," he nervously replied.

"Have a nice rest of your day," Damone said.

While Monroe was escorting their visitor downstairs, Damone told Lewis to check the monitoring system to make sure it was working, and they had the councilman filmed. In fact, the room was wired for both audio and video. And Jalen Bryant had assumed it was.

Councilman Bryant drove six blocks to a parking lot near a small park. When he got there, he found three men waiting for him. One was his campaign manager, Kordell Glover. The other two were FBI agents. Satisfied he had not been followed, Bryant parked his car and joined the three men in the agents' car.

"How did it go?" the older, male agent, Jeff Johnson, asked from the front passenger seat.

"About like we expected," Bryant replied. "He acted offended. His two thugs even stripped me down to check for a wire."

"You okay?" Kordell asked.

"Yeah, I'm fine."

"You weren't followed?" the younger female agent, Tess Richards, asked.

"No, I drove around. No one was after me," Bryant assured them. "He's not what he seems to be. I'm sure of it."

"We tossed the bait at him," agent Johnson said. "Give it time. He'll come back for something."

When Lewis and Monroe were done escorting Bryant out and checking the monitoring, they joined Damone in his office. They took the comfortable, leather armchairs in front of his big desk.

"I want this place swept for bugs at least twice a week," Damone said.

"I'll see to it," Lewis replied. "That shifty tech guy…"

"Conrad Hilton?" Damone asked.

"Yeah, him. He's quick and thorough. Comes highly recommended," Lewis said.

"He did a good job setting up the monitoring system, too," Monroe said.

"Make sure he does my apartment, too."

Monroe's phone rang, he answered it, briefly listened then said, "I'll be right there."

He put the phone away and said, "Rondall is here with five of his guys."

Damone shook his head in disgust and said, "I told him I would see him alone. Bring him up by himself. Put him in the conference room," Damone looked at Lewis and said, "While Monroe does that, shut off the monitoring equipment in the conference room please, Lewis."

Five minutes later, Damone had finished informing Rondall Brown what he had done with the two Muslims. The victims of the Friday night murders were members of Rondall's gang, the Northside NWA. Of course, Damone had lied to him. He told Rondall that the Muslims were dead.

Rondall stood up, quite angry and stomped around the conference room.

"I told you I wanted to take care of them!" he yelled pounding an indignant fist against his chest while glaring at Damone.

"You told me, did you?" Damone calmly replied. "You told me? Who are you to tell me anything? I decided what was best for business and to keep the peace. You don't get a vote."

"Yeah? We'll see about…"

"Don't," Damone calmly, but clearly warned him. "They insulted Muslim women. It was a foolish thing to do…"

"Muslim women? Muslim women?" Rondall sneered. He was standing now at the opposite end of the table, staring down at Damone. Almost silently, Monroe slipped into the room behind Rondall. He stood by the door holding his hands together. Rondall turned, saw him and his demeanor changed immediately.

He looked at Damone and quietly said, "I accept your decision."

"Good," Damone said. He got up and walked down the table to where Rondall was nervously looking at Monroe. Damone and Rondall went through a series of hand gestures while Monroe opened the door.

Damone went back to his office while Monroe escorted Rondall back to the first-floor exit. When Damone entered his office, Lewis was there waiting for him.

EIGHT

Marc entered the suite of offices he shared with his friends to find most of them laughing. He stood in the doorway with a quizzical look on his face. It was Barry Cline, one of the other lawyers, who was the first one to notice him.

"I just had a call from a woman who should be on our top ten list of dumbest potential clients," Barry told him.

"What?" Marc asked, laughing a bit before even hearing the story.

"Woman wants to sue Target for discrimination," Barry began. "She went to Target with a Target coupon and was told she couldn't use it because it had expired. She told the Target clerk that she was out of town when the coupon came out and since it wasn't her fault, Target should allow her to use it to buy the item."

"What? How…what?" Marc said.

"It wasn't her fault because she was out of town and Target should still honor the coupon."

"That expired," Marc said.

"Right. But it wasn't her fault," Barry repeated.

"And…I'm sorry," Marc said, "I'm trying not to laugh. What is her discrimination claim? Is she black or gay or what?"

"Maybe there's a religious thing here," Connie Mickelson chimed in. "Maybe she's a Druid and this was their holy time and she was hanging out in the forest."

"I asked, and she didn't have anything specific. In fact, she got mad and said, quote, I thought that's what lawyers were for, to come up with things like that. I, politely as possible told her it wasn't a case I'd be interested in," Barry said.

"Don't tell me you gave her my phone number," Marc said. "I'm still pissed about the last time you did that."

"No, no, I didn't," Barry said. "In fact, she said she was going to sue me, too."

"I'm just glad someone else got this call. I've had my share," Marc said.

"Oh, please," Connie replied. "I was getting calls like this when you were still a twinkle in your daddy's eye."

"How did your case go?" Barry asked.

"What case?" Connie asked.

41

"The Kullens," Marc replied. "The most dysfunctional family since the Borgias. I got another postponement. Dr. Butler promised to have her psyche eval done by Friday. She said she's trying to decide if she should laugh then move to a different state and hide from them."

"What are you going to do with it?" Carolyn Lucas asked.

"I have no idea. I'm hoping something will come to me after I get the shrink's report. I told Lorraine to give me a good recommendation."

"You cannot let this bunch of lunatics go to trial," Connie said.

"Maybe I should," Marc said. "Let the courts and justice system deal with them. I'll think of something.

"Oh, more news," Marc continued. "I found out Margaret is getting married."

Marc was referring to his ex-lover, Judge Margaret Tennant. They had recently split-up for the third or fourth, but definitely final, time.

"How do you feel about that?" Carolyn asked.

Marc looked at Carolyn, smiled and said, "I'm fine, Mom. In fact, I wish her well. She's a terrific lady and I hope she's happy."

"There you go," Connie said. "Me, I always hope my exes die a slow and painful death."

"Right after you squeeze them for all the money you take them for in the divorce."

"Earned every penny," Connie said barely able to avoid joining in on the laughter.

"And now," Marc said. "You'll have to excuse me. I'm going to go into my office, crawl under my desk and sulk for an hour about Margaret. My safe space."

"Shut up!" Barry almost yelled. "You got the best consolation prize of all time: Maddy."

"I'd be very careful if I were you," Marc said. "Don't let her find out you called her a consolation prize."

"Good point," Barry agreed. "I better make sure my health insurance is current in case she ever finds out I said it."

"Okay, so I won't be sulking," Marc said as he walked toward his office.

Marc was at his desk, more precisely seated with his back to his desk. He was leaning on his credenza, the window open behind it watching the traffic on Charles and Lake. A beautiful summer day was enticing him to set aside his work and play hooky for the afternoon. Marc leaned out a little further to watch two teenage girls in shorts crossing the intersection. Realizing that at his age, his daughter would extremely chastise him for looking at girls that young no matter how cute they were. As his guilt was kicking in for leering the way he was, the intercom on his phone buzzed. It startled him and he banged his head on the window.

"Owww!" he said a little too loudly.

Rubbing the back of his head, he answered his phone.

"Maddy's on line two," Carolyn told him. "Why are you yelling?"

"Never mind," Marc said as he answered Maddy's call.

"Hey, what are you doing?" he asked trying not to sound guilty.

"I'm sitting in my car a couple of houses down from my philandering subject," Maddy said. "How did court go this morning?"

"You must be bored," Marc said.

"I am," Maddy replied. "I should know better than to take a divorce case."

"Why did you?" Marc asked.

"The money's good and Harriet was good to me when I was starting out," Maddy reminded him, referring to a divorce lawyer friend of Marc, Maddy and Connie Mickelson. "Oh, shoot! That reminds me. You're not gonna believe what I found out this morning."

"What?" Marc asked, the pain from the thump on his head subsiding.

"Harriet's client, the wife I'm doing this for, is Vivian's niece."

"Seriously? Does Vivian know what you're up to?"

"I doubt it. Get this. Her name is Nicolette Osborne. She is forty-seven and two years ago she left her first husband after twenty-two years for number two, Bradley Osborne, now age twenty-nine."

Marc chuckled then said, "Are you kidding?"

"No, he's twenty-nine and this is marriage number three for him. And right now he's in the house I'm watching, having a little afternoon romp between the sheets with another forty-something divorcee."

"Is he cute?" Marc asked trying to bait her.

"I guess, maybe," Maddy replied. "In that pretty, bad-boy kind of thing that does nothing for me," Maddy lied.

Marc laughed and said, "You liar. You probably have enough pictures of him to fill a photo album."

"Wait a minute," Maddy said turning serious. "Hang on a second. Someone pulled into the driveway."

Maddy set her phone on the passenger seat and picked up her small, Bushnell binoculars. She watched as a woman exited the black Lexus sedan and started walking toward the front.

"What is this?" she whispered to herself while she watched. When the woman reached the front door, she turned her head so Maddy could see her face.

Maddy picked up her phone as she watched the woman enter the house. "Marc," she said, "it's Nicolette, the wife."

Maddy tossed the glasses onto the passenger seat and said, "I need to get in there."

"No, wait!" Marc yelled. "Don't go in there! She may have a gun."

Maddy was out of her car and hurrying toward the house, phone still at her ear. When she reached the driveway, she heard the shots.

"Pow, pow," two quick shots, a pause, then three more quick ones, another pause and one final shot.

Maddy stopped in the driveway and knelt down behind the Lexus the woman was driving. "Shots fired, Marc. Call 911 and give them this address," she said then told him the street address.

"Madeline? You stay the hell out of there," Marc yelled into an empty phone.

Maddy slipped her phone into the back pocket of her jeans. By this point, she was holding her 9 mm Beretta in her right hand. She waited a few seconds then sprinted to the house.

"Six shots," she whispered to herself. "Maybe that's all she had."

Maddy got to the front door and listened for roughly twenty seconds. Hearing nothing, she quietly turned the doorknob then threw the door open, jumped in and went to one knee. Holding her handgun in front of her, she swept the room with it until she saw Nicolette calmly sitting in the living room.

"Let me see your hands," she barked out an order pointing the gun at her.

Nicolette held up both hands, palms out and said, "The gun is on the table," indicating the coffee table in front of her. On it was a .38 caliber six-shot revolver.

"I was about to call the police," Nicolette calmly said.

Without lowering her gun, Maddy took a chair directly across the room from her. She retrieved her phone and called Marc.

"Are you all right?" Marc said.

"Yeah. I'm in the house. Nicolette is here, and I have her. Did you call the police?"

"Yes, they're on the way and so am I. Connie's with me. If traffic is okay, we'll be there in twenty minutes," Marc said.

"Call 911 and tell them to send an ambulance ASAP. Tell them I'm in the house and everything is under control and I have a gun."

"Have you asked her any questions?"

"No," Maddy replied.

"Don't. In fact, tell her you have a lawyer on the way and that she is to keep her mouth shut. Don't ask her any questions. You are now a witness for the state. Got it?"

"Yeah, you're right. Okay," Maddy said. "Hurry."

Maddy put the phone away and said, "My name is Maddy Rivers and I'm…"

"I know who you are," Nicolette interrupted. "Aunt Vivian speaks very highly of you."

"Please, listen to me," Maddy said. She then told her what Marc had said about being quiet.

"I understand," Nicolette said with a rueful smile. "Believe me, I know plenty of lawyers."

The house was located in the fairly affluent suburb of St. Paul of Shoreview. By the time Marc and Connie arrived, there were two Shoreview police squad cars and two others from the Ramsey County Sheriff's patrol in front of the house. There was also an unmarked Sheriff's investigator's car and an ambulance, all with their lights flashing. The normal crowd of people, neighbors mostly, was gathering across the street.

Mark parked on the street behind Maddy's car and he and Connie hurried toward the house. As they did, the ambulance slowly pulled out of the driveway and drove off. As it did, a hearse from the medical examiner's office took its place behind the Lexus.

Marc explained who they were to the deputy who had stopped them. The deputy used his radio to have the lead investigator come out of the house.

A minute later, two plainclothes cops came outside; a black man whose name was Kendell Walker and a younger white woman, Ruth McGowan. They joined Marc and Connie on the driveway next to the coroner's hearse.

45

"What can you tell me?" Marc asked.

"Two dead. A man and a woman naked and on the bed. Looks like three shots each," Walker said. "We recovered a .38 revolver that was on the living room coffee table. All six shots were taken. From the size of the wounds, that is likely the murder weapon."

"I need to see my client," Marc said.

"Sure, follow me," Walker said.

He led both of them into the house. They showed IDs to the deputy at the door who recorded their names. When they entered the living room, Walker asked Marc if he knew Maddy.

"Um, yeah, we're acquainted," Marc said. "Ms. Mickelson will represent her…"

"She's not a suspect. She's a witness," Walker tried to protest.

"I'm representing Madeline Rivers," Connie said with authority.

"Take Maddy outside and wait for me," Marc told Connie. "I need to talk to Mrs. Osborne alone."

When they were alone, Marc pulled a chair up next to Nicolette.

"How are you holding up?" he asked.

"Terribly," she replied. "Are they going to arrest me?"

"Yes, they are," Marc admitted. "Look, you need to know, I can't represent you after today."

"Why? Aunt Vivian knows you."

"Because I have a conflict. The woman who found you…"

"Maddy?"

"Yes, her. She is going to be a witness for the state. We have a personal, romantic relationship. It would be unethical for me to represent you because of that. In fact, it might be unethical for me to be this involved.

"I know some terrific lawyers," Marc continued. "I'll talk to Vivian and we'll get you someone good. Until then, keep quiet, don't talk to anybody, especially anyone in jail. They might put someone in with you and try to get you to talk. Don't do it.

"You'll be brought before a judge, probably sometime tomorrow. We'll find a lawyer for you and have him or her meet with you yet today."

"Hey," Marc heard Connie's voice from behind. "Tony's here and he brought Vivian. Harriet Kennedy is here, too," she said referring to Nicolette's divorce lawyer.

"Can Harriet come in?" Nicolette asked.

"Yes, I'll have her come in," Marc said.

"What about Aunt Vivian?"

"No," Marc replied. "They won't let her in."

When Marc joined Connie, she was with Harriet Kennedy. Connie told Marc, "Harriet and I have been talking. We don't think Maddy should give a statement to the cops."

"She was working for me and my client. Anything she saw or heard is privileged," Harriet said.

Marc looked at Maddy then back at Harriet. "We can take that position today, but it won't fly. She's a witness to a crime that was outside the scope of her employment. A judge will make her talk."

Marc saw Vivian coming toward them and he held up a hand to stop her. "I don't want you to hear any of this."

"Privileged?"

"Yes."

"Okay," Vivian said then walked away.

"If that happens, okay," Harriet said. "But for now, I'm the one who is really Nicolette's lawyer and Maddy's employer." She turned to Maddy and said, "Sorry, kiddo, but I'm not letting you talk to the cops today."

"Okay by me," Maddy said.

Marc's phone rang, he looked at the ID and said to Harriet, "Why don't you tell the investigators. I need to take this call."

Marc answered his phone by saying, "Did you get her number?"

Marc had called the office and asked Carolyn to find the number of a female lawyer he knew. Her name was Adison Greer and she was a bit of a feminist crusader. Despite that, Greer was a very capable lawyer who would do a great job with Nicolette's case.

"Yeah, here it is," Carolyn said and read it to him.

A short while later, while Marc was on the phone with Adison Greer, Nicolette was being escorted out. She was now officially under arrest and wearing handcuffs.

Vivian went to her and tried to hug her but was stopped by the deputy. Marc told Greer what was happening and assured her he would make sure Nicolette knew Greer would meet her at the jail.

With Nicolette in the back seat with a female deputy, the sheriff's car drove off. The little group on the front lawn of the crime scene could only watch her go.

NINE

Shelly Cornelius nervously paced about on the thin carpeting in her apartment's living room. For almost an hour she could hear the fighting between the couple across the hall. Shelly paced and chain-smoked Salems while trying to stay calm. This was their third big, loud fight in five days and Shelly was scared to death for her neighbor and good friend, Karenna Hines.

Karenna's boyfriend, 22-year-old Mikal Tate, was a part-time gangbanger, part-time junkie and, by Shelly's opinion, a full-time asshole. Karenna insisted when Mikal was not using, he was a decent boyfriend. But then Karenna at 19 already had two babies by Mikal.

Shelly stopped next to her second-hand coffee table. She reached down, stubbed out her cigarette in the metal ashtray and lit another one. As she set the plastic lighter on top of her cigarettes, she heard a loud crash from across the hall. A moment later, Shelly heard Karenna's door slam and Karenna pleading with Shelly to let her in.

Shelly quickly opened the door to find a battered Karenna crying and staggered into Shelly's arms. Her nose, lips and left ear were bleeding. The left of Karenna's face was swollen and bruised and there were bruises around her neck where she had been choked.

Shelly closed the door and activated all four locks. It was likely a futile gesture. If Mikal wanted to kick it in—he had done it before—the locks would offer little resistance.

Karenna was on her knees at the table, blood and tears running down her face trying to light one of Shelly's cigarettes.

"My god, baby," Shelly said as she knelt down next to her. "Let me look at you."

Shelly wiped her friend's tears then went into the small kitchen. She returned with a washcloth and a butcher knife.

While Shelly wiped the blood, tears and snot from Karenna's face, she said, "I swear, girl, if that asshole comes in here after you, I will stab that motherfucker in the throat, I swear it."

"No, no, you can't…"

"Where are the babies?" Shelly asked referring to Karenna's children, a two-year-old boy and a nine-month-old girl.

"My Momma's," Karenna said.

"I'm calling an ambulance. Your ear looks bad."

Karenna took a drag on the cigarette and as she blew out the smoke said, "I can't hear with it. He hit me, but he doesn't mean to," she quickly added. "It's the dope."

"It's because he's a mean sonofabitch," Shelly said while punching in 911 on her iPhone.

MPD officer Colby Houston came out of a Super America station on Plymouth Avenue carrying two coffees. His partner, Ross Marcott, was leaning on the side of their patrol car two spaces from the door.

"Thanks, Colby," Marcott said as he reached for the paper cup. He blew on it to cool it off, took a sip then heard their call sign come over the radio. Marcott answered it with his shoulder mic.

"There is a disturbance involving an EMT vehicle," the dispatcher said. She gave them the address and what little information she had received from the person who called it.

"We're a minute away," Marcott told the dispatcher. "Will respond ASAP."

Less than 90 seconds later, Colby Houston, with lights flashing, stopped behind the ambulance. The officers quickly got out to deal with the scene on the yard in front of the apartment building.

One of the EMTs was holding a small towel to his bleeding nose. The other was looking at his partner. The one with the broken nose also had the beginning of a black eye showing. The one helping him had a swollen left cheek.

There were two women on the ground next to the EMTs' gurney which had been tipped over and was lying on its side. One of the women was trying to help the other while screaming at the young man prancing around yelling obscenities at everyone, including the cops.

A furious and raging Mikal Tate was stomping around the small yard. He pointed at the EMTs and yelled, "I told you not to take my woman. I told you, I warned…" He stopped when he saw the two police officers.

"What?" Mikal said looking at the cops. "Hey, dude, I warned them."

"You talk to him," Marcott told Colby. "I'll check the girls."

Colby was a 28-year-old black man with a talent for cooling out angry black youths. While Marcott went to check on Karenna and Shelly,

Colby approached Mikal with his hands out in a non-confrontational gesture.

"Easy, man, easy," Colby said as he slowly approached Mikal.

"It's cool," Mikal replied holding up his hands in a don't shoot gesture.

"What's the problem?" Colby asked when he stopped a couple of feet from Mikal.

"They try to take my woman," Mikal said pointing at the EMTs.

"Okay, let's just chill out and talk about it," Colby said still holding his hands up.

Mikal, in his incoherent, drugged out-state, prattled on trying to justify his assaults on the EMTs, Shelly and Karenna. While this was taking place, Marcott was with Shelly and Karenna. Seeing Karenna badly beaten he gestured for the EMTs to join him.

The bleeding nose had stopped and the EMTs had lifted up the gurney. They were helping Karenna to her feet when they heard Colby Houston yell something.

While Mikal was telling his tale, for a brief moment, Colby turned his head to look at his partner. In that instant, Mikal stepped toward him and sucker punched him in the ear. As Colby was going down, Mikal jumped on Colby and slammed him to the ground. As he lay on top of the stunned policeman, Mikal jerked Colby's gun out of its holster. Mikal stumbled to his feet, took a step back, pointed Colby's gun at him and muttered, "Motherfuckin' pig..."

What the EMTs and Ross Marcott heard Colby Houston yell were two words: 'gun' and 'don't'.

Marcott turned to his partner and saw him lying on the ground, his left arm extended. Marcott also saw Mikal Tate pointing a gun at Colby. In an instant, Marcott's twelve years of police work and training took over. He drew his sidearm and quickly aimed it. Three loud, rapid, explosions came out of the business end of his .40 caliber.

The first shot hit Mikal in the middle of his ribs on his right side. The second under his right armpit and the third between his ear and right eye. Either of the first two would have killed him, eventually. But the third one dropped him dead on the ground.

It took four or five seconds for Shelly and Karenna to realize what had just happened. When it did, both of the young women started screaming the most vile, foul, obscenities Marcott had ever heard. And they were screaming them at him.

Both EMTs ran to Mikal. They checked him over and immediately knew he was gone. They also knew that they needed to get him out of there. In less than thirty seconds, while the two women continued to berate Ross Marcott, they grabbed the gurney, tossed Mikal onto it then shoved Mikal's body in the ambulance and took off.

Colby got to his feet. While this was going on, he came to his senses, started breathing again and radioed the incident in. Within minutes, there were four more squad cars at the scene. Another one was taking a sobbing Karenna and Shelly to the Hennepin County Medical Center.

As the ambulance with the dead Mikal Tate in it pulled away, Marcott, with Shelly and a hysterical Karenna still screaming, quietly said to Colby, "Please tell me you had our body camera on."

"I did," Colby whispered back. "But I'm not sure what it recorded."

TEN

Damone Watson used the TV's remote to turn up the volume on the 65-inch, High Def Sony in his office. He had been monitoring events in the city for the past two days. It was now Monday morning and the news was getting worse. Damone did not like bad news. Bad news stirred things up. Chaos was bad for business and events were becoming more and more chaotic.

Damone placed the remote on his desk and tersely said, "Lewis, get that white bitch on the phone. I need to know what the hell is going on in city hall."

The white bitch he was referring to was his city council concubine, Patti Chenault.

"You got it, boss," Lewis said.

While Lewis sat with his phone to his ear, Monroe came in with more bad news.

"I just got a call from our friend at Cedar/Riverside. The holy man wants to know if this protest is going to get out of hand. The last time something like this happened, there was serious trouble between the Somalis and Americans," Monroe said. The holy man he referred to meant Imam Sadia. The trouble was between Somali street gangs and African American street gangs. Damone had brokered—enforced would be a more accurate description—a tenuous peace between them. But there was definitely no love lost between the two groups. In fact, there was a good deal of racial prejudice involved with Somalis looking down on African Americans as not black enough.

"Call them back and tell them I am working on it," Damone replied.

"No answer," Lewis said. "It went to voicemail. I left a message, she is to call immediately."

Damone pointed at the TV screen. On it was the good Reverend Ferguson. Next to him were two young black women, one of whom looked battered.

"Those two girls must be the ones involved with Ferguson's victim. The moron he's trying to turn into an Eagle Scout honor student. Find them and bring them to me. Pay them if you have to."

At that moment, the white bitch was in a meeting at the mayor's office. Along with Jalen Bryant, they were there representing the city council. Also present was the City Attorney, Trudy Spencer and her top deputy, Gail Symanski and the Chief of Police, Marvin Brown and his top deputy, Reggie Terrell. The mayor had requested this meeting to discuss the events outside the Old City Hall Building. Another mass protest was taking place, larger than the recent one regarding the white supremacist rumor.

All of the attendees were seated in a conference room watching a television. They were viewing the same thing Damone Watson was watching and at the same time. On camera, in front of a collection of microphones was the righteous Reverend Lionel Ferguson, all six-feet-five, three hundred pounds of him. In front of him, once again blocking Fifth Street except for light rail traffic, was an angry crowd ready to explode. The media would report their number at twenty thousand. The actual number was barely five thousand. Still, large enough to cause serious problems if things got out of control, which seemed likely.

"Once again," Reverend Ferguson's voice boomed over the crowd, "one of our innocent, young brothers was wantonly murdered by a racist white cop! An unarmed black man, preparing to attend college this fall on a scholarship, was gunned down for the crime of being born black! Mikal Tate had his entire life before him. A life where he could and would make a difference. A fine young man, a father of two beautiful children, two children who will grow up without their father..."

"Shut this off before I throw up," Chief Brown demanded.

"...who was taken from them in front of their mother!"

Reverend Ferguson paused and looked over the crowd of both black and white faces. There was a low, stirring sound, an almost animal-like growl coming from them in anticipation of Ferguson's next words. A palpable sense of anger, frustration and fury waiting to explode.

Ferguson turned to his right, placed an arm around the shoulders of a young black woman and gently pulled her to the podium. Holding Karenna as closely as possible to hide her injuries, Ferguson leaned into the microphones and quietly, sadly continued.

"And this is the mother of the two boys whose father was taken from them. And her friend next to her. Both of them witnessed the shooting and both are prepared to swear that Mikel Tate was unarmed acting peacefully and the entire sordid mess was another outrageous overreaction and an act of brutality by a racist white cop. Racist police that run rampant across this country."

Ferguson paused again to embrace Karenna Hines while she wept into his chest. He held her for a calculated twelve seconds then went back to the microphones. He again moved his head back and forth looking over the crowd for several seconds.

"What do you want?" he finally bellowed.

"Justice!" the mob screamed back.

"When do we want it?"

"Now!"

For the next three minutes, Ferguson repeated this over and over.

"Shut it off," Chief Brown said again.

This time Mayor Fogel did what the Chief requested.

"This is unadulterated bullshit," Gail Symanski said. It was Gail who would had the unenviable task of dealing with this case in court for the city. "It's time we find the balls to stand behind our police officers."

"Let me remind you," City Attorney Trudy Spencer chimed in, "we have two EMTs, one of whom needed medical treatment because he was assaulted by Tate who verify the officer's statements one hundred percent."

"There are political considerations…" Patti Chenault started to say.

"Fuck political considerations," Symanski almost yelled.

"That kind of language is not acceptable," Mayor Fogel said.

"We could probably quiet everything by hiring an outside firm to do an investigation," Fogel's Chief of Staff, Mary Heyer, said. "Perhaps a reputable law firm."

"That's a great idea," Symanski said. "Let's spend a million bucks of the taxpayer's money for a 'cover-your-ass' commission. Or, I have a thought. How about we do what we are paid to do, do our jobs and let the police finish their investigation."

While the outspoken Gail Symanski was taking the lead on their behalf, the Chief and Deputy Chief, both in dress uniforms, sat quietly. The city attorney's office and police department had the same attitude toward criminals; they should be locked up. This was a constant source of friction with the mayor's office and city council. Because of Symanski's willingness to speak truth to power, it had been decided beforehand by Trudy Spencer and Chief Brown to turn Symanski loose.

"What do you think, Jalen?" Chief Brown asked Jalen Bryant.

"I agree, I think that's the thing to do. Let the internal investigation be completed. Then we'll see at that point. Right now, it looks like a good shooting. If so, we need to take a stand and not give in to the mob."

"Mr. Mayor?" Chief Brown asked.

"Yes, I suppose that's the thing to do," Fogel quietly said.

"You need to meet with Reverend Ferguson," Chief Brown said.

"Is that necessary?" Fogel said looking around the room for some help.

"Yes," Symanski said.

Chief Brown looked at Fogel's Chief of Staff and said, "Set it up, Mary. I'll be there and," he turned to look at Trudy Spencer, "Trudy will be there too."

"How about you, Jalen?" Brown asked Jalen Bryant.

"I'll be there, no problem," Bryant said.

"Today, this afternoon," Trudy Spencer said. "We can't let this fester."

"I'll set it up now and let you know the time," Mary Heyer replied.

On the way back to the city attorney's office, Chief Brown and Deputy Chief Terrell walked along with the two women from the city attorney's office.

"If that man ever found a backbone," Gail Symanski said to no one in particular, referring to Mayor Fogel, "he might be able to walk upright."

"Now, now," her boss said laughing quietly. "He is in charge."

"That's what worries me," Symanski replied.

"Aren't you worried about your job?" Terrell asked Symanski.

"I turn down one or two job offers a month," Symanski said. "So, no, not really."

"Thank you for coming, Reverend," Mayor Foley said to Ferguson. "Please come into the conference room where we can discuss things."

It was now 3:00 P.M. and Ferguson had agreed to meet with the mayor. The protestors were still on the streets around City Hall except now the temperature downtown was topping ninety-five and at least half from the morning crowd were gone.

Fogel held the conference room door for the reverend. Waiting inside were the same people who had met that morning.

Ferguson dropped his large frame in the empty chair at the head of the table. While he did this, he gave the attendees a warm smile and greeting. He knew each of them and they, in turn, were well acquainted with him.

Fogel took the chair at the opposite end and started things off. "Thank you for coming, Reverend Ferguson. As I told you on the phone, we," he continued waving an arm around the table at the others, "want to bring you up to date on the tragic death of Mikal Tate."

"Murder," Ferguson said.

"Chief Brown," Fogel said, ignoring the comment.

"We've interviewed all of the witnesses and the only ones who appear to have changed their story are the girlfriend of Mikal Tate, Karenna Hines and her neighbor Shelly Cornelius," Chief Brown said.

Reverend Ferguson was leaning back in his chair, his fingers locked together over his ample stomach. While Brown was speaking, Ferguson looked on with a mask of a total indifference on his face. He was tempted to fake a yawn just to emphasize the point.

"On Friday night, at the scene, both women gave a statement to our detectives. Their statements corroborated the obvious evidence of the beating Ms. Hines received from Mikal Tate. Their statements were absolutely consistent with the other witnesses, the EMTs, who were both assaulted by Mikal Tate, one of whom has a broken nose. The women's statements were also consistent with the statements of the two officers involved."

"What are you suggesting, Chief?" Ferguson asked.

"I'm not suggesting anything," Brown replied. "The statements they gave Friday were typed up and signed by the women."

"Obvious police coercion," Ferguson said. "Anything else?"

"Yes, we'd like you to cool down the rhetoric and give us a chance to complete our investigation," Brown said.

"Why? Let's assume for a minute that your investigation finds what you claim to be a valid, legitimate, police shooting. So, what? You can't be trusted. Why should we believe you? The police are murdering young black men in this country everyday…"

"That's a lie and you know it," Deputy Chief Terrell interjected. "Every honest study ever done refutes that nonsense. All you're doing is stoking race hatred."

"White racism is everywhere," Ferguson said with a smile.

"Tell him," Gail Symanski said to her boss.

Trudy Spencer looked at Ferguson and said, "If our investigation exonerates these two police officers, we will fight any lawsuit brought against the city. We're all done caving in just for public relations purposes."

"We'll see. Besides this isn't about money. It's about justice," Ferguson said.

"Reverend, Mikal Tate was out of his mind from smoking crack and snorting heroin," Chief Brown said. "He beat his girlfriend, attacked two EMTs who tried to help her, assaulted a police officer, stole his gun and was about to shoot him. A black police officer with a family, you got the wrong martyr here."

Ferguson stood up and said, "Good day, gentlemen, ladies." With that, he left as calmly as possible.

Waiting for Reverend Ferguson in his church office was Philo Anson. When Ferguson got back to his office, the two of them spent over two hours together. When Philo was satisfied he had enough dirt on the cops, he hurried back to the Star Tribune building. His story, with an across the page headline, ran the next day on the paper's front page.

By 10:00 A.M., because of Philo's story, the Northside 4th Precinct was surrounded and shut down by the mob. Three hundred officers from other parts of the city were called in to assist. Wearing riot gear, they managed to keep a lid on things with only a few minor injuries and no arrests. Philo Anson celebrated with a night on the town in the company of a high-priced, beautiful call girl.

ELEVEN

Marc Kadella waited patiently while seated in the jury box of Judge Noran's courtroom. There were six or seven other defense lawyers—he wasn't sure because one of them looked like he could be a defendant—hanging about waiting to talk to the prosecutor. The prosecutor was a young black man Marc vaguely knew with the city attorney's office. It appeared that Marc's was the only felony case scheduled for a pretrial. The city attorney only handled misdemeanors.

While Marc waited for his clients and Jerry Krain to arrive, he looked over the gaggle of defense lawyers. By the obviously inexpensive suits they wore, he was reminded that very few lawyers, let alone criminal defense lawyers, got rich practicing law. Marc was doing well compared to most, but it was still a tough, competitive way to make a living.

The door opened and his clients, all three of the Kullens, came in; the stepfather, Ambrose Kullen, age 57, the mother, Susan, age 56, and Susan's son, Troy Fontaine, age 32. They all wore the same sullen expression.

Marc went through the gate in the bar and waved them forward to greet them. He shook hands with all three and told them to sit in the front row. Troy sat first, three empty seats from his mother who sat in between Troy and Ambrose. While they were doing this Marc saw a familiar face come in from the hallway.

"Hey, Jennifer," Marc said to the prosecutor. "Please tell me you're here for me."

"I'm here for you," Jennifer Moore replied. "Let's find a place to talk."

Jennifer checked in with the judge's clerk who told her the jury room was available. The two of them went in and took chairs at the table.

"Where's the Nazi?" Marc asked, referring to Jerry Krain.

"He's in trial, so this got handed to me late yesterday," she replied, indicating Marc's case. "Interesting reading," she said with a touch of sarcasm. "I read through the case file—in fact, I couldn't put it down—and I'll tell you what Marc, the next time I go to a family reunion, I'm going to give everyone there a big hug. Some of them may have some issues, but at least they're not this bunch."

"Well, um, yeah," Marc said rolling his eyes at the ceiling. "They, uh, don't always get along too well."

"They don't get along too well? Let's see," Jennifer began. "Ambrose, the stepfather, and Troy, the stepson, get into an argument about a TV show." She picked up a sheet of paper and read, "They were arguing about who should win the American Idol contest. Really?"

"So, I'm told," Marc hesitantly replied.

"They start throwing punches, trash most of the house including smashing the TV. All the while Susan, Troy's mom, is screaming hysterically.

"She gets them settled down until Troy runs out to the garage and comes back wielding an axe. Ambrose hikes it into the bedroom, slams and locks the door while Troy is after him with the axe."

Jennifer looks up from her notes, smiles and says to Marc, "This is my favorite part.

"Troy starts in on the door with the axe. He smashes a hole in it and does... is this really true?" she asks Marc who silently nods his head knowing what's coming.

Jennifer continues to read from her notes. "...does a Jack Nicholson imitation from The Shining, sticks his face in the hole he cut in the door and says, 'Heeeere's Johnny.' At which point the old man blows a hole in the door a foot from the idiot stepson's head with a .357 magnum.

"Is that pretty much it?" Jennifer asked.

"Well, they did settle down then," Marc said trying not to laugh.

"The cops come because Susan has called them and arrest both of these geniuses. And, it is now the ninth time in the past twelve months the cops have been called to break up a fight at this place. Either between Ambrose and Troy or Ambrose and Susan. You won't see this one on Leave it to Beaver," Jennifer said.

"What do you mean?" Marc asked. "You don't see Wally and the Beav getting into it like this while Ward and June look on?"

Jennifer laughed and said, "I'm having a hard time keeping a straight face with this. You want to do what now with the All-American family?"

Turning serious, Marc said, "They've been seeing a shrink..."

"I saw her report," Jennifer said.

"And she thinks they understand they need anger management," Marc said.

"They need a year or two behind bars," Jennifer replied.

59

"What good will that do? You put either or both of these knuckleheads in jail they'll come out worse than they are now." Marc continued, "Plead each of them to a gross misdemeanor assault, sentence them to a year on the county and suspend it for a couple of years. They agree to anger management counseling and supervised probation to make sure they do it."

"Nope, they plead to third-degree assault with twenty-four months in a real prison suspended but hanging over their heads. Five years probation, two supervised, three unsupervised, if they complete the therapy," Jennifer said. "And Troy needs to move out. He's thirty-two. When is he gonna cut the cord?"

"I told him that. Make it part of the package," Marc said.

"How did you get this case, anyway?" Jennifer asked.

"The wife is a cousin of a former client. They were recommended to me. I quoted them a fee that I thought would make them run screaming out the door. Instead, Ambrose wrote a check."

"Serves you right for being greedy," Jennifer smiled.

"They're not getting a refund," Marc said. "Should we go see the judge and get this over with?"

"Krain's gonna be pissed, but I got the okay from Steve to make this go away," Jennifer said referring to her boss, Steve Gondeck. "Let's do it."

"Krain's always pissed. You're doing him a favor giving him something to be pissed about. That will actually make him happy. He won't have to find anything else today," Marc replied.

TWELVE

"Come in, Reverend," Damone said to the Reverend Ferguson.

Lewis had escorted Ferguson up to the second floor where Damone was waiting for them in the conference room. Damone saw them through the window in the door and quickly jumped up to hold it open for him. As Ferguson strolled into the room, Damone held out his hand. Ferguson almost reluctantly shook it then took the chair at the head of the table. Damone took a seat to his right.

"Thank you for coming. I've wanted an opportunity to meet you since moving to this fair city. You're a legend in the community and-"

"Don't give me your shuck and jive bullshit, boy," Ferguson said. "I know who and what you are so what do you say we cut to the chase and get down to business."

Damone stared at the man for several seconds with a perplexed look on his face. While he did this, he lightly brushed the fingers of his right hand on the polished tabletop while leaning on his left elbow.

"I, ah, I don't understand. I'm not sure what you mean," Damone said.

Lewis had retreated to a chair in the corner of the room behind the large minister. Ferguson shook his head, wiggling his fleshy face and replied,
"Get him out of here," referring to Lewis.

Without moving his head, Damone shifted his eyes to his aide and nodded once. Lewis stood and silently left the room.

When the door clicked shut, Ferguson said, "You're a drug dealer and a gangster."

When Damone opened his mouth to protest, Ferguson cut him off. "Don't bullshit me, boy. You think I was born yesterday?"

"I talked to the two girls," Damone quietly said. "Karenna Hines and her friend, Shelly Cornelius."

"I know you did. Did you think I wouldn't find out? Do you think I give a fuck?"

"Such language from a man of the cloth," Damone said quietly, maintaining his nonchalant attitude. "That collar you wear is a nice prop. I want you to stop this nonsense. You know those two cops are innocent..."

"So, what?" Ferguson almost bellowed. "It makes the point that needs to be made. White cops gunning down young black men is epidemic in this country."

Damone tilted his head back and laughed. "We both know that's not true. No, you're just exploiting a tragedy for your own purposes. How much money have you taken in from contributions? Enough for that new Mercedes?"

"This is absurd coming from a drug-dealing gangster," Ferguson said. "All right, gangster-boy. You want me to shut it down? Why?"

"Because it's not true, what you're saying. And what the community needs are good relations with the police."

Ferguson laughed until tears came to his eyes. "Not good for the community? Oh shit, boy. That's rich."

He took a deep breath to regain control, then said, "Okay, I want a hundred grand. No, make that one twenty, every month. I'll get you the bank account information. Oh, and I'll take that new Mercedes. Make it a really nice S-Class sedan. Black. I'll look good in it."

"Where do you propose I get that kind of money? Even I don't have a car like that," Damone said.

Ferguson pushed his large frame away from the table stood and looked down at Damone. "If you want to stay in my city, if you want calm in my city, that's the price. And I'll want an answer and the first payment in two days."

Damone turned his head toward the door and silently nodded. Lewis, who had been watching through the window, stepped in and held the door open.

"Thank you for coming by," Damone said. "Have a pleasant day, Reverend. Lewis will show you out."

While Damone waited for Lewis to return, he remained seated where he was. He lightly drummed his fingers on the table while thinking about what to do. He looked up when he heard the door open and both Lewis and Monroe joined him.

"You know, maybe we can use this trouble the good reverend has created for our purposes," Damone told them. "Monroe, give Jeron a call and get him on the phone for me or have him call me as soon as possible," Damone said, referring to his brother in Chicago. "Do you have a new phone for me?"

"Yes, boss," Monroe replied. He reached in his coat pocket and handed Damone a new burner phone. "You want me to give him that number?"

"Yes, do that. Tell him it's urgent and thank you."

Monroe made the call to Chicago and while they waited for Jeron to come to the phone, Lewis said to Damone, "You asked me to remind you about the accountant."

"Yes, I remember. He'll be here in forty minutes," Damone said after checking the time. "What does he want?"

"He wants to talk to you about supply," Lewis said.

"Okay," Damone replied while taking the phone from Monroe. "Jeron?" Damone asked.

"Yes," he answered.

"Give me a minute," Damone said. He stood up and said to his aides, "I need to take this in my office. Shut off the recording equipment in there."

When Damone was seated behind his desk, he continued the call to his brother.

"How are things?" Damone asked.

"We're holding our own but not making the progress I had hoped," Jeron replied.

"Your numbers are fine," Damone said. "We knew Chicago would be difficult…"

"It's like the Old West on a Saturday night. Shootings, shootings and more shootings. Most of these fools take more pride in being gangsters than businessmen," Jeron said.

"We knew that when we set out," Damone reminded him. "Keep your eye on the ball. Remember what our goal is and why we are doing this."

"Of course, brother," Jeron said. "What do you need?"

"I have a delicate job. I need a professional—not some street thug who's going to spray the streets with bullets. I need a surgeon, not a fool. Do you know anyone like that?" Damone asked.

"I know *of* someone like that. At least I have heard of someone like that. Someone the Italians have used."

"You don't know who he is?"

"I don't know anything about him," Jeron answered. "Nothing. I'm not even sure he exists. One of our Italian friends told me about him. At first, I thought he was bragging, but he assured me he wasn't. He doesn't know who he is either. He doesn't know if it's a man or a woman. He's a ghost, a whisper, a phantom."

"The real-life boogeyman," Damone said. "And he is good?"

"They say the best. Very careful and expensive. At least according to our Italian friend," Jeron replied.

"This sounds exactly like what I need. Find out what you can. How do we get in touch with him? Find everything you can."

"When do you need him?" Jeron asked.

"As soon as possible. There is too much trouble and protesting on the streets here…"

"I've seen it on TV," Jeron said. "How can you use this man to stop it?"

"It's not important for you to know. At least not over the phone," Damone answered. "Do what you can to get this man for me."

"Today, brother. Right now."

"Good. Call back today," Damone replied.

While Damone was in prison, he spent a significant amount of time educating himself. With his innate intelligence being as high as it was, he was able to grasp a good deal of knowledge simply by reading a broad array of books. Especially business books.

One of his absolute favorite subjects was how a small number of companies, primarily DeBeers, control the diamond market. Like most people, Damone believed that diamonds derived most of their value from their rarity. In fact, diamonds are not rare at all—just the opposite. They are quite plentiful. The price and value of diamonds are controlled by manipulation, controlling the supply that is allowed onto the market.

The cartels do this by storing diamonds in large, well-guarded vaults. In fact, they have literally tons of diamonds, 'stores', that will never be allowed on the market. And despite the fact that DeBeers claimed to have stopped hoarding diamonds in 2000, they had not stopped hoarding, and nothing had changed.

"Come in, Donald, have a seat," Damone pleasantly told his next appointment.

The man's name was Donald Leach and Damone found him while in prison. Leach was a mathematical wizard. In fact, Damone believed Leach lived in his own little world of numbers and equations. He was not quite that bad. His social skills were not the best, but he was not as bad as a typical techie. Leach was just more comfortable with numbers than ordinary people. He also had a problem; Donald Leach had an opioid drug addiction that he had no desire to kick.

In the late 90s Leach had been in a car accident. He had been in a car driven by a client that was hit by a drunk driver. His client was killed, and Leach awoke two days later in a hospital. Several broken bones, a concussion and a wrenched back were the result of the accident. Of course, Donald Leach was prescribed hydrocodone for the pain and Donald Leach was still hooked.

Leach did a six-year stretch in prison for helping several small businesses defraud the state of Illinois. He was able to hide several million dollars' worth of revenue to avoid Illinois' sales tax. A divorce came to one of his clients whose wife—the proverbial woman scorned—made a call to the Illinois Department of Revenue. The cheating husband was arrested, sang like a canary and Leach went to prison.

While in prison, he was able to feed his habit by coming to the attention of Damone Watson. On one of his daily trips to the library, Damone found out that one of the new librarians, Donald Leach, was an accounting wizard. Damone had been using him ever since.

"What do you need to talk to me about?" Damone asked Leach.

"We're hearing grumblings about supply levels of oxy," Leach said.

"Good," Damone replied. "That's precisely why we're controlling supply. It keeps local prices at a premium."

"I know that," Leach acknowledged. "It's mostly coming from Northern Wisconsin, outstate here in Minnesota and North Dakota. Our people in Omaha and Des Moines are doing fine. Some of these guys, especially in the oil fields in North Dakota, are starting to make noises about finding another source. They're not that far from Denver."

"What do you suggest?"

"I've run the numbers and another eleven percent for North Dakota, six percent for Northern Wisconsin and seven percent for Northern Minnesota. I think the price will stay up, but even if it drops a little, your net will be the same."

"Sounds reasonable," Damone said. He looked at Lewis and said, "Take care of it."

"No problem," Lewis replied.

Leach handed Lewis a single sheet of paper with the amounts of opioids to be released from their supply. It also had coded names and addresses on where they were to be sent.

Lewis scanned the list and said to Damone, "I'll have them shipped by tomorrow. Is this the new normal amount to these places?" he asked Damone.

"Until we decide differently," Damone said.

Damone looked back at Leach and asked, "Anything else?"

"Yes, I think we need to take another look at going to a local supply net," Leach said.

"No," Damone said. "I know the numbers and the cost of supply from California and Mexico. I appreciate your concern. We're not going to start using local doctors and pharmacies for supply. I simply don't want to and I'm not going to. They're too unreliable and can bring too much heat. Producing rock here," Damone continued referring to turning cocaine into crack, "isn't as much of a risk. The local politicians treat it as no worse than weed. Oxy's different. The heat's too much. We're staying low key."

"The way it's done," Damone continued, "our suppliers in the states get prescriptions for oxy by using junkies to go to crooked doctors. They write out the prescriptions for whatever, thirty, fifty or eighty-milligram tablets. Then the junkies are taken around to pharmacies who are in on it. They fill the prescriptions, the junkies are paid with oxy, usually a one-day supply, and the rest get sold.

"A lot of this is going on down South and out West. Everyone is making a ton of money. The doctors, the pharmacists, the suppliers, the drug companies and let's not forget, the politicians who are in no hurry to stop it.

"In Mexico, it's even easier. They simply manufacture the stuff themselves and cut out all of the middlemen. They ship to other places who turn it around to ship it to the states. UPS, FedEx and others are making a lot of money, too.

"So, no, we don't need to get involved with that. And by controlling supply, we can charge a premium price. Usually, the street price is around a dollar per milligram. An eighty-milligram pill would sell for eighty bucks. By the time it gets to the street the cost per pill is less than twenty. Because we tightly control supply, we're getting even more per milligram, a buck and a quarter to a buck and a half per dose. May not sound like much, but it adds up pretty quick."

THIRTEEN

Charlie Dudek parked his car—one that was nice, dependable, but not noticeable—a two-year-old, dark blue Buick LeSabre in the lot of the Kansas City, Kansas South Branch Library. Charlie was here to check his business email account.

So as not to draw attention to himself and to make sure no one was watching him, he spent fifteen to twenty minutes in the fiction section browsing. He found two books, a Jack Reacher and a new one by Michael Connelly. Although he personally thought the Jack Reacher books were absurd, he found them entertaining. The idea of one man getting into as much trouble as Reacher hitchhiking around the country stretched fiction to the limit. He liked Connelly's writing and his knowledge of the LAPD.

Charlie took the books and found an unoccupied computer. He quickly opened his email account and found an inquiry from earlier that afternoon. He recognized the sender, a wiseguy from Chicago, as someone discreet and reliable, although the man's discretion was unnecessary. He had no idea who Charlie was or where he lived and knew it was a bad idea to try to find out.

The message was short and to the point. Charlie was given a name, address and phone number of someone in need of his services. He memorized the information and deleted the email. Because of the job's location, by the time he was back in his car, Charlie had decided to take it. The reason being the message included a cryptic two-word note: 'Very challenging'. And the city it was in, Minneapolis, brought back memories and a tiny emotional rush. There was a woman in Minneapolis who Charlie had become quite smitten with. He had not thought of her for a while. She was way out of Charlie's league and he accepted that. But, the thought of possibly seeing her again was too hard to resist. Maddy Rivers did that to a lot of men.

Charlie Dudek was a professional assassin who lived a quiet life in a suburb of Kansas City, Missouri. If his neighbors ever found out what he did—they believed he was a traveling salesman of some kind—they would be shocked down to their toes.

One of the things that made Charlie so effective was the fact that he was about as ordinary looking as any man could be. At five-feet-eleven inches, one-hundred sixty-five pounds, he was the epitome of the average of the American male. His light brown hair was totally unnoticeable and if five people saw him and described him, there would be five different descriptions. If this was not enough, over the years, Charlie had become an expert with disguises.

What did not show from his appearance was his background. Charlie had spent ten years in the Army, the last four with the super-secret Delta Force. He had been trained by the very best instructors to kill in so many different ways he could not remember all of them. Charlie was also absolutely fearless. In fact, he was a pure sociopath. During the battle for Tora Bora in Afghanistan, when the U.S. was hunting Osama bin Laden following the 9/11 attacks, it was Charlie who went into the caves and only Charlie whoever came out.

By 2:00 P.M., Charlie had everything he would need—clothes, weapons and disguise kit—packed and ready. Before he left, he went to his next-door neighbor to let them know he would be gone on a business trip. They would keep an eye on his house while he was gone. What he really liked was to see their kids and say goodbye. To be called Uncle Charlie always made him feel good. Like someone actually cared about him.

The next morning in his motel room, Charlie took a minute for one last review of the new face reflecting back in the bathroom mirror. Satisfied his neighbor back in Kansas City would not recognize him, he finished dressing for his meeting.

Charlie had arrived in the Twin Cities the previous evening around 8:00 P.M. He had a reservation in an out of the way motel in a suburb south of St. Paul. Having been here twice before, Charlie was fairly familiar with the area, especially its freeway system. From his current location and freeway access, he could be anywhere in the metro area in thirty to forty minutes. He could also be gone in less time than that.

Shortly after checking in, he had called Damone and set up today's meeting. First things first, he would meet with Damone, find out what the job is, then settle on a price. Charlie's ultimate goal was five million in an offshore account then retirement. Still in his early forties, he would be there in a few more years; if he could give up what he did.

Charlie had chosen the place for this meeting having been there once before on a previous trip. He set the time, 10:15 this morning, on the public park walkway directly above Minnehaha Falls in South

Minneapolis. Charlie would sweep Damone for any electronic recording device, but in case he missed something, the noise from the waterfall would stifle anyone trying to listen in.

Charlie arrived before 9:00 and took up a position in the park on a bench overlooking the area. He had insisted Damone come alone but knew that was unlikely. At 9:40, Charlie saw them.

At this time of the day, even on a weekday, there was already quite a few people wandering around. When he saw the three men he briefly wondered if he should leave. His concern was for Damone's intelligence. Did he not realize that three black men would stand out like a red flag in this place?

"Well, let's find out," he quietly said to himself.

The three men separated. Charlie watched as Damone walked toward the falls and Lewis and Monroe split up to cover him. Charlie went for Lewis first and then Monroe. Neither man saw him coming.

"It's a really nice area, isn't it?" the elderly man asked Damone.

"Uh, yeah, it is," Damone agreed.

They were standing on the walkway bridge above the falls leaning on the stone fencing directly over the waterfall. The old man took a small device out of his back pocket and said, "Move over a few feet so we can talk."

It took Damone a couple of seconds to realize this old man was who he was meeting.

"Away from these people," Charlie said referring to the dozen or so standing near them mostly taking pictures.

"Hold still," Charlie said. He used the device he held and quickly waved it over Damone. Satisfied he was not wired, Charlie put it away.

"Your men won't be coming to help you," Charlie said.

With the roar of the water rushing over the falls, there was little chance of being overheard. And picking them up on any directional listening device was all but impossible.

"Relax," Charlie said after seeing the look in Damone's eyes. "They're fine. They should be back at your Tahoe by now. What do you need me for?"

It took Damone almost fifteen minutes to explain what he wanted. When he finished, Charlie was thoughtfully quiet for another couple of minutes.

"I can't guarantee that. What you're asking will be very difficult," Charlie said.

"I know," Damone agreed. "Can it be done?"

"Sure," Charlie replied. "I didn't say impossible. I said difficult. But, because I like a challenge, I'll give it my best shot. It will take several days of surveillance…"

"I know."

"…then I'll let you know if I think I can do it. Let me check this out and see what I can come up with. If I don't think it's going to happen, I'll call you and then you can decide what you want to do. I'm not suicidal or interested in spending the rest of my life in a cell. Understood?"

"Absolutely. I'll tell you now, one way or another I need it done. I do want you to call me if you can't do it this way. How much?" Damone asked.

"What were you told?"

"One hundred," Damone said, meaning one hundred thousand dollars.

"That's normal. But I won't charge you extra for the difficulty. Like I said, I like a challenge. I'll get you the wiring instructions. Just so we understand each other, no one has ever dared to stiff me."

"Deal," Damone said then stuck out his hand for a deal-sealing handshake. Instead, Charlie handed him the two handguns he had taken from Lewis and Monroe then simply turned and walked away.

FOURTEEN

During the past few days, since the death of Mikal Tate, the initial outburst of rage over his death had cooled. The media, especially Philo Anson at the Minneapolis Star Tribune tried to keep it inflamed. Despite their blatant efforts to sell newspapers, most people were waiting for the police investigation to conclude.

On June 12, the case was submitted to a grand jury. Reverend Ferguson did his best to help the two women involved—Karenna Hines and Shelly Cornelius— avoid testifying, they were both subpoenaed and forced to face the grand jury. Like most people, when seated in a witness chair in front of a grand jury and facing possible perjury charges, they both told the truth. It took the grand jury less than twenty minutes to No Bill the case and exonerate the police. Apparently, they concluded that if you assault a police officer, steal his gun and point it at him in a threatening way his partner is justified in the use of deadly force. Convincing the public of this was an entirely separate matter. On top of that, despite being warned that it was a mistake to do what he wanted to do, Mayor Fogel was about to make a huge mistake.

Kordell Glover, Jalen Bryant's mayoral campaign manager, paced about and checked his watch over and over. He was in the basement of the City Hall Building waiting for Bryant. Jalen was invited to attend this morning's meeting in the mayor's office and Glover wanted to talk to him beforehand. Glover was at the entrance to the tunnel under Fifth Street leading to the large Hennepin County Government Center. It was almost ten o'clock and the pedestrian traffic coming and going through the tunnel was still fairly heavy.

Glover checked his watch again, 9:54, then saw Jalen heading toward him. Relieved, he waited patiently for his client.

The two men shook hands, then Jalen said, "What more do we need to talk about?"

"Nothing, really," Glover replied. "I just want to make sure we're on the same page."

"Relax, Kordell. We are. Stay as neutral as possible and don't let anyone take my picture if Foley is going to be in it. I still think I should make a statement on behalf of the police. This was a clean shooting."

"Why did he shoot the kid three times?" Glover asked. "That will be the question. I hear Ferguson is going to use that to demand a trial. It was an overuse of force. An opportunity for a white cop to kill a young black man."

"Who was about to shoot his black partner," Jalen reminded him.

"Hey, I'm with you on this. It was a clean shooting. Go to the meeting and if anybody asks, give them a noncommittal quote about it being a tragedy and everyone needs to keep cool kind of thing. We'll get the endorsement from the cops, don't worry. Why is he doing this the day before the Fourth of July?" Glover asked.

"Because he's not a deep thinker. He says he wants to get it out to the public as soon as possible—no cover-up. Besides, this way, more people will be off work tomorrow to help burn the city down," Jalen replied.

"That would help us," Glover said.

"I'll pretend I didn't hear that," Jalen said. "I have to go," he continued as his elevator arrived.

"Thank you for coming," Mayor Fogel said to the crowd assembled in his conference room.

Instead of taking his chair at the head of the table, Fogel stood at that place. On the table was a small podium on which Fogel placed his papers.

Seated around the conference room table were the main players. At the other end of the table was Reverend Ferguson. The others around the table were Hennepin County Attorney, Felicia Jones, the Chief of the MPD, Marvin Brown, City Attorney Trudy Spencer, Jalen Bryant and Patti Chenault. Seated along the wall, each behind his or her boss, were deputies and assistants. Also in attendance, and sitting at the table, Bible in hand, was Damone Watson. On the same side of the table as Damone were three more community leaders from the black community.

Mayor Fogel's Chief of Staff, Mary Heyer, was going around the table handing out copies of a report. As she did this, Fogel began the briefing.

"The police department, in conjunction with the FBI who graciously assisted, has completed their investigation of the death of Mikal Tate," Fogel began.

"Try calling it what it was: a cold-blooded murder of an unarmed young black man by a white, racist cop," Ferguson said.

Mary Heyer placed a copy of the report in front of Ferguson. He picked it up and disdainfully tossed it the length of the table at Fogel. The report hit the podium in front of Fogel which caused the mayor to jump backward.

The room went silent while everyone waited for the mayor to respond. When it became obvious that he would not, the city attorney, Trudy Spencer did.

She was seated three chairs from Ferguson facing Fogel. She swiveled her chair around, crossed her arms on the table, leaned forward and glared at the abusive minister.

"Is this what you call being open-minded?" she snarled. "You don't even wait..."

"I know what's in this stack of lies," Ferguson said dismissively. "You are going to let this racist cop go free without even facing a trial, aren't you? Go ahead, deny it."

"I'm not going to deny it," Spencer said. "It was a justified shooting. Even those two girls you were able to get to lie for you told the truth in front of the grand jury."

"That's ridiculous, woman," Ferguson said as if speaking to a child. "You and your cops threatened and intimidated two poor, young, black girls into telling you what you wanted to hear."

"That will make for an interesting opening statement at your next press conference," Felicia Jones said.

"Are you, or are you not, going to bring charges against this racist cop?" Ferguson thundered, then slammed his fist on the table.

By now, there was a definite stirring along the wall behind Ferguson. There were a dozen or so members of the black community either seated or standing. Several heads were nodding in support of the reverend.

"He had the black officer's gun and was about to shoot him!" Spencer yelled back at him.

"There is no proof of that," Ferguson said more calmly. "Besides, that should be something for a jury to decide. Not white government bureaucrats."

The murmuring and head bobbing along the wall picked up.

While all of this was taking place, Damone Watson sat silently keeping his own counsel. At one point, he suppressed a laugh when he saw the panicked look in the eyes of Mayor Fogel. Other than that, he simply watched with detached silence.

Felicia Jones leaned back and motioned for her chief of felony litigation, Steve Gondeck, to come to her. The two of them exchanged several whispers, then the county attorney turned back to Ferguson.

"You want us to spend a half a million dollars or more on a criminal trial we don't believe in and can't win. Is that it? Just to placate you," Jones firmly said to Ferguson. "Not to mention that doing so would be extremely unethical."

"That's a laugh," Ferguson said with a fake chuckle. "Lawyers and ethics. What a joke."

Ferguson glared back at Jones and said, "It's not to placate me. It's to show the black community that justice is not an empty word."

"How much are you going to make on a civil suit against the city?" a female voice from behind Trudy Spencer was heard asking. When Trudy heard it, she clenched her teeth and tried to swivel her chair around before it got worse. Too late, her chief assistant, Gail Symanski, was already on her feet.

"I resent that," Ferguson replied.

"Yeah, fine, resent away," Symanski said flipping the back of her hand at him. "Answer the question."

"I don't have to answer any damn fool question from you, woman," Ferguson indignantly said.

"You can do it now, or if a civil case is brought, I'll put your fat ass on a witness stand, and you can answer it then," Symanski said. She looked at Trudy who was drawing a finger across her own throat in a sign for Symanski to stop. "Well?" Symanski asked.

Ferguson nervously looked around the room and saw over twenty pairs of eyes watching him.

"I, uh, I have advised, um, Mikal Tate's family that they have a, ah, right to bring suit. There was, um, nothing, I mean well, nothing decided about a, ah, donation to the church they might make from any proceeds. That would be up to them."

"Uh-huh," Trudy sarcastically replied. "As their spiritual adviser? Have you started shopping for your new Mercedes?"

"I'm leaving," Ferguson said. "I won't take this abuse. But," he continued after rolling back his chair and standing and pointing a long finger at Fogel, "if you insist on this cover-up, the politicians in this room will regret it at the polls."

With that, all of the black attendees, except for Damone and Jalen Bryant, followed Ferguson out the door. None of them bothered to take a copy of the investigation report with them.

A minute or so after they left, Damone picked up his copy of the report and his Bible. He looked at Fogel and said, "Mr. Mayor." Then he smiled at those still in the room, wished them a good day and quietly left.

After another moment of silence, Chief Brown said, "Well, that went better than I thought it would."

This broke the ice and elicited laughter from those still in the room––everyone except Mayor Fogel.

Trudy swiveled around again to look at her top assistant, smiled at her and said, "You just can't keep your mouth shut, can you?"

Symanski sheepishly shrugged and replied, "You know me. Because you do know me, I figure it's your fault for bringing me along. You know I can't help it."

"True enough," Trudy said.

"Gail, you slammed him, and he had it coming," Steve Gondeck said. "If Trudy fires you, come across the street. We'll find a place for you."

"I'll keep it in mind, Steve, thanks."

Having finally gathered himself together, Mayor Fogel, who had taken Damone's empty chair, said, "We need to decide what to do next. We have released a statement to the media about the findings already."

"So they can start reporting it on their noon news shows," Mary Heyer chimed in.

"Any suggestions?" Fogel asked.

"To do what?" Chief Brown asked. "It was an obviously legitimate, justified use of deadly force. My guys were exonerated. The FBI and DOJ are both on board with that. What more is there to do?"

"I think we should consider making a financial settlement offer to the family," Fogel said.

"Absolutely not!" Chief Brown thundered. "It will open the floodgates for this type of extortion."

"And law enforcement across the nation already believe their civilian governments don't have their back," Deputy Chief Terrell added. "That causes more crime. More civilian and police casualties. You're telling the criminals to go ahead, take a shot at a cop. If he shoots back, the city will pay."

"That's an overreaction," Mary Heyer said.

75

"Since this doesn't involve the county, it is strictly a city matter, we're leaving. I don't want to hear more," Felicia Jones said. The room went quiet while Jones and Steve Gondeck left.

"Along with the city's liability insurance and what we, the city can do," Fogel said, "we can offer them six million dollars right now to wrap it up and make it go away. Opinions?" Fogel asked looking at the others.

He turned first to City Councilwoman Patti Chenault.

"I think it's probably the thing to do," she replied.

"Mr. Bryant?" Fogel asked Jalen.

"No," Jalen answered. "I think we need to stand with our police department on this. Plus, it's way too early to make such an exorbitant offer. This isn't Baltimore or New York. Let's not get carried away."

"I assume you're a no, Marvin?" Fogel asked Chief Brown.

"Definitely," Brown replied.

"Trudy?" Fogel asked Trudy Spencer.

"Gail, go ahead," Spencer said.

Symanski stood up and looked over the others. "Let me see if I understand this," she began by addressing the mayor and his overpaid, glorified secretary, "You want to pay six million dollars to the family of an unemployed, high school dropout junkie for a wrongful death case that the city legally has no liability for?"

"You can't say we have no liability," Fogel protested. "I'm a lawyer too and I'm not so sure."

"Yeah, okay, whatever," Symanski said with obvious disrespect.

She held up a sheet of paper she had been holding in her hand and said, "Would you like me to enlighten you about the family? The mother," she continued reading from the paper, "of Mikal Tate is an alcoholic crack whore with eight arrests and three convictions for prostitution. The father, Emmanuel Tate, is far worse. He is forty-two and has spent seventeen of the last twenty-four years in prison…"

"There are the two boys, the sons of Mikal Tate," Chenault said.

"Fine," Trudy replied. "Set up a college fund for them. Give their mother a hundred grand to raise them. Six million? Every drug dealer in the Upper Midwest will be after Karenna and Tate's mother and father.

"We can win this thing at trial for a lot less than six million," Trudy Spencer said. *Otherwise, Jalen Bryant will shove this right up your ass in the election*, she thought.

76

FIFTEEN

"You're pretty quiet this morning," Marc said to Maddy. "You okay?"

"Yeah. I'm fine," she said with a small smile.

"This is nothing today. You won't have to do anything," Marc said.

"Oh, yeah, I know. But what if the judge asks me something?"

"Answer her truthfully, but don't get carried away. If she asks you a question, answer just that question. And it's okay to ask her to repeat it if you're not sure what she is asking. Don't worry. You'll be fine," Marc assured her then reached over and squeezed her hand.

They were in Marc's car on I-94 crossing the Mississippi River bridge into St. Paul. The motion to prevent Maddy from testifying in Nicolette's trial was today in Ramsey County. They were on their way to attend it.

"What happens if the judge rules I don't have to testify?"

Marc paused for a moment before answering her. As he was about to, a guy in a huge pickup truck swerved in front of him causing Marc to hit his brakes.

"Asshole!" Marc yelled then hit his horn.

The driver of the pickup looked in his mirror then flipped him off.

"Don't," Maddy sternly told him. "Let it go. The last thing we need is to get in a fight with some redneck idiot. Be a little patient."

Marc looked at Maddy and said, "That's great. You're telling me to be patient. Have you ever watched the way you drive? One hand on the wheel, one hand on the horn."

"That's different. Now, answer my question," she said.

"Why is it always different?"

"Move along," she snarled.

"Yes, ma'am. What was the question?"

"What happens if...."

"Oh, yeah. Well, if you aren't allowed to testify, I think the state's case is over. Without you, they can't tie her to the time of the shooting or the gun. The M.E. can give a time of death, but it's not that precise. Greer can argue they were already dead when she got there. There were no prints on the gun. It wasn't registered to Nicolette, her husband or anyone she knows."

"The gunshot residue on her hands and clothes?" Maddy asked.

"She was at a shooting range she regularly goes to that morning. Didn't I tell you that?" Marc asked.

"No."

"Yeah, she's been a sport shooter for many years. There's video of her there earlier that day," Marc said. He looked at Maddy and continued, "Lucky for her no one saw what she was shooting with."

"What was she…"

"I don't know, but it doesn't look like she had a long gun with her."

"She was practicing with that handgun," Maddy quietly said.

"Maybe, but there's no evidence of it," Marc said.

"What about you calling 9-1-1?"

"They can make me testify that I was the one who did it," Marc said. "But they can't make me testify how I knew to do it—where I got the information. I got it from you and if I try to say that, Greer will object. It's hearsay."

"You think the judge will rule I can't testify?" Maddy asked.

Without hesitation, Marc answered. "No, I don't for a couple of reasons. One, it's too crucial to the state's case. And what you saw and heard is not really a privileged communication from a client in the normal sense of that word. No one is asking you to divulge what a client told you only what you personally saw. Plus, you witnessed a very serious crime. I think she'll risk being overturned on appeal rather than let a double homicide case slide."

Marc and Maddy entered the Ramsey County Courthouse through the Fourth Street entrance. The Art Deco twenty story building is a rare jewel in the era of glass and chrome office buildings. Built during the Great Depression, it came in under its $4,000,000 budget and ahead of schedule. Unheard of for a government project in more modern times.

"Oh my god!" Maddy exclaimed. "That's beautiful!"

The two of them were walking through the first floor to get to the elevators. What had grabbed Maddy's attention was a 60-ton, 38-foot tall white onyx statue of an American Indian. Originally named the Indian God of Peace, the PC police forced its renaming in 2012 to the Vision of Peace. Since it dominated the first-floor lobby, it was hard to miss.

"Haven't you ever been in this building before?" Marc asked.

"Yeah," Maddy replied while she read the plaque on the statue's base. "But I always came in the Kellogg entrance."

"Impressive, isn't it?" Marc asked.

"I'll say. It's beautiful," Maddy replied.

"One of my favorite buildings," Marc said as they continued toward the elevators. "Love the Art Deco style. Very classy."

"They should build more like it," Maddy said.

"Too expensive," Marc said.

They reached the elevators—the very last ones in Minnesota to give up the tradition of attendants on them—and waited for their ride.

"Do you know this judge?" Maddy asked as the doors for their car were opening.

"No," Marc replied.

The elevator doors opened and waiting in front of Room 1416 were Tony Carvelli, Vivian Donahue and Nicolette Osborne's divorce lawyer, Harriet Kennedy.

After greetings were completed, Kennedy said, "Nicolette and Adison are inside."

"Who's the judge?" Marc asked.

"Suzanne Kelley," Harriet answered him. "You know her?"

"No, uh uh," Marc said. "Never heard of her."

"Adison likes her. Liberal feminist and relatively new to the bench. A couple of years. This is probably her first big homicide case," Harriet said.

"That could be good," Marc agreed. "She'll want to be careful and a little concerned about being overturned on appeal."

"You really think so?" Vivian asked.

Marc looked at her and said, "I don't know, Vivian," he shrugged. "It's a theory. To be honest, I don't know any more than you do. This is an unusual motion. There doesn't seem to be any cases directly on point. We'll see."

"Why am I so nervous?" Maddy asked.

"Good question," Marc replied.

"You're the subject of this thing," Carvelli said. "No one likes to have their name tossed around in court."

"Probably," Maddy said.

Marc opened the door and looked around. There were ten or twelve people, mostly elderly court watchers, seated on the benches. He saw three reporters that he knew for sure and two more who could be. The only one seated at the tables was Nicolette Osborne. The lawyers were in chambers with the judge.

Vivian went in first and a very forlorn looking Nicolette turned to see her aunt striding toward her. Vivian, followed by Marc and Kennedy, marched right through the gate. Maddy and Carvelli took seats directly behind the bar.

Vivian and Nicolette embraced then Nicolette said, "Thank you for coming. I feel better already."

Nicolette looked at Maddy and said hello and nodded at Carvelli.

"You shouldn't talk to each other," Marc said referring to Nicolette and Maddy.

"Sorry," Nicolette said.

"It's okay," Marc replied. "Just for the sake of appearances, ignore each other."

Nicolette looked at Maddy who shrugged her shoulders and said, "Sorry."

Before Nicolette could say anything else, the door behind the bench opened. Leading the way was Nicolette's lawyer, Adison Greer. She was followed by the two prosecutors, Kevin Cheng and his second chair, Polly Connors.

"We kicked it around and the judge decided to do this in chambers," Adison quietly said when she reached the table. "She wants Madeline back there, too." Adison looked at Marc and said, "I told her you were Madeline's lawyer, so you get to sit in. And you, Harriet, in case she has any questions about Madeline's employment. Sorry," she said looking from Vivian to Tony.

Marc whispered to Vivian, "I think this is best. Let's keep this out of the papers."

"I agree," Vivian said. "We'll be fine waiting here."

They trooped single file into the judge's chambers. Judge Kelley, in her robes, was seated at her desk. To her right, her court reporter was setting up his equipment. The judge amiably greeted everyone and told them to find seats.

The prosecution took the two chairs to the judge's left. Adison Greer moved her chair a couple of feet away from Kevin Cheng before sitting down. Nicolette was seated to Adison's left.

Marc, Maddy and Harriet Kennedy sat down on the judge's sofa.

"All set?" Judge Kelley asked her court reporter.

He nodded his assent then Kelley turned to the small crowd in her chambers. She read the case title and court file number into the record then paused.

"Starting with the prosecutors, I want each of you to give your name and who you represent for the record," the judge told them.

Cheng went first and then everyone else around the room identified themselves, including Maddy. When they finished, the judge started again.

"We are here on a motion by the defense for an order of suppression to exclude the testimony of a witness for the state. That witness is Madeline Rivers and, as noted, she is present," Kelley said.

She looked at Adison Greer and continued, "The basis for that motion is Ms. Rivers, at the time of the event at the center of this case, was working as a licensed private investigator. Ms. Rivers, please read your investigator license number into the record."

Maddy found her billfold in her purse, opened it and read the number off of the license.

"Ms. Rivers was in the employment of the defendant's lawyer, Harriet Kennedy. Is that correct, Ms. Kennedy?"

"Yes, your Honor, it is," she replied.

"Okay," Kelley continued turning back to Adison Greer, "let's hear it, Ms. Greer."

"Your honor," Greer said beginning her argument, "the state wants to use Ms. Rivers as a witness for their case against my client for the death of Charles Osborne and Morgan Ellison. The defense is requesting that the court disallow Ms. Rivers' testimony on the grounds of attorney-client privilege.

"First of all, your Honor, Madeline Rivers did not actually witness the shooting deaths of the two victims."

"She saw-" Kevin Cheng started to say but was stopped when Judge Kelley held up her hand to him.

"You'll get your chance," Kelley said.

"As I said, your Honor, she didn't see anything. She may have heard some gunshots, but that has not been determined.

"Further, this was not a casual occurrence. Madeline Rivers was performing her duties as a private investigator on behalf of Harriet Kennedy, the defendant's lawyer, and by extension, of course, the defendant herself. As you likely know, anything Ms. Rivers did in the course of her duties is obviously covered by attorney-client privilege. Or anything she may have seen or heard during the performance of her dutics is privileged. She cannot testify. To allow her to testify would be an obvious reversible error."

"Objection," Cheng said. "She has no idea if this would be reversible error and it is inappropriate for her to even bring it up."

"Overruled. She's a lawyer, Mr. Cheng. In a motion such as this, she is entitled to state her opinion. Are you worried that I might not have thought of that myself? Trust me. It occurred to me.

"You may now continue," Kelley told Greer.

"Since Ms. Rivers cannot be allowed to testify, then the indictment must be dismissed."

Judge Kelley held up her hand to Cheng to stop him from interrupting again, which he was about to do.

"The gun found in the living room must be excluded. They have no way of tying the gun to my client.

"The gunshot residue test they performed is out because they had no probable cause to perform it and…"

"She was sitting in the living room five feet from the murder weapon!" Cheng almost yelled.

"…and, even if it's allowed, the GSR found on her hands and clothing came from a shooting range earlier that day. Mrs. Osborne has been a competition shooter for twenty-five years. We have proof she was at the range that day.

"In short, your Honor, without the testimony of Madeline Rivers their case falls apart. My client should not have to go through the ordeal of a trial to clear her good name. This must end now. Thank you."

"Mr. Cheng," Judge Kelley said, indicating he could proceed.

"This is preposterous," Cheng jumped right in and said. "She, Madeline Rivers, was sneaking around peeping through keyholes…"

"Objection!" Maddy jumped up and yelled.

While suppressing a smile, Judge Kelley quietly said, "Ms. Rivers, please sit down."

By this time, Marc had a hold of Maddy's arm and was gently trying to pull her back onto the couch.

"Watch it, buster!" Maddy said to Cheng. "That's not what I do."

Kelley looked at the court reporter and told him to strike everything Maddy said from the record. Her last remark clearly embarrassed Cheng and drew laughter, even from the normally stoic court reporter.

Before continuing, the judge pointed a finger at Marc and then a still steaming Maddy. She then held that finger to her lips to make sure Marc got the message. Marc silently nodded his assent.

"My point, your honor," a flustered Kevin Cheng said, "was she was working on behalf of a divorce lawyer on an entirely separate matter. She was not involved with this criminal case. Plus, there was no communication in the common meaning of that word. The only thing the defendant said to her was," Cheng looked at his notes and said, "'I was about to call the police.' The defendant told Ms. Rivers that after Ms. Rivers entered the house and found her calmly sitting in the living room. If the court wishes, we will stipulate that this statement was privileged and not allow it to be heard by the jury..."

"Of course, they will," Greer said. "Because it's actually exculpatory."

Judge Kelley held up a hand to Greer to silence her.

"There was no communication covered by privilege. Madeline Rivers is a material witness to a double homicide. The state's case must have this crucial testimony."

"Ms. Greer?" Kelley asked.

"Your Honor, hypothetically, let's say I am representing a man accused of bank robbery. Then assume, after I have been retained, while driving in my car, I see this same man running out of a bank carrying a bag. Does the prosecution suggest I have an obligation to come forward and testify? That what I have seen my client do is not privileged? Of course, it is."

"No, it isn't," Cheng said.

"Why? What's in the bag? For all I know it could be his lunch. If I tell the police about this, they could try to use it against my client for the crime he is accused of for which I am representing him," Greer said. "There are no fingerprints or DNA on the gun. It is not registered to my client, her ex-husband or the deceased woman he was having an adulterous affair with. In fact, the gun was stolen. It could have belonged to anyone. An ex-boyfriend or even ex-husband of the deceased."

"Your Honor, it comes down to Madeline Rivers must be made to testify as to what she saw and heard while outside the crime scene. There is no communication that privilege would apply to. This would make for an interesting law school or bar exam question," Cheng continued. "but we have a double homicide. A premeditated, first-degree double homicide. Her testimony is crucial to the state's case."

Kelley held up both hands, palms out and said, "Enough. I'll take it under advisement and make my ruling."

Greer commandeered the jury room and brought everyone in after leaving Kelley's chambers. Everyone found a seat around the table before Greer began.

"Well?" she said looking at Marc, the criminal defense lawyer.

"I have no idea," Marc said. "If I had to guess, I think she'll rule Maddy has to testify. I think it's the 'no communication' argument. Plus, this was a serious crime. Sorry," Marc said looking at Nicolette.

Nicolette grimaced a bit then said, "That's what Adison thinks, too."

"What do you think?" Marc asked Maddy trying to break the tension. "She thought she'd try her hand at being a lawyer," Marc said looking across the table at Vivian and Carvelli.

"Shut up," Maddy said trying not to smile. "He made me mad."

Marc then told Vivian and Carvelli about Maddy's objection.

"Way to go, kid," Carvelli said. "I'm proud of you."

"Actually," Greer interjected, "she was pretty good. Emphatic and passionate."

When the laughter stopped, Greer said, "Seriously, Maddy. It was good. You slapped him pretty good and he noticeably dialed it back."

"See," Maddy said looking at Marc. "I'm a natural."

"So, now you're bragging that you're a natural lawyer?"

"Ah, I'm not sure I meant that," Maddy replied.

Carvelli, driving one of Vivian's cars, a new Bentley, drove Nicolette home. Vivian was in the back seat with her niece and neither said a word.

Carvelli pulled the car into the driveway of Nicolette's Lake of the Isles home and parked. He jumped out and opened the driver's side back door.

"The thought of going back to jail…" Nicolette quietly said letting her words hang in the air.

"You're a long way from that," Vivian replied. "One step at a time."

The women exited the car and embraced in the driveway.

"Thanks, Tony," Nicolette said.

"If you need anything, call," Carvelli said. "Anytime, day or night."

"Thanks, I will."

As they watched Nicolette walk up the sidewalk to the front door, Vivian said, "I'm really worried about her mental and emotional state. She doesn't seem as strong as she used to be."

"Maybe some counseling," Tony said.

"I'll see what I can do."

SIXTEEN

"I think that's Connie and Albert, three or four cars ahead of us," Marc said to Maddy.

They were in line at the Corwin Mansion on Lake Minnetonka. Vivian was hosting her annual summertime, invitation-only, charity event. Every year, on the Saturday evening of the last weekend in June, Vivian held an informal bash to collect for some cause or other. A 'soak the rich' party. If Vivian Donahue invited you to her party, a no-show RSVP was not acceptable.

"What kind of car does he drive?" Maddy asked referring to Connie's date, Appellate Court Judge Albert Spears.

"That is a 1957 Chevy Bel Air," Marc admiringly said of the classic car the judge was driving. "And it's a beauty," Marc said.

"Guys and cars," Maddy said.

"That car, in the shape it's in, can sell for up to a hundred thousand dollars," Marc said as he inched forward toward the valet parking.

"Seriously? Guys and cars," she said again.

They saw Judge Spears stop and the parking attendants open the doors for them. One of them replaced the judge at the wheel to park it.

"Watch," Marc said. "Spears will watch the kid drive away."

That is exactly what the judge did, with an anxious look on his face.

"Worried about his baby," Maddy said watching Spears.

"My favorite couple," Marc and Maddy heard a familiar voice coming from behind them. They were in Vivian's backyard ten feet from her pool taking in the scene. As usual, those in the scene were taking in Maddy. Her hair was done up and she was wearing a new fashion pantsuit. It was white, loose in the legs and bare shoulders. Very fetching and it covered the knife and bullet scars.

"Hi," Maddy said as she and Vivian hugged. Marc and Vivian exchanged cheek kisses then Vivian got in between them. She took both by an arm and started leading them toward a reserved table.

"Have I told you how happy it makes me to see you two together?" Vivian asked.

"Let me think," Marc said. "Not for at least forty-eight hours."

"Shut up, smartass," Vivian lightly said.

"Feel free to slap him," Maddy replied.

86

"He'd like it too much," Vivian said. "We have a table for you."

Connie's office had a table reserved for all of its members. Everyone else was already there with spouses or dates. Introductions were made to the few new faces. While this was taking place, Marc nodded at Tony Carvelli.

"Always the ones to be fashionably late," Carvelli said.

Without moving his head, Marc moved his eyes to look first at Maddy then back at Carvelli. Marc raised his eyebrows and was holding an arm against his chest pointing a finger at Maddy.

"Of course," Carvelli said. "Waiting for the Princess."

"I didn't say that!" Marc quickly said while holding up his hands, palms out and taking a step back.

Maddy's eyes turned to slits, her lips pursed together as she looked first at Marc then Tony.

"Worth the wait," Judge Spears said. "Every minute of it."

"Thank you, your Honor," Maddy said looking at Spears. She looked back at Marc and Tony and said, "At least there's still one gentleman left."

"Hey, he just beat me to it," John Lucas, Carolyn's husband said. "Owww," he yelped after Carolyn gave his ribs a sharp elbow.

For the next hour, the banter around the table, the good-natured back and forth, continued. The band began to play at 9:00 and a few minutes later Marc and Maddy were the first ones on the portable floor. After the third song, Judge Spears broke in to spin Maddy around the dance floor.

While Marc walked back to their table, he saw Vivian across the pool speaking with Tony Carvelli. Carvelli saw Marc and motioned for him to join them.

"What's up?" Marc asked them.

"Vivian hasn't heard from Nicolette for two days," Carvelli said.

"It's been, what," Marc began, "ten days since the hearing? Have you been in touch with her?"

"Just about every day," Vivian answered. "I spoke with her Thursday and she assured me she would be here tonight. It's almost nine thirty and she's not here. I called a couple of times and she didn't answer."

"I told her I'd run over and check it out," Carvelli said.

"You want me to ride along?" Marc asked.

"Would you two do that for me?" Vivian asked.

87

"Of course," Marc said. "Do you have a key to her house? Do you know where it is, Tony?" Marc asked.

"Yeah," Carvelli said. He held up a piece of paper. "The lock and alarm combinations."

"Let me tell Maddy, then we'll go," Marc said.

The Saturday night traffic was light and with Carvelli's heavy-foot driving, the drive was barely fifteen minutes. On the way, Carvelli called the MPD non-emergency number. He identified himself—the person taking the call knew him—and requested that a uniform patrol meet them at Nicolette's. When they arrived, Carvelli parked in the driveway. The squad car was in front of the house.

"Hey, John," Carvelli said to the MPD sergeant while shaking the man's hand.

The three of them met in the yard and Carvelli introduced the cop, John Hendrik, to Marc.

"The lawyer," Hendrik said, "Should've worn gloves."

"Hey..." Marc started to protest.

"I'm just giving you a little jazz," Hendrik said with a grin. Turning serious he asked Carvelli, "What do we have, Tony?"

As they crossed the front yard to the door, Carvelli gave him a quick rundown of the situation. Carvelli read the numbers by a streetlight off the note Vivian had given him. He punched them into the lock and opened the door.

"Go ahead, John," Carvelli said.

The policeman went in first, carrying a flashlight and his service pistol. Carvelli, also carrying a gun, followed by Marc trailing.

They went through the main floor then the sergeant went upstairs. He found her in the bedroom.

While the crime scene unit and the medical examiner worked inside, Tony and Marc waited in the yard. They had gone upstairs and looked through the door into the bedroom. Nicolette was lying on the bed, very pale with blue lips, arms at her side, unmistakably dead. On the nightstand next to her were three or four pills, an empty pill bottle and an empty bottle of Grey Goose.

"Let's finish clearing the house then I'll call it in," Hendrik had said.

"You should call Vivian," Marc said. "Maddy's called three times in the last ten minutes. I don't want to call her back until Vivian knows."

By this time, they had been standing around in the yard for a half hour. Vivian would be getting worried.

"I know," Carvelli acknowledged. "I'm hoping we hear from the M.E. soon."

Five minutes later, one of the crime scene techs came out through the front door. He was carrying a clear plastic bag. From all of the lights of various cars and emergency vehicles lighting up the place, they could see there was a piece of paper in the bag. The tech walked directly to them and handed Carvelli the bag. Tony held it so Marc could read along. It was handwritten with the flair and precision of a woman.

> *Dear Aunt Vivian,*
>
> *Ever since my surgery three years ago, I had a benign tumor removed from my thigh, I have had an opioid addiction. Gary and the kids had no idea.*
>
> *It has gotten worse since I met Chip. In fact, he was my main supplier, which is why I killed him. He told me he was leaving me and cutting me off. I could not deal with it.*
>
> *Now, with the specter of prison looming, I could not face it.*
>
> *Please don't show this note to Gary. Tell them I still love him and of course, the boys, and I am terribly sorry, but I cannot go on.*
>
> *Nicky*

"The M.E. is ready to call it a suicide. Unless we find something, and it doesn't look like it, that's what this is. The house is clean. We'll finish going through it but..."

"You'd better," Carvelli quietly said. "You should know, her aunt has a lot of clout."

"Hey, we do our job."

"I know," Carvelli said. "I just thought I'd give you a heads up. This thing will go to the chief and the mayor."

"Really?" a now concerned tech asked.

"Yeah. Don't worry. The aunt is very sensible. Here," Carvelli said handing the man the note back.

The tech went back inside while Carvelli pulled out his phone. Before he called Vivian, Marc spoke to him.

"This makes sense, the opioids. Her husband, Chip, the gigolo and his latest squeeze both had them in their system."

"From the autopsy?"

"Yeah," Marc said.

With that, Carvelli put the phone to his ear while Marc used his to call Maddy.

SEVENTEEN

Vivian Corwin Donahue was seated front and center at the gravesite. To her left were her two grandnephews, Nicolette's two boys, Paul, age 15, and Tad, age 12, named for his dad's father. Next to them, the third seat to Vivian's left, was their dad, Gary Anderson. To Vivian' right was her favorite escort, Tony Carvelli. Nicolette was being interred in the family plot at Lakewood Cemetery.

The only attendees were family with a few exceptions allowed by Vivian. Marc Kadella and Maddy Rivers were among them. They were all seated under a lawn canopy solemnly listening to the minister's final words. Being Lutherans, the ceremony was relatively short and sweet.

Vivian Corwin Donahue was the current matriarch of the Corwin Family. They were one of the most socially prominent, politically connected and old-money wealthy in Minnesota. Their lineage could be traced directly back to the 1840s when the family patriarch, Edward Corwin, immigrated to the mostly empty prairie that was Minnesota at that time, started farming and began building an agricultural empire that was worth billions today.

The minister completed the service and the crowd started to disperse. Everyone had already paid their respects to Vivian and given sincere condolences to Gary and the boys. While Carvelli stepped aside to patiently wait, Vivian gave the boys a hug, then gave one to Gary.

"At least she's not in pain now," Gary said to Vivian. "I'm just sorry I wasn't able to…"

"Stop, Gary," Vivian quietly said. "You had these two to take care of. What happened to Nicky was not your fault. Meet someone. Get on with your life."

"I have met someone," he replied.

"Good, I'm glad. Bring her around. I'd like to meet her. Is she good with the boys?"

"Yes, they seem to get along pretty well, all things considered. The boys tell me we should get married," he said with a smile. "You'll get an invitation."

"I'd better," Vivian chided him.

Carvelli escorted Vivian away from the grave toward the limo they came in. Along with Vivian to his right, on Carvelli's left arm, was Vivian's favorite granddaughter, Adrienne. She was home from college for the summer and staying with her grandmother.

"I feel terrible about the boys," Adrienne said. "Don't people think about the damage they do when they do that…commit, you know…"

"Suicide," Carvelli said for her. "I have no idea what anyone is thinking about at that moment."

"She was in a lot of pain. Addicted to drugs, looking at prison after throwing her life away. She wasn't strong enough to deal with it," Vivian said. "I just wish she had reached out, to me or someone…"

"Don't do that," Carvelli said. "You just got through telling Gary not to accept the guilt. Don't start finding reasons to take it on yourself."

Vivian was walking with her left arm looped through Carvelli's right arm. She looked at him, gave him a pained smile, patted him on the shoulder and said, "Thank you, Anthony. You're right. It's just so very sad."

Marc and Maddy, along with the limo's driver, an ex-cop friend of Carvelli's currently working for another ex-cop friend, were waiting for them.

"I think these are worse than homicides," the driver, Dan Sorenson, said to Marc and Maddy.

"Think so?" Marc asked.

"Yeah, I do. A murder may seem senseless, but they don't normally leave the guilt behind that a suicide does," Sorenson quietly said.

A few seconds later the people they were waiting for arrived. Maddy gave Adrienne and Vivian big hugs and wiped a tear from Adrienne's cheek.

"You'll be okay," Maddy told her.

"We're meeting the probate lawyer at Nicolette's house tomorrow morning at ten," Vivian told Maddy. "You're welcome to…"

"I'll be there," Maddy assured her.

Vivian looked at Marc and said, "We'll go through the place, make an inventory and get it ready for an estate sale."

"If I knew anything about probate…" Marc started to say.

"Stop," Vivian said. "I know plenty of lawyers. It's just the ones I know are boring corporate types. None do the interesting things you do."

"I'm not sure interesting is the word I would use," Marc replied.

"We should go," Carvelli said.

Dan Sorenson opened the limo's back door then said his goodbye to Marc and Maddy when his passengers were aboard.

"Estate sales don't usually net much money," the probate lawyer, Ken Frost said.

It was the morning after the funeral and Vivian, Adrienne, Carvelli, and Maddy were standing in the living room of Nicolette's house. They were here to make an inventory to prepare for the sale.

Vivian looked around the immediate area and said, "It's amazing what we collect even in a short lifetime. Then we're gone and what does it matter?"

"You're acting a little melancholy this morning," Carvelli said to her.

"I have some forms for you to use," Frost said before Vivian could reply. "For each room, kitchen, bathrooms, bedrooms," the lawyer said as he handed a small stack of paper to Carvelli. "The rest of the estate seems to be pretty straightforward," he continued looking at Vivian. "Her money was in a few investment accounts. She had named Osborne as the beneficiary of all of it…"

"Do his heirs inherit?" Maddy asked.

"No, he died before her, so the accounts and her remainder estate passes to the secondary beneficiaries, the two boys. She even set up trusts for each of them," Frost explained. "Nicolette stands to inherit from him if we find anything."

"Even if she killed him?" Adrienne asked.

"That was never legally adjudicated," Frost replied. "I have an assistant doing a search on him. If we find something, the boys will likely get it."

"Good!" Vivian replied.

"Unless you have any questions, I'm going to leave you to it," Frost said.

"Thank you, Ken, for stopping," Vivian said.

"No problem, Mrs. Donahue. If you have any questions, call my cell number."

"Will do," Vivian replied. "Well, I guess we should get at it."

Each of them took a different area of the house and started the inventory.

Carvelli chose the basement. It was fully finished and there were four rooms, including an unused, full bathroom. He went through the two smaller rooms in about an hour.

He moved into what looked to be a TV room but had become a storage room. Carvelli found several boxes filled with items that obviously belonged to the late Chip Osborne. They were stacked up against a sofa. When he moved them to open and look through them, Carvelli noticed something. The carpeting the boxes covered showed a definite sign of wear from the sofa being moved. It looked as if the sofa had been pushed back and forth to and from the wall many times. His curiosity piqued, Carvelli moved it himself.

Along the wall, all the way around this room, was decorative wainscoting. He had expected to find something behind the couch, but everything looked in order. Carvelli checked the area out thoroughly wondering why the sofa had been moved so much. There was plenty of dust built up behind it, so it was not from vacuuming. He even looked under the sofa and carefully checked the back of it.

When he finished, to help himself get up off of his knees, he placed his right hand on the paneling. That's how he found it. One of the panels was not completely flush with the one next to it. If he had not felt it with his hand, he would not have noticed it.

Still on his knees, he carefully examined the two panels. At the bottom, where the paneling met the baseboard, he found a small opening. Using his pencil, he placed it in the opening, and one of the panels easily swung outward. It had been hinged to open from left to right. Inside the panel, neatly stacked, were several plain brown boxes that looked to be 3 inches deep by 4 inches high by 6 inches long. There were 6 altogether. Next to them, also neatly stacked, was money, cash and a lot of it—at least fifty or sixty thousand dollars.

"Drug stash," Carvelli whispered. "Looks like Chip had a nice little business going."

Carvelli ran up the stairs and out to his car. From the trunk, he took out a pair of latex gloves and a digital camera then hurried back inside. He found Vivian and Maddy together in the kitchen and told them both to come downstairs.

While the two women watched, he quickly took 8 photos of everything inside the wall hideaway. Carvelli then opened one of the boxes and held it up while Maddy took 3 shots of the contents.

"What are they?" Vivian asked.

"OxyContin, oxycodone," Carvelli said. "Opioids."

He held one of them up in the light and said, "These are 80 milligrams worth between eighty and a hundred bucks each on the street. I'd guess there's five hundred, maybe more, in this box. Worth between forty and fifty grand in one box."

By removing the box that he was holding, a book that the boxes were covering was revealed. Carvelli removed a few more of the boxes then brought out a 6 x 9-inch book. He stood and sat on the back of the couch. With Maddy and Vivian looking over his shoulder, he paged through what was obviously a ledger.

"This is his customer list," Carvelli said. "Recognize any names?"

"Unfortunately, I do," Vivian quietly said.

"Really?" Maddy asked.

"Yes, I do," Vivian said again. "These are not street people. They are well-to-do, upper middle class and even wealthy people. Do you mean to tell me they were buying drugs from Chip Osborne? Opioids?"

"I think so," Carvelli replied. "At least that's what I think this is."

"I know kids at school," they heard Adrienne say. All three of them turned and saw her standing at the bottom of the stairs.

"My god, Adrienne! Please tell me you're not..." Vivian exclaimed.

"I'm not, Grandma. But these drugs are easier to get than beer. It's everywhere. I know a guy who overdosed and died. I went to his funeral," Adrienne said.

"Come here, child," Vivian said.

Tears were running down Adrienne's cheeks as she walked quickly into her grandmother's arms.

A couple of silent minutes passed, then Vivian said, "Anthony, we have to do something about this."

"What do you suggest? You need to understand something. This is a mountain to climb. There is so much money being made. Everyone— the drug companies, crooked doctors, politicians, pharmacists, you name it—is in this up to their eyeballs."

"We can at least go after the dealer who sold to Chip Osborne and killed my niece," Vivian said.

"What do you want to do about this?" Maddy asked Carvelli, pointing at the stash in the wall.

"We need to call the cops," Carvelli said. "Turn it into them."

"Why, so they can keep the cash and sell the drugs themselves?" Maddy asked. "There's a good chance that will happen."

"Maybe," Carvelli solemnly said. "But they're not getting this," he said holding up the ledger. He looked at Maddy and said, "Maybe we should stop looking the other way. Let's think about this. I'll call Minneapolis and get them out here. But this goes in the trunk of my car. If we do go after this," he continued tapping a finger on the ledger, "this will be a place to start."

EIGHTEEN

The first two days following the leak by Reverend Ferguson of the internal investigation of Mikal Tate's death brought on the largest protests in Minnesota since the Vietnam War. The leak was done through Philo Anson. The first day, with a couple of hundred Black Lives Matter members in front of a crowd of at least five thousand, the protest brought Downtown Minneapolis to a virtual standstill.

Each day it started around 4:00 P.M. on Sixth Street under the Government Center Building. The more or less peaceful parade went West along Sixth to Hennepin Avenue. There it turned South, went two blocks to Eighth Street then back East. When it reached Fifth Avenue, a block East of the Government Center, it went North back to Sixth Street.

The protestors did this until 11:00 P.M. By then, except for a few hardcore marchers, the crowd had dwindled to almost nothing. But the real damage was done during the 4:00 to 6:00 rush hour. The downtown commute was virtually frozen in place.

On the third day, the less-than-enthusiastic protestors, those that were there for the fun, started to melt away. On the fourth day, the crowd was down to barely one thousand. But these were mostly the angry, whipped-up-by-Ferguson, hardcore participants.

Philo Anson parked the Jaguar in the Star Tribune lot. He whistled a tune he had heard on the radio as he passed through security. Philo was on top of the world. His ego told him he personally was responsible for shaking the foundation of the City's government. And he could not have been prouder. When he reached his desk, there was a terse, hand-written Post-It note on his computer screen.

'See me immediately' was written on it followed by the word 'Proctor'. Vince Proctor was Philo's editor. A note like this, written and slapped on his screen like that, was not likely to be good news.

Normally, Philo would hang up his suit coat, then wander to the break room for coffee. He would then take an hour to stroll around the room allowing his co-workers to congratulate him—or so he believed—for his latest piece of brilliant writing. The tenor of Proctor's note told him today was not the day for such indulgence.

Before Philo reached Proctor's glass-enclosed office, Proctor was on his feet and coming out his door. He came out and abruptly said, "Follow me. They're waiting."

A silent, short ride up on the elevator brought them to the publisher's office. The 'they' who were waiting for them was the publisher, managing editor, and chief counselor. None of them looked happy to see Philo.

"Come in, please," Aidan Smith, the paper's publisher told them. "Have a seat," he continued, indicating the two armchairs in front of his glass-topped desk.

The other two people in the room were Carl Bedford, the managing editor, Proctor's boss, and Blane Weathers, chief counsel for the paper. Bedford was standing by a window leaning on the sill and the lawyer was seated next to and slightly behind Aidan Smith.

Smith made introductions then reached across his desk and handed a multipage document to Philo.

"Mr. Weathers and I had a meeting with the city attorney early this morning. With the okay from the mayor and city council, Ms. Spencer gave us this copy. They are also sending copies to all media outlets," Smith said.

"We got a copy ourselves ahead of the others because, according to Trudy Spencer," Blane Weathers said, "your riot-inducing article was extremely one-sided and highly inflammatory. In fact, she claims the only source you used was Reverend Lionel Ferguson."

"Is that true?" Proctor's boss, Carl Bedford, asked.

"He was a significant source, yes," a slightly nervous Philo replied. "Not the only one. He was at the meeting when the mayor told him, and others, that their investigation exonerated the cop who shot Mikal Tate. Ferguson assured me it was a total cover-up. Check my stories word-for-word. I made it clear that the information used came from sources who were briefed by the mayor and city and county attorneys. I told the truth. We're covered."

"Yes, we know," the lawyer said. "And you're right. We're covered. Sort of. You made it sound like others in the meeting agreed it was a cover-up but named no one."

"I even checked with the mayor's office. All I got was a 'no comment'," Philo said. "What's the problem?"

Aidan Smith stood up and looked out the fifth-floor window at the Vikings' new stadium a few blocks away. While he did this, the room remained silent. Finally, he turned back and looked from Proctor to Philo.

"Okay, here's what I want. You," Smith said looking at Philo, "take that report and go through it line-by-line, item-by-item. Write up a thorough, unbiased, objective article for the front page of tomorrow's paper.

"I want it edited by both you and Carl and ready for me by 3:00 P.M.," Smith told Proctor. "Any questions? Are we clear?" he asked Proctor and Philo.

Both men said, "no, sir" and "yes, sir" in unison.

As the two of them walked back to the elevator, Proctor said, "I guess the report is pretty credible. At least that's what Bedford told me."

"Tell me something," Philo bitterly said. "When did they start worrying about unbiased, objective reporting?"

"This is different. It's not about our beloved president. It's about a local cop who we crucified and maybe unjustly."

Philo Anson stormed out of the Star Tribune building. He had completed his article to cover the paper's ass, but that was not enough. What the higher-ups wanted was an apology from Philo personally for inciting the protests. At least that was the impression Philo got out of the meeting. He submitted his article and decided to let his boss, Vince Proctor, make the changes.

When he reached his car, Philo checked his watch. It was a few minutes past 3:00. Instead of driving off, he realized he had time for a quick drink then go to the protest. There was a bar across the street from the parking lot, the Front Page, that attracted a clientele from the paper. Normally Philo steered clear of the place not wanting to fraternize. It was still early enough that the bar would not be crowded. It was also close enough to ground zero of the protest that he could walk there by 4:00 and leave his car in the paper's lot.

Charlie Dudek, in disguise, was hanging out in front of the Government Center. He was wearing an old, battered Twins' baseball hat, wrap around, very dark sunglasses and a scraggly beard. He had a loose fitting, dark-brown, long-sleeve shirt, well-worn jeans and sneakers. Charlie looked like a street person just hanging out with the protestor crowd. For the past three days, he had been scouting his target by walking along with the protestors. Mostly he was checking out the TV cameras.

Charlie had found a place along the protest route where he might be able to pull it off. It was risky in the extreme, but the idea of it got his juices moving. He had not done anything this risky in years. Besides, he reminded himself, if the opportunity was not there, he would walk away and get him somewhere else.

Rob Dane had been with the MPD for 6 years. In the army at 18, 8 years with the 82nd Airborne, then back home to Minneapolis. His high school girlfriend, Leah Johanson, had stayed loyal and waited for him. Three months after his discharge, they were married, and a month later, Rob was an MPD cop. Now, five years and two little girls later, he was extremely happy and on the list for promotion to sergeant.

"Be careful tonight," Leah told him while watching him dress for duty.

"I will, babe," Rob said and smiled at his wife. Leah was a classic Scandinavian-Minnesota girl. Blonde, blue-eyes and girl-next-door pretty. Rob truly believed he was the luckiest guy alive. And their two little copies of the mother had Daddy wrapped around their little fingers.

"It's actually calming down a bit. They yell a lot, but so far, no real violence."

"I wish they'd stop spitting on you. It's disgusting," Leah said.

"You know something?" Rob said while hitching his belt around his waist, "It's more degrading for the ones who act like that. They really don't understand how bad that makes them look."

"It's still disgusting," Leah said. "Remember, helmet and vest."

By 4:30 the protestors were again marching West on Sixth. Charlie had fallen into his usual place, but today he was quietly walking along. In fact, he had stuffed earplugs in each ear to keep the noise out. Each night he would end up with a headache from the same overdone chant— "No justice, no peace"—over and over. They had not even begun the march when it started up.

Couldn't someone please come up with something new? Charlie again started thinking. *That same tiresome, banal, clichéd chant had passed its sell-by date years ago.*

While he walked along, once in a while, Charlie would pump his fist in the air like everyone else. Behind the glasses, Charlie's eyes were in constant motion. He was looking for something in particular and was relieved not to see them—TV cameras. The first two days they had been everywhere. Starting yesterday, there were very few and today, so far none.

Philo Anson was on the very far left end right behind the Black Lives Matter sign holders. He was getting hot, tired and sweaty and started to wish he had not stopped for a drink. Or if he had just one instead of a quick three, that would have helped.

Philo was in the exact same spot as the previous three days. He was a step to the left of Reverend Ferguson and six or seven feet in front of him. They had walked less than three blocks and Philo was already feeling it. The Nicollet Mall was coming up and he was thinking he might slip away there. Philo looked ahead and saw the same cop who was there yesterday, twenty feet from the Mall's corner. Today, with a smaller, less raucous crowd, there were fewer cops and they were spaced out a bit farther apart.

A few feet before he reached the helmeted cop, Philo looked back to see if Ferguson was watching him. A small crowd of admiring, ass-kissing sycophants, Philo thought, was close to the reverend. Philo also noticed a scruffy looking, likely homeless guy, shuffling along and coming up behind and to the right of Ferguson. Philo removed his phone from his pocket and took a few pictures.

Charlie had been gradually creeping up on the fat man as the crowd moved along. After two blocks, even with earplugs, he would have paid each one of them a crisp C-note to stop the inane chanting; "No justice, no peace, no justice, no peace."

When they were halfway down Sixth Street on the third block, he looked ahead and saw his mark. He could see a little man in a shirt and tie just ahead of the reverend turn and look at him. The man looked to be on the verge of collapse.

When the fat minister was fifteen feet from his mark, Charlie made his move. He stepped up directly behind the reverend and grabbed his shirttail in his left hand to hold him for a second or two, then reached around him on his right, pinning Ferguson's right arm to his side. For the second or two it would take, the long-sleeve brown shirt would fool the mark into believing it was Ferguson's arm and hand pointing a gun at him.

Rob Dane had been on station at his normal spot, twenty feet from the corner of Sixth and Nicollet Mall. Today the protest was actually a little boring. The numbers were way down and his colleagues down the line had reported very little cursing at them and, so far, no spitting.

Rob looked East along Sixth and watched the Black Lives Matter sign get closer. Every time he saw one, he wondered the same thing, *How many back lives are saved across America every day by blue lives? Someone should do a study.*

Rob watched the sign holders go by then saw Reverend Ferguson close behind. Ferguson seemed to stutter step then looked at Rob with a mask of rage on his face. It was then he saw the arm come up and point right at him.

Without hesitation, Rob's army and police training took over. He drew his sidearm, went into a shooter's stance and yelled "gun" at least three times. He also fired three quick shots into the large man's chest. Two went through Ferguson's heart, and the third through his left lung. Ferguson was dead by the time he hit the street.

Rob Dane maintained his shooter's stance for another two or three seconds. As Ferguson's large body fell, for Rob, the entire scene took on an eerie, almost ethereal silence and slow-motion, film-like quality. It took that long for his conscious brain to realize what he had done and for the crowd to react. When the people around Ferguson finally realized what happened, all hell broke loose.

As quiet as a whisper, Charlie Dudek vanished.

NINETEEN

"I'm telling you, I saw a gun. That fat reverend, Ferguson, was glaring right at me. He had hate in his eyes. I was watching him and the next thing I saw was his right arm come up. He had a gun in his hand pointed right at me. I drew and fired."

A tired, anxious, frustrated and a little bit scared Rob Dane finished giving his statement, for the third time, to Internal Affairs. The two I.A. cops were Lt. Kevin Scott, a white man, and Sgt. Bowie Jackson, a black man. Both were veterans and had the reputation of being fair, honest and very thorough. Also in the interrogation room at the downtown headquarters was Arturo Mendoza. Mendoza was a lawyer brought in by the police union to represent Rob.

Lt. Scott shut off the recorder on the table. He looked at his partner who shook his head indicating he had no more questions. It was after 9:00 P.M. and they had been at it since 6:00.

Scott looked across the table at Rob and said, "All right, officer. That's it for tonight. I have to tell you that you are officially on paid administrative leave pending our investigation. We will need your badge and your gun and the second one you have on your inventory card.

"Off the record," Scott continued, "I have to tell you, no one's come up with a gun and nobody else saw it…"

"He had a gun, goddamnit!" Rob yelled. "I told you, it was a small automatic. A thirty-two or twenty-five."

"Stop," Scott said. "They're looking. The investigation is just starting. You need to go home."

"A suggestion, officer," Sgt. Jackson said. "You may want to get your family out of the house for at least a few days. This isn't going to calm things down."

"I know," Rob quietly replied. "Her parents have a lake place up North. I'll see if they can take her and the kids up there. I'm gonna need a lawyer…"

"The union will pay me to take your case. If you're not comfortable with me, we'll find someone else who is contracted with the union," Mendoza said. "I won't be insulted if you want someone else. You need to be comfortable with who you have."

"Don't you want it?" Rob asked. He knew Mendoza a bit. A couple of his fellow officers had used him, and Mendoza had done Rob and Leah's Wills.

"Yes, I do," Mendoza said. "But you have to decide. Think about it and give me a call. You have my card. Call anytime."

While Internal Affairs was wrapping up the statement of Rob Dane, Philo Anson was in his favorite "gentlemen's club" enjoying the show. There were two girls, in particular, he was especially fond of. Both were long-legged, five-hundred-a-night Russians. Given his luck today, he was thinking about a thousand-dollar, hot tub threesome treat. Unfortunately, because of this afternoon's event, Philo was having a hard time concentrating.

Philo was less than ten feet away from both Reverend Ferguson and the cop who shot him. When he heard the shots, he froze for 2 or 3 seconds before he saw what happened. First, he looked at Ferguson lying in the street. His feet and arms were twitching because his heart was dead but not his brain. When Philo thought about the sight, he closed his eyes and shook his head. He knew that image was going to give him sleep problems for quite a while.

He stared at Ferguson for several more seconds then turned his head toward the source of the shots. A cop in a shooter's stance, his gun still pointed at the dead man, was yelling something Philo could not make out.

Running down Sixth on both sides were at least a half dozen cops. Panic took over Philo and he ran to Nicollet Mall and hid behind a tree. He stayed there, terrified, for two or three minutes while the police surrounded the body and sealed off the area. It was then Philo remembered he was a reporter.

He carefully stood up and cautiously walked over to the scene. Inexplicably, none of the now 8 or 10 cops around Ferguson paid any attention to him. He managed to walk up to the body within three feet. Philo, phone in hand, stood there for almost ten seconds taking photos before a police sergeant spotted him.

Two of the cops grabbed him while the sergeant grappled with him to get his phone. All the while Philo was yelling that he was a reporter with the Star Tribune. This finally caught the sergeant's attention and he allowed Philo to show his ID. At which point, phone in hand, Philo was not very pleasantly escorted away.

On the way back to the Star Tribune building he emailed the photos of Ferguson's body to his company email. He also called Vince Proctor to let him know what he had. An eyewitness account and photos of Ferguson's killing. Proctor had not even heard the news yet.

Tomorrow's front page story was written and ready for the morning's edition by six o'clock. The big argument with the top management was over the photos. Philo wanted them all in the paper, including the one he had sneaked of the cop shooter, Rob Dane. The brass decided to use one photo of Ferguson on an inside page but refused to run the cop's photo. Sensibly, they decided it would be irresponsible to run the photo until they knew for sure he was the accused shooter.

As a side benefit, the apology story Philo had reluctantly typed up earlier that day lost its juice. Instead of a below the fold, A Section front page article, it went to the B Section of the Metro news.

Philo sat at the bar ignoring the strippers, staring at a photo on his phone. It had been a stroke of blind, dumb luck, he realized. But, nonetheless, there it was in full color and crystal clear.

"That's something about that big mouth black guy that got popped today," the bartender said bringing Philo back to reality.

"Huh? Oh, yeah," Philo said while shutting off his phone. "I was there. I saw it."

"Seriously?" the scantily-clad bartender responded. "Did you write it up for the Strib?"

Philo was a regular enough customer so that the bartender knew him and what he did.

"Yeah, I did," Philo said beaming. "A Pulitzer Prize!"

"You want another one?" the bartender asked referring to Philo's twenty-dollar watered-down brandy soda.

"Uh, no, I think I'm gonna take off, Colleen. Thanks."

Philo, feeling pretty good, left a twenty on the bar and headed for home.

When the shots were fired, the crowd panicked and ran. Charlie Dudek joined them. In the two to three seconds after the shots were fired and the stampede began, Charlie was able to tuck the gun away in his back waistband. Getting out of the area was easy.

Charlie had rented a car using a fake license and credit card. Knowing ahead of time where he would try to set up the cop, he parked it two blocks away. It was less than two minutes after the shooting when Charlie was in the car and on the street driving out of downtown. Because of rush hour traffic, it was more than an hour later when he pulled into the motel.

Ever the cautious, careful professional, after removing the disguise and a quick shower, the last thing he did was wipe down the room for prints. The shooting occurred shortly after 4:30 and Charlie was heading south on I-35 by 6:15. The only disappointment came because he had not found time to see Maddy Rivers.

Damone Watson, along with Lewis and Monroe, was watching Damone's office TV. Every local station was running the story about Ferguson. Damone flipped channels and silently watched in amazement. The professional had pulled it off. He had suckered a cop into shooting Damone's number one pain-in-the-ass.

"I don't get it, boss," Monroe said. "I thought you wanted things to calm down. How does this help us?"

"Mikal Tate was a good shooting. The city will throw some money at it and it will go away. This will give the cops and the media something to do. Take their attention away from our business. Then there's the fat dearly departed Reverend Ferguson."

"Oh man, look at that shit," Lewis said.

A young black man had sucker punched a female reporter while she was on camera. The young woman dropped like a rock, clearly unconscious. The cameraman continued to film while the assailant celebrated with several of his friends.

An angry Damone stood up behind his desk, pointed a finger at the TV and said, "I want them. All five of them. Get out there, find them and bring them to me. That is not what is needed right now. Whatever sympathy we had for the community is now gone!"

"We have a meeting with the Muslims in an hour, boss," Lewis said.

A calmer Damone looked at him, nodded and said, "Thank you, Lewis, for reminding me. All right," he continued looking at Monroe, "You go find them. You know who to go to. These young fools will be bragging about putting this girl in the hospital. Idiots. Get them here tonight." Damone reached in a desk drawer and came out holding a rubber band wrapped bundle of money. He tossed it to Monroe and said, "Here. Pay whatever you have to, spread it around and find them."

"You got it."

Lewis parked the Tahoe behind a Muslim bakery near Cedar/Riverside. The bakery was one of the dozens of small businesses in the Somali community forced to do the bidding of Damone and his Muslim allies but paid well for their services. Before Damone was out of the SUV, his man, Saadaq Khalid, was out the back door to greet him.

"What is it?" Damone asked Saadaq after the traditional greetings.

"Sadia is getting greedy. He wants an increase in supply and a larger piece for himself personally. His head is getting larger every day. He acts as if everything is run by him."

"And what is he doing with the money he receives now?" Damone asked.

"I don't know," Saadaq admitted.

"Make that your priority. Find out. Why does a holy man need more Earthly possessions? It could be useful. Now, let's go see the Imam," Damone said.

"Our supplies run out too fast," Ahmad Gurey complained to Damone. Gurey was the Imam's man who handled the drug business on his behalf. Imam Sadiq was in attendance but chose not to speak. He did not entirely trust anyone, especially Damone.

"They're supposed to," Damone said.

"Increase the supply," Gurey said loud enough to make it sound like a demand.

"Watch your tone," Saadaq told him.

"Apologies," a chastened Gurey said. Gurey looked at the Imam who stared back. The Imam obviously disapproved of Gurey, his man, backing down so easily.

"Raise the price," Damone said.

"We just did, a month ago," Gurey said immediately realizing his mistake.

"Did you know about this?" Damone asked Saadaq.

"No, I did not," a fierce-looking Saadaq answered while glaring at Gurey.

"This was your idea?" Damone said looking at the Imam.

Realizing he had pushed a little too far, Imam Sadia meekly nodded and shrugged his shoulders.

"I see. Well then, this meeting is over. I will not agree to either an increase in supply or price," Damone flatly stated, re-establishing his authority. "I will send the accountant to you to go over your revenue. You will cooperate with him."

He turned to leave, then said to Saadaq, "Find out exactly what they did."

"Yes, sir," Saadaq replied.

"I should have your bodies buried where they will never be found. What were you thinking?"

Damone was talking to the five young men who were involved in the assault on the female reporter. The one who had struck the woman, Rodney Stone, was standing in the middle of the group. All five were lined up against a wall in Damone's conference room.

Damone was sitting on the edge of the conference room table. Lewis and Monroe patiently waited in opposite corners of the room. When none of the five terrified young men responded to Damone's question, he stood up and moved to Rodney. He leaned down so his nose was less than an inch from Rodney's.

"Well?!" Damone bellowed.

"I, ah, we just, I guess, got caught up, you know, in the excitement," Rodney stammered.

Damone flashed his right hand at Rodney's face and slapped him as hard as he could. His head snapped back and hit the wall. Blood began seeping into his mouth from the loosened teeth and his knees began to buckle.

Damone looked them over slowly, staring back and forth for a full minute.

"I slapped you like the bitch you are because you aren't man enough to be punched. Sneak up on a woman and hit her when she isn't looking? That is disgusting cowardice. And then dance around like fools to celebrate it? And you expect to be treated with respect?!"

He stared at them again for another thirty seconds. Damone leaned forward again nose-to-nose with Rodney.

"If you're thinking about getting even with me, to come after me to earn respect, you will die a painful death—all of you. Then I will go after your families. Speak of this to no one. Now get out."

TWENTY

The funeral for Reverend Ferguson turned into a riot. The service was held at Ferguson's church, North Memorial Baptist. It was presided over by the last person that should have been chosen. A minister from Chicago, a fire-breather, more anxious to stir up racial animosity than Ferguson, had flown in. It would have been far better for the black community to bring in someone less controversial. Instead, this man, Reverend Cleveland Hawkins, was invited to perform. Unknown to the church board that brought him in—for a healthy fee—was the irony of that selection. The Reverends Ferguson and Hawkins were well acquainted with each other. Hawkins was getting rich hustling Chicago. Ferguson had tried to get a piece of the Chicago action and was driven out by Hawkins. There was no love lost between them.

Hawkins was also well known as a man who did everything he could to stir up racial animosity. He was living quite well from the proceeds. Not surprisingly, the funeral service had little to do with the dearly departed Ferguson. Hawkins spent an hour at the pulpit raging against police racism and white injustice.

Because the church was filled to capacity loudspeakers were set up outside. A crowd of at least two thousand were listening outside the church. By the time Hawkins, an excellent orator, finished, the worshippers were seething.

The chaos started when the service was over—the six men seated in front as pallbearers wheeled the casket out front. A hearse was waiting, and the funeral procession was starting to form. Unfortunately, when the mob saw the casket, a couple hundred surged forward to get it.

Three of the pallbearers were knocked down and almost trampled. The others fled for their lives. The coffin, with its cargo aboard, had to weigh well over four hundred pounds, was hoisted up and carried off. For the next three hours, the coffin was passed around and held aloft by the mourners. They paraded it around the North Minneapolis neighborhood—it was almost dropped at least a dozen times—until Reverend Hawkins got to the front. Along with a couple of local thugs brought in as bodyguards, they led the mob to Parkland Cemetery.

They got the casket to the burial site and the crowd calmed down enough to hear the graveside service. Once that was finished, a couple of hundred of the mourners, a small percentage, rampaged through the streets.

While 90% of the people who attended the funeral ducked for cover, this out-of-control bunch ran wild. They set cars on fire, looted stores, burned others down in a night of mayhem—the worst since the 60s. And the police, by order of the mayor, backed by the city council, were told to stand down and made spectators of the carnage. Of course, they were allowed to protect themselves and others. Most of the cops interpreted this exception rather liberally. By morning, there were over a hundred arrests on various charges of assault.

Fortunately, after midnight, a cold front moved in which brought a steady day of rain. Between the rain and the courage of the firefighters and police, the fires were put out and order was restored.

The cost became clear right away. In the rubble of the burned-out buildings, the bodies of seven people, including three children, were found. Most of them were Asian Americans trying to protect their property. Autopsies would prove five died from gunshot wounds. Despite their best efforts, the police were unable to charge anyone with any of the killings. The entire community was too intimidated to say who had done what.

Damone was in his apartment dressed in a beautiful, blue silk robe. He was with Lewis and Monroe and they were watching the news on various channels. It was 10:00 A.M. of the morning following the riot. Damone had expected a violent reaction—in fact, he welcomed it—but this was more than he wanted. He had no interest in black people killing yellow people. He was quite upset with that, especially the four children.

"They're mostly Koreans," Lewis reminded him. "They move in, run their businesses, but don't hire our brothers."

"They move in, work eighteen-hour days along with their families to build a business to become successful. It's a lesson our brothers, as you call them, should learn," Damone replied. "Well, it serves our purpose. The attention of the authorities will be elsewhere for months."

Damone placed his empty China cup on its saucer on the coffee table then stood up.

"Time to go," he said. "We have meetings to attend."

Lewis' phone rang. He checked the caller ID and held up an index finger, indicating to Damone to wait a moment while Lewis took the call.

111

"Yes, he's here. Just a moment," Lewis said into the phone. He covered the mouthpiece and said, "It's the mayor's office. They have an announcement to make and they want you to attend."

"About what?" Damone asked.

"She didn't say."

"Probably announcing the cop has been indicted," Damone quietly said, "What time?"

"Eleven."

"Tell her I'll be there."

"Thank you for coming," Mayor Fogel announced. "I'm letting you know what has happened and then we'll all go in the media room for a brief press announcement."

In the mayor's conference room, besides Damone, were six other leaders of the African American community. All of them had guessed the meeting was about an indictment of Reverend Ferguson's killer, Officer Robert Dane. By the extremely pleased look on Fogel's face, they could see they were correct.

Technically this should be an announcement from the office of the Hennepin County Attorney. All felony prosecutions for the county are handled by her office. Fogel insisted on making the announcement here and at the press briefing. He needed to do something after last night's mayhem. Something to show the city government was still functioning.

The only other official in the room was the County Attorney herself, Felicia Jones. Noticeably absent, because they were not invited, was Jalen Bryant and any other members of the city council. Fogel had no intention of sharing this spotlight.

"I'll get right to it," Fogel said. "The investigation of the shooting death of the Reverend Lionel Ferguson has been completed. The investigation turned up no exculpatory evidence to exonerate Officer Robert Dane. The case was submitted to the grand jury who returned a three-count indictment—one count each of first and second-degree murder and first-degree manslaughter.

"Comments, questions?" Fogel asked looking over his audience.

"Are you going to go all the way with this or are you going to make a plea deal that lets him off easy?" one of the men asked, a minister from a South Minneapolis church.

Knowing this was not his place, Fogel stepped aside and Felicia Jones took the question.

"No, we are not going to make a deal," she emphatically said. "Unless, of course, more evidence turns up that we are not presently aware of."

"There it is, the weasel words," a different invitee said.

An annoyed Felicia Jones glared at the man and said, "We cannot know what will turn up. It is our intention to have this cop's balls. Good enough?"

No one in the room said a word.

Marc arrived at the office to find no one working. Everyone, including Connie and the other two lawyers, was seated in the common area watching the television.

"Where have you been?" Barry Cline asked him.

"Court," Marc replied looking at the TV.

"Downtown?" Barry asked. "You didn't go…"

"No," Marc replied. "Hastings," he said referring to a suburban Dakota County city. "What's going on?"

"They just announced the indictment of that cop who shot Ferguson," Connie Mickelson said.

Barry and Marc looked at each with an uneasy look in their eyes. Then Barry said, "Word on the street, and from the courthouse and cops, is they should be thanking this guy."

"What?" Connie asked. "He shot him down…"

"Lionel Ferguson was no choir boy," Marc said. "Cops claim he was making a nice living shaking down drug dealers and other street-side, urban entrepreneurs. What did they indict him for?"

"Three counts," Connie replied. "One each first and second-degree and first-degree manslaughter."

"Who's his lawyer?" Chris Grafton, the fourth lawyer in the office, asked.

"Don't know," Marc replied. "The cop union will probably provide him with one."

"Would either of you take it?" Grafton asked Marc and Barry.

They looked at each other, then Marc said, "I don't think so. That's a lot of heat coming from this one."

"Would be a challenge," Barry said.

"True. But I don't know. Besides, I haven't been asked. He'll get a lawyer or two through the union."

While the press conference announcing the indictment was taking place, five police officers, two in uniform and three in plain clothes, drove up to Rob Dane's home. They arrived in two cars, one a squad car, and parked in the driveway. They were led by a tall, black man: Lt. Owen Jefferson of the homicide division. Before they reached the door, Rob was there to let them in.

"I watched it on TV," Rob said when they were all in the living room.

"Where are Leah and the kids?" Jefferson asked.

"Her parents' place up North," Rob said. "I just got off the phone with her when you guys drove up."

"Good, I'm glad they're okay," Jefferson said. "Well," he sighed, "let's get on with it. Marcie?"

Marcie Sterling, a homicide detective, stepped forward and said, "Robert John Dane, I am placing you under arrest for the murder of Lionel Ferguson. You have the right to remain silent, anything…" she continued until she was done reading him his rights. When she finished, she asked if he understood them. He answered affirmatively.

The phone rang and the male detective, Donnell Green, answered it.

"It's his lawyer, Arturo Mendoza," Green told Jefferson.

"Let him talk to him," Jefferson said.

In less than a minute, the phone call was finished.

Rob said, "He'll meet us downtown."

"Okay, let's go," Marcie said. She turned to one of the uniforms and nodded. He removed a pair of handcuffs from his belt and stepped behind Rob.

"In front," Jefferson told the uniformed cop indicating that he should cuff his hands in front. "Go easy. Rob, we have a warrant to search the house, garage and your car. Do you want a copy for your lawyer?"

"Sure," he said.

Green peeled off a carbon of the search warrant, showed it to Rob then folded it neatly and placed it in Rob's shirt pocket.

"I'm really sorry about this, Rob," Jefferson said.

"There was a gun, Lieutenant. Someone must have seen it. Please keep looking."

"We will," Marcie assured him.

114

TWENTY-ONE

"That's a little odd," Maddy said as she re-entered Marc's bedroom.

"What's a little odd, babe?" Marc asked.

It was almost 7:30 A.M. and Maddy was already dressed and ready to go. Marc was struggling with his tie.

"Here, let me help you," Maddy said.

Marc dropped his arms to his side, lifted his chin and while Maddy was fixing the tie, said, "Why do women like to do this?"

"It's very flirtatious," Maddy replied. "And a come-on. Let's you know we're very interested because we want to touch you. But in your case, there you go," she said as she finished, "you need the help."

"I would have gotten it," Marc said indignantly.

"Eventually. Tony wants to meet me for breakfast," Maddy said while they went into the living room.

"Carvelli's out of bed already? That is odd. Turn on the TV. We must be under attack by Martians," Marc said. "What does he want?"

"Don't know. He just asked me to meet him at Sir Jacks on Chicago," Maddy replied.

"He didn't ask for me?"

"No, in fact, I'm not supposed to tell you this, but he told me not to let you come with," Maddy replied.

"Great. That can only mean he's up to something criminal and he doesn't want me to know about it. Now I have to go."

"No, I told him…"

"Yes! I don't care. End of discussion," Marc emphatically said.

Maddy tilted her head and gave him her best bedroom eyes come-on. Normally, this would make just about any man fold.

"Won't work," Marc said. "I'll get it later anyway."

"It's such a turn on when you act so manly," she said teasing him.

"That won't work either. Now, let's go."

"Just for that," Maddy said as they went through the kitchen door and into the attached garage, "we'll see about you getting it later."

Marc laughed and said, "Now there's an empty threat. You mean I might get a good night's sleep."

"You're playing with fire," Maddy said, walking around Marc's SUV to her new Audi.

"Really? You want to put some money on how long each of us can hold out?" Marc asked.

Maddy stopped, thought for a moment, and then meekly said, "No, I guess not."

Carvelli had the last booth on the left up against the back wall. He was reading the restaurant's copy of the morning Star Tribune when he looked up and saw them come in. He frowned upon seeing Marc, then waved to them.

Maddy slid in first across from Carvelli. While Marc sat next to her, Carvelli leaned on the table, his chin in his left palm, looking at Maddy.

"He forced me. He threatened to withhold sex," she told him.

"Folded like a cheap suit," Marc said.

"Well, if he's going to resort to torture, I guess I'll let it go," Carvelli said.

Carvelli poured each a cup of coffee then the waitress arrived. They hastily ordered breakfast before getting to it.

"What are you up to?" Marc, the lawyer, sternly asked.

"I'm not sure yet," Carvelli replied. "I found that ledger at Nicolette's house..."

"Oh, yes, I remember," Marc said, "the evidence you withheld from the police."

"Oh, hell," Carvelli lightly waved a hand. "I suppose if you want to get technical about it."

"I'm amazed I've been able to keep my license as long as I have hanging around you," Marc said.

"Shush," Maddy said lightly slapping Marc's hand. "Let him talk."

"Thank you, darling," Carvelli said. He leaned toward Maddy, squeezed her right hand and asked, "What do you see in him?"

She looked at Marc and then turned back to Carvelli. "It's hard to explain."

"Irresistible sex appeal," Marc said.

"Okay," Carvelli said. "Time to move on.

"I have Chip Osbourne's client ledger. Vivian and I went through it and she knows about half the guy's customers. Mostly women. Vivian thinks they all belong to the country club Chip worked at, including Nicolette."

"What about Gary, Nicolette's first husband?" Maddy asked.

116

"No. Vivian called him and asked. He told her he never really liked that crowd. Anyway, to cut to the chase, I'm going undercover to find the source. Vivian wants these guys busted."

"Excuse me?" Marc said. "Isn't that what we pay the police for?"

"Whoever this is, has a line into the cops or city hall. Probably city hall," Carvelli said. "I talked to a couple guys in narcotics at MPD. They tell me they've been shut out for months. They think whoever's running things has really tightened things up. Gang shootings are down and supply, especially oxy and crack, are being tightly controlled."

"So, they need somebody from the outside," Marc said.

"Somebody who can start at the street-level and work his way up," Carvelli said.

"You're playing a very dangerous game, my friend," Marc said. "These cops you talked to, how much information did you give them? Can they be trusted?"

"I gave them nothing. Just that I had someone I knew overdose and die. Nothing else. I was acting a little cautious and let them believe I was just curious for the family. Although I do trust these guys and I don't think it's the cops."

"You're biased," Maddy said.

"I recognize that, my love. But I still think it's more likely leaks from the mayor's office or the city council," Carvelli told her.

"I'd bet on the city council," Marc said. "They all think the solution to crime is throwing taxpayers money at basketball programs for gangbangers."

Their food came and they ate for a few minutes. Maddy finished first and pushed her plate aside.

"You need to go see Jake Waschke and the guys," she told Carvelli.

"Yep," Carvelli agreed. "That's my next stop." He looked at his watch and said, "We're meeting at Jake's at nine thirty."

"We?" Marc asked.

"Not you, cowboy," Carvelli said. "The lady and me."

"What are you planning to do if this works? If you find out who this is?" Maddy asked.

"We'll decide that if we get there and hopefully get enough to bust them," Carvelli answered her.

"You should go, and I have to get to the office," Marc said.

117

Maddy parked behind Carvelli on the street two doors down from their destination; Jake's Limousine Service. The business was owned by an ex-MPD detective named Jake Waschke. Jake had foolishly gotten himself fired from the job and sent to prison for a couple of years. He had fabricated evidence of a murder case believing he was protecting his brother. Marc Kadella was the lawyer for the man Waschke did this to. It was Marc who had discovered it. Waschke took it like a man and accepted responsibility for what he did—a refreshing departure from society's norms.

"He's got two more cars," Carvelli said to Maddy as they approached the garage doors. There were two new Cadillac limos parked in the driveway.

Jake's business also provided good paying, easy, part-time employment for quite a few retired cops. Jake and three of those retired cops were waiting for Maddy and Carvelli.

The building had two large garage doors for access for the cars. On the left was Jake's office and behind him, the maintenance area. Maddy and Carvelli entered through a customer door to the left of the garage doors. When they got inside, they were in front of the large window for the office.

They both waved at Jake who was seated at his desk, his feet up on an open desk drawer. The two of them went in and found the three ex-cops waiting for them along with Jake. All four stood when they came in.

"Well, thanks guys," Carvelli said when he saw them stand. "I had no idea…"

"Get out of the way, Carvelli," Dan Sorenson said lightly pushing him aside. "Hello, beautiful," Sorenson said to Maddy.

"Hi, Dan. Hi, guys," Maddy replied as she gave Sorenson a quick hug.

"Have you dumped the lawyer yet?" another one, Tommy Craven, asked.

"Not yet," Maddy replied with a laugh.

"And you'll be the last to know," Jake said to Craven. "You guys are ridiculous," he added.

"Ah, they're like adorable puppies," Maddy said. "Especially the big guy, here," she continued as she stepped up to the fourth man, Franklin Washington. Franklin was a large black man who would throw himself in front of a train for Maddy. And she knew it. Franklin got the serious embrace. They all sat down and Carvelli took a few minutes to give them a quick version of why he wanted to see them. When he finished, he sat back waiting for questions.

"And you don't want to go to the cops for what reason?" Jake asked.

"There's a leak. Either in the Department or City Hall. Whoever is running things is well informed," Carvelli said.

"According to Andy Clayton?" Sorenson asked, referring to the narcotics cop Carvelli had talked to.

"Yeah," Carvelli said.

"Andy's no fool," Jake interjected. "He's been around a while."

"I know," Sorenson quickly and defensively said.

"You need a legend," Craven said. "An undercover legend." Tommy Craven knew this business. He had been a great undercover cop when he was on the job.

"I can't go to the department," Carvelli said.

"Then go to the Feebs," Craven said referring to the FBI. "They're great at it. They can access anything for it. They'll build you a profile no one can crack."

"Locals?" Carvelli asked Craven.

"Normally, I'd say yes. But, if you're right about the leak, then that would be risky."

"What about the DEA?" asked Franklin.

"I don't think they'd help," Jake said. "I know they used to be fanatics about protecting their turf."

"They still are," Carvelli said. "I talked to Andy about them and he says they're all cowboy assholes. They don't cooperate with locals unless they have to; and even then, it's a one-way street."

The room went silent and after a half minute, it was Maddy who had the answer.

"Paxton," she said.

"Yeah, I forgot about her," Craven said. "You think…?"

"I think we need to make a trip to Chicago," Carvelli said. "Is she still there?"

"Yes," Maddy replied. "I talk to her every couple of weeks. She asks about you," Maddy slyly said giving Carvelli a playful poke in the ribs.

"Give me a break," an embarrassed Carvelli said.

119

"Why, Tony, you're actually blushing. That's adorable," Maddy said.

"She's a hottie," Sorenson said while the others all looked at Carvelli with sneaky smiles and wide 'aren't you lucky' eyes.

"I am dead serious, Tony," Maddy said. "I tell you what. We'll go to Chicago. You ask her out to dinner, and I'll bow out. What do you say? Vivian won't care. Trust me."

"I guess we're going to Chicago," Carvelli said. "You call ahead and let her know what we need."

"I will," Maddy replied.

TWENTY- TWO

Catching a plane between Minneapolis/St. Paul and Chicago is about as hard to do as finding a cab at an airport. There is a flight between them 25 to 30 times each day. The pilots wave to each other as they pass in the air.

The day after the meeting in Jake's office, Maddy and Carvelli were on a 10:30 A.M. flight to O'Hare. Scheduled for an hour and a half, it was barely an hour after leaving that they arrived. By using her badge and DOJ credentials, Paxton O'Rourke was waiting for them at the end of the ramp.

Paxton O'Rourke, an Assistant United States Attorney, was assigned to Chicago. Marc, Maddy, and Carvelli had originally met her while she was a lawyer with the Army JAG Corps. Marc was defending a man falsely accused of treason. Paxton was the lead prosecutor.

Paxton won the trial and the soldier, an army major, was convicted. Subsequent events would prove his innocence and the verdict was overturned. Even though she won the case at trial, the Army was in need of a scapegoat. Paxton was allowed to resign but landed on her feet with the Department of Justice.

Both Maddy and Carvelli had each packed a single piece of luggage for the two days they were to be here. After a nice reunion of smiles and hugs, the three of them headed out of the airport.

"So, tell me all about you and Marc. You know, I had a little thing for him myself," Paxton said to Maddy. They were walking together arm in arm with Carvelli trailing behind.

"Well," Maddy started, "the sex is amazing."

"Shut up!" Paxton almost yelled then laughed. "I don't want to hear that."

By now, both women were laughing hysterically drawing looks from other people. Carvelli slid back a little further from them.

Upon leaving O'Hare, instead of heading toward the city, Paxton took I-294 South. Paxton, of course, was driving with Maddy in the front passenger seat and Carvelli in back. It was Carvelli, a Chicago native as was Maddy, who first noticed it.

121

"Hey, where are we going?" he asked. "This doesn't look like we're going downtown."

"We're not," Paxton replied. "We're heading for Schaumberg. I'm going this way to avoid the traffic and tolls on I-90."

"What's in Schaumberg?" Carvelli asked. "Sean O'Rourke, Uncle Sean," Carvelli immediately said, answering his own question referring to Paxton's retired FBI agent uncle.

The drive South then Northwest to her uncle's took less than a half hour. Apparently, Paxton believed speed limit signs were only a suggestion.

When they reached Sean's mini-colonial, Carvelli was the first one out of the car. He paced up and down on the boulevard while the women waited.

"What's wrong?" Paxton asked.

"I don't like sitting in back while someone else drives, I don't like not driving and…" he paused.

"Go ahead, you sexist dinosaur. Say it. You don't like women drivers," Paxton said.

Carvelli looked at Maddy somehow expecting help. Maddy smugly looked back and said, "What she said."

"How many speeding tickets have you gotten?" Carvelli asked hoping to change the subject.

"How many have I been given or how many are on my record. A lot and none. Somehow I manage to magically make them go away."

Paxton looked toward the house and saw a man coming at them across the yard.

"Hey, Uncle," Paxton said.

"Hello, Tony," Sean greeted Carvelli. He turned to Maddy, held out his arms and said, "And, of course, the beautiful Miss Madeline."

They hugged and Maddy said, "Hello, Sean. It's nice to see you again."

Paxton jogged to the front door and hugged the woman waiting for them. Her name was Helen Gregg and like Sean, a retired FBI employee. Introductions were made then they went inside.

Helen served refreshments then they got down to why they were there. Maddy had given Paxton the reason for their trip and Paxton had told Sean and Helen. Carvelli explained what and why he was going to do in more detail and what he needed.

"You need a bulletproof legend," Helen said.

"Right. Whoever is running the drug business in the Cities has political clout. We believe there's a leak in the MPD or City Hall. He has a source. He'll be able to check me out and I have to appear legit or he'll smell it. Whoever it is, isn't a fool."

"Well, you've come to the right place," Sean said. "My lady friend here spent the last ten years at the Bureau doing just that."

"I did a lot of work with DEA and Witness Protection," Helen said. "I still have contacts in the government to build one for you that your mother wouldn't breach."

Maddy started laughing and after ten seconds or so Carvelli asked her, "What's so funny?"

Maddy stopped laughing, drew a deep breath and said, "The idea that you have a mother."

Even Carvelli had to laugh at that.

"Yes, I have a mother and she loves me very much."

"If you say so," Maddy said.

"Okay, let's leave his mother out of this," Helen said. "Paxton told me a bit about what you wanted. Starting you off as a street-level dealer is actually a problem. Your age and hot Italian looks don't lend itself to that."

Carvelli put on his best Italian charm face, looked at Maddy and said, "See, hot Italian looks."

"Tell her about the customer ledger, Mr. Hot Italian Looks," Maddy said.

"I found the customer ledger for this Chip guy who was dealing the opioids," Carvelli said. "It's a pretty high-end list and they're likely jonesing by now. Even if they have found a new source, I can still use that to move in."

"You're going to have to feed these people," Sean said. "At least some."

"And without the locals in on what you're up to, you could get yourself jammed up pretty good," Paxton replied.

"I've got some cover with former cops I trust and now you," Carvelli replied. "Can't be helped. What about your contacts with the Feds? Can they be trusted?"

"I know a couple of people. They'll stick their necks out a bit for me," Helen said.

"Okay, let's do it. How do we start?" Carvelli asked.

"Have you ever done undercover before?" Sean asked.

"Yeah, a couple of times for a short while," Carvelli replied.

"Then you know the risks," Sean said.

"I'm aware. And I know how to handle myself. Plus, I already have a safety net set up."

"How about a disgruntled Witsec Mafia guy? You've been working a job in a mortgage office shuffling paperwork and you can't take it anymore?"

"That wouldn't be a lie," Carvelli said. "If I had a job like that, I'd eat my gun."

"Good, 'cause it's all set," Helen said. "You've been employed by Lake Mortgage, a real mortgage company that operates as an FBI front for us here in Chicago. You quit and haven't been seen for a couple of months."

"What did I do for Lake Mortgage?"

"You were a loan processor. You handled credit checks and the paperwork. There's a website, a listing in the phone book, legit phone numbers. If anyone calls asking about you, the person answering will go into their computer and find everything all on the up and up," Helen said.

"Ah, what's my name?"

"Oh, yeah," Helen laughed. "That could come in handy. Tony Russo. Anthony. I kept your first name for convenience. We have all the documents. Passport, social security, credit cards—they're legit but don't get carried away. The statements will go to an address you choose."

"Jake's," Maddy said.

"Yeah, that would be good. Jake's Limousine Service. I don't know the street address, but he's got a website."

"I'll find it and take care of that," Helen replied. "Now, we'll go downstairs and get a couple of different photos. One for the slightly used passport," she added, "and one for your Minnesota driver's license. We'll have you all set to go by tomorrow. You have a flight back?"

"Yes," Maddy said. "Five o'clock, United out of O'Hare."

"Good. Okay, let's get some photos and I'll get them to my source," Helen said.

"Then I'm taking everybody to dinner," Sean announced.

"We'll come back and spend this evening and tomorrow going over your new identity," Helen said. "By the time I'm done with you, you'll believe you are Tony Russo."

"What if they really dig too deep?" Maddy asked. "We don't want his mother to worry."

"Smartass," Carvelli growled.

"It wouldn't take much to run into a Witsec wall. If they get law enforcement to do it, whoever it is will recognize it as Witsec and that you're gone."

"That will actually verify what they want to hear about me."

Maddy and Carvelli exited through the upper-level doors of the Minneapolis/St. Paul International Airport. Waiting for them, leaning against his Buick SUV parked at the curb, was Marc Kadella. Maddy almost jumped on him and then turned to Carvelli.

"Let me introduce you to Tony Russo. A former wiseguy, tired of life as a schmuck in Witsec about to become a major drug dealer."

"I'm not surprised. I always knew there was a gangster right below the surface," Marc said.

Carvelli held a finger to his nose and pushed it to bend it. "I feel liberated."

"Did he take Paxton to dinner?" Marc asked Maddy.

"No, but they did sit awfully close to each other when Sean took us out," she replied.

"Hey, will you two stop talking about me as if I'm not here?" Carvelli asked.

"Stop it. Don't tell me you don't find her attractive," Maddy said.

"What about Vivian?" Marc asked.

"Don't worry about Vivian," Maddy replied. "We've, ah, talked a bit about this."

TWENTY-THREE

Arturo Mendoza, Rob Dane's union provided lawyer, was starting to wonder if he had made a huge mistake. Following Rob's arrest, Arturo had represented him through his first appearance. Rob entered a not guilty verdict and then bail had been arranged. The first appearance was in front of Judge Eason in the arraignment court. Eason, who was under media and public pressure to deny bail, decided to figuratively flip them off by setting bail at half a million. Martin Eason was a couple of months from retirement and did not much give a damn.

Arturo had been contacted by at least two dozen big-name criminal defense lawyers soon after. Arturo was no naïve virgin. He had been around long enough to know what they were after; publicity. He was also honest with himself. This case was going to generate a lot of heat and he might be a bit over his head.

The police union set up a GoFundMe account for Rob. Donations came in from all over the country including several from well-known black conservatives. Within a few days, Rob had the money and was able to make bail. Eason restricted him to his home and ordered a monitoring bracelet to be attached. Leah and the girls were still at her parents' cabin up North.

Arturo sat down with Rob and went over the list of lawyers offering their help. With Arturo's recommendation, they had selected one. A well-known man from California who had successfully represented a long list of Hollywood celebrities for a variety of misdeeds, including murder.

This morning Arturo was slowly making his way across the second Floor Atrium of the Hennepin County Government Center along with three other lawyers, starry-eyed minions of Sheldon Burke, the lawyer Arturo had brought in.

Trailing in the wake of the great man while he held a slow-moving press conference, Arturo was getting annoyed. First was the constant ego-feeding Burke required. That was not too bad. With his own gaggle of ass-kissers in attendance, Arturo felt no need to join in. Second, a companion to the ego-feeding was the vanity attention. Burke was a tall, one-time very handsome man. Now in his sixties, his hair needed replenishment, his face needed makeup and wrinkle cream and body-parts were sagging and expanding.

None of this was much of a concern for Arturo, although it was a source of amusement. What really bothered him was the man's attitude toward their client. Arturo was becoming concerned that Rob Dane was being treated as an afterthought; secondary to the great man's needs. Which, of course, included making sure the GoFundMe account was still in place.

Regarding the client, Rob had made it abundantly clear that he did not want any delays. Despite their best efforts, the police had not located a gun on or around Ferguson. Not surprisingly, given the makeup of the crowd, no one would admit to seeing a gun. No one would admit to seeing anything except the cop who shot the now sainted Lionel Ferguson.

Rob believed that his testimony and the testimony of character witnesses on his behalf would create reasonable doubt. He wanted to get his life and family back as quickly as possible. Unfortunately, the great man did not agree. His strategy was to stall as long as possible. Although it was becoming obvious this was a strategy to milk the publicity.

Arturo, knowing this would annoy Burke's ego, got in between him and the minicams. "We're supposed to be upstairs in Judge Tennant's court in five minutes," Arturo told Burke.

One of Burke's toadies almost pushed Arturo aside. Burke put on a big smile showing his highly polished mouthful of expensive teeth and stopped for the cameras.

"Well, I heard Judge Tennant is waiting for me, so I better go. Don't want to get her upset," he told the reporters.

Burke and his entourage entered Courtroom 1745 with a flourish, as if he was expecting trumpets to announce him. Instead, he found an almost empty room. Judge Tennant's clerk, Lois, was seated next to the judge's bench. To Burke's right, seated at one of the tables, were two people, obviously lawyers.

They passed through the gate as the prosecutors stood to greet them. Burke's assistants took chairs in front of the bar while Arturo and Burke stopped to meet the prosecutors.

"Hey, Steve," Arturo said shaking the man's hand. "Good morning, Jennifer," he said to the woman lawyer.

"Steve," he began the introductions, "this is Sheldon Burke. Sheldon, Steve Gondeck and Jennifer Moore. Steve is the head of felony litigation for the county attorney and Jennifer is a very capable prosecutor in her own right."

"So, rolling out the big guns against me," Burke said shaking Gondeck's hand.

While Burke shook hands with Jennifer, Steve Gondeck was thinking, *It's going to be a pleasure to hand this blow hard his ass.*

"You're looking for a continuance?" Gondeck asked Burke.

"That's right. We can't possibly be ready to go to trial in sixty days."

"It's actually less than that," Gondeck said. "The clock has been ticking since he pleaded not guilty and demanded a speedy trial."

"Yes, yes," Burke replied as if speaking to a child. "We can waive it anytime we want."

"Where's your client?" Jennifer asked.

"I decided it's not necessary for him to be here," Burke said with a patronizing tone.

Jennifer looked at Arturo, a man she knew and respected, who moved his eyes toward the ceiling.

"Does he know about this?" Gondeck asked. "He seemed quite adamant when he requested..."

"Now, Steve," Burke interrupted him. "That's a privileged communication."

While this was taking place, Lois had called back to Margaret Tennant to let her know everyone was in court.

"All rise," the deputy said, interrupting them as he led the judge and her court reporter in from the back.

"Keep your seats," the judge quickly said as she ascended to the bench. She silently waited for her reporter to set up while Burke and Arturo went to their table. When the reporter indicated she was ready, Judge Tennant began.

"Off the record," was the first thing she said.

"Mr. Burke," she began while looking at him with a slight smile. "First let me welcome you and your team to Minnesota..."

"Thank you, your Honor. It's a-"

"… and don't you ever keep me waiting again and don't interrupt me. Do I make myself clear?"

Burke had started to rise when he spoke to thank her. Halfway up he froze in place. Fully admonished, he sat back down and said, "My apologies, your Honor."

"Mr. Mendoza," Tennant said to Arturo, "you know better."

Judge Tennant then went on the record and read the case name and court file number for the reporter.

"It is my understanding that the defense is now willing to waive the right to a speedy trial. Is that correct, Mr. Burke?"

Burke stood and politely said, "It is, your Honor."

"Why?" Tennant asked.

"Your Honor, I have only recently been retained. I've barely had time to study the police report. We cannot possibly be ready within the statutory sixty days."

"Mr. Gondeck, what is the state's position?" Tennant asked.

"We could go today, your Honor," he replied. "This is not a complicated case. The only discovery left to be provided is the toxicology report from the victim's autopsy."

"You have provided all of the other discovery to the defense?" Tennant asked.

"As I said, your Honor, this is not a complicated case. The fact that the defendant did the shooting that caused the Reverend Ferguson's death is not in dispute."

"It seems to me you're a little light on motive," Tennant said. "It's not a legal necessity, but you're likely going to need that for first-degree."

"We believe we have sufficient motive, your Honor," Gondeck replied.

Tennant turned back to Burke and asked, "Where's your client? Does he know what you're up to?"

"I decided his presence was not necessary and any communication with my client is privileged," Burke said.

"Oh, I see," the judge replied. "You decided his presence was not necessary and the information about this motion, telling your client about it, is privileged.

"Okay, here's what I'm gonna do. I'm denying your motion to waive a speedy trial until you bring Mr. Dane in and I hear from him. Was there anything else?"

129

"Yes, your Honor," Gondeck stood and said. "It has come to my attention that Mr. Burke is quite fond of press publicity…"

"I object," Burke jumped up and bellowed.

Judge Tennant motioned with her hand for him to sit down while saying, "Overruled. It's come to my attention, also."

"As I was saying, your Honor," Gondeck continued, "Mr. Burke has been holding sessions with the media almost daily. The state asks for a gag order to be put in place. This case is already inflammatory enough. Let's not make it worse."

Gondeck sat down and Burke started to rise. As he did, the judge held up an index finger and silently used it to stop him and indicate she wanted Burke to sit down.

"Mr. Mendoza, I want to hear from you about this," she said.

Arturo stood up to address the court. "Your Honor, we strongly oppose any gag order. We're all grown-ups here. We know these things never really apply to the prosecution."

Gondeck started to stand to object, but Judge Tennant held up her hand, palm out and used it to sit him down.

"I know both Steve Gondeck and Jennifer Moore, your Honor. I don't doubt they will obey your order. But let's face it. Police departments and prosecutor's offices leak like a bucket with a hole in it and Mr. Gondeck will not be able to prevent it. Gag orders only stop one side from using the press, the defense."

Gondeck started to stand again and again Tennant held up her left hand to stop him.

"I'm going to issue the order," she said. "Even though he has a point," she continued looking at the two prosecutors, "I'm going to be personally monitoring the news about this case. If I see a lot of leaks coming from either side, there will be consequences. Do I make myself clear?"

Both tables acknowledged her admonition.

"Mr. Burke," she continued, looking back at him, "now that you won't be holding news conferences, you should have more time to prepare for trial. If you want to have me reconsider my ruling, bring Mr. Dane in with you."

The judge continued by asking, "Anything else?" When no one spoke, she adjourned.

The elevator car on the ride down was empty except for the defense lawyers. There was an awkward silence until Arturo Mendoza broke it.

"Did you or did you not get Rob Dane's permission to waive speedy trial?" he indignantly asked Sheldon Burke.

Burke casually replied, "I thought so. Didn't I tell one of you guys to talk to him?" he asked the three baggage carriers.

They all looked back and forth at each and then shrugged and shook their heads.

"Minor oversight, I guess," Burke said.

"Minor oversight? That's a serious ethical violation," Arturo said.

"Oh, come on," Burke said with his patronizing smile. "Every lawyer knows what's really best for his client. Don't make too big a deal out of it. We can't get his permission for every little thing that comes up. Relax."

A dumbstruck Arturo Mendoza stared wide-eyed at Burke while thinking, *What the hell have I done allowing this arrogant fool into this?*

TWENTY-FOUR

The good-looking passenger in the two-thousand-dollar, gray, pinstripe Italian wool suit was third to disembark. He smiled at the flight attendants who had worked the first-class section where he sat, then thanked the captain for a smooth flight.

At six feet, one hundred ninety trim pounds, with a perpetual three-day beard and the wrap around Ray Bans, the swarthy man could turn female heads. Tired from traveling, he was in a hurry to get through the airport to his awaiting transportation.

Without a word, not even the traditional Muslim greeting, the man with the wrap-a-rounds got in the back seat of the mini-van. The driver, a Somali cabbie, scurried to place his suitcase in the back, then got in the driver's seat. This was the third time this same lackey had picked him up at the Minneapolis/St. Paul airport. He liked that because the cabbie knew better than to make small talk with him.

Despite the fact that the passenger had spent the better part of two days traveling, he felt refreshed just by being here. The Middle East was nothing like this. The bright-green foliage everywhere and the enormous amount of space these people had accented their affluence. The only significant downside was the humidity. While not as hot as the Middle East, it could be considerably more uncomfortable.

The mini-van left the airport and the driver got on an old stretch of freeway, County Road 62. As he drove toward downtown, his passenger stared out of the window at the rain. *A very scary man*, the driver thought.

The mini-van stopped in front of a Marriott near the Cedar/Riverside Somali community. The passenger got out and waited out of the rain under the hotel's canopy. The driver retrieved his suitcase and hurried inside. By the time the man with the sunglasses reached the front desk, the clerk was ready for him. He paid with a legitimate American Express card under the same name as his Italian passport. He left instructions for a wakeup call, then spoke the only word he ever did to the driver. "Go," he said.

Relieved that he was no longer needed, the driver made a hasty retreat. He waited until he was back in his mini-van cab before cursing to Allah about, once again, receiving no compensation for his work.

132

Four hours later, at 2:00 P.M., Damone was in a meeting at his office. The thirty-two-year-old gang banger he was meeting with was doing his best to make excuses.

"I'm tellin' ya, bro," he said for the fourth or fifth time, "crack ain't what's happenin' like it used to be. It's smack that they want," Jimmy Jones said.

Jimmy Jones was one of four people—two black men and two white men—that managed both a crack and opioid distribution unit. Each had their own geographic location in which to operate. And none of them knew each other.

Jones had been doing this same song and dance for twenty minutes. Damone was seated in his usual place; the head of the table. Lewis and Monroe were at the opposite end and Jones was to Damone's right in between Damone and Lewis.

Damone had several sources on the streets giving him price information. Jones was partially correct; heroin was the number one street demand. There was still plenty of market for crack cocaine and it drew a lot less attention from the police. Heroin required more maintenance, more cutting and much more overhead to get it on the street. Crack, per gram, was still more profitable. But, Damone also knew he was being scammed by Jimmy Jones.

"The average price of rock on the street is down two and three quarters percent in the last twelve months," Damone quietly said. "Your overall quantity of sales is actually up over three percent during that same period. Yet the profits are down almost ten percent. How do you account for that, Jimmy?"

After saying this, Damone leaned forward, crossed his arms on the tabletop and stared at Jones with a blank expression. He sat motionless this way for more than a long minute watching the sweat break out on Jones' forehead.

Finally, in a friendly way, Damone said, "I like you, Jimmy. I really do. Here's the deal. It's not me, it's Lewis and Monroe. They don't like you. They believe you're skimming."

Jimmy turned his head, licked his lips and nervously looked at Lewis and Monroe. They both stared back with a completely dispassionate expression.

"I try to convince them that you wouldn't do that. You don't want to make me look like a liar and a fool, do you, Jimmy?"

"Um, ah, no, boss, no," Jimmy stammered.

"You see, they're in charge of the crack business. Their pay and bonuses are tied to your sales and profits. Just like sales at General Motors. Do you understand that?"

"Ah, I guess, sure."

"The better you do, the better they do. You understand?"

"Yes, sure," Jimmy quickly replied.

"In fact, well, I hate to say it, but they want to fire you and replace you with someone they can trust."

Turning very serious, Damone looked at Jimmy's eyes and said, "You do understand that if I give them the okay to fire you, it doesn't mean you'll just lose your job, don't you?"

Jimmy's head swiveled back and forth between the two men opposite Damone and Damone himself.

"Yes, sir. Yes, sir." Jimmy said.

"I don't want to hear any more about smack from you. You were hired to do a job. I can easily replace you. Do your job, knock off the bullshit, boy, and you might see a few more birthdays. Now, get out."

By this time Monroe was at the door holding it open. Jimmy's feet barely touched the floor as he fled.

"I got a text from Saadaq a couple of minutes ago," Lewis said. "The recruiter's back and they want to meet."

"When?" Damone asked.

"Whenever you're ready," Lewis replied.

Damone looked at his watch and asked, "Anything else for a while?"

"No, not until later. You're supposed to meet with that senator, Halane, later. Seven o'clock," Lewis said.

"Call Saadaq and see if now is okay."

Lewis made the call, received an affirmative answer and the three of them left.

Damone and Imam Sadia were seated in tall, comfortable armchairs looking through a one-way mirror. Lewis and Monroe stood against a wall a few feet behind their boss. In the room next to them, the scene they were observing, were three people. Damone, as usual, held his Bible in his lap.

In the room they were watching, to their right, was a Muslim man seated at a small, cheap desk. Behind and to his right was Saadaq. To their left, sitting in a chair identical to theirs, was the quiet man wearing the wraparound sunglasses. In the center of the room seated in an uncomfortable, unpadded, armless chair, was a young Somali man. He was facing the man at the desk while everyone else watched.

The man at the desk had the same lighter skin complexion as the man with the sunglasses. The two of them had taken over recruitment of holy warriors in Minneapolis about a year ago. Their two predecessors had been killed by a Russian bomb in Syria.

For the next two hours the man at the desk, Dawoud, questioned a total of three Somali teens. The three of them had been recruited together and had spent the past six weeks being interrogated and indoctrinated. They had lived in the building they were in, an abandoned store, the entire time. Not once had they been allowed to leave. Today was their final exam.

When it was over, Dawoud and Saadaq briefly conferred. Then the man with the sunglasses looked at the mirror and silently nodded his head. All three of the recruits had been found acceptable.

The next phase would be to get them to their destination. This was so highly classified that the recruiter, the man with the sunglasses, would not reveal it to anyone. Even the recruits would not know until they arrived in the Holy Land. Once there, the people waiting for them would let them know where they would go to begin their fight for Allah.

Dawoud went with the three recruits while Saadaq and the recruiter joined those who had watched.

"How many does this make?" Damone asked.

"For us, these will make it fourteen. Why do you want to know?" The mystery man asked in a barely accented English.

"Just curious," Damone replied.

Doing business with the Somalis, Damone had known all along that they were recruiting local Somalis and sending them to terrorist groups. That was why he was allowed to attend the session today. Minneapolis was the Number One terrorist recruiting area in America.

The four of them, while Lewis and Monroe continued to wait, held an impromptu meeting. As usual, the Imam argued for more product. And, as usual, Damone politely refused.

Saadaq accompanied Damone to the Tahoe when the meeting was over. It was parked alongside the building and Lewis and Monroe were waiting.

"What have you found out about the Imam?" Damone asked.

"He's keeping at least two mistresses," Saadaq replied. "And we believe there are one or two others."

"Muslim women?"

"No, American whores," Saadaq replied.

"Anything else?"

"He must be putting money away somewhere. He is skimming from both you and his employees."

Damone sadly shook his head then said, "Keep digging. Gurey should know. Lean on him. He is a weakling."

"Will do," Saadaq replied.

TWENTY-FIVE

Tony Russo, formerly Tony Carvelli, was sipping his unsweetened glass of iced tea. Acting the part of a refugee from Witsec, Tony was wearing a thousand- dollar, light gray, sharkskin suit and white silk dress shirt. His companion was a forty-year-old, elegant looking woman with a two-hundred-dollar hairstyle. She was also a thousand-dollar a night prostitute whose birth name was Gretchen Stenson. Gretchen was a high-end prostitute that Tony had known for over twenty years. He first busted her as a seventeen-year-old high school girl turning tricks and running three of her high school friends.

Tony was wondering how he was going to cover her cost on his expense report for Vivian. He was hoping that swearing Adrienne, Vivian's granddaughter, to secrecy would hold up.

The woman they were watching was the trophy wife of a senior partner in a large, white-shoe law firm. Vivian knew both the husband and wife. The woman was in Chip Osborne's ledger and Adrienne had helped them find her. Using Adrienne to locate the woman and meet Gretchen might have been a mistake. As soon as Adrienne found out what Gretchen did, she could not have been more curious. Fascinated even.

The two of them had ignored Tony at lunch a couple of days ago while they talked. Adrienne wanted to know everything about Gretchen's business. The best line was Gretchen explaining how she got into it.

"Well, Adrienne," she said to the question. "When I was in high school, I went down to the guidance counselor and he gave me the usual aptitude tests. The test results came back, and he told me a lawyer or hooker. I asked, 'what's the difference?' and he said, 'Hookers have more self-esteem, a better reputation and make more money!' So, here I am."

By now, Adrienne was laughing hysterically and Tony was looking on in horror.

"Relax, Tony. I'm not going to do it. It's just, I don't know, curiosity."

"Tony," Gretchen said, "there isn't a woman alive who hasn't wondered what it would be like to go to a hotel with a strange man and get paid for sex. Especially at her age."

"Really?" Tony asked looking at Adrienne.

"Uh, I plead the fifth," Adrienne said.

"Here it is," Gretchen said. They were in the Highland Hills Golf and Tennis Club having lunch. They had used Adrienne's membership card which had her name as Adrienne Grant, not Donahue or Corwin.

The woman they were watching was Lois Collier. A long-legged, bored thirty-year-old blonde married to a fifty-eight-year-old man. She was alone at a table near the tennis courts, sitting under an umbrella with an alcoholic drink. A striking brunette, wearing white tennis clothes, sat down opposite Lois. She reached across the table with both hands and took both of Lois' hands in hers.

"That was it," Gretchen said. "That was the drop-off."

"Are you filming?" Tony asked

"Oh yeah," Gretchen replied.

On their table, Gretchen had placed a knockoff, light gold, Coach shoulder bag. You don't punch a hole for a camera in a real one. In the purse was a video camera focused on the table barely thirty feet away. In less than five seconds after the exchange, Lois put the pill in her mouth and downed the rest of her drink.

"She was hurting," Gretchen said.

"We need to find out who the other woman is," Tony said.

When he said this, both women stood up and exchanged an air kiss. Lois grabbed her tennis bag and they parted. While they watched, the brunette joined two other women at another table. Before she sat down, she discreetly put her right hand in her bag and came out with her fist clenched.

"I got an idea," Gretchen said as she shifted the camera-purse to film the new table. "You go watch Lois and see where she goes. I'll stay here and wait. I'll keep an eye on her."

Tony stood up and Gretchen said, "If Lois leaves in her car, come back. It's the brunette. It's the brunette we need to talk to."

For the next fifteen minutes, Gretchen watched the brunette as she made her rounds. She went to a total of six tables and serviced ten women. By then Tony was back.

When she finished at the sixth table, they watched as she headed toward the clubhouse.

"I'll be back," Gretchen said. She grabbed her purse and went after the brunette.

Gretchen got inside just in time to see her go down a hallway to the left of the club's member service counter. There was a sign on the wall telling Gretchen she was going exactly where she had hoped; the restrooms.

When Gretchen got inside the Ladies' restroom, the brunette was already in one of the stalls. Two other women were finishing up at the sinks. Gretchen set her purse on the counter and fiddled with her hair until the two women left. She then quietly locked the entrance door. In less than a minute, a toilet flushed and the brunette came out. Gretchen decided to go right at her.

"Who's your source?" Gretchen demanded. She had walked up behind the woman while she washed her hands. Startled, she straightened up and turned around. Gretchen was staring at her with a tough, no-nonsense look on her face.

"My what? My source? I don't…" She started to stammer.

Gretchen grabbed her blouse under her chin and pulled her toward Gretchen's face. "Don't go there, honey. I got you on film going from table to table dropping off today's dose."

By this point, the brunette was clearly terrified. This woman who was glaring at her was not from any debutante school she had attended. This woman was clearly hard as nails and meant business.

"Do you want to see it? It's in my purse," Gretchen said still gripping the woman's blouse.

"No," she barely managed to croak.

"Relax, honey," Gretchen said then released her. "We're going out there and the guy I'm with is gonna have a chat with you. We know Chip was your supplier. We want to take over. You'll all be made well again."

There was a knock on the door after someone tried to open it. Two seconds later the knocking became louder and more urgent.

"Let's go," Gretchen said.

Gretchen marched the woman arm-in-arm through the country club like they were two old friends. On the way to the parking lot she called Tony and told him to meet them. The women were waiting next to

Tony's car; a leased, burgundy colored Lincoln Continental courtesy of Vivian Donahue. While Tony drove, the women sat in the back seat.

"What's your name?" Gretchen asked.

"Wendy Merrill," she replied.

"Okay, Wendy," Gretchen said. "We're going to a little park about a half mile up the road. We know of a nice spot for the three of us to have a little chat. When we're done, we'll take you back to your car."

"Are you police?" Wendy nervously asked.

"No," Tony replied. "We're not with any law enforcement agency of any kind."

"Okay," she said much more calmly. "Then what do you want?"

Without answering her, Tony turned into the park and drove to a small pavilion. He parked and the three of them went to a shaded bench about a hundred yards from the car.

"My name is Tony Russo and her name's Gretchen," Tony said. Wendy was sitting in between them. "I knew Chip and what he was up to. I want to take over."

Wendy said, "Chip never mentioned anyone named Tony."

"Yet, here I am. And how do you think I pulled that off?"

Carvelli looked like a serious gangster. With his sharkskin suit, Italian loafers, a diamond pinky ring and rose-tinted glasses, he looked like he could star in a Goodfellas sequel.

Wendy stared at Tony for three or four seconds then turned to Gretchen. Gretchen stared back with the same impassive look Tony had. It was then Wendy burst into tears and began sobbing. She covered her face with her hands, bent over and put her head between her knees.

Tony looked at Gretchen with a 'what did I say?' expression. Gretchen frowned, rolled her eyes, shook her head and mouthed the word "men" at him. Uncertain what to do, Tony sat and looked helplessly at her. Gretchen let it go on for almost a minute.

"All right," Gretchen said. She pulled on Wendy's shoulders, forcing her to sit up. Without any empathy in her voice, she said, "Stop feeling sorry for yourself. Get a grip. How did you get into this in the first place?"

"You don't give a damn," Wendy whined to her. "Why do you want to know?"

"Oh, you're looking for sympathy," Gretchen said. "Well, honey, you'll find it in the dictionary somewhere between shit and syphilis.

140

Now, I want to know how a pampered, country club princess could become a junkie, drug-hustler."

"Fuck you, bitch!" Wendy snarled.

"That's better," Gretchen said. "Now, I do want to know."

Wendy looked at Tony who gently said, "Go on, let's hear it."

"About three years ago I hurt my knee in a skiing accident. I went to a doctor who prescribed pain medication—thirty milligrams of Percocet. He thought the knee would heal by itself.

"After a few months, it hadn't healed, so I had surgery. I didn't realize it, but by this time I was hooked. I was taking twice the amount of Percocet prescribed.

"Anyway, I had the surgery and he increased the dosage to fifty milligrams. By this time, I was taking two or three hits of fifty milligrams every day. I knew a couple of the girls at the club were taking them too. That's how I met Chip. The knee healed, but now I was taking them to get high. And I became involved with Chip…"

"You were sleeping with him?"

"Hell, half the woman at the club were screwing him. For the drugs," Wendy said. "Yeah, I was too. Why not. My husband pays zero attention to me."

"That's always the excuse," Gretchen said. "And then you started selling for him and turning tricks."

"No, no, I never turned tricks. He tried to get to me to, but I wouldn't. Some of them did. They were having fun they said. Going down on guys in the back seat of cars for their dope money while their husbands are working.

"It's disgusting. Our husbands are successful professionals. They provide us with a nice life. But you know what, we're all arm candy. Our lives are so dull and boring we resort to drugs and hooking to liven it up."

"What's your husband do?" Tony asked.

"He's the managing partner of a mid-size brokerage. He makes over a million dollars a year and you know what? I'd give it up to get clean and away from him. He's an arrogant, self-centered control freak."

"Who's your supplier?" Tony asked.

"I can't tell you that."

"I told you," Tony said. "We're taking over. I have Chip's customer ledger and…"

"How did you…"

141

"None of your business. I have it and that's that. Now, who is your source?"

"A black guy by the name of Jimmy Jones," she quietly said.

"Good. Now, you're going to introduce me. After that, if you really want to, we'll help you get clean," Tony said. "But you're going to work with me for a while first."

"Really? You'd help me…"

"If you really want it, yes,"

"Why?" Wendy asked. "I don't get it. Why would you want to help me get clean?"

"Because you're gonna help me and for now, that's all you need to know."

Wendy looked back and forth between the two of them and said, "Deal."

"That's him," Wendy said. "The guy with the cornrows and red leather jacket."

Tony had dropped off Gretchen and then Wendy had taken him to where Jimmy Jones lived. They were parked on Dupont, a half block north of 28th Street watching a small apartment building. A shiny, black Escalade pulled up and parked in front and four men got out.

"I think Jimmy owns the apartment building. It has two apartments in the basement, two on the first floor and two on the second," Wendy said. "Jimmy lives and works out of one of the second-floor places."

"Let's go," Tony said.

They hurried across the street and reached the four men as they started into the building. One of the men, a fairly large, serious looking black man stepped in front of Tony and stuck his right hand in Tony's chest.

"Are you right-handed?" Tony asked him.

"What? Are you a cop? Get lost," the bodyguard replied.

By now the others, especially Jimmy, were watching.

"Get your hand off of me or you're gonna have to learn to wipe your ass with your left hand," Tony quietly said.

The man started laughing along with his friends, everyone except Jimmy. He had recognized Wendy and figured this had something to do with business. He silently watched to see how this little drama would play out.

142

When the bodyguard laughed, Tony snatched two of his fingers in each hand. As he spread them apart, he also bent the man's hand back which caused enough pain to drop him to his knees.

"No, no, no," the man pleaded.

The pain was excruciating. It felt like his fingers were being torn apart and it ran all the way up his arm to his shoulder.

Tony dropped the man's hand, looked at Jimmy and said, "Mr. Jones, a few minutes of your time, please."

"Check him," Jimmy said meaning pat him down for weapons. "Then come on up."

Across the street in an apartment one building down, a man and a woman were watching and filming the action. While Tony and Wendy crossed the street, Tony, looking for traffic, turned his head toward them. The man was watching through binoculars when he did this.

"Are you serious?" he said while continuing to watch. "Carvelli, what the hell are you up to?"

The man's name was Jeff Johnson and his partner was Tess Richards. They were the two FBI agents working with city councilman Jalen Bryant to bring down Damone Watson.

TWENTY-SIX

On the way back to the country club and Wendy's car, the two rode in silence most of the way. About a mile from their destination Tony could see Wendy was not doing well.

"You okay?" he asked.

"Huh, me? Yeah sure. I'm good. Um, good, why what?" she said too fast.

"You're jonesing," Tony said; a statement, not a question.

"Me? No, why do you ask? No, I'm good, really. I'm just, you know…"

"An opioid addict and you need a hit," Tony answered her. "Go ahead. I'm not a cop. Do what you gotta do."

Wendy scrambled through her handbag and came out holding a small pill. She quickly popped it into her mouth, leaned her head against the car's window and relaxed.

"Feel better?" Tony asked with an obvious tone of disapproval.

"Hey, you're not my dad, you're not my…"

"Husband, mom or guardian angel," Tony said. "Seventy thousand people died in this country last year from what you're doing," he quietly continued. "How much longer before you're sticking a needle in your arm?"

Wendy did not answer. By now, the dope was doing its work and she was mellowing out.

"Feeling better?"

"Yeah," she said and smiled. "Who are you?"

"I told you. I'm taking over for Chip, but I don't use that shit. You want to get your life back, I can help you," Tony said. They were in the parking lot, stopped behind Wendy's Mercedes. "You're going to help me. Give me your cell number and I'll call. Be ready whenever I need you."

Wendy wrote the number on a slip of paper, handed it to him, got out and hurried to her car.

"Look at me," Tony said. "Are you okay to drive?"

"I don't know. I'll go inside and wait with some friends for a couple of hours. I'll be okay by then. I promise," she added when he continued to stare at her.

"No booze," he said.

"No, I don't do this and drive. I'll be okay."

By the time Tony drove out of the parking lot, he was on the phone to Maddy.

"How did it go?" she asked.

"Okay. He's checking me out. He said he would call me with news in a couple of days."

"You know he took your picture while you were in there, don't you?"

"Yeah, and if the leak is a cop and he sees it…"

"You could be in a lot of trouble."

"I know. I'm thinking the next time we meet…"

"If there is a next time."

"I'm gonna play the badass wiseguy and not let them frisk me."

"I was thinking," Maddy said. "There is a cop we can trust. Owen Jefferson."

"Yeah, we can trust Owen. You think I should go to him?"

Maddy paused for a moment before answering. "Yes. Maybe we should have Marc write up something. A written, ass-covering letter in case you get busted. Give a copy to Owen, Marc could keep one and send one to Paxton."

Tony thought it over then said, "I've heard worse ideas."

"Wow. High praise indeed."

Ignoring the sarcasm, Tony said, "Let's talk to Owen first. I'll call him now then call you back. See if he has time now."

A half-hour later, Tony and Maddy walked into the homicide division at the downtown MPD offices. They could see Jefferson waving them to come into his office. As they walked through the room, the place went completely silent. Tony stopped and looked around at the detectives. Every one of them, including the women, were staring.

"You guys act like you've never seen me before," he said as he swiveled his head around the room.

"Yeah, it's you we're looking at, Carvelli," one of the older cops, a friend of Tony's, scoffed. "Get the hell out of the way. Hey, Maddy," the man said.

"Hi, Ron," she said smiling back. "How's your wife?"

This provoked laughter from the cynical crowd.

"She's fine. I hear you're dating a lawyer," he said.

145

"Sorry, yeah, it's true," she replied.

"Maddy, Maddy, Maddy," he said shaking his head in sorrow. "First you're hanging out with this jamoke," he said referring to Carvelli, "and now you're dating a lawyer. We gotta have a chat about your taste in men."

"It's worse than you think, Flaherty," Carvelli said. "He's a criminal defense lawyer."

"Great," one of the other men spoke up. "Now we gotta have an intervention and a deprogramming like they do with cult members."

By now, Tony and Maddy were at Jefferson's door and Maddy was laughing. "You think it's that bad?" she said.

"Probably worse."

Jefferson came around his desk and ignored Carvelli's handshake attempt. He took Maddy's hand in both of his, flashed a big grin and welcomed her.

While he did this, Carvelli stood there with his hand still extended looking at the wall behind Jefferson's desk.

"This dreary place always seems to light up a bit when you visit us," Jefferson said.

"Thanks, Owen," Carvelli replied.

"Oh, yeah, sure, you too, Carvelli," Jefferson said.

They took their seats, then Maddy pointed a finger at Jefferson and said to Carvelli, "This is the guy I should be dating."

"Absolutely," Jefferson beamed.

"Yeah, and he could bring his wife and kids along," Carvelli said.

"With him, I could wear heels and he'd still be taller than me," Maddy continued referring to Jefferson's six-foot five-inch height.

"Of course, there is the wife and kids thing," Carvelli said.

Before Jefferson could respond, Carvelli said, "Forget it, Owen. By the time she got done with you, you wouldn't have enough money to go out by yourself."

"And I'd probably be singing soprano," Jefferson wistfully said. "Okay, getting serious, what did you need to see me about?"

"Where to begin?" Carvelli rhetorically asked.

"Nicolette," Maddy said.

Carvelli nodded in agreement and started in with the murders of Chip Osborne, his girlfriend and Nicolette's suicide. For the next twenty minutes, with Maddy filling in some minor details, Carvelli laid it all out for him.

When he finished, the first question Jefferson had was: "So, you think there's a leak in either the department or city hall?"

"And so do some cops I've talked to. Guys in narcotics," Carvelli said.

"Hmmm," Jefferson hummed. "I won't say it isn't possible to be coming from the department, but I'd bet on city hall. The department leaks like a sieve sometimes, but mostly feeding reporters little tidbits for the prosecutors. Hell, I've done that. So, what do you want from me?"

"Someone in law enforcement to have my back. Someone who knows what I'm up to who can provide cover," Carvelli answered.

Jefferson leaned back in his chair, covered his mouth with his left hand and stared at Carvelli, obviously thinking it over. After a minute or so he leaned forward and placed both arms on his desk.

"How many toes are you going to step on if you do this?" Jefferson asked.

"I don't know," Carvelli said. "Not the MPD. The guys I talked to in narcotics, straight guys that we both know, tell me they're all pretty frustrated because the intel they get is bad as soon as they get it. They go for a bust and poof, everybody's gone. They try to flip street dealers and can't get them to budge. There's a leak, Owen."

"What about the Feds. The FBI or DEA?" Jefferson asked.

"I don't know and I don't care."

"We have the Feds covered," Maddy interjected. She turned to Carvelli and said, "Our friend."

"Yeah, I know," Carvelli replied.

"Who's your friend that has you covered with the Feds?"

Maddy looked at Carvelli and raised her eyebrows as if silently asking, Should we tell him?

"An AUSA," Carvelli said. "Who shall remain anonymous, for now."

"Oh, I see. You want me to cover your ass, but you won't trust me with your Fed's name," Jefferson replied.

"Owen, give me a break. Right now, it's best not to-"

"Yeah, yeah," Jefferson said with an indifferent wave of his right hand.

"This person is not local," Maddy said. "We'll see about getting permission to tell you."

"Okay," Jefferson replied. "From you, I trust. You," he continued looking at Carvelli, "are lucky you brought her along."

"Why do you think I did? I think there's a lot going on here, Owen. More than just drug dealing. There could be some serious takedowns coming," Carvelli replied.

"Or, we may be putting you in the ground," Jefferson said.

"Always possible. I won't tell you who, but I have some guys watching my back."

"How is Jake?" Jefferson asked.

"Great," Carvelli grumbled at the realization Jefferson could guess who he was referring to. "He's good and doing well. You should stop and see him."

"I don't know," Jefferson said. "He's persona non grata in the department."

"Half the brass, including the chief, have been by to see him. And they use his limos when they have a need," Carvelli said.

"Seriously? Well, in that case, I will," Jefferson replied. "Okay, I'll do it. Write up what you're up to and I'll put it in my personal safe deposit box at my bank."

"Good. Thanks, Owen," Carvelli replied.

"Keep me in the loop as much as you can. I can't get you any money…"

"We have a couple of sources for that," Maddy said.

"I'll have Kadella write it up and Maddy will get it to you," Carvelli said.

"Speaking of which," Jefferson said looking at Maddy. "Are you and Kadella still an item?"

Maddy smiled and said, "Yeah, yeah we are." She had a noticeable sparkle in her eyes when she said it.

"Girl," Jefferson smiled back at her and said, "you're in love, aren't you?"

"Yeah, I am," she admitted.

"Well, I guess you could do worse," Jefferson told her. "And that's high praise from a cop for a defense lawyer."

TWENTY-SEVEN

While Maddy and Carvelli were meeting with Owen Jefferson, Marc was at his desk dealing with the business side of practicing law. He was working through his monthly bills. There was a knock on his office door and Connie Mickelson, the landlord, walked in before Marc could respond. Instead of sitting in one of the client chairs, she moved one next to a window and opened it.

"Do you have to do that in here?" Marc asked.

Connie had a cigarette in her mouth and a plastic lighter in her hand.

"Yeah," she replied. She took a long drag then blew the smoke out the window.

"My office is too smoky and I need some fresh air," she said.

"Did it ever occur to you to go outside? It's nice out," Marc said. "Here," he continued as he handed her his rent check.

"Go all the way outside just to smoke a cigarette? It sounds like a lot of work. How's business? You okay for money?" Connie asked.

Connie Mickelson was everyone's dream landlord. Having practiced law herself for forty years, she was well aware of the ups and downs. The building they were in, the Reardon Building on Lake Street and Charles Avenue was an inheritance from her father, along with a good deal of money she never talked about. If any of her tenants were having financial problems, Connie was always understanding.

"I'm good," Marc replied. "Things have become much more consistent, allowing me to do fewer divorces. Give me a murderer ahead of a pissed off wife, any day."

"Speaking of divorce, you up for handling my next one?" Connie asked.

"What? When did you get married?"

"The judge is making subtle hints," she said.

"Does he know your track record when it comes to successful marriages? As far as that goes, when are you gonna learn?"

"I figure sooner or later I'll hit the right one," Connie said laughing.

"Your problem is, you like getting married, you just don't like *being* married," Marc told her.

There was another knock on Marc's door and Barry Cline came in.

"She's thinking about getting married again," Marc told him.

"Wow. Hey, that's great Connie. About time you settled down. We're all very happy for you," Barry said.

Marc laughed while Connie gave Barry a dirty look. "Very funny, Mr. Sarcasm."

"Who's the lucky sailor this time?" Barry said.

"You know, smartass, I haven't raised your rent…" Connie said then paused. "Come to think of it," she continued, "I haven't raised your rent ever. It sounds like it's about time."

Barry, who was still standing, rushed over to her, bent down, put his arms around her and kissed her cheek. "I meant every word of it. Don't do anything hasty."

Turning serious, Barry took a seat and asked, "Is this the judge? Spears?"

"Yeah," Connie replied.

"How many times has he been married?" Marc asked.

"None," Connie said.

"Really? None?"

"He was waiting for someone with a lot of experience," Barry said.

Even Connie had to laugh at this.

"How old is he?" Marc asked.

"He'll turn seventy next year, then retire," Connie answered.

"Connie, you've been married to a retired guy. Remember how well that worked out?" Marc asked.

"The more I think about it, Vern might've been the best one. He was always fishing and I was always working."

"Wasn't he the one who asked for the divorce when he met a younger woman while fishing?" Barry asked.

"Yeah, now that you mention it, there was that little problem," Connie wistfully said.

Barry had not closed Marc's door and Carolyn yelled into the room that Marc had a phone call.

"Who?" Marc yelled back.

"An Arturo Mendoza," she replied.

"Oh, oh," Connie quietly said.

"What's this about?" Barry asked. "He wants you on the team?"

"Oh boy," Marc said wondering what he might want. Of course, they all knew who Arturo was representing. The call was a bit disquieting.

150

"I'll take it, Carolyn, thanks," Marc yelled out. "Close the door," Marc said to Barry.

"You want us to leave?" Barry asked.

"No, that's okay," Marc said.

He picked up the phone, punched the blinking light and said, "Arturo, been a while, what's up?"

"I got a problem, Marc. A big problem," Arturo replied. He then explained everything about his difficulties with Sheldon Burke and his entourage. When he finished, there was silence on the line for several seconds.

"And?" Marc finally asked.

"When Rob found out Burke tried to get a continuance, he blew a gasket. Fortunately, Burke wasn't there. I was the one who told him.

"He wanted to fire Burke on the spot. I calmed him down, for now, and told him I would talk to you. Would you be willing to meet with him? I'm pretty sure I can get you paid and…"

"Let's not get ahead of ourselves, Arturo," Marc said.

"He swears Ferguson pointed a gun at him…"

"That no one else saw or found," Marc said. "I'll tell you what, Arturo. I'll meet with him. No promises."

"Thanks, Marc. I appreciate it."

"When and where?" Marc asked.

"You name it."

"Your guy's on home monitoring?"

"Yeah, he is," Arturo replied.

"Okay, his place at five o'clock this afternoon? What's his address?"

While Marc was discussing the call with Connie and Barry, Carolyn knocked and opened the door.

"Maddy's on line two," she said.

Connie and Barry stood up to leave and before Marc took the call, Barry said, "If you take the case, every cop in America will think you're a hero."

Marc looked at him and asked, "Is that good or bad?"

"I'm not sure either," Barry said.

"Hey," Marc answered his phone. "Where are you?"

151

"We're just leaving Owen Jefferson's office. We're outside the building. He needs something from you, Tony does."

"What?"

"He needs you to write up a history of all this, so Owen has a clear record of it to cover Tony's ass if he gets in a jam," Maddy said.

"Not if he gets in a jam, but when. Okay, but I need him here to help with the details. What are you doing later this afternoon?"

"Um, I can make myself available. What's up?"

"We have a meeting at five. I'll tell you when you get here," Marc told her.

"We'll be there in a little bit," Maddy said. "Can you do the letter Tony needs for Owen Jefferson?"

"Sure. We'll email it."

"No, no email. They can be traced," Maddy said. "I'll deliver it."

"Does it look okay?" Marc asked.

Carvelli was reading the letter to Jefferson. He was sitting behind Marc's desk in his executive chair while Maddy looked over his shoulder.

"Yeah, that should be fine," Carvelli said when he finished. "What do you think?"

"Looks good," Maddy agreed.

Marc regained his chair and typed a short cover letter to go with it. While he did this, Carvelli gave Jefferson a heads up. In addition to Jefferson, Marc would send a copy to Paxton O'Rourke and printed one for himself.

"I don't know what else we can do," Marc said. "You and I need to get going," he said to Maddy.

"You're really looking into helping Rob Dane?" Carvelli asked.

"Yeah, I guess," Marc replied. "What do you know about him?"

"Not much. Word I've heard is he's a good cop. I don't know about any disciplinary problems. From what I hear, everyone who knows him is pretty shocked by what happened."

Before Marc and Maddy reached the front door, it was opened and Arturo Mendoza was standing in it.

"Thanks for coming," Arturo greeted them.

He led them into the living room where Rob was waiting. Marc introduced Maddy to both men. Ron was in a recliner near the TV. Marc and Maddy took the couch and Arturo an armchair by Rob.

Before anyone had a chance to say anything, Rob blurted out, "He had a gun. He pointed it right at me and…"

"Whoa," Marc said and held up a hand to stop him. "Slow it down."

Marc looked first to Arturo then at Rob and asked, "Why am I here?"

"My lawyer won't listen to me," Rob replied. "He doesn't seem to care what I want. All he does is what he wants."

Marc looked at Arturo and asked, "Why won't you listen to him?"

"Very funny, smartass. You know he's talking about Burke."

"I know. I just thought I'd try to lighten the mood a bit," Marc said looking at Rob, who had laughed at his joke.

"That's probably the first good laugh you've had since this thing started," Marc said.

"Yeah, it is."

"Start at the beginning," Marc said. He looked at Arturo and said, "I take it that the fact he shot the bullets that killed Ferguson is not in dispute."

"No, it isn't," Arturo replied.

"Okay," Marc said. He looked at Rob and said, "I want you to tell me everything. Go slow and speak the way you would to an eight-year-old kid."

"He means that," Maddy said, which brought a smile to Rob's face.

Rob started at the very beginning of the protest parades. The very first day of duty. With Marc asking an occasional question, usually to clarify a point, Rob went through the entire story up to today.

When he finished, Marc told him to tell it again.

"Why? That's what happened?"

"Indulge me," Marc said.

"Okay," Rob said, a little frustrated.

Fifteen minutes later, he finished it for a second time. Only this time, Marc did not ask any questions.

Marc turned to Maddy and asked, "What do you think?"

"I think he's telling the truth," she said. "There were just enough minor inconsistencies to be truthful."

"Well, thanks for the vote of confidence," Rob sarcastically said.

"Clients lie to their lawyers all the time," Marc quietly replied. "I don't know you. You seem like a straight guy, but I've been fooled lots of times."

"He got the shooting absolutely the same," Maddy said.

"Yes, he did," Marc agreed. "You've probably been over it in your head a couple of hundred times."

"At least," Rob replied.

"His story is also consistent with the police reports, which he has not seen," Arturo said.

"Any witness statements?" Marc asked referring to written witness statements.

"No," Arturo replied. "They have interviewed at least a hundred people and didn't write any of it down for discovery. That's why their investigation report is barely two pages and doesn't have anything."

"How did that picture of Ferguson's body lying in the street get into the paper the next day?" Maddy asked.

"One of their reporters was on the scene, this Philo Anson guy," Arturo said.

"The cops who were closing off the crime scene let him walk right up and take pictures," Rob told them. "I saw him parading with Ferguson every day. He's not cooperating with the cops. Or so I've heard."

"Are you getting inside information?" Mark asked referring to friends in the department.

"Well, yeah. I've talked to some friends in-"

"You better stop it now," Marc told him. "Until this is done, you don't have any friends in the department."

Marc looked at Arturo and Rob and asked, "So what do you want from me?"

"I thought you'd figure it out," Rob said.

"I have to hear it," Marc said.

"I want you to take over my defense," Rob said.

"Are you sure?" Marc asked.

"Yeah, you've got a good reputation and I wish we'd gone to you in the first place."

"You have to understand something, Rob. I would be coming in late. And, I won't work with Sheldon Burke."

"That's no problem," Rob said. "I'd love to fire his ass."

"What about money? Ms. Rivers here doesn't come cheap."

"There's money in a GoFundMe account. A half a mil that was used for bail. That will be available, assuming he doesn't skip. There's more from the union and still some in the GoFundMe account," Arturo said.

"Okay, sounds like money should be covered." Marc looked at Arturo and said, "I don't second chair…"

"No problem," Arturo said. "Whatever you want me to do. You call the shots."

"Who's the judge?" Marc asked.

"Margaret Tennant," Arturo answered.

"Oh, oh," Maddy said and looked at Marc.

"Oh, oh?" Arturo asked. "What does that mean?"

"Ah, we, ah, had a personal relationship…"

"Romantic," Maddy said. "Do you want to recuse her?"

"I don't know. Probably not. That could be a bit insulting. I'll talk to her." He looked at Rob and said, "It's kind of up to you, too."

"Will she be fair?" Rob asked.

"We parted on good terms. Even if we didn't, she wouldn't let that affect her. Besides, I hear she's engaged, so it'll be okay."

"I'm looking forward to seeing her again," Maddy said. "She's a nice lady. Besides," Maddy continued. "Steve Gondeck might recuse her for us."

"No, no he won't," Marc said. "Prosecutors have to deal with judges all the time. To recuse one is risking their wrath. No, Margaret will recuse herself before Steve does."

"Are you in?" Arturo asked.

Marc had a leather folio with him. He removed a two-page document and handed it to Rob. Rob glanced it over then gave it to Arturo.

"You should read it," Marc told Rob.

"It's a retainer agreement that means I owe you my soul," Rob said.

"And the souls of your children," Arturo added while reading.

"This is fine," Arturo said when he finished.

After it was signed, Marc and Maddy stayed for another hour. Marc went through the entire file Arturo had and they discussed everything that had happened up to that point, again.

While Marc questioned Rob about specific details, Arturo wrote a letter for Rob terminating Team Burke.

On the drive back to the office, Marc gave Maddy her first assignment.

"This reporter, what's his name?"

"Philo Anson," Maddy told him.

"What the hell kind of name is that? Philo Anson?"

"I don't know," Maddy said. "Finnish?"

"Maybe. Anyway, I have a feeling he knows more than he's telling. Put that at the top of your list.

"When we get back, I got a job for Jeff," Marc said referring to Jeff Modell, the office paralegal. "He can find every article or anything this Philo guy as written. He knows something, and we need to know what it is."

TWENTY-EIGHT

"You have the dedication of the Damone Watson Park this afternoon at three," Lewis reminded his boss.

Lewis, Damone and Monroe were meeting in the living room of Damone's third-floor apartment. Following a late night the previous day, Damone had slept in. Meeting with Imam Sadia and his bootlickers was becoming more and more tedious. The never-ending demands and the Imam's attitude were wearing on Damone. If he trusted the Imam more, he might have taken him into his confidence. Since that was out of the question, Damone could only feel relief that he had not allowed the fool to know his true business.

Monroe filled the coffee cups of all three men while Lewis continued.

"Delmar has a report about that reporter for you, Philo Anson. He says it's pretty important," Lewis said.

"Okay," Damone replied. He looked at Monroe and said, "Go in the kitchen and call him now."

Damone looked at Lewis and asked, "Do I have time now?"

"Yes," Lewis said. Lewis looked at Monroe and said, "Tell him to drop what he's doing and get over here right away."

"Will do," Monroe replied as he walked off to make the call.

"Jimmy wants to see you," Lewis said.

"Jones?"

"Yes, boss. He says he has found a white man to take the place of the tennis player to service the country club set..."

"The tennis player?" Damone asked.

"Chip Osborne," Lewis reminded him.

"Why do I need to see him? Why doesn't Jimmy decide for himself?"

"Don't know. He just said this guy should be okayed by you personally."

"A street-level dealer? He better have a good reason for it. Call him now. Tell him to get here right away. Then he can wait while we meet with Delmar."

"The surveillance guy is coming in today to sweep the building," Lewis said.

"What time?"

"Two-thirty. Monroe will stay with him while we attend the ceremony at the park."

"Anything else?"

"The phone call to Chicago from Jeron at noon."

"He's on the way," Monroe said as he re-entered the living room.

"Yes, I remember the call with Jeron," Damone said. "I'll want to meet Delmar in the conference room. I want it taped. Make sure the equipment is working."

"Come in, Delmar," Damone politely said as Monroe led the young hacker into the conference room.

"Have a seat, please," Damone said gesturing to the conference table armchair to Damone's right. This particular chair had the best location for filming.

"What do you have on this reporter?" Damone asked.

"Well, sir," Delmar began. Being in Damone's presence always made the younger man a bit nervous. Even though he was merely making a report to him, today was no exception.

"Um," he continued looking at his notes, "he pretty much is what he seems to be. He's a progressive liberal, or at least he claims to be..."

"You don't get a job with that newspaper unless you are," Lewis said.

"...from a well to do farm family in Wisconsin. He lives well, better than a reporter on what they make."

"How so?" Damone asked.

"Well, um, Mr. Watson, he has a townhouse that goes for four-hundred-grand. No mortgage on it. He drives a two-year-old Jaguar that appears to be paid for. His credit cards show a taste for high-end strip clubs and call girls. The five-hundred to a thousand bucks a night type."

"How can he afford that?" Lewis asked.

"He can't. Not on what they pay a reporter," Damone said.

"Now for the interesting stuff," Delmar said, warming to the subject. "He's the reporter that has done most of the stories in the paper that have fueled the racial problems. And he was the one who got the pictures of Reverend Ferguson lying in the street after the cop shot him. I made copies of all the newspaper stories he wrote," Delmar said as he handed a large envelope to Damone.

158

"So, he was there when Reverend Ferguson was killed," Damone said.

"Yes. He wrote it up for the paper. It's in the envelope."

"I'll read it later," Damone said. "Anything else?"

"I got a copy of his resume from the paper's files. It's in there," Delmar said referring to the envelope.

"Is that it?"

"Yes, sir. Do you want me to keep digging?"

"No, I don't think so. At least not for... oh, wait. There is something. Can you get into the computers of the Hennepin County Attorney's office?"

"Probably," Delmar said. "I haven't tried for a while, but I was able to in the past. What do you need?"

"Get in there. Find out if he's on the witness list for the state against the cop. See if they have a written statement from him. Get what you can. And find out what you can on this cop, the one charged with shooting Ferguson."

"Okay," Delmar said.

Damone pointed a finger at Lewis then at Delmar. Lewis removed an envelope from his sports coat pocket and slid it across the table to Delmar.

"A little something extra for your trouble," Damone said.

Inside the envelope were twenty, one hundred-dollar bills. Delmar the junkie would spend it on his habit effectively giving it back to Damone.

"We have to find out exactly what this reporter saw," Damone said.

The three of them were still in the conference room after Monroe came back from escorting Delmar out. Damone was still at the head of the table, tapping the fingers of his left hand on the highly polished tabletop.

"We need to know if he saw our out-of-state friend set up that fat Ferguson for the cop."

"Grabbing and shaking down reporters isn't a good idea," Lewis said.

"I know," Damone agreed. "But this one might be susceptible to a cash inducement. I don't want him to know where it's coming from."

"We might be able to use one of his expensive hookers," Monroe said.

159

Damone looked at Monroe, nodded his head and pointed a finger at him. "That might work. There should be information in there," Damone continued, pointing at the envelope with Delmar's report. "Check into it. See what you can do."

"Jimmy Jones is waiting," Monroe said.

"Oh, yeah. I forgot. Okay, fetch him."

Monroe held the door for Jimmy Jones. As Jimmy entered the conference room, remembering the last time he was there, Jimmy's eyes nervously darted about the room. Instead of taking a seat at the table, he stood at the end opposite Damone waiting for permission.

Two or three seconds went by, then Damone silently pointed at the chair to his right. Jimmy hurriedly sat down.

"Thanks for seeing me…"

"I hear you have a replacement for your white boy," Damone said, interrupting him. "Tell me."

"Well, he's, ah, older and he, ah, looks like an eye-talian gangster. He seems to know his business. He had that white bitch who worked with Chip Osborne with him," Jimmy said.

"Her name?" Damone calmly asked.

"Oh, yeah, uh, Wendy something," Jimmy answered.

"Wendy Merrill?" Damone asked.

"Yeah, I think that's her name."

"Why do I know your employee's names better than you?"

"I know her, boss. I just forgot her name for a minute," Jimmy replied.

"Why are you so nervous, Jimmy? What have you been up to?"

"Nothing! I swear, boss," Jimmy almost shouted.

"What's this man's name?"

"Tony Russo," Jimmy replied. He reached in his coat pocket then handed a photo to Damone. Carvelli was wearing red-tinted glasses, a different hairstyle and nose putty. Enough of a disguise to fool any casual acquaintance.

"Tony Russo?" Damone said holding the photo. "Pretty common Italian name."

"He has Chip's customer book," Jimmy said.

"How did he get that?" Damone calmly asked.

"He said he had started working with Chip," Jimmy replied.

"You believe him?"

Jimmy shrugged and said, "Wendy, you know, agreed. And he has Chip's customers."

"If he is what I think he is, he could get his own supply and go into business for himself," Damone said absently flicking the photo with his fingers.

Damone slid the photo down the table to Monroe. Both Monroe and Lewis looked it over, shrugged and shook their heads.

"What else did he tell you?" Damone asked.

"He said he was tired of pushing papers like some sucker for a mortgage company in Chicago. So, he split and moved here a few months ago," Jimmy replied. "He seems cool. I asked him a lot of questions. He knows the business. Wendy was trying to supply Chip's customers but she ain't worth a damn. She needs help."

"Does he have money to buy product or are you gonna give him credit?" Damone asked.

"He says he has money."

"It's your call," Damone told him. "Don't be wrong."

"I'll let him have enough to get him started and then, we'll see how he does," Jimmy said finally relaxing.

"Okay," Damone replied. "Any other employees that you don't know about?"

"Huh?"

"This guy, this Tony. He was working with your boy Chip and you didn't know it," Damone said. "Any others?"

"No, no, boss," Jimmy said.

"How would you know? Get your crew tightened up, Jimmy. You're supposed to know this. You don't just collect the money. Stay on top of them. Tighten it up. And lay off the rock."

"I ain't…"

"Shut up! Don't treat me like a fool."

"Yes, sir," Jimmy replied, the anxiety back.

"Get out. One week, I want you to give a detailed report to Lewis on this Tony Russo and all of your employees."

After Jimmy had fled, Damone told Lewis to get the photo and information about Tony Russo to Delmar to check him out.

"I think he's a refugee from Witness Protection," Damone said.

"Sounds like it," Lewis agreed.

"Let's find out."

At precisely noon, Damone's burner phone for the day rang. The three of them were in Damone's second-floor office waiting for this call.

"It's Jeron," Lewis said as he handed the cheap flip phone to Damone. Damone waited until Lewis and Monroe left before answering the call.

"Are we ready?" Damone asked without even saying hello.

"They won't be able to change this month's shipment," Jeron replied. "It's too late. The shipment for the first and second weeks of October," Jeron replied.

"First thing next month," Damone said. "Good. That is sooner than I thought. How were you treated?"

"Like a prince," Jeron said. They were referring to a week-long business trip to Mexico Jeron returned from the night before. "We are a favored customer," Jeron said.

"They are animals," Damone said. "When we are ready, we should deal with them."

"Everything is proceeding better than we had hoped," Jeron reminded his older brother. "Now for the next, more profitable phase."

"Yes, you're right. Stay in touch. Take care, brother," Damone said then ended the call.

Fentanyl-laced opioids from China, Damone thought. *Yes, more money from the next phase.*

TWENTY-NINE

"Yeah, Russo," Tony Carvelli said answering his drug dealer phone.

"Yeah, it's me," he heard the caller say.

"Me who?" Carvelli gruffly said to make the caller tell him even though he knew exactly who it was.

"It's me, Jimmy," Jimmy Jones replied.

Upon meeting Chip's wholesale provider, Jimmy Jones, Carvelli decided to act the tough guy with him. Despite the entourage/bodyguards he had surrounded himself with, Carvelli could sense Jimmy was not a tough guy.

"Okay, tell me," Carvelli said. "What did you find out?"

"We can do business," Jimmy replied. "When can you come by?"

"An hour," Carvelli abruptly said.

"Yeah, that'll do, see you then," Jimmy said, but he was talking to himself. Carvelli had hung up.

"I'm in," Carvelli said into his phone.

He was in his car a few minutes after receiving the call from Jimmy, on his way to pick up his "partner", Wendy Merill. He had called her first to get her ready, then placed his current call.

"What do you need?" Jake Waschke asked.

"Get one of the guys to follow me."

"Dan Sorenson's here," Waschke replied.

"Good. I'll be there in ten minutes."

Carvelli entered the limo service office in his disguise and greeted his friends. Jake and Dan were the only ones there.

"What do you think?" he asked them as they stared.

"Looks good," Waschke replied.

"Are you kidding? It's a huge improvement," Sorenson said.

"Very funny, smartass," Carvelli said.

"Seriously," Waschke said. "If they had a picture of you as Carvelli, I don't think they'd make the connection unless they knew you."

"What do you need from me?" Sorenson said.

"Just cover my back. I'm going to meet these mutts and I need some backup. When I leave, I want you to wait to tail me and see if anyone else does first. Use your phone. Stay in touch."

"You got it," Sorenson assured him.

Carvelli parked on Dupont across from Jimmy's apartment building. With a nervous Wendy beside him, he crossed the street. Waiting on the stoop were two of Jimmy's thugs, including the one Tony had put down the first time he was here.

They stood when Carvelli reached them and indicated he should raise his hands to be searched. Instead, he shook his head.

"No, not again," Carvelli told them. "I'll tell you right now, I'm carrying and I'm gonna keep it."

There are four steps leading up to the building's front door. Carvelli was standing on the bottom one and the two guards were two steps above him. Wendy was on the sidewalk behind Tony. Carvelli took two steps back to get on the sidewalk. Wendy moved further away.

"If your boss wants to do business with me, he better realize now I'm not some street punk. Call him," Carvelli said.

The big one with the sore right hand called upstairs.

"Yeah. That Russo guy's here. He won't give up his piece."

He listened for a moment then asked Carvelli, "Did you bring money?"

"I'll talk to your boss," Carvelli replied.

"He's bein' an asshole. He won't tell me," the guard said into his phone.

He listened for a moment, said "okay" and ended the call.

"You can go up," he said. He pointed at Wendy and said, "Not you."

Carvelli had taken a step up on the stoop. Without stopping, he said, "She's with me. Now get of the way."

Wendy hurried to get behind him as the second guard held the door for them. Once inside they started up the stairs.

"What's wrong with you?" Wendy whispered. "Are you trying to get us killed?"

"Relax," Carvelli said. "I know what I'm doing. We'll be fine."

Watching from his car a half a block away, using small binoculars, Dan Sorenson suppressed a laugh. He saw the entire mini-drama and

164

knew the wiseguy Tony Russo had just put Jimmy Jones and his pals in their place.

"Mr. Russo," Jimmy said greeting Tony as he was led into the apartment. "Please come in. And the lovely Wendy. Please welcome. Something to drink?"

Carvelli and Wendy sat down on a couch facing Jimmy who was in a wingback chair behind a small table in the living room. The guard who had opened the apartment door stood silently behind and to the left of the couch. His hands were crossed in his front and he was holding a large, chrome, semi-auto handgun. Probably a .45.

"I'm not here to socialize, Jimmy. Let's do a little business so I can get on with mine," Carvelli told him.

"Whatever you say, Mr. Russo," Jimmy said flashing a smile with a mouthful of gold-filled teeth. Jimmy reached down on the floor and picked up a small, brown, paper bag. He removed two boxes identical to the ones Carvelli had found in Chip's hidey-hole in Nicolette's basement. He placed the boxes on the table.

"Here's your dope. Now, let's see the money."

Carvelli removed a plain, white envelope from his inside coat pocket and stood up. With two steps he was at Jimmy's table. He leaned down and while placing the envelope in Jimmy's hand whispered in his ear, "If your guy even blinks, I kill you. Keep your hands on the table."

Carvelli stood, looked at the gunman and smiled. The guard stared back with a totally inexpressive look on his face.

"No, no, my man," Jimmy said holding up both hands. "I don't do business that way. I ain't no crazy Colombian. I'm a businessman. We can do a lot of business if we just treat each other with respect. This ain't no rip-off."

By now, Jimmy was counting the cash in the envelope. Two-hundred used one hundred-dollar bills. When he finished counting, he stood and extended his hand.

"We good," Jimmy said.

The two men shook hands and Wendy stood and moved to the entrance to the living room. Her purse was over her left shoulder and in her right hand was a small .22 caliber semi-automatic handgun.

"Just like I promised, four hundred, fifty mills and two-fifty eighties," Jimmy said referring to the number and size of the opioids then sliding the boxes to Carvelli. "Forty grand on the street. I get twenty percent. One week."

"No problem," Carvelli said. "Let me have that paper bag."

"Sure," Jimmy smiled again. "No charge."

"Cute," Carvelli replied as he put the boxes of pills back in the bag. "These will go fast. I have a lot of connections."

"Back East?" Jimmy asked.

"I'm going to want to meet your boss and soon. I'm looking for a source to move a lot of weight. I ain't working with some Mickey Mouse street wholesaler," Carvelli said ignoring the question.

"Hey! No need to be insultin'," Jimmy said. "But meeting my boss, I don't know. I doubt he'll want to."

"It will be worth his while," Carvelli assured him.

As Carvelli pulled the rented Lincoln away from the curb to drive away, Wendy said, "I thought I was gonna pee in my pants back there. Chip practically threw himself at Jimmy's feet and you try to start a gunfight. What the hell?"

"Just showing him, he's not dealing with Chip anymore," Carvelli said.

"No, shit!" Wendy said. "But you know what?"

"Hmmm?"

"That was the coolest thing I've ever done. I've never felt so alive. I wish I had your balls," Wendy said.

Sometimes I wish I did, too, Carvelli thought as he looked at Wendy with a smirk.

Carvelli had barely turned the corner on 28th Street to go east when the Cadillac DTS pulled out of the apartment parking lot. There was only one person in it. One of the guards, the smaller one, was driving it. He immediately punched the gas to go after Carvelli.

Dan Sorenson pulled away from the curb and hit Carvelli's phone number. He made it through the same green light the Caddie did on 28th as Carvelli answered the call.

"He's in the beige Cadillac a couple of cars behind you," Sorenson told Tony. "The smaller guard from out front of the apartment."

"Yeah, I see him," Carvelli replied looking in his mirror. "You want to get in front of him and block him at a light?"

"Will do," Sorenson said.

Wendy was listening to Carvelli's side of the conversation.

"Are we being followed?" she asked.

"Yeah, we are," Carvelli said. "But I have a friend who's gonna cut him off. I don't want them following us."

Sorenson got ahead of Jimmy's guy and at Garfield Ave, Carvelli had his chance. The light turned yellow and he sped up to get through it. At the same time, Sorenson hit his brakes and forced Jimmy's guy to stop. By the time he realized what had happened, Carvelli was gone.

Wendy had turned around to see if anyone had run the red light. Satisfied, she looked at Carvelli. A silent twenty seconds went by before she spoke.

"You're not who you say you are, are you? You're a cop of some kind. You're too cool. Too smooth. You've done this stuff before and I don't buy this BS that you're a gangster."

Carvelli kept going heading toward downtown now. All the while Wendy kept looking at him waiting for a response. Instead, he pulled out his phone and made a call.

"Did I wake you?" he asked when the call was answered.

"It's afternoon, Tony," Gretchen Stenson said. "What do you think I do all day? Screw and sleep? I have a normal life just like everybody else."

"Sorry, you just, you know, keep unusual hours."

"Did you make a deal?" Gretchen asked.

"Yeah," Carvelli told her. "Now comes the tricky part. We'll be at your place in ten minutes."

"Good. I have to tell you," Gretchen said, "this is kind of exciting."

"I know, you've told me. See you in a little bit."

"Well, are you going to answer my question?" Wendy asked.

"I'm not going to tell you much right now. I don't know how much I can trust you. But, if you want to stay out of jail," he continued, turning to look at her, "and get a life back, this is your best chance. Well?"

Wendy thought about it then said, "For some reason I can't figure out, I trust you. So, yeah, I'm in."

They drove for another couple of minutes when Wendy suddenly spoke up again. "I almost forgot. I know for a fact Chip never paid Jimmy more than ten percent of the gross. Not twenty."

"Hmm. Interesting," Tony replied. "Good to know. I'll find the right time to use that."

THIRTY

"I'm thinking you're going to need some help," Marc told Maddy. The two of them were sitting in the living room of Marc's townhouse. "I don't know how many people the cops have questioned, but I think it's safe to assume a lot."

"You don't have any statements in the discovery," Maddy said, a statement not a question.

"That doesn't mean much," Marc said.

"What about some of Tony's guys? They're all ex-cops. They should know how to interview a witness," Maddy said.

"That's what I was thinking," Marc agreed. "Plus, they're working for a cop defendant. Interesting how cops can quickly change their minds about lawyers when it's one of their own."

Maddy narrowed her eyes, stood up and walked to where Marc was sitting. She uncrossed his legs, sat down on his lap and lightly kissed his left ear. With her arm around his neck, she snuggled and kissed his cheek.

"It's not gonna work," Marc said. "You're not coming with me this morning."

"Oh," she said and lightly slapped him on the shoulder. "But I want to see-"

"Get up, you're wrinkling my suit pants," Marc said.

"-Margaret."

"Come on," Marc said and swatted her on her rear. "Get up. I have to go."

"Oooh, you keep that up and we're not going anywhere," she purred then laughed.

"If she stays on the case, and I'm sure she will, you'll see plenty of her. Call Tony and see about getting some help. We don't have a lot of time to prepare."

"I will," Maddy said. By now they were both standing facing each other. Marc was silently looking at her.

"What?" she asked.

"Aren't you going to fix my tie?"

Maddy looked at him and said, "Nah, you're on your own."

"Great. We're already starting to act like an old, married couple."

Maddy stopped, crinkled her nose and said, "You're right. It's too soon. Come here."

She fixed the knot in his tie, they kissed and went out together.

Marc entered the very familiar Courtroom 1745 in the downtown Government Center. His motion in front of Margaret Tennant was scheduled for 10:00 A.M. and Marc was a little early. Sitting in the front row was Arturo Mendoza. The prosecutors were not there yet.

Margaret was conducting a motion on a civil case when Marc got there. As he walked up the center aisle, Margaret looked at him and they flashed each other a smile. He looked at Margaret's clerk seated next to the bench. Marc had known Lois for several years. This morning, while one of the lawyers prattled on, she looked back at him, narrowed her eyes and gave him a stare of disapproval. Knowing Lois, the way he did, Marc had to cover his mouth to avoid laughing. When she saw this, she smiled back at him.

At 9:55, Margaret stopped the insurance defense lawyer midsentence.

"You keep repeating the same argument," Margaret told the man. "Do you have anything new to add?"

"Well, um, no, your Honor," the lawyer replied.

"I'm granting the plaintiff's motion, Mr. Lockhart. Your argument is not persuasive, and the *Bailey* case is clearly dispositive."

"Your Honor," the same lawyer began, "I must object…"

"You're free to pursue an interlocutory appeal, Mr. Lockhart. Of course, you'll be appealing to the same court that decided *Bailey*. That's up to you. Anything else, gentlemen?"

When neither side said anything, she gaveled an adjournment as Steve Gondeck and Jennifer Moore came through the front doors.

"On the next matter, I'll see counsel in chambers," Margaret announced.

On their way back to the judge's chamber, the lawyers, all of whom were well acquainted, gave each other a pleasant greeting. When they were all seated in front of the judge's desk, Margaret started the discussion off the record while her court reporter set up next to her desk.

"You didn't seek recusal," she said looking at Marc.

"I have no problem with you presiding, Judge. I know you well enough to know you'll be fair and impartial," Marc replied.

"Does your client know, Marc?" she asked.

"Oh, yeah, that reminds me," he said. He reached in his portfolio and removed a manila folder. He took out two sheets of paper and handed one to the judge and one to Steve Gondeck.

While she read it, Judge Tennant asked, "Mr. Gondeck, are you aware that Mr. Kadella and I were involved in a personal, romantic relationship?"

"I am, your Honor," he replied. "I talked it over with the Felicia Jones. We are satisfied with you presiding."

"Are you?" Marc asked Margaret.

"Yeah. I've thought it over and as long as there is full disclosure, I'm okay. Both of you should know, if you want me out, now is the time to say so and I promise I'll understand and not hold a grudge."

When neither side made a comment, she continued. "Okay, let's put this on the record."

Margaret's court reporter had been patiently waiting. Margaret read the case name and number and the lawyers, in turn, noted their appearance.

"Mr. Dane is not joining us?" she asked Marc.

"No, your Honor. I didn't feel it was necessary."

Judge Tennant made a brief statement for the record regarding her previous relationship with Marc. When she finished, in turn, both the defense and prosecution agreed that it was not necessary for her to recuse herself. The judge also noted that the defendant had been fully informed and waived recusal in writing.

"Now, Mr. Kadella, your request to reopen the issue of a change of venue."

Marc looked like he was going to say something, so the judge held up a hand to stop him.

"As you are obviously aware, this issue was previously argued by your predecessor, Sheldon Burke. The court found insufficient grounds to support a venue change.

"I have carefully read your pleadings and was unable to find enough new facts to change my original decision. Do you have anything new to present today?"

"No, your Honor," Marc had to admit.

"If anything, the local atmosphere and media coverage have cooled off," the judge said.

"I'm very concerned about what is going to happen once jury selection has begun," Marc said.

"I'm not unsympathetic, Mr. Kadella, but it's also your client who won't waive time…"

"I couldn't persuade him to, even for this, your Honor," Marc admitted.

"In that case, we'll go forward and see what happens," Tennant said.

Thanks for stepping in it, Marc, Steve Gondeck thought.

"Moving on. I understand there are discovery issues, Mr. Kadella," Tennant said.

"The problem is there has not been any discovery given to us…"

"That's not true!" Gondeck almost jumped up to say. "He has…"

"Mr. Gondeck, wait your turn," Margaret told him.

"They have gone over my client's life with a magnifying glass. They've served search warrants on his house and cars. They've tried to get them for his parents' and in-laws' homes. They confiscated computers, including the ones the kids use for school. Laptops, cell phones, you name it. They've scooped it all up. And, so far, we have seen nothing."

"We're hearing from people he hasn't seen in years that the county attorney's investigators are questioning them," Arturo Mendoza added. "People going back to kindergarten. They're trying to get someone to claim Mr. Dane is a white supremacist. And, again, we have seen nothing forthcoming from them about any of this. We can't even bring a suppression motion because we don't know what to suppress."

"What about it, Mr. Gondeck?"

"We're working on it diligently, your Honor. We're almost done. If the defense wants a continuance, we will not object."

"What about it, Marc, um, Mr. Kadella?"

"He won't budge, your Honor. This case is playing hell on him and his family. We're down to twenty days," Marc replied.

"I know," the judge said. "Monday, October 3rd. You're almost done?" she asked Gondeck.

"Yes, your Honor. A few more days," he replied.

"Witness statements," Arturo said.

"We don't have anything written," Gondeck said.

"We want, we absolutely have to have, the complete list of everyone you've talked to, even if you don't plan on calling them or including them on your witness list."

"If we found anything exculpatory, we would have told you!" Jennifer Moore spoke up for the first time.

"I'll be the one to decide that," Marc said. "Witnesses may see things and tell cops things that the prosecution might not think is important. That list, I want today. Names, addresses, phone numbers, any notes you might have about what they told you. We gotta have it, now."

"Do you have this on your computer file?" Margaret asked Jennifer.

"I'll see, your Honor," she answered.

"Delivered to the defense by noon tomorrow," Margaret said. "The rest of it," she continued, looking at Gondeck, "by noon Friday. If they don't have it by noon Friday and you try to get it into evidence, you'll have a tough road to convince me. Understood?"

"Yes, your Honor," Gondeck replied.

"We'll have a list of prospective jurors by Friday also. And, you will both exchange witness lists by five p.m. next Friday, the twenty-first," Tennant said.

"Anything else?"

When no one responded the judge said, "Okay, we're adjourned."

As they were packing up to leave, Margaret asked Marc, "How's Maddy?"

"She's good," Marc said.

"I heard a rumor the two of you were, um…" she smiled.

"Yeah, we are," Marc admitted. "And I heard you're getting married."

"True," she replied.

"Do I know him?"

"I doubt it," Margaret said.

Marc leaned on her desk and whispered, "Be happy, Margaret. Okay?"

"You, too," she replied.

When the four of them were almost back to the empty courtroom, as they were about to enter through the back door, Steve Gondeck gently took Marc's arm.

"You and Maddy? Really?"

"Yeah, Steve," Marc said, "it's true."

Putting on a forlorn, broken-heart act, Gondeck said, "That's it. I might as well get it over with. My fantasy was all I had to live for."

"I'm calling your wife," Jennifer said.

172

"Huh? Oh, yeah. I forgot about her," Gondeck said. "Never mind. Leave it alone."

"You won't have to kill yourself," Jennifer said

"If that's all I thought she'd do to me…"

"The good news is, Steve," Marc said, "Maddy'll be hanging around the trial. I'll be sure to have her wear something distracting."

"She could wear a burlap Burkha and he'd be distracted," Jennifer said. "Come to think of it, I would be too and I'm not gay," she added.

THIRTY-ONE

When Marc arrived back at the office, he found Maddy and the office para-legal, Jeff Modell, in the conference room. First, Marc stuck his head in Connie's open door to say hello.

"You got a problem," Connie said.

She got up from her desk and led him into the conference room. Maddy was seated across from the door with a stack of printouts in front of her. Jeff was going through three boxes of discovery documents they had just received.

Maddy looked up and said, "Hi."

Jeff ignored them completely.

"Anything interesting?" Marc asked Maddy referring to the stack of paper in front of her.

"Interesting isn't the word I would use, but I am getting into his head   a   bit," Maddy replied.

What she was reading was the life of Philo Anson. She was also devising a way to go at him.

"We just got this stuff from Gondeck?" Marc asked Jeff.

"Yeah, looks like records of everything they found during their search. I won't know if they found anything until I get through it, but it doesn't look like it so far."

"It's only some of it," Marc said. "You can bet there will be an even larger paper dump on Friday. Most of which will be worthless junk."

Marc turned to Connie and asked, "So, what's the problem?"

"You didn't let me finish," Jeff said. "This stuff here," he continued, referring to the paper dump in the boxes, "appears to be smoke just to give us something to do."

"And they'll try to hide things in there," Marc said.

"They did. I started going through the box on the bottom first. Sure enough, in the middle of all the junk, I found a smoking gun," Jeff said.

"Your guy's been involved in four civilian complaints for excessive use of force," Connie told Marc.

"Shit," Marc quietly said as he slumped down in one of the chairs.

"Let me have them," he told Jeff.

Jeff slid a two-inch stack of papers across the table to Marc.

"They were hidden in two boxes, spread out so we might miss them," Jeff said.

"That's not like Steve," Maddy said. "Is it?"

"He's under a lot of pressure to win this. To get a solid conviction," Marc replied.

"He'll offer second-degree with a small break on sentencing," Connie said, "at the courthouse door."

"Maybe," Marc said. He looked at Jeff and asked, "Have you been through these?"

"Enough to know that they are all from African Americans."

"Perfect," Marc said.

"Why hasn't he charged this as a hate crime?" Maddy asked.

"Don't know," Marc replied. He took out his phone and while scrolling for a number, added, "He still might."

The phone he called rang once and was answered.

"Arturo, we've got a problem."

"What?" Arturo asked.

"I'll meet you at Rob's in fifteen minutes and explain it then."

"Okay," he heard his co-counsel say as he ended the call.

"What about my lunch?" Maddy asked.

"Mom, will you take her across the street for me?" Marc asked Connie.

"Sure, but she's buying," Connie replied.

Marc had called ahead, as did Arturo, to let Rob Dane know they were coming. Marc made the turn onto Rob's street and saw Arturo pull into the driveway. Before Arturo got out of his car, Marc pulled in behind him. The two of them walked up to the door together to find Rob holding it open.

Greetings were a bit brief and perfunctory while they went into the living room. Marc and Arturo took the couch, so they could use the coffee table for the documents they brought. Rob took a chair across from them.

"This feels kind of serious," Rob said looking back and forth at his lawyers.

"It is," Marc replied. He pulled a manila folder out and placed it on the table.

Marc tapped the folder and said, "What do you suppose this is?"

Puzzled, Rob replied, "I have no idea."

"Do the names, Jorell Clark, Levon Turner, Romain Robinson and Faaruq Noor sound familiar?"

"Oh, shit," Rob said. "I had forgotten…"

"Did you think the prosecution would miss these?" Marc asked. "Civilian complaints against you. All by African Americans except Faaruq. I assume he's Somali."

"Oh yeah, he's Somali," Rob defiantly said. "Did you read the incident report? I was exonerated. In fact, I was exonerated on all of them," he continued, annoyed.

"Take it easy, Rob," Arturo said. "We are wondering why you kept this from us."

"I didn't," Rob said. He paused then said, "Okay, maybe I did. But only because I was totally cleared of all of them."

"Tell me about Faaruq Noor," Marc calmly said.

"Let's see," Rob said. "I was cruising Little Mogadishu, ah, sorry, Cedar/Riverside when a call came in about a gang disturbance at a local park. Gold Medal Park.

"I turned the lights on…"

"Your emergency lights?" Arturo asked.

"Yeah, but not my siren. Anyway, I was there in a minute or so and found a squad with two officers already on the scene.

"There were two cars of American blacks hassling the Somalis. In case you didn't know, they don't get along. The Somalis treat African Americans with racial contempt. Not black enough.

"There were a lot of mouths going off on both sides. Especially this Faaruq guy.

"One of the other cops on the scene was Sergeant Dave Powell. Dave's a black man and usually good at calming these things down.

"Dave got in between a couple of these guys and tried to cool it off. He told the Americans to get back in their cars and take off.

"The other cop was Officer Diane Logan. She's a good cop who can normally take care of herself. She was trying to get the Americans settled down and back in their cars. I was standing next to Faaruq who had shut up by now.

"The shit started when Dave Powell put his hand on the chest of the ringleader of the Somalis. His name is in the report. This guy slapped Dave's hand away and pushed him. Dave is ex-Marine and nobody's chump. In about two seconds he had the Somali leader on the ground trying to cuff him. That's when all hell broke loose.

"This Faaruq asshole sucker punched me in the neck and pushed me down. I found out two or three of them each went after both Dave and Diane.

"Faaruq jumped on top of me and tried to stab me in the face. I was able to hold his right hand, the hand with the knife, away while he tried to get my gun. I let go with my right hand and punched him as hard as I could. I fractured his cheekbone, his jaw and knocked out four teeth."

"With one punch?" Marc asked.

"One punch," Rob answered. "He was out cold. By this point, there was a mini-riot going on. Lucky for us another eight or ten squads got there and put the whole thing down."

"Was this on the news? In the paper?" Arturo asked.

"Sort of," Rob said. "The Star Trib had a story in the Metro section the next day.

"The headline was that the police were under investigation for overreaction to a minor problem, that's what they called it, 'a minor problem', in the Somali community.

"I found Faaruq's knife with his prints on it. I had enough sense to bag it as evidence.

"Just about all of the cops there received excessive force complaints. We did get an honest investigation, and everyone was exonerated.

"Everyone who was arrested, twenty in total, had the charges dropped. Including Faaruq who was arrested in the hospital for the attempted murder of a police officer."

"And Faaruq signed a waiver agreeing not to sue the city," Marc said.

"Yep," Rob said. "All of them did. Signed a waiver."

"Why doesn't this stuff get more news coverage?" Marc asked.

"Because the local media and politicians don't want people to know about Somali gangs and crime in the Somali community," Arturo said.

"At least you got a good shot in on the little shit," Marc said. "What about Jorell Clark?"

"Oh, him," Rob said as if recalling who he was. "I was one of five or six officers and a couple of detectives responding to a shooting on the Northside. One dead, one wounded and taken to the hospital. It was over some kind of gang turf dispute.

"It was two years ago during the summer. A pretty good crowd had gathered and a few of us were walking through the crowd asking if

177

anyone had seen anything or knew anything. I look at Jorell Clark and without a word, he throws the soda he's drinking at me. A can. Only he missed me and hit a seventy-year-old woman in the head and knocked her down.

"I went after Jorell and tackled him, rolled him on his stomach and cuffed him. One of the other officers had gone to the victim to help her.

"I dragged his ass back and arrested him for assault. His gang buddies bailed him out and the woman dropped the charges. He filed a complaint against me. Then he failed to show up or cooperate with the case and it was thrown out.

"As for the other two..."

"Levon Turner and Romain Robinson," Marc reminded him.

"Right. Levon was arrested on a warrant by two other cops during a traffic stop. I had rolled up and was doing backup. Levon clearly resisted arrest and got thrown on the ground and cuffed. My dashcam had the whole thing on film. I never touched him.

"Romain Robinson was sort of the same deal. He was arrested on a first-degree murder charge; his girlfriend and her six-year-old daughter. He did both of them with a knife during a domestic assault. We were warned armed and dangerous. And that was putting it mildly.

"There were nine cops involved in taking him down. I held one leg while another cop held his other leg. That was all I did.

"Romain is six-foot-seven and at least three hundred pounds. He wasn't very cooperative. In fact, he was tossing cops around like beanbags. We were lucky no one was seriously hurt, especially Romain."

"I remember this," Marc said. "Wasn't he the one screaming police brutality on the ground while a dozen people were filming?"

"Yep, that was Romain and it made great film for the local TV stations. Look, every time we get an uncooperative perp and he has to be taken down by force, they always scream about something. 'You're breakin' my arm' or 'my back' or 'I can't breathe.' That guy in New York a few years ago who died in custody. The one who got busted for illegally selling cigarettes? He yelled 'I can't breathe' as clear as I just said it, eleven times on film. Sorry, but if you really can't breathe, you can't yell 'I can't breathe' like that once, let alone eleven times."

"What happened with Romain?" Arturo asked.

"There was one video that showed the whole thing, especially Romain tossing cops around. That exonerated everyone. Of course, that was never shown on TV. Romain got consecutive thirty-year sentences. He won't be out for a while."

The three of them took a brief break and then Marc got down to business.

"You have to understand something, Rob," Marc began. "This can't happen again—you failing to tell us something. If we hadn't found this," he continued holding up the folder with the complaint documents in it, "they could've sprung this on us and made you look like a racist."

"I get it," Rob said.

"Do you? Let me be clear. This is a must win case for them. You shot and killed a prominent member of the black community. It just about started a race war. They are putting your life under a microscope. By the time they're done, they will know how many times you pulled Polly's ponytail in third grade. How many times you had detention in middle school. How many times you ever picked on a black kid. Do you get it?"

"Yeah," he meekly replied.

"I want all of it—your life back to the cradle. And don't hold anything back. If you think it will hurt you, we have to know so we can deal with it. Talk to your friends, mom, dad, you name it. Report cards, school records anything you got in trouble for. If you saved someone's life, we need to know it. Your military record..."

"I didn't think they could get at that," Rob said.

"Why, what's in there?" Marc asked.

"Actually, nothing but..."

"Don't assume they won't find something. And I want it all by next Monday." Marc said.

"Okay. I don't have anything else to do."

"When is your family coming home?"

"A few days before the trial starts," Rob said.

"Good. Did you talk to your parents and in-laws about attending the trial?"

"Yeah, they're in."

"Good. Okay, I guess that's it for now. If I think of anything, I'll call. You too. Any questions, call.

"And Rob, nothing is too trivial. Whatever you think of, write it down. This is covered by privilege, so we won't have to show it to the prosecution," Arturo told him.

179

"One last thing," Marc said. "I am having a psychiatrist check you out. I just want to be sure…"

"No way," Rob began to angrily protest. "If that gets out my career as a cop will be over."

"She'll be discreet and…"

"No, and that's final. I'm not copping to insanity…"

"What about PTSD? And if you're found guilty your career…"

"No! End of discussion. I was checked out for PTSD before I left the army."

"It can come up years later," Arturo said.

"No."

Walking to their cars, Marc said to Arturo, "We may be able to use these civilian complaints to our advantage. If they try to use them, and I think they'll have to for motive, we can throw it back in their face."

"Maybe," Arturo agreed. "We'll see how it plays out."

"We'll need to talk to all of the cops involved," Marc said.

"Put Maddy on it. They'll sing like canaries for her."

THIRTY-TWO

"Yeah, yeah, I'm coming," Tony Carvelli grumbled as he groggily went to answer the pounding on his front door. He unlocked the door, flung it open and without looking to see who was there, yelled, "What?"

Carvelli stood in the doorway in a black T-shirt and black boxer briefs. At the door were two people, a man and a woman. Both were dressed in similar, boring, off-the-rack business suits, probably from J.C. Penney.

Calmly Carvelli looked at both, then said to the man, "Well. What an unpleasant surprise. And to what do I owe the pleasure, Agent Johnson?"

"Mind if we come in?" FBI Agent Jeff Johnson asked.

"Probably," Carvelli said. "Oh, what the hell, come on in, Jeff."

Carvelli turned to go inside and the two FBI agents followed him.

"Find a chair," Carvelli said. "I'll start the coffee," he continued as he went into the kitchen.

The two agents had barely sat down on his couch when they heard him yell, "Six o'clock! In the morning?"

Carvelli stomped out to the living room, stopped and stared at them. "What the hell is wrong with you people? Is it really six o'clock? This had better be good."

By this point, Agent Johnson was laughing and his partner, Tess Richards was holding a laugh in.

Carvelli stomped off and a minute later came back wearing a pair of gray sweats. With an annoyed look he sat down in an armchair across from his guests.

"You want to wait until you've had some coffee?" Johnson asked.

Carvelli sat silently thinking over the question. He could hear the coffee maker in the kitchen and decided waiting would be a good idea. A couple of minutes later he went into the kitchen and came back carrying a single cup.

The two Feebs looked at him with an "Are you serious?" expression then Johnson says, "You're quite the host, Carvelli."

Carvelli laughed and said, "I'm just kidding. I poured two cups for you. They're on the counter in the kitchen."

"Do you mind, please?" Johnson asked Tess.

"No, I'll get them."

She returned and handed a cup to Johnson.

"Thanks, Tess," he said. "Now, the reason we're here, we need to know what you're up to."

"I was sleeping until you showed up."

"That's not what I meant, and you know it. What are you up to with Jimmy Jones and his crew?"

Carvelli sipped his coffee and with a puzzled expression said, "How do you..." and then he realized the answer to his question.

"You're set up on him. Why? Why is the FBI sitting on a street-level drug dealer? Shouldn't you be tapping the phones of Republicans?"

"Very funny, smartass," Johnson said. "Now answer the question."

Carvelli said, "I'm going into the retail drug business. Now, why is the FBI and not the DEA set-up on Jimmy? You show me yours and I'll show you mine."

"You know, we could bust your ass right now," Johnson said.

"Except you know that would be a really bad idea," Carvelli answered him. "Hang on. Let me make a phone call," Carvelli told them.

He went back into the kitchen and called Marc who answered right away sounding awake.

"Sorry," Carvelli said. "I hope I didn't wake you or Maddy."

"I was up and Maddy is at her place. What's up?" Marc replied.

Carvelli quickly told him what was going on with the two FBI agents in his living room.

"You know this agent, Johnson?" Marc asked.

"Yeah. Straight as an arrow," Carvelli replied.

"What about the woman?" Marc asked.

"If she's with Jeff, then she is too and whatever they're up to is legitimate."

Marc went silent for a minute or so then said, "It's your call. I don't like the idea of any more people knowing what we're up to, but they know something. What do you think?"

"I'll tell them a little, they'll tell me a little then we'll see," Carvelli replied.

"Okay," Marc agreed. "Be careful."

"I'm doing undercover," Carvelli told them when he went back to his chair.

"We know that. Why else would you be in disguise? But who are you doing it for?"

182

"I can't tell you that. I will tell you it's not for any law enforcement or government agency. Your turn."

"Sorry, can't do it," Johnson said.

"Okay, be that way. Then Jimmy will be getting an anonymous phone call to let him know the Feds are watching him."

"You sonofabitch! I'll have your ass…"

"Stop it," Tess quietly said. She put a hand on Johnson's shoulder and pulled him back before he jumped up. "Think about it, Jeff. He could be just what we need; someone getting in on the inside. Tell him. You said yourself he was a straight guy you could trust."

Johnson took a deep breath then Carvelli left to go into the kitchen. When he returned, he had the coffee and filled everyone's cup. By then Johnson had calmed down.

"Okay," Johnson began. "I'm gonna lay it all out for you, or, as much as we know. But, Tony, you have got to swear to me that what is said here does not leave this room. You tell no one. Not even your lawyer friend, Kadella and his girlfriend, Madeline Rivers. And none of your ex-cop friends."

"Okay," Carvelli agreed.

"No one in the local field office or the U.S. Attorney's office knows anything about this.

"A few months ago, the two of us were called to Washington. The Director himself briefed us. That's why you gotta keep quiet. We, including you, could end up in prison if it gets out.

"Anyway, the two of us, we're told to come back here and find out what's going on with the local drug business, especially opioids."

"Why not the DEA?" Tony asked.

"There's something big going on. Bigger than DEA drug trafficking. We don't even know what."

"Besides, you know what cowboys they are," Tess interrupted. "All the DEA higher-ups care about are pictures in the news of themselves and big drug busts."

"Yeah, okay," Carvelli agreed.

"We came back and started quietly poking around," Johnson said. "Our boss and the U.S. Attorney were specifically told to mind their own business.

"Anyway, you know a local guy by the name of Damone Watson?"

"Yeah, I know who he is," Tony said. "Reformed gang banger and now a Bible-thumping, community organizer and soul saver."

"Yeah, well that's the image. We think he is the center of the drug business," Johnson said. "And the guy running things in the Somali community as well.

"And we believe that what we're really doing here is trying to find and trace a huge money laundering business being run by Somali gangsters with Damone Watson at the head," Tess said. "We weren't told this, but that's what we've come to suspect."

"What makes you think it's Damone Watson? He's supposedly totally reformed and doing great things for the black community in both Minneapolis and across the river in St. Paul."

"Because we were able to tail your pal Jimmy twice to Damone's community center that serves as his office and home," Johnson said. "We even tried to get both a normal wiretap warrant and a FISA warrant to put listening devices in there. Turned down for both."

"Why do you need a warrant?" Carvelli innocently asked.

"Because that's what we would have to do legally," Johnson said obviously aggravated with Carvelli's cavalier attitude toward the Constitution.

"I'm just kidding, relax. Besides, if he is who you think he is, he's not some Mafia moron. He'll have the place swept often enough to quickly find them.

"So, you think this Watson guy is a phony and is probably Jimmy's boss?"

"Looks like it," Tess answered.

"Is Washington on your asses yet to make more progress?" Carvelli asked.

"A little yeah," Johnson said.

"I told Jimmy I have big plans and that I would have to meet his boss and soon," Carvelli said.

"Perfect!"

"There's a leak," Carvelli said. "Somewhere in Minneapolis. Either the city council or the MPD. I'm betting the city council."

"I would, too," Johnson said.

"The city council falls all over this guy, Watson," Tess said.

"Well, we'll see," Carvelli replied. "We better stay in touch. Every day if we can. Are you sitting on Jimmy or filming?"

"We have a camera on the front of his place twenty-four hours a day. Sometimes we watch him. So far, we have identified most of his crew."

"I'll want that," Carvelli said.

Tess reached in her jacket pocket and removed a two-page document.

"Here's what we have. If you can fill in some blanks, do so," she said.

"We have his crew, but we don't know any other wholesalers working for Watson."

"Okay," Tony said as he looked over the list. "I'll see what I can come up with."

"Are you selling to this guy's customers? Chip Osborne?" Tess asked.

Carvelli looked at Johnson then Tess. Before he could say anything, Johnson did.

"There are some things you don't want to ask. Some things best left unsaid, Tess."

"Have you ever done undercover work?" Carvelli asked.

"No," she replied looking a bit embarrassed.

"It's okay that you haven't," Carvelli said. "It's not a character flaw. Doing undercover, the idea is to look and act legitimate to the assholes," Carvelli said. "These are very nasty people. If they get even a tiny whiff that you aren't who you say you are, they'll kill you without a second thought. You have to be realistic. If I'm going to make my way to the top dog, I have to deliver."

"I understand," Tess said. "Sorry I asked."

"Don't be," Carvelli said with a reassuring smile.

THIRTY-THREE

Two hours after the FBI agents left Carvelli's home, he parked the rented Lincoln two doors down from Jake's Limo Service. There was a meeting scheduled. Although Carvelli was not actively involved with Rob Dane's murder trial, since he would know everyone, Marc asked him to attend anyway.

Carvelli made the short walk to Jake's garage and recognized several cars parked nearby. He entered the building through the customer service door and went into Jake's office. Once inside, he found a dozen people, almost all ex-cops, sitting around doing what cops do when together; trading insults.

Carvelli went around the room shaking hands while Marc talked to Jake and Franklin Washington at the desk. By the time Carvelli made his way back to the desk, Dan Sorenson was there as well.

"Put the makeup and glasses back on Tony," Sorenson said.

"Don't go there," Carvelli replied knowing an insult was coming.

Marc looked at him and asked, "How did it go?" Obviously referring to Carvelli's early morning visitors.

"Okay," Carvelli cryptically replied.

"All right. Let's get started," Marc said.

Marc stood at the end of Jake's desk to address the small crowd.

"I wasn't here when you were hired to do some investigation," he began.

"Where is Maddy?" one of the ex-cops asked, one Marc did not know. "Imagine our disappointment that she's not here," the man continued with a smile.

Another ex-cop, one that Marc did know, named Tommy Craven, leaned over, cupped his hand and whispered into the inquisitive man's ear.

"Oops," the man said. "Look, um, sorry, I, ah didn't know you and Maddy were, ah…"

"Never mind," Marc laughed. "I'd like to get a brief, verbal report from each of you about how it's going. First of all, before we start, did any of you get a written, signed statement from anyone you interviewed?"

There were eight ex-cops involved; three black men including Franklin, two white men including Tommy Craven and three women.

Two black and one white. All of them shook their heads to indicate the answer was no. These were the people who were interviewing everyone on the list that the cops and prosecutor's investigators had interviewed––the list provided to Marc with one-hundred-fifty-three names on it.

"Okay, good. Tommy," he continued, looking at Craven, "you want to get us started? Anything of interest?"

"Craven was in a chair and stood up to address the crowd. Not much, so far," he said. Reading from his notes, he continued, "Of the twenty names on my list, I've interviewed fourteen in person and three by phone. The other three called me a few names my mother would disapprove of, then slammed a door in my face."

"What name could someone possibly call you that your mother would disapprove of? Remember, I've met your mother," Carvelli said.

Tommy waited for the laughter to die down before starting again. "Anyway," he said trying to get back on track. "None of them saw anyone with a gun. Most of them didn't even see the shooting. The ones that slammed the door on me were holding the Black Lives Matter banner. The rest were pretty close to Ferguson, but every one of them said they didn't see the shooting. They heard the shots but didn't react until they saw Ferguson on the ground. By then people were screaming and running for cover.

"But," Tommy said, "not sure if you ever met her." He paused and pointed a finger at a black woman sitting a couple chairs to Tommy's left.

"Sorry, no, I don't think so," Marc said.

"This is Sherry Bowen. Sherry looks twenty-five, but don't let that fool you. She's like the rest of us, retired off the job. You want to tell him what you found, Sherry?"

"Sure," she said, then stood. "Most of my list were dry holes, too," she began. "I'm from Texas, originally. A dry hole is…."

Marc smiled and said, "I get the reference. Please, go ahead."

"I did find three girls, three black teens, who were there. None were on my list. I was told about them by someone who was who thought they might have seen something. They were friends and had attended every protest, mostly for the fun of it."

Sherry was speaking from memory now but held a notepad in her hands.

187

"Their names are," she recited from her notes, "Tonya Howard, age sixteen... they're all sixteen. The others are Bethany Morris and Ronnie Mitchell. I got addresses, phone numbers, parents' names, too.

"They all say they saw a shabby looking old white man following behind Reverend Ferguson. They say he looked like a homeless guy which is why they noticed him. He looked out of place. Ferguson was on the left-hand side of the street, just a few feet from the curb, according to the police report," she continued.

"Yeah," Marc said, thoroughly engrossed by now.

The girls were more in the middle about fifteen or thirty feet away from Ferguson. Pretty close to him. But, they said, because the crowd size was way down on the day of the shooting, they had a clear look at Ferguson."

"Did they see a gun?"

"No, and I pressed them on it. They weren't looking at him when they heard the shots. And they told me they didn't want to get any closer to him, to Ferguson."

"What, why?" Marc asked.

Sherry paused for just a moment before continuing. "Because the girls said they had heard some rumors around the neighborhood about Ferguson and young girls. And some other things that he was into. I pressed them on this, but I didn't want to push them away. I'm sure they know more than what they told me."

"Like?"

"Not sure. Like maybe they knew a girl or two who might've been, I don't know, seduced, molested, I'm not sure. You're gonna love this, Mr. Kadella..."

"Marc," he replied.

"Marc. They all went downtown and were interviewed by an old, bald white man. They told him about the homeless guy running away from Ferguson. Why they weren't on our list I don't know."

"You believe them? They're credible..."

"Yeah, they're nice kids and they said they would be willing to talk to you if their parents would let them."

"What happened to the homeless guy?" Marc asked.

"The girls heard the shots—they know what gunfire sounds like—but at first they weren't sure where it came from."

"I heard that a lot," Tommy Craven said and almost all of the others nodded in agreement. "Shots fired in-between buildings. The direction they come from can easily fool you."

Sherry continued, still looking at her notes for accuracy. "One of the girls, Bethany, got it right. She thought the shots came from exactly where they did. She turned just in time to see Ferguson go down. And she saw the homeless guy sprinting—her word—away and disappeared into the crowd. By now everyone was running, and the girls did too."

"And the girls swear they told this to the investigator?" Carvelli asked.

"Yep, They do, Tony."

Marc looked over the crowd and asked if any of them had anything at all like this. They all shook their heads and several quietly said no.

"Anybody say anything about this homeless guy behind Ferguson?"

This elicited the same response.

"What do you think?" Marc asked Carvelli who was standing next to him.

"I think you guys should go back at them, again," Carvelli said. "At least the ones who were willing to talk to you. See if you can get some more sightings of this old, homeless guy."

"Especially if anyone else saw an old man sprinting from the scene," Marc said.

"Sherry, great job," Marc said. "Now, babysit the girls and see if you can get a better description of him. You know, clothes or anything."

"They weren't really sure about that, so I told them to think about it. I gave each of them my card…"

"Hold it," Marc said. "Did the investigator who talked to Tonya give her his card?"

"No, that's right. He didn't. I remember asking her. She said no and couldn't remember his name. Just showed her his badge. An old white guy, going bald. Of course, an old white guy to a sixteen-year-old black girl could be anyone over thirty."

"We'll find him," Marc said. "Maddy can get that easily enough. I have money for everyone," Marc announced.

On Jake's desk were eight, plain white envelopes, each with a name on it. He asked Carvelli to hand them out while he talked privately with Sherry.

"Start nosing around the neighborhoods and see if you can come up with more on Ferguson," Marc told her. "Anything about the rumors the girls heard."

"Will do," she replied. "And I'll stay on these girls. I am positive they know more. Maybe even a name or two. Although I'm not sure how that helps Rob Dane."

"I don't either. At least not yet," Marc admitted. "But we need to dig some more. Rob swears there was a gun. We don't have to prove absolutely that there was a gun. Just enough to create reasonable doubt."

"Lawyers," Sherry said then shook her head and smiled.

"One last thing," Marc announced to the entire group. "We don't have a lot of time so, if anyone can't make this their priority, please speak now so we can replace you. No hard feelings, it's just the clock is starting to tick pretty fast."

When no one backed out, Marc thanked them all and the meeting ended.

THIRTY-FOUR

"You're not gonna scare the shit out of me again, are you?" Wendy asked Carvelli.

The two of them were in the rented Lincoln, a car Carvelli was becoming very fond of. He had parked across the street from Jimmy's apartment and they were going in for more product.

"Probably," Carvelli replied as he exited the Lincoln.

The same two guards were on duty on the front stoop. As Carvelli and Wendy approached, the smaller of the two men opened the front entryway door for them.

"He's expectin' you," the man said.

"Well, thank you," Carvelli replied smiling at both men. "Have a great day, fellas."

"You need more product?" Jimmy asked. "Who you sellin' to?"

They were in Jimmy's office and Jimmy was seated behind the same table, the same man with the same chrome .45 was silently standing guard. Only this time the gun was stuffed down the front of his pants.

"Let me tell you something," Carvelli said looking at Jimmy. "I don't like your man there staring and threatening me with a gun. If anything ever gets out of hand, I'll put a bullet in his forehead and then one in yours. And yeah, I know about the Mac you have strapped to the underside of this table. You might possibly get me, but I doubt it. You better believe I will get you. Get your hands up on the table."

Jimmy smiled his gold-capped smile and slowly placed his hands on the tabletop. He looked at the guard and silently tilted his head, a signal for the man to take a break.

"Yeah, I need more product," Carvelli said finally replying to Jimmy's initial question.

"This is the third time in less than a week," Jimmy said as he placed the boxes with Carvelli's supply on the table.

Carvelli removed the envelope with his payment from his suit coat pocket and tossed it on the table.

"It's all there," he said.

"You're doin' twice the business old Chip did. How?" Jimmy asked.

191

"What do you care? You're still overcharging me. You're getting yours," Carvelli said as he checked the contents of the two boxes.

"Maybe it's time I take a look at your customer list," Jimmy said rubbing the fuzzy, scraggly, goatee on his chin.

"Then again," Carvelli said looking down at him, "maybe not. When do I meet your boss?"

"He says maybe someday, but not for a while."

Carvelli handed the two boxes to Wendy, who was sitting on the couch. He turned back to Jimmy and said, "Maybe I'll find a new supplier."

Jimmy grinned again, laughed and said, "There ain't no other supplier, my man. This is it. We runnin' it all. You do with us, or you don't do nothin'."

"I'm tired of making these trips here," Carvelli replied.

By now Jimmy had sliced open the envelope with a sharp switchblade. He ignored Carvelli while he looked over the contents.

"Seems to be okay," Jimmy said.

"Count it later. I want to get credit. I'll pay cash for…"

"Uh, uh," Jimmy said. "No credit. At least not for a while. You doin' good, but I need to see more."

"Great," Carvelli said. "Well, nice doing business with you again, Jimmy. I'll be in touch."

"Call me when you need me, Mr. Rossi."

"That went well," Wendy said as Carvelli drove away. "Except for the part about the gunfight."

"Let me tell you something about these guys," Carvelli said as he drove and kept an eye on his mirror. His phone rang, Dan Sorenson was calling.

"The whole bunch, including the two guys out front, just pulled out in a black Escalade," Sorenson said. "It looks like they're going somewhere in a hurry."

"Stay with them. See where they go."

"I am," Sorenson replied. "Where are you?"

Carvelli told him the intersection he was passing through. He was again heading toward downtown.

"They're not after you. I think they're heading toward the freeway. 35W. I'll stay in touch."

"Are they following us?" Wendy asked.

"No."

"You were telling me about these guys," she said.

"Oh yeah. These are street punks—that guy with the chrome .45 in his pants, if he tried to pull that thing out quickly and shoot it, he'd be lucky not to blow his own balls off, which wouldn't be the worst thing. These guys are not trained Navy Seals. They do their thing by fear and intimidation and a willingness to commit murder. It's powerful and works, but they're not trained soldiers or law enforcement. Essentially, they're bullies who think doing time in prison is some kind of badge of honor. If you stand up to them, they'll back down to do business with you."

"Are we going to Gretchen's?' Wendy asked.

"Yeah," Carvelli said. "We'll get things together for you two to get your friends their scores. I have to go somewhere. You okay with that?"

"Yeah," Wendy said. "I like her. Gretchen, I mean. What does she do?"

Carvelli smiled and thought about what he should tell her. "I guess she'd be okay with me telling you. She's an, ah, let's see, she's an independent businesswoman."

"Doing what?" a now seriously curious Wendy asked.

"She's in the, ah, I know, personal hospitality business. She's very good, exceptional in fact, and quite expensive."

Wendy sat quietly thinking about this then said, "I don't know what…" Then it dawned on her. "She's a hooker! Is that it?"

By now she was leaning forward as far as the shoulder strap would allow. She stared at Carvelli who was trying not to look at her.

Wendy swatted him on the arm and asked, "Well?"

Carvelli nodded his head up and down a couple of times, then said, "Yeah. She's a high-end call girl. Makes a damn good living."

"Wow!" Wendy said as she sat back in her seat. She stared at Carvelli and said, "That's fabulous. I would never have guessed. She's so, I don't know, smart, educated, sophisticated even. Now I really like her.

"How do you know her?" she asked.

"That, we're not getting into. Not for a while, at least," Carvelli replied.

"You're a customer," Wendy said.

"No, I'm not."

"Yes, you are, tell me all about it. I'm an adult. I want to know," Wendy said.

Carvelli looked at her, shook his head and said, "I am not, nor have I ever been, a customer. We're friends and that's it. As for the rest of it, use your imagination."

"Can I ask her about it? Will she be offended?" Wendy persisted.

"Go ahead and ask. I don't know what she'll tell you. Except, she'll probably tell you not to get into it. The nosiness, I mean."

"Oh, I hadn't thought of that," Wendy said. "Hmmm. Now I really want to know."

"Look, Wendy, it isn't what you see in the movies. None of her clients bear any resemblance to Brad Pitt or George Clooney, just so you know," Carvelli warned. "Or even me, as far as that goes."

Tony and Wendy took the elevator up to the twelfth floor of Gretchen's high- rise condo. When Gretchen let them in, having been here a couple of times before and knowing where it was, Wendy announced she needed to use the bathroom and went there. Gretchen led Tony into the kitchen and turned on the sink's faucet to cover their conversation.

"Is she jonesing?" Gretchen asked, wondering if Wendy needed a pill.

"Probably," Carvelli replied.

"Have you told her what you're up to yet?"

"No," Carvelli said shaking his head. "I'm not sure how much I can trust her. We'll see."

"She needs help," Gretchen said.

"I know, and it worries me."

"What if she ODs and dies?"

"Don't even say that," Carvelli said.

"Are we going out today?" Gretchen asked.

"You're into this, aren't you?" Carvelli asked.

"Into what?" Wendy asked as she came into the kitchen.

Gretchen shut off the water and replied, "Yeah, sort of. It's a little risqué. A little dangerous. It's a bit of a thrill, though."

"Tony told me what you really do," Wendy said.

"Oh, he did, did he?" Gretchen asked looking at Carvelli with her eyes narrowed to slits.

"She, ah, um, kind of asked, so, I, ah, didn't think you'd mind."

"It's cool," Wendy said. "I wish I had the balls to do it the way you do."

"Don't glamorize it, Wendy," Gretchen said. "It can be a tough business. For instance, I've been put in the hospital three times by assholes."

"Let's get this done," Carvelli said.

For the next hour, they went over their delivery list for the next two days. They packaged the pills in small, sealable, plastic bags and used Post-It notes to identify the customers. Between the three of them they had it down to such an organized procedure, they were finished and ready to make deliveries by 5:00 P.M.

Carvelli paid the women with his expense money, being careful not to use drug sale money. Every dime of that would be saved and accounted for. He also took possession of the inventory.

Carvelli dropped both women off at Wendy's car. They would go to the country club to take care of business and make deliveries. Carvelli left them to drive to Vivian Donahue's mansion on Lake Minnetonka.

THIRTY-FIVE

Lewis and Monroe were sitting together at a small table for two. They were a couple of rows away from the runway over the middle of the horseshoe- shaped bar in Gentleman Jim's. It was a so-called gentleman's club in the Warehouse District north of downtown Minneapolis. It was also Philo Anson's favorite titty bar and hooker pick up joint—an expensive strip club.

Damone's two guys had been watching both Philo, who sat at the bar with his back to them, and the girls. They were each nursing their second weak, ridiculously expensive, vodka soda waiting for Philo's date. It was after 10:00 and she was late. For what they had paid her, she was testing their patience.

A third smiling, buxom, white girl leaned over their table looking for lap dance money. Lewis whispered in her ear, stuck a twenty between her breasts and she left happy. As she walked away, Philo's date sat down next to Philo at the bar. Her working name was Bianca and she was a beautiful, biracial, copper-toned girl not even old enough to be in a bar. She was also an acquaintance of Monroe's.

While they watched and waited, Lewis was keeping time. Less than ten minutes after she arrived, Philo was following her out the front door.

"How long?" Monroe asked.

"Eight minutes," a dejected Lewis answered.

Monroe smiled and held out his left hand to his friend. Lewis peeled a twenty from his stash and slapped it into Monroe's hand.

"I'm surprised it took her that long to reel in the white boy," Monroe said as the two men stood.

Maddy Rivers had been after Philo for almost ten days. Her usual method for dealing with someone like him would be to coincidentally sit down next to him in a bar. Philo was making that method difficult. So far, he had either worked late and gone straight home or stopped at a strip club.

As an investigator, Maddy had tried twice to follow a mark into a strip club. Unfortunately, a single woman that looks like she

196

Maddy is a little out of place. The good news was if she ever needed a job, the managers of both places had offered her one.

Maddy was in her car across from Gentleman Jim's waiting for a chance at Philo. A few minutes ago, she had seen a young woman go in by herself. She looked classy enough, but the signs still read 'hooker'. Sure enough, less than ten minutes later, she saw the girl come out with Philo in tow.

Maddy watched the two of them climb into Philo's Jag across the street and three cars down from her. The car's headlights came on and illuminated two large black men who exited the bar as the Jag was pulling away.

Maddy saw the two men hurry to a light-colored SUV and she instinctively knew Philo was about to be followed. She slumped down in her seat as they drove past. Maddy waited until they were a block away then pulled out to follow them.

"Come on in, sugar," Bianca said as she unlocked the apartment door.

Philo followed her in and was surprised to find a tastefully furnished and decorated apartment. Bianca took his hand and led him to a sofa that matched the living room furnishings. He took off his outer coat and tossed it on the end of the couch. Bianca gently pushed him down, but when he tried to grab her, she playfully pushed him away and stood.

"Not so fast, honey," she quietly said with a seductive look. "For what I charge, we take our time and let you get the full enjoyment."

"Okay," Philo said with a big grin.

"You were drinking brandy, I think," she said walking toward a dry bar set up across the room.

"That'll be fine, baby," Philo replied.

A minute later, she returned with a snifter of brandy on the rocks. She sat next to him, her legs curled under her and handed him his drink. While he took a sip, she lightly ran her fingers through the hair on the back of his head. Philo put his hand on her knee and tried to slowly move it up under her dress.

The exterior door burst open and slammed against the wall. A very angry looking black man came storming into the apartment with murder in his eyes. Philo, a little too buzzed to understand what was happening, sat and stared, his mouth open and an uncomprehending look on his face.

When the man came in, Bianca jumped up and let out a panicky short scream. "It ain't what you think…" she tried to say.

"Yeah! Then what the fuck is it, bitch?!" the man yelled. He stepped over to Bianca, grabbed her hair and yanked with his left hand. In his right hand, so Philo could clearly see it, he snapped open a nasty-looking switchblade knife.

"Well?!" he screamed in Bianca's face.

"I can explain…" she tried to say.

Finally, realizing there was a problem, Philo put his drink on the coffee table and started to stand.

"Look," he said, "there's been some kind of mistake and…"

"Sit down!" the angry man screamed.

"Put the knife down, Lemar," they all heard a man's voice say from the doorway.

Lemar turned toward the door as Lewis and Monroe came in, Monroe holding a gun at his side.

"What?" Lemar asked, a look of fear replacing the anger. "Okay, okay," he said as he let go of Bianca and knelt down to drop the knife on the floor.

Bianca backed up, her hand raised in the air saying, "We ain't done nothin'. We were just…"

"Shut up, bitch," Lewis said. He looked back at Lemar and said, "What have you been told about this?"

"We, ah…"

"What have you been told?" he repeated more loudly.

By now, a thoroughly confused Philo could only watch as if this drama being played out had nothing to do with him.

"What have you been told about running Murphy's?" Lewis asked again.

"It's just some white boy," Lemar said, trying to defend himself.

"You ain't supposed to be doin' it to anyone and this ain't some ordinary white boy."

Lewis bent down and picked up the knife. He folded the blade into the handle, put it in his jacket pocket then looked at Philo.

"You all right, Mr. Anson?" he asked.

Surprised that this man knew his name, Philo picked up his drink and in one swallow tossed it down.

"Yes. Yeah, I'm okay," he said.

"Good, I apologize for this," Lewis said, then gave Bianca and Lemar a nasty look.

"The man we work for would like to have a word with you. I know it's late, but he keeps odd hours. Do you mind?" Lewis asked. "Monroe will drive your car since you've been drinking, and they might have drugged you. You can ride with me. It's not far."

Maddy had followed Philo and the car following him to the apartment building. Only a few minutes had passed when she saw the two black men escort Philo out of the building. One of the men got in to drive Philo's Jag while Philo and the other man got in the Tahoe.

While using a few tricks—turning off her headlights, pulling over and stopping with lights off—Maddy was able to easily follow them. When they reached their destination, she saw them drive into Damone's parking lot. Maddy stopped on the street after cruising past and seeing them enter the building. Although it was not the best neighborhood for a white woman to be in at night by herself, she decided to risk it and wait. Maddy drove up a block, turned around and parked a half block away on the opposite side of the street. With a handgun in her lap, she watched the parking lot and waited.

Despite the lateness of the hour and the cool, late September weather, there was a ball game being played next to the parking lot. Maddy made herself comfortable and half watched the game, half watched the parking lot.

"Come in, Mr. Anson. Please, have a seat. I've been meaning to meet you for a while now," Damone cheerfully told Philo

Lewis and Monroe had escorted Philo up to Damone's second-floor conference room. Having called ahead, they knew Damone would be waiting.

"I'm sorry about this, the way this came about," Damone continued. He had stood up and was holding the chair for Philo to

199

take. The seat was the one to Damone's right; the one best suited for filming.

"You've met Lewis and Monroe," Damone said as he sat down again. "They have been watching those two who tried to rob you tonight for a while now. It isn't the girl, it's that pimp," he continued saying the word 'pimp' with clear disgust.

"No, I mean, thanks," Philo said. "They saved my ass. I had no idea. The girl, Briana, she seems nice and well, she's beautiful and hard to resist."

"Yes, I can understand that. Men are a little too susceptible to the pleasures of the flesh," Damone said while placing his left hand on his Bible. "Fortunately, God is forgiving.

"I wanted to meet you because of your fair coverage of the troubles the city is experiencing this summer. I read your paper every day and am very impressed."

For the next ten minutes, Damone went over a list of articles Philo had written. By the time he finished, Philo's ego had been sufficiently primed.

"I was especially impressed with how you were able to get a picture of poor Reverend Ferguson's body lying in the street. Where were you when he was murdered? If you don't mind my asking."

"Oh, no, not at all, Mr. Watson."

"Damone, please," he said with a smile and turned his eyes toward Lewis and Monroe.

"Damone, okay," Philo said.

It took him almost fifteen minutes to describe, in detail, where he was and how sincerely he participated in each day's protest. By the time he finished bragging, it almost sounded like he was among the protest leadership.

"As I understand it," Damone said, interrupting Philo to shut him up, "you got the photo of Reverend Ferguson lying in the street, the one in the paper?"

"Yes, I did," Philo sadly said. "It was terrible, but I had to do it. I had to forget the shock and horror and be a professional. Much like Abraham Zapruder who filmed the assassination of Kennedy. Very heroic of him to take that risk."

"Yes, it was," Damone agreed, still filling Philo's head with flattery to make him get on with it.

"Well, I saw Ferguson lying in the street, obviously dead. Within seconds there were cops around him. But I didn't let that deter me. I barged right through them and using my phone, took seven pictures."

"Seven? The paper only printed one. Do you have the others still on your phone? I'd love to see them," Damone said.

Philo paused for a moment then said, "Ah, no, no, I don't. The paper took them."

He's lying, Damone thought.

"That's a shame," Damone said. "Well, the reason I'm asking about it is because there is a rumor out there," he continued, waving his hand toward the windows, "that there was an unidentified man, a white man, near Reverend Ferguson. Did you see anyone like that?"

"You know, I, ah, I did actually. I mean, I'm not sure how near he was. In fact, he had been around for every protest march. I saw him, now that you mention it. I remember thinking he kind of looked out of place. He looked like a homeless guy. You know, a bum, really. He seemed to be just hanging around."

"Did you ever get a picture of him? Maybe in the background of another photo?" Damone asked.

"No, uh, uh," Philo answered. "The only pictures I took at all were the ones of Ferguson in the street."

"None of the cop who shot him?"

"No, I wasn't sure who shot him. Not right away. I heard some cops talking. That's how I got his name for the paper," Philo said.

While he told the story, Philo was very careful not to mention that his first instinct was to run. Philo figured there was no reason to muddle up a good story with irrelevant facts.

"Well," Damone said. "Thanks for stopping by. And don't worry about what happened tonight. I'll see to it that it won't happen again."

Maddy had become so engrossed in the late-night ball game she almost missed him. It startled her for a couple of seconds when she noticed Philo's Jag pulling out of the lot. It took a moment to get her bearings, then she quickly went after him.

To her disappointment, Philo hurried straight home. Maddy was hoping Philo's drinking problem would cause him to stop at a bar other than a strip club. She was beginning to realize following him was a waste time.

When Philo got to his townhouse, the first thing he did was pour a double shot of Cognac. To calm himself, he drank it down in two swallows. He poured another one, then went into his den.

He turned on his laptop and, while waiting for it to warm up, he removed the SIM card from his phone. He placed it into a USB port adapter and uploaded the pictures he had taken at the crime scene onto his computer. He then downloaded them onto a memory stick. When that was done, he deleted the photos from his laptop and the SIM card. Fifteen minutes and another drink later, he changed his mind and reloaded them onto his phone.

THIRTY-SIX

Marc was in the office's conference room with Arturo and Jeff Modell. It was almost noon on the Friday he was to receive all of the final discovery. Fortunately, there were only two more boxes. If Gondeck were being true to form, most of it would be a waste of time, Jeff's time.

What they were currently reviewing was the list of prospective jurors—a list of one hundred fifty names of Hennepin County residents. For each name, there was some bio information: age, marital status, address, employment and race. This last piece, race, was always a delicate matter and normally not allowed. With the significance of the racial aspect of this trial, Judge Tennant risked being overturned on appeal and had it included.

"What do you think?" Arturo asked.

"I hope you don't have plans for the weekend," Marc replied. "We'll send this to Grayson and let them run it," Marc said. Grayson was Grayson Trial Support, a jury consulting firm in Boston. The police union insisted on using them and agreed to pay for it.

"While they're doing that, we'll go over it ourselves…"

There was a bit of a commotion in the outer office at that moment. All three men turned to look through the conference room windows to see Maddy come in.

"Ah, there she is," Marc said. He was expecting her.

A moment later, after making the rounds in the office, she joined them.

"So, you're not having any luck with the reporter. Tell us about last night," Marc said.

When she finished telling them about tailing Philo, the hooker and the two guys and then Philo and just the two guys, it was Arturo who responded.

"That sounds like Damone Watson's building," he said. "What would he want with the reporter? Especially that late?"

"So, Philo goes into an apartment with the hooker, the two black guys follow and a few minutes later they escort Philo out?" Marc asked.

203

"Yeah. And they were in the strip club and I'll bet anything they were watching Philo. I think it was a setup. I'll bet that when she got him in her apartment, a guy came in, angry, maybe waving a gun and the rescue was a setup.

"When I followed Philo to the strip club the two black guys were in front of me. They were following him, too. Why else would they do that? Follow him to the strip club, then leave right after him and coincidentally show up at the hooker's and drive him to-"

"Damone Watson's," Arturo said.

"Okay," Marc said. "But what does Damone Watson, the city's new community organizer darling, have to do with this?"

"Are you getting side-tracked?" Jeff asked.

"Maybe," Marc answered him. "But Philo took the photo of Ferguson that was used in the paper. The caption gave him credit. He must've seen the homeless guy."

"And?" Arturo asked. "You think he saw something?"

"I don't know, maybe, yes," Marc replied. He looked at Maddy and said, "Let's get a subpoena and go after him."

"Let me try something, first," she said. "Trust me," she continued when she saw Marc give her a suspicious what-are-you-up-to look.

"Okay," Marc quietly said. "When are you going after him?"

"Tonight, or tomorrow. As soon as I can get at him, but I need to talk to Tony," Maddy said.

"Oh man," Marc said shaking his head. "Try not to commit any more felonies than you have to and please be careful."

"And you," Maddy said looking at Marc, "don't ask questions you don't want to know the answer to.

"Now you get to work on your jury list. I've got a list of cops to meet this afternoon. Have you thought about using Tony's hacker? Paul?"

"I resent that," Jeff said. "I'm a pretty good hacker, myself."

"Not like this guy, Jeff. Be thankful you're not. And, yeah, we might use him," Marc told him.

Maddy had the list of every cop involved with Rob and the civilian complaints against him. She had talked to each one on the phone already. They all sounded eager to cooperate and would have done so over the phone. A phone interview of a potential witness is not the same as one done in person.

She started with the two cops first on the scene of the mini-riot between Somalis and African American gangs. Sergeant Dave Powell and Officer Diane Logan agreed to meet with her on their lunch hour. Having read the complaint and hearing it from Rob, Maddy was pretty well versed in what happened.

Powell and Logan corroborated both the official account and Rob's.

"We were all lucky Rob punched that guy. If he had stabbed Rob and gotten his gun, we would've all been in serious trouble. The complaint was filed because Rob smashed the side of the guy's face. The doctor who patched him up, a Somali himself, didn't believe one punch could do that much damage. But I saw it. A strong man fighting for his life, no problem."

Without even being asked, both Powell and Logan agreed to testify.

"I'll tell you something else," Powell said. "The word is, they're out to show Rob is a racist and that's why he shot Ferguson. I don't buy it. I know Rob. He's no saint, just like all of us, but I've never seen or heard any reason to believe he's a racist. And we've all heard some things about the dearly departed Lionel Ferguson. He did something to get Rob to do that. Maybe not on purpose, but Ferguson did something."

"Was there a gun?" Logan asked. "We've heard Rob says there was."

"Rob insists there was. Pointed right at him," Maddy replied.

"If he says it, I believe it," Powell said.

The rest of her day went basically the same way. Maddy interviewed every one of the cops who were involved in the complaints. All of them said the same basic things about each incident. And they all offered to testify.

She also asked them about Ferguson's reputation. Many of them had heard rumors, but none could swear to any of it.

At 4:00 P.M., she was finishing up her notes from inside her car when her phone rang.

"Maddy Rivers," she answered.

"Maddy, it's Sherry Bowen," she heard the caller say.

"Hey, Sherry. What's up?"

"Can we meet, like, right away?" Sherry asked.

"Now?"

"Yeah, now if you can," Sherry replied.

"Okay. Where?"

Sherry gave her the name and location of a restaurant on the North side and Maddy agreed to meet her.

Maddy knew Sherry Bowen, so when she entered the restaurant, she spotted Sherry right away. Maddy slid in opposite Sherry. They were in a horseshoe-shaped booth in back by themselves. There were two girls between them. Sherry introduced them as Kendra Parker and Tonya Howard.

"Tonya is one of the girls I talked to about the shooting of Lionel Ferguson. She was at the scene when it happened. This is her friend, Kendra, who has had a bad experience with Ferguson."

"Kendra's sister is more my friend," Tonya said. "Kendra is a senior this year and I'll be a sophomore."

"How old are you, Kendra?" Sherry asked.

"Seventeen, I'll be eighteen in October," she quietly replied.

"Are you okay to tell me about Reverend Ferguson?" Maddy softly asked.

At that moment the waitress appeared. Maddy ordered coffee and another soda for the girls.

"He raped her," Tonya blurted out as soon as the waitress left.

"Tonya," Sherry said, "let her tell it."

"Sorry. But he did and she's not the only one."

"Tonya," Sherry chastised her again.

"Sorry."

"What happened?" Maddy asked. "Can you tell me?"

"I ain't goin' to the police or court," she said.

"No one's talking about that," Maddy said. "I'm just trying to find out what kind of man he was."

"He's an asshole and it's a good thing someone shot him," Tonya said.

"Tonya!" Sherry said again.

The waitress brought their drinks and left, then Maddy tried again.

"It was at church," Kendra began. She explained to Maddy and Sherry about how she became involved with Ferguson and the church. She alluded to the fact that she had been a problem for her mother growing up. When she became involved with Ferguson, her mother was very happy.

"He was good, at first. Helping me understand that going to school, getting an education and doing good with my life was the way up. He was doing the same thing with other girls, too. And some boys.

"We became close, too close. I don't know where my father is. I know who he is, but he's never been around. Reverend Ferguson was the first black man to even take an interest in me, ever tried to help me. Momma is always so busy workin' two jobs and all.

"Then after a few months, I was at church alone, in his office. We was studyin' the Bible and he was explainin' to me about how we should comfort each other, like the Bible says. He was holdin' my hand and lookin' at me in the eye and the next thing I know, he's on top of me, kissin' me and pullin' my pants down. I was so scared and shocked. I didn't know what to do.

"Then, at one point, he asked if I was willin' to comfort him. I think I said yes, then he was in me and…"

At this point, Kendra was getting teary-eyed. They stopped for a moment to let her collect herself. A couple of minutes later she continued.

"I wasn't a virgin. I'd been with a couple of boys. Boys I liked who said they loved me and then we would do it. But they always used a condom. We learned that in school. The fat ass reverend didn't use no condom and I was scared I might be pregnant, but I got my period, so I knew I was okay. I never went back to church. After, I found out he did other girls even younger than me. As young as eleven or twelve."

"Did you tell your mother?" Maddy asked.

"No, I was too ashamed. I just wanted to forget it. But I told my sister. When he got shot, I was happy, and she wanted to know why. So, I told her."

"Her sister told me," Tonya said.

"Please, you can't tell anyone. You promised," she pleaded, looking at Sherry.

"We won't," Maddy said. "I would like the names of some of the other girls."

"I have those," Sherry said.

"I don't understand what this has to do with who shot Ferguson," Tonya said. "That white cop shot him, didn't he?"

"That hasn't been proven yet," Maddy said. "Right now, we're just investigating. Part of an investigation into a case like this is the background of the victim."

"He's no victim," Kendra sullenly said. "He's a child molester and an asshole and got what he deserved."

THIRTY-SEVEN

"Have one of the ex-cops check with guys still in the department. See if they can find out who this guy is. Try detectives. They would be the ones to work with him," Marc told Maddy.

The two of them were in Marc's office discussing Rob's case and Maddy's investigation. So far, she was not having any luck finding out who the prosecution's investigators were since there were no written reports done—probably because they had not discovered witnesses who saw much. There were no names of investigators from written reports.

"In fact, try to get a list of all of them, everyone who they have working for them. Even those who did not work Ferguson's shooting. I'll put them all on my witness list," Marc said.

"Okay," Maddy agreed. "What do you want me to do about the reporter, Philo Anson?"

"What do you think? You know, I've kind of missed you," Marc said going off on a tangent. This was the first time they had seen each other for almost four days. Trial preparation is time-consuming for everyone involved.

"Me too," Maddy replied. "When this is over, maybe we should take off for a few days. Go lie on a beach somewhere."

"Hold the thought," Marc said.

"Now, what about Philo?" she asked.

"We need to find out what he saw," Marc said.

"I've been thinking, and I hate this idea, maybe I go after him in a strip club dressed up like a hooker. See if I can get him out of there and into a motel room where Tony is waiting."

"I don't like that, but…"

"We're running out of time. At least he likes a better class of strip clubs," she said.

"You looking to apply for a job?"

Maddy put on her best come-hither look and said, "I do private shows only."

"Don't say that right after I tell you I've missed you," Marc said.

Maddy audibly sighed and said, "Yeah, me too."

209

"Philo," Marc said. "Try the next couple of nights. Coordinate with Tony if you think you can get him. No felonies!"

"Me? Tony? Cross the line and bend the law? I'm insulted and if he were here, he'd be too."

"No wonder I worry about you," Marc said. He was about to say something else when a thought occurred to him.

"What's Gabriella's phone number?"

"Home or work?" Maddy asked as she removed her phone.

"Her cell number," Marc replied.

Maddy found it on her phone and read it to him while he dialed. It rang once then Marc heard a familiar voice.

"Hi, Marc," she cheerfully said.

"Hello, gorgeous, how have you been?"

"Hey! Watch the flirting," Maddy said.

"Let me talk to my buddy," Gabriella said referring to Maddy.

"Not yet. I need a favor. If you can't do it, just say so," he replied.

"Okay."

"You guys had cameras covering the protest marches that went on, the ones that Reverend Ferguson was in when he got shot, didn't you?"

"Sure," Gabriella said. "The station had two or three handhelds for the first couple of days. I think the third day, too. We blew it and missed the day he was killed if that's what you're looking for."

"That would've been nice, but I was wondering if Maddy or I could review the film you have. Anything with Ferguson in it, even the days before the shooting."

"I don't know," Gabriella said. "I'm not sure the station would allow outside personnel to do something like that. The county attorney requested it and we turned them down. Hunter thought there would be a subpoena coming, but they dropped it," she said referring to her boss, Hunter Oswood.

"If they didn't let Gondeck do it, they wouldn't let me," Marc said.

"They would fight you over a subpoena..."

"And probably win," Marc said. "What if I asked for something very specific?"

"Like what?"

"I'm looking for film of a homeless man, or someone who looks like a homeless guy, hanging around Ferguson during the protest marches."

"I could ask," Gabriela said. "Why do you want this guy?"

"Off the record and promise me you won't use this or any part of it?" Marc said.

"Sure," Gabriella replied. "But I want an exclusive interview after the trial."

"You drive a hard bargain," Marc said. "We have witnesses who say they saw this guy both before and after the shooting. He was right behind Ferguson and we would like to find him."

"A homeless guy? Good luck. You could check out Tent City along Franklin Avenue."

"Waste of time," Marc said. "Unless we have a photo."

"I'll check with management and let you know. I'd be willing to look through the film myself," Gabriella said.

"Thanks, kid. I appreciate it."

"Let me talk to Maddy."

"Should I leave the room while you two talk about me?" Marc said into the phone.

"You're not that interesting," Maddy said loud enough for Gabriella to hear her.

Marc let the two women gab for three minutes then pointed at his watch and mouthed the words "we have to go" to Maddy.

She nodded and said, "We need to leave. I'll talk to you soon."

After ending the call, Maddy said, "She's dating someone."

"I gathered that," Marc replied.

"An anchor for another station who claims to be getting a divorce," Maddy told him.

"Are you serious?" Marc asked. "What is she thinking?"

"That's when I said we need to talk," Maddy replied.

Marc parked in front of a well-kept house and yard. They were in a residential area in the Near North neighborhood of Minneapolis. The house was a brown and white, two-story sitting up above street level. There were fourteen concrete steps, including a landing, to the top of the hill. By the time they reached the top step, a serious looking black man was standing on the porch waiting for them.

211

"Mr. Howard?" Marc asked when they reached the porch.

"Bill," the man replied and put out his hand to Marc.

"Marc Kadella," Marc said as they shook hands.

"And you must be the girl who talked to Tonya and her friends," Bill Howard said. "She said you were very pretty. She didn't lie."

"Thank you," Maddy said as she also shook the man's hand.

"We weren't expecting you," Marc said. "I talked to Mrs. Howard and she said you would be at work."

"I took a half day off. I want to know what's going on with my daughter," he replied.

"Absolutely," Marc said.

"Are you going to let these nice people in or make them stand on the porch all day?" They heard a woman's voice say through the screen door.

Inside they met Tonya's mother, Sheila Howard, and found Tonya waiting in the living room. They all found seats, Sheila served coffee and cookies and Bill Howard started the discussion.

"So, you want Tonya to be a witness at the cop's trial," he said.

"That's a maybe at this point, sir," Marc said.

"She didn't see much," Bill replied.

"I understand," Marc continued.

"And to be blunt, while I know that fat Ferguson was a phony asshole…"

"Language," Sheila said.

"I'm not sure I want my child involved in this. Especially if you get him off. Sorry, but that's how I feel."

"You're entitled to feel whatever you want to, and you have to look after her," Marc said. He looked at the family photos lining the window sill in front of the bay window. Several were of a young man in an Army uniform. The uniform of an army ranger.

"Let me ask you this," Marc said. "What if your son shot and killed someone overseas? And what if he truly believed it was justified? Wouldn't you want him to get the best representation? The fairest trial? One that all of the evidence was told in court?"

Bill looked at a picture of his son, turned back to Marc, smiled and said, "Okay, you got me there. Of course, I would. All right, girl," he continued, "tell the man what you saw."

Tonya told Marc what she had already told Maddy. Marc let her go and only asked three or four questions to clarify a few points. When she finished, Marc thanked her.

"The other two girls, her friends…" Marc hesitated, trying to remember their names.

"Bethany and Ronnie," Maddy said.

"I've talked to their parents on the phone and they are willing to testify if Tonya does. They're nervous. I really don't believe you have much to worry about. This isn't a gang shooting and by the time this trial is over, the good Reverend Ferguson won't look so righteous anymore."

"You'll only use her if you have to?" Sheila asked.

"Of course," Marc replied. He looked at the sixteen-year-old Tonya and asked, "What do you want to do?"

"I'll testify," she said. "I won't lie…"

"Absolutely not," Marc said, "You just listen to the questions carefully and tell the truth. You didn't see the actual shooting so don't say that you did. But, I have to know, you did see the homeless man walking right behind Ferguson. Then when you heard the shots, you saw him running away along with everyone else."

"Yes, I'm sure of that," Tonya said. "But I did not see the shooting or see a gun."

"Then don't say you did. In fact, I want you to say that. Say you didn't see the shooting or a gun. We will go over your testimony again before trial, so you're prepared and not nervous. We will not put words in your mouth. You just stick to what you honestly saw and did."

"All right. I will."

Marc looked at the parents and asked, "Are you two okay?"

"Yes," they both said.

Marc and Maddy were halfway down the front steps when Maddy's phone rang.

"Hey," she answered after checking the ID. "Did you find out anything?"

"Yeah," Gabriella replied. "I talked to Hunter, the news manager, and his boss, Madison, and they okayed me to go through our film and see if the homeless guy is there."

213

"Great," Maddy said in the phone. She then moved the phone away from her face and said to Marc, "Good news from Gabriella-"

"Hold on!" she heard Gabriella say. "There are conditions."

"Just a second," Maddy told her. "Tell Marc."

By now they were at the bottom of the stairs standing on the sidewalk. Marc took Maddy's phone and said hello.

"There are conditions. First, we want to know why we're doing this…"

"I can't tell you that without violating the court's gag order. I'm right up to the line now. If Margaret finds out she may find it amusing to put me in jail just for old times' sake. If that's a deal breaker then, so be it."

"Okay, I'll tell them that. Second, we get exclusive interviewing rights after the trial. Promise me you're going to win."

"I promise I'm going to win," Marc quickly complied.

Gabriella was laughing and had a difficult time speaking. "You can't promise that," she said.

"Why not? I'm a lawyer. Of course, I can tell you that. Anything else?"

"Yes. Before we let you see anything, they will want a proprietary property agreement to protect the station."

"No problem," Marc said. "As long as I can use what we find in court if you find him."

"And if the station balks at that?'

"Keep this between us," Marc said. "I'll subpoena everything and because I'll be able to honestly say I saw what you have and need it for my case, the judge will give it to me."

"You think so? The station has pretty good lawyers and…"

"…and I've got a first-degree murder defendant. Gabriella, I don't want to get into a pissing contest with your bosses. Be a doll, check the film and see what you can find. We'll take it from there."

"I will," Gabriella replied. "Give the phone back to your better half."

While Marc drove, the two women talked all the way back to Marc's office.

THIRTY-EIGHT

Lewis knocked sharply twice on Damone's office door and went in without waiting for a reply. Damone was at his desk proofreading a speech he was to give that night at a fundraiser for Jalen Bryant. Damone had finally endorsed Bryant in his mayoral campaign. He would prefer the current office holder, the eminently unqualified featherhead, Dexter Fogel. A useful idiot.

Fogel was disqualified from seeking another term. Bryant's opponent, Betsy Carpenter, was the same level lightweight as Fogel. Should he win, Bryant would be too difficult to control. Damone was trying to have it both ways. Endorse Bryant then help Carpenter win. Damone decided for appearances he would support Bryant publicly. He already had a scandal to use to defeat him—an October surprise.

"What is it?" Damone asked.

"It's Saadaq," Lewis said referring to Damone's main link with the Somali's. "He says it's important."

Lewis handed Damone the burner phone they were using for today.

"Yes," Damone answered.

"I just found out something and in case you are unaware of it, decided I better call right away," Saadaq said.

"What?"

"Did you know that the Imam is a significant shareholder in the bank?" Saadaq asked.

The bank Saadaq was referring to was the Cedar/Riverside State Bank. This bank was a state-chartered bank set up specifically for the Somali community. It was also the least regulated bank in the state. The last thing the state's politicians and the regulatory agency wanted to do was offend the Somalis.

"I am aware he owns a small piece of it. Something like five percent," Damone replied.

"No, not even close," Saadaq said. "From what I have found it, through the bank's outside auditor, a Christian woman with Decker Flagg," he continued referring to the accounting and auditing firm the bank used, "the Imam is the real owner of almost seventy percent."

215

The phone went silent for so long that Saadaq finally asked, "Are you there, sir?"

"Yes, yes. I'm still here. Are you sure about this?"

"Yes, she showed me the real list of shareholders. Imam Sadia is listed as owning five percent. But there are others who are shareholders in name only, I am positive, who account for another sixty-three percent and are doing Sadia's bidding. I have a copy of the list for you."

"Thank you, Saadaq. Bring it to me personally, please. You have done well," Damone said.

Damone looked at Lewis and was about to tell him when Lewis' phone rang.

"Take it," Damone said, referring to the call.

While Lewis was speaking to one of their wholesalers, Damone thought about the call from Saadaq. The bank he referred to was a significant part of their money-laundering. Millions of dollars each month from Damone's business, the Somali's business and Chicago went through more than three dozen Somali businesses and then the bank. Because the government, both state and federal, are reluctant to regulate Somali Muslim businesses, they are very safe "laundromats" for money-laundering. Due to the high volume each month, and the fact the bank was opened specifically as a laundromat for cleaning money, the bank's fees are only fifteen percent. Still very profitable.

What had angered Damone was the duplicity of Imam Sadia. He was not only skimming from the sales but making even more on the laundering end.

"That was Jimmy," Lewis said when he ended the call. "The white boy was back again today for more product. In a very short time, he has become our number one salesman."

"Good for him," Damone said still distracted by Sadaaq's phone call.

"Jimmy said he is becoming more insistent on meeting you," Lewis said.

"Why?" an annoyed Damone asked.

"To cut out Jimmy, I think," Lewis said.

"I can understand that," Damone replied.

Lewis' phone rang again. He checked the ID, looked at Damone and said, "It's the Chenault woman."

216

"It's about time. Answer it and if it is her, give her today's number and have her call."

Instead, Lewis listened then told Damone, "She wants to stop by. She has information."

"When?"

"Anytime."

"Tell her now."

When Lewis ended the call, Damone told him, "You go and see Jimmy. Tell him that I want this dago to see you first. You meet him, size him up and see what he wants, then I'll decide. He's a little too insistent."

"On my way," Lewis said.

Monroe knocked on Damone's office door, opened it then stepped aside. Councilwoman Patti Chenault strolled in then tossed her jacket onto a chair. For a woman in her late forties she was still quite good looking; sexy even. Damone was on the phone watching her as she came toward him and seductively sat on the corner of his desk next to him. As she did this, she hiked her skirt up enough for him to see the lace garter and no underwear.

"I gotta go," Damone said into the phone. "Another meeting just came in."

The councilwoman sat with her legs crossed and dangling. Damone watched her expression as he ran his left hand under her skirt to the top of her thigh. He slid the hand up and down on her thigh until he could feel the heat.

"So, what did you find out?" he asked while watching her breathing increase.

Instead of answering him she got down on her knees in front of him.

Playfully she looked up at him as she unbuckled his belt, unzipped his pants and pulled everything down to his ankles.

"Later," she said, then hungrily went to work as Damone gasped with pleasure.

Afterwards, she returned to her perch on Damone's desk as he pulled up his clothing. It took them both, especially Damone, another minute to breathe normally again. When he was calmed down, he asked her again.

"I found out he is exactly what he seems to be," she began. "He was in witness protection, got tired of it and walked away. They had him set up outside of Chicago working in a mortgage company and he apparently got bored. They don't force people to stay in protection."

"Why was he in witness protection?"

"That I cannot get to. I can't even find out what his real name is, where he comes from or if he was a mob guy, a witness or what."

Chenault is the chair of the city council's Public Safety and Emergency Management standing committee. In that capacity, she can always think up a good excuse to run a background check on people. She is supposed to have some reasonable grounds to do so, but a good lie is a good lie.

Carvelli's drug dealer phone rang and he looked at the ID. It was his nominal boss, Jimmy Jones. Tony was in the Lincoln with Wendy a block away from Gretchen's condo.

"Yeah," he answered the phone saying.

"Hey, dude…"

"Don't call me dude," Carvelli gruffly told him. "I hate that. Do I look like some asshole who spends two weeks playing cowboy on a vacation?"

"Huh? What you talkin' bout?"

Carvelli smiled at the response before asking, "What is it, Jimmy?"

"Listen, I got someone here who wants to meet you. You'll want to meet him. Now."

"I'll be there in ten to fifteen minutes," Carvelli replied.

Carvelli parked the Lincoln in his usual spot across the street from Jimmy's. He had dropped off Wendy at Gretchen's so they could make the rounds of upper- class opioid junkies while Carvelli went to Jimmy's apartment.

Carvelli crossed Dupont and found the thug with the chrome .45 waiting for him. He was standing in the building's foyer with the same tough guy look and the chrome .45 was again tucked down the front of his pants.

"Hand it over," the man said referring to Carvelli's gun.

"Ain't gonna happen," Carvelli replied.

"I said-" the guard started to say.

Before he could finish, Carvelli had the barrel of the .45 pressed against the man's forehead and his free hand on the man's throat. Upon seeing this through the window in the door, the two guards out front came in.

"Out," Carvelli ordered them without turning his head.

"It's okay," the man with the gun in his face nervously told them.

Still pressing the gun against his forehead, Carvelli said, "He's right, fellas. We're all friends here. What's your name?" he asked the frightened guard.

"Duwayne," the man nervously replied.

"Duwayne says it's okay. You guys can go back outside.

"Duwayne, huh?" Carvelli said when the door closed. "I like that name. What do you say, Duwayne? Let's go upstairs and have a chat. We'll all be friends."

"Sure, uh huh, okay," he gulped.

Carvelli followed Duwayne up the stairs and into the apartment. They walked through the entry into the living room. Jimmy was again sitting behind the table. In a comfortable armchair was a man Carvelli did not recognize.

Jimmy looked at his man, shook his head and asked, "Now what?"

"The man just won't listen!" Duwayne said almost pleading.

When he said this, Carvelli noticed a slight smile come and go on the man in the chair.

At that moment Carvelli learned two things. The man in the chair was not the man, but he was close to him. And, he was serious and not to be trifled with.

"Okay, go," Jimmy told him. "Give him his gun back."

"What's the magic word?" Carvelli said.

"What?"

"Give him his gun back, *please.*"

Jimmy looked at Carvelli, sighed and said, "Give him his gun back, please."

"In a while," Carvelli said.

Duwayne turned and left as Carvelli stepped over to the man in the chair.

"Tony Russo," he said extending his hand.

The man took it and said, "Lewis."

"Nice to meet you, Lewis," Carvelli said.

219

"Why you always gotta bring the drama with you?" Jimmy asked.

"I told you, I don't like people threatening me with guns," Carvelli replied.

Carvelli took a seat on the couch and in less than ten seconds, Duwayne's gun was emptied and dismantled. When he finished, he tossed the pieces on the couch to his left.

"Jimmy here tells me you want to become a bigger player. Why should we do business with you?" Lewis asked.

"I have," Carvelli said, pausing as if thinking about the question, "connections in significant geographic locations. They are already in the business, but the way they get supplies is a pain-in-the-ass. And it's under too much scrutiny. Running around with junkies to doctors, clinics and drugstores is no way to do business and get supplies. You seem to have a steady stream of supplies coming in. Steady and reliable."

"How do you know we're not getting our supplies the same way?" Lewis asked.

Carvelli smiled, looked at Jimmy, looked back to Lewis, pointed a thumb at Jimmy and said, "Because you seem smart enough to know better than to send Jimmy here into a clinic or a drug store. He'd be lucky to come out with his dick still attached."

Lewis laughed until there were tears in his eyes. He leaned forward with a fist extended to Carvelli for a fist bump, then said, "That's a good point."

Jimmy was sitting with his eyes glaring at Carvelli. Lewis saw this, then spoke.

"Relax, Jimmy. He meant no disrespect. There are some things you are good at and some things you're not. It's true for everyone.

"I tell you what," Lewis continued looking at Carvelli, "let me check with the man about a meeting. I'll get back to you."

THIRTY-NINE

Carvelli heard his personal phone ring in the console of the Lincoln. He took it out, checked the ID and answered it.

"Hey, Paxton, what's up? Why are you calling me on your personal phone?"

"I just left the office," Paxton O'Rourke replied. "We have a problem."

"And that is? Hey, watch it, asshole!" Carvelli yelled at a driver who cut in front of him, turned on his blinker and hit his breaks to make a quick left turn.

"You better not be talking to me like that," Paxton said.

"No, no, some jerk just cut in front of me," Carvelli explained.

"Really? You guys brag all the time about how nice people in Minnesota are," Paxton replied.

"Yeah, right. That must be why I carry a gun," Carvelli said.

"Maddy told me you carry a gun because of all the people you've pissed off over the years."

"It's a talent, what can I tell you?" Carvelli laughed. "Now, what is our problem?"

"I just left a meeting with my boss, the US Attorney, the local FBI SAIC and local DEA chief," Paxton said. "They think there's a link between a Chicago drug dealer and you guys. They're thinking about expanding the task force to include the Twin Cities."

"Which would mean they're gonna flood us with another fifty Feebs and Drug Cop Cowboys," Carvelli said. "You have to stop them, Paxton. I'm almost inside. I met with a guy I think is number two on the food chain. If we get another fifty Feds up here stomping around, they'll blow the whole deal. You gotta stop this, Paxton."

"How long before you get inside?"

"Not sure. Could be tomorrow, could be a couple of weeks."

"Should I go to my boss and tell him?"

"Can you do that without you getting—oh shit!" Carvelli yelled, then slammed on his breaks. There was silence for a few seconds while Paxton asked "What?" several times.

"Ah, nothing," Carvelli said.

"You almost hit somebody, didn't you?" Paxton asked. Carvelli did not answer right away and she continued, "Well? Did you?"

"Um, yeah, but it's okay."

"I hope you get a ticket for distracted driving," Paxton said.

"You're the one distracting me. I keep seeing you in lacy lingerie and…"

"That does it!"

"I'm kidding. Will you get in trouble if you tell your boss what's going on and you haven't told him?"

"I don't know. I could probably do it and make it look like I'm not involved," she replied.

"Then maybe you better. Can he be trusted? We've got a leak here and it could get some people killed. Like me."

"Yes, he's been a cop and a local prosecutor. He's not a politician."

"Then tell him. We can't have this. Maybe later, but not right now. There are some things going on that I can't tell you about. I gave my word."

"Okay. I'll do that. What are you guys up to, otherwise? I should come up there for a couple of days."

"You should," Carvelli said. "Tonight, Maddy and I are running a sting on someone. He's got information for Marc's trial."

"Oh man. I am so jealous. I'd love to come up and watch this, but I can't tonight."

"Go talk to your boss and stay in touch," Carvelli said.

"I will," she replied. "Oh, and uh, you want some photos of me in lingerie?" she seductively added, then started laughing. "Best I can do is my army green boxers and T-shirt."

"I'll take 'em," Carvelli laughed.

"He's heading for the Warehouse District," Maddy said into her phone.

"You sure?" Carvelli asked.

"Either that or Whole Foods," Maddy said. "We're stopped on Washington and Third. I can see a Whole Foods from here. Call me crazy, but I don't think that's where he's headed."

"Hey, now that you mention it, I heard somewhere that Whole Foods was expanding into the adult entertainment business," Carvelli replied. "You may be on to something."

"You should consider doing stand up," Maddy said. "Nope, he went past Whole Foods."

"Okay, I'll get over to the Marriot and wait in the room. Stay in touch."

It was after nine o'clock on a pleasant Saturday evening. The Warehouse District, also known as the North Loop, is known for its vibrant nightlife of bars and restaurants. Maddy had previously followed Philo here on several other occasions. There were a couple of gentlemen's clubs Philo seemed to prefer in the area. Tonight, she drove by as Philo pulled into the private parking lot of Sadie's Salon.

"Damn," Maddy quietly said to herself as she drove by. Dressed the way she was, she wasn't sure the parking lot attendant would let her in.

She drove up to the next corner, did a quick U-turn and back to the parking lot. As she pulled up, she unbuttoned a third button on her black silk blouse to expose her black lace bra. The attendant was a little too distracted to care what she was dressed like.

After paying the ten-dollar parking fee, she quickly found an open space. It was toward the back of the crowded lot and only three spaces from Philo's Jag,

Before she got out of her car, she jerked her head forward. All of her hair fell forward, then she quickly jerked it all back and gave her head a shake. Maddy checked her makeup and hair. Satisfied she looked sufficiently trashy, she finished the style by pushing up and squeezing her breasts together.

"If this doesn't get him, I'm probably getting too old," she quietly said.

To complete the ensemble, she was wearing a black mini-skirt, black stockings, a leather jacket and six-inch heels.

The bouncer supposedly collecting the ten-dollar cover charge took one look, then opened the door for her. Maddy flashed him a smile and went in quietly saying, "Still got it."

"This is a really bad idea. If she-"

"-finds out she's gonna kick our butts. Yeah, I know. You've said it at least five times. Sorry, but I agree with Tony. Especially in this place. It's a little sleazy, and someone needs to cover her back."

This was a brief conversation between Dan Sorenson and Tommy Craven, two ex-cop pals of Carvelli's. They were walking toward the entrance of Sadie's Salon; the same door Maddy went through two minutes ago.

"Have you ever been here before?" Sorenson asked.

"Once."

"We'll go in and slide to the left. As soon as we find a table, we'll look for her. She'll probably be at the bar."

"When she spots us, and you know she will, I'm blaming it on you and Carvelli," Tommy said.

They paid the cover and once inside did what Sorenson suggested, they took a sharp left and found a table in a dark part of the audience.

When Maddy got inside, she walked slowly along the bar. It took barely four or five seconds to spot Philo. He was seated at the far end of the bar and one of the girls was right in front of him. Maddy made her way toward him as the girl bent over and almost slapped Philo across the face with her boobs.

This is going to be worse than I imagined, Maddy thought.

When she was five feet from him, the girl turned around, bent her knees and waved her butt at him from less than a foot away from his face. Fighting her instinct to flee, Maddy thought, *Please, tell me she's at least wearing a thong.*

Philo slipped a bill into the strap of her bikini bottom. She flapped her boobs at him again, then saw Maddy take the seat next to him. When that happened, the stripper moved off.

Philo had not looked at Maddy until the girl moved off. Annoyed that some bimbo had caused her to leave, he turned and started to say, "Thanks a lot for ruining…"

"Sorry," Maddy said. "Was she your sister?"

"Um, ah, no, ah, my what? My sister? No, what," a flustered Philo responded. Realizing Maddy was pulling his leg, Philo laughed and took a long look at Maddy's crossed legs.

"Sorry, I didn't mean to chase her off," Maddy said. "Buy me a drink to make up for it."

"Huh? Oh, sure," Philo said. "What…"

"Vodka tonic with a lime."

Philo turned his head to get the bartender's attention. At that moment, Sorenson and Tommy Craven came in and tried to sneak into the crowd. When they reached their table, they looked toward the bar and saw Maddy staring right at them.

It took Maddy less than a minute to get Philo talking about his favorite subject: himself.

"Really? Wow. You're a reporter with the Star Tribune," Maddy said. "That must be interesting."

Philo went off on a ten-minute soliloquy about his coverage of the protests during this past summer.

Maddy did her best to seem interested and then he got to the good part.

"I'm the guy who took the pictures of Ferguson lying dead in the street. It went nationwide. I'll probably get a Pulitzer Prize for it."

To help him think she was a bit of a fluff head, Maddy pretended ignorance. Philo practically puffed out his chest when he explained what a Pulitzer was.

"I have a few other photos that the prosecution and cops would love to know about," Philo slyly told her.

"Really? Where?" Maddy asked. "I'd love to see them!" she practically squealed.

"Well, we'll see," Philo said trying to sound cool and mysterious.

Halfway through her second watery drink, they got down to business. Maddy told him about a room she had nearby. They quickly settled on a five hundred-dollar price which Philo thought was a bargain.

Philo was ahead of her as they walked toward the door. As they did, Maddy turned and stared once again at her two babysitters. Both Sorenson and Tommy tried to act innocently as if they didn't notice.

The two ex-cops waited a few minutes, then hustled out to the parking lot. They were just in time to see Maddy exit the lot with Philo right behind her.

As they hurried toward Sorenson's car, Tommy said, "We are in deep shit with her."

"Stop it," Sorenson said. "What is she gonna do?"

"You want her mad at you? Women hold grudges forever," Tommy said as he was opening the passenger door.

While Sorenson was starting the car, he said, "That's a good point. Marge is still mad at me about things I did before we were married. And that wasn't even in this century."

"I'm gonna blame it on you and Carvelli. I'll tell her you guys made me do it."

FORTY

Maddy slipped the room's key card into the slot. The red light went off, the green light came on, and she opened the door. By this point, Philo was already getting a little aggressive and too close to her.

"Easy, tiger," Maddy said as she gently pushed him back a little bit.

A light came on illuminating the bed as they walked in. There was a closet on both sides of the foyer, and before Maddy took two steps, Philo was on her with his arms around her waist.

Maddy grabbed his right hand, bent it back, twirled him around twice, pulled him into the room then flipped him onto the bed. Philo landed on his back staring up at the ceiling. Between the alcohol and her tossing him around, Philo was dizzy, the room was spinning, and he was quite confused.

He laid there for almost a minute before the room stopped spinning. Maddy was standing at the edge of the bed towering over Philo's head waiting for him to say something.

"Wow! That was fabulous. This is gonna be the best ever!" Philo almost howled with delight.

Maddy looked down at him, smiled and said, "I hate to burst your bubble Philo, but it's not going to be anything. I'd like you to meet someone," she continued pointing at the dresser toward the foot of the bed.

"You do like to make an entrance, don't you?" Carvelli said. He was leaning against the dresser silently waiting for Philo to notice him.

Philo turned his head toward the dresser, saw the man leaning on it, jumped up and off of the bed away from Maddy, stumbled and fell.

"No, not again," he said as he staggered to his feet.

"Relax, Philo," Tony said. He stood up straight and held his hands up palms out. "No one's running a game on you. We just want to talk."

"You're a hard guy to track down for a private conversation," Maddy said.

"About what?" Philo nervously asked.

Maddy looked at Carvelli and said, a bit sarcastically, "You want to call your two buddies and have them join us?"

With a sheepish look, Carvelli said, "Oops. Hey, I can explain..."

"Yeah, I know, Dad," Maddy said.

"We worry about you. All of us do. So..."

"That's very sweet. Now, call them."

"I'll kick 'em loose for the night."

"Hey! Over here," Philo said. "Remember me?"

"Sit down," Carvelli barked pointing at an armchair.

Philo meekly sat down on a chair next to a small table. Carvelli took the chair across from him and Maddy sat on the edge of the bed.

"You're a hard guy to get ahold of," Carvelli repeated.

Philo was nervously looking back and forth at his two kidnappers. "Who are you and what do you want?"

"Don't you ever return your messages? We've left several…"

"Hey, this is kidnapping," Philo worked up the nerve to say.

"It is not," Carvelli said. "You came here of your own free will…"

"Quite eagerly, in fact," Maddy said.

Philo quickly stood up and said, "Okay, I'm leaving."

"No, you're not. Now sit down. We just want to talk to you. We have a few questions, then you can go," Carvelli said.

"Tell him," Maddy said.

"Okay," Carvelli replied. "We're private investigators working for Rob Dane's lawyer. We have some questions."

"Why didn't you just call me?"

Maddy leaned forward, took an open-hand swipe at the side of his head and deliberately missed. "We've left messages!"

Philo ducked then said, "Sorry, I can't always find time for every call I get."

"We want to know what you saw," Carvelli said.

"Nothing," Philo quickly replied. "Can I go now?"

Maddy leaned forward again with her right-hand palm out and Philo put up his left arm for cover and ducked again.

"I didn't even ask you what you might have seen," Carvelli said.

"You're working for that lawyer, Kadella. He represents Robert Dane, the guy who shot and killed Reverend Lionel Ferguson. How am I doing?" Without waiting for a reply, Philo continued, "You want to know if I saw the shooting and the answer is no. Now can I go?"

"Calm down. What did you see? You were right there. You got pictures of Ferguson in the street. We've been told there was a homeless guy hanging around close to Ferguson the entire four days of the protests. Did you see him?"

"Maybe. Why?"

Carvelli leaned on the small table and looked directly into Philo's eyes. "Why are you making this so hard? We think he was there and saw it all. Rob swears Ferguson pointed a gun at him. No gun was found. So, either he or you picked up the gun and took off with it."

"Hey, I didn't take any gun. And yeah, I saw the guy you're talking about but, well, after the shooting, I took off when I saw Ferguson on the street. I went back and took pictures of the body. That was it."

"We want copies of every photo you took that day," Maddy said.

"No chance. The paper has them. You may have heard of the First Amendment. Besides, all they have are shots of Ferguson lying in the street," Philo replied.

"I thought you said you had more?" Maddy asked.

"I was just trying to impress you," Philo meekly admitted.

"Did you use a camera or your phone?" Carvelli asked.

"My phone. Why?"

"We want the SIM card," Carvelli said.

"No way. I'm not gonna give you that. There's nothing on there. We, uh, the paper, uploaded the pictures and then I deleted everything. Besides, if I gave you the SIM card, wouldn't I have to give it to the cops? There's nothing on there that would help you."

Maddy started to say something, but Carvelli cut her off. "Okay, you can go. Go ahead, take off."

"That's it?" Philo asked.

"Yeah, that's it," Carvelli said. "If we think of anything, I'd appreciate it if you could just return our calls."

"Yeah, okay, sure," Philo replied a little too quickly.

"What was..." Maddy started to ask as soon as the door closed behind Philo. Carvelli held up a finger to stop her. He went to the room's door and listened for a moment. He grabbed the door handle and quickly jerked it open. Carvelli looked up and down the hall. Satisfied, he returned to his chair.

"He's lying," were the first words he spoke. "I could see it in his face."

"As soon as you asked about the SIM card," Maddy said, "a light bead of sweat broke out at his hairline."

"And his eyes shifted back and forth, twice. Something on the SIM card made him nervous," Carvelli added. "He's lying. But what about?"

"We could get a pro to steal his camera. I know a couple of them," Maddy said.

"I could find a dozen," Carvelli replied. "But, if he does have anything in his phone, give him an hour, and it will be gone. And your feminine charms aren't going to get it out of him now that he knows you."

Maddy looked at him with a twinkle in her eye and a devious smile. She leaned toward him as Carvelli said, "What?"

"Know anyone who has honed her feminine wiles to professional status?"

Carvelli looked at her with a puzzled expression. It took a moment, but the light went on. "Gretchen!"

"Gretchen," Maddy agreed. "Besides, I'd love to meet her."

FORTY-ONE

Marc, Arturo, and Jeff Modell were, once again, in Marc's conference room. It was Monday morning and they were one week from jury selection. Arturo and Jeff were again going over the list of prospective jurors. They had received the report from Grayson, the jury consulting firm, first thing that morning. The two of them were comparing Grayson's suggested jurors with their own. While they did this, Marc was going over his trial book.

The trial book is a three-ring binder with sections for each part of the trial. Most lawyers preferred the convenience and organizational ability of a good laptop. There were still those who preferred the physical book, such as Marc. To be on the safe side, Jeff always loaded the physical book onto a laptop just to have a back-up.

Arturo and Jeff had been at it for about a half-hour. Arturo started with the first name on the list, a retired Marine officer, and worked forward. Jeff started with the last name and worked back. Their job was to break the one hundred and fifty names into five categories. A one was a "must have," a two was "acceptable," a three "marginal," a four "keep off" and a five was "poison." It was a slow and tedious process, and they would work on it until the twelve jurors and six alternates were officially selected and sworn in.

"How is it going?" Marc asked.

"So far," Arturo said, "their guesswork, Grayson's, is pretty much the same as ours. You know, we're basically looking for jurors who are the exact opposite of what we usually have. People who love cops and believe they can do no wrong."

"I know," Marc replied and chuckled. "I'll work on it too as soon as I am done here."

There was a knock on the door and Sandy, one of the assistants, stuck her head in.

"Hey, Maddy's on line one. She says to tell you that you're supposed to always carry your cell phone, so she can get a hold of you any time."

"I know, that's why I don't."

"Oh, wait till I tell her that one," Sandy replied.

"She knows," Marc said, then punched the flashing light on the office phone.

"Hey," he said.

"Hi," Maddy replied. "We finally got the name of the bald investigator for Steve Gondeck. The one who talked to the girls and blew them off."

"I remember," Marc said. "What is it?"

"His name's Dirk Shepherd. Forty-four years old. He did twenty with Duluth PD and retired as a sergeant last year. He's double dipping with Hennepin County."

"Love those guys who spend their lives to get two pensions off the taxpayers," Marc said. "What else do you have? Dirk Shepherd," he said to Arturo.

"I'm in my car. I'll be at your office in ten minutes and help with the jury list and write up a bio on him for you. He seems pretty straight."

"He's on Gondeck's witness list," Arturo said.

Marc passed that along to Maddy and then ended the call.

"He's not on ours," Jeff said.

"That's okay. We'll subpoena him. Margaret will let him testify."

"What's Gondeck going to do? Complain he didn't have a chance to interview him?" Arturo added.

"Good point," Jeff said.

A couple of hours later, after they were about forty names through the list, Marc called for a lunch break. Arturo reminded him he had to go back to his own office for the afternoon.

As they were packing up, Maddy received a call from Gabriella Shriqui.

"I think I found the guy you're looking for," Gabriella told Maddy.

"Hey," Maddy said to Marc. "She thinks she found your guy. Here," Maddy said handing him her phone.

"What do you have?" Marc asked.

"We got him," she said. "Quite a few times and always in the vicinity of Ferguson. And we made several prints for you. We even blew one up. I had Hunter and some others look at it. Marc," she continued, "no one could swear to it positively, but we all think he's wearing a disguise. Makeup and some facial putty to change his face. And he's always wearing a hat and wrap-around sunglasses."

"When can I come in?" Marc asked.

"Now would be a good time. I'm rehearsing at three," Gabriella said.

"I'll bring your pal and we'll be there as soon as we can get there."

On the way to the Channel 8 building west of downtown, Marc called Carvelli.

"Hey, I may need your hacker, Paul," Marc told him.

"For what?"

Marc briefly told him about the homeless guy in the crowd of protestors and what Gabriella had found.

"Okay," Carvelli said. "I'm downtown now. How about I meet you at Channel 8 and we'll all take a look?"

"Fine, see you then."

The three of them, along with Gabriella and a woman from the makeup department, were in a small room viewing tape and photo prints the station had made. It took more than an hour and a half, especially with the station's make up expert giving her take. At one point Gabriella's boss, Hunter Oswood, the news director, joined them. He brought a non-disclosure, proprietary property agreement for Marc to sign. Basically, it protected the station's rights to the film and Marc agreed he would use it only in court and not sell it.

"What do you think he did?" Oswood asked.

"Hunter, I can't get into that without violating the judge's gag order," Marc said.

"The judge is his ex-girlfriend and she'd probably love to throw his ass in jail," Gabriella told her boss.

"Now that would be newsworthy," Oswood laughed.

"Please don't use that," Marc said. "A couple of other stations already have, and the chief judge had to issue a statement that there had been full disclosure and there was no conflict."

"Gabriella gets an exclusive interview after the trial?" Oswood asked.

"She does," Marc said.

"Okay, good enough," Oswood said, then left.

"There is one other thing I want to show you," Gabriella said. "Watch."

She ran the film of Ferguson, with the homeless man behind him, during the first two days of the protests. It was the part of the film taken when they were going past Rob Dane's position just before the corner of Sixth and Nicollet. As they did, the homeless man made an obvious effort

232

to look over the area, including the buildings. Gabriella allowed the film to continue showing the protestors walking away until they were out of range.

The filming of the third day was different. For the first two days, it appeared the man was also checking out the cameras. On the third day, there were very few cameras and he appeared to be looking for them. What was really odd was once the homeless man reached Nicollet Mall, he turned right and hurried away.

"What do you think?" Marc asked Carvelli.

"Run it again," he said.

Gabriella ran the part where the homeless man hurries away two more times

"He didn't pick up the gun and run off after the shooting," Carvelli said. "He was the one who pointed the gun at Rob. He had his escape route scouted out ahead of time."

"You cannot use that," Marc emphatically told Gabriella.

"I know," she agreed.

"He may have found the gun and ran off," Carvelli said. "But I don't think so. He was doing recon the first three days and he found his spot and his pigeon. This guy, if I'm right, is no homeless guy just hanging out."

"I didn't think so either," Gabriella said.

"He could be, but I don't think so. No, this is a pro's pro," Carvelli said still staring at the frozen image of the man scurrying away.

"I'm sorry we didn't get any film on that fourth day when Ferguson was shot," Gabriella said.

"Nobody else did either. At least according to our witnesses and Philo," Maddy said.

"If one of the other stations had, they would have run it by now," Marc said. "It would be the Zapruder film for this event."

There was silence in the little room while everyone waited for Marc.

"We need to do one of three things. Find out why he did it and who put him up to it, find out who he is, or somehow come up with a witness who can put that gun in his hand," Marc said. "Do you have anything else?" he asked Gabriella.

"No," she said. "We've been through our film with a magnifying glass. Unless you want film of him finishing the protest march."

233

"I might," Marc said. "Do you have film of him doing the entire route for the first two days?"

"Not specifically on him the entire way. But bits and pieces of him walking along with Ferguson until the end of the protest. And it's odd. Everyone else was raising a fist and shouting. He was faking it. Or, at least, not showing much enthusiasm."

"Yeah, get me that film on a DVD, will you?"

"Sure," Gabriella said.

"I'll pay…"

"Never mind," Gabriella smiled.

"I'll get this over to Paul today," Carvelli told Marc.

The three of them were in the parking lot of the TV station. Carvelli was holding a print of the best facial shot of the homeless man. He was still wearing the wrap-around sunglasses and a battered baseball cap. He was also sporting what looked to be a five or six-day beard.

"Paul can clean it up, get rid of the shades, the hat and stubble. He'll probably have at least four or five possibilities."

"I'll get a few prints of it first," Maddy said. "Then I'll get together with some of the guys and we'll take it to Tent City and any other places where homeless hang out."

"Go ahead and do it, but we won't find him that way," Marc told her. "This guy isn't homeless."

"Probably not," Carvelli agreed. "I got a feeling this guy's a pro."

"If that's true, then why was he brought here and by who?" Marc said.

"Whom," Maddy corrected him, then quickly said, "I'm sorry. Bad habit."

"Okay, grammar Nazi. Whom."

"Play nice, kids," Carvelli said. "Do you need to take a timeout?"

"Yeah! Actually, we do," Maddy said.

"No kidding," Marc agreed.

Carvelli's phone rang. He looked at the ID and answered it.

"Yeah," he said.

He listened for a minute, looked at his watch and said, "That'll be fine. See you then.

"My Feebs," he told Marc and Maddy. "They want to see me today. I'll get this to Paul and see what the Feds want."

"Hey, I need to come with. I need prints of that one," Maddy said.

"We'll take my car and then I'll drop you off back at your car before I see Paul. Let's go."

FORTY-TWO

Damone was at the table in his office going over financials with his accountant, Donald Leach. The amount of money the opioid business was making shocked even Damone. The amount of profit from each pill multiplied by the millions his network was selling, outstripped every drug he had ever peddled.

The crack cocaine business, while still quite lucrative due to its addictive capability, was still very good. But the overhead, especially the labor involved, was significantly higher. Opioids required no manufacturing facilities. They almost sold themselves and there was money for everyone. Doctors, pharmacy companies, you name it, they were all swimming in cash. Fentanyl was even better and deadlier.

"What is this all about?" Damone asked pointing at a spreadsheet for crack cocaine. Sales were down as were profits, but costs had risen.

"Demand is down all over the country," the accountant replied.

"And so is the price of cocaine," Damone said. "So why are costs up?"

"Because of the labor force we have to carry," Donald answered. "We can't just fire people. They tend to get pissed and go to the cops."

Damone went quiet thinking over the problem. Crack was still quite profitable, but not as profitable as opioids and heroin. He did not want to get into heroin because of the manufacturing costs. Heroin—street heroin—was something he had done before, and it had earned him twenty years in prison. Damone had already tried to wholesale out crack away from the Cities. Because of the margins for opioids, the salesmen were not anxious to deal crack.

"I know you don't want to hear this but…"

"We should get into smack," Damone finished for him. "Let me think about it," Damone said.

"The money, the laundered money, it is going where it is supposed to go?" Damone asked.

"With the exception of what our friends around Cedar/Riverside are helping themselves to, yes," Donald answered.

"And you're pretty certain that we are short eight million so far this year?" Damone asked for the fourth time during this meeting.

"At least."

"Very well," Damone said wrapping up the meeting. "I have some things to think about. But, for now, at least, we will maintain the status quo. We may not be making as much with crack as we could with street-smack, but there is not nearly as much heat. The word 'heroin' scares everyone. It's like the word 'cancer'."

Damone went to his desk and retrieved a plain white envelope.

"These are your copies," Donald said while Damone went to his desk. Donald neatly stacked the financials for him and placed them in a large envelope. The date of the meeting was prominently displayed on it.

"Here you are and thank you, my friend," Damone said. He handed Donald the envelope with ten thousand dollars in it.

He escorted the accountant out and found Lewis and Monroe waiting for him. The three of them took the back stairs behind Damone's office up to the third-floor apartment. They found chairs in the living room after Damone had served coffee.

"That problem has been taken care of?" Damone asked after taking his seat.

"Yes, sir," Lewis replied.

Lewis and Monroe had spent the night in a motel in Superior, Wisconsin. Superior is a city across from the Lake Superior port in Duluth. The two of them had taken a speedboat roughly twenty miles into Lake Superior where they dumped their cargo; two twenty-year-old gang bangers who had tried to defy Damone. They were trying to set themselves up in the dope slinging business. They had received a warning from one of Monroe's guys. Instead of heeding the message, Monroe's man had been found in an alley with three in bullets in the head. The word went out through the black community, and by noon of the day he was found dead, yesterday, Monroe had them both.

Lewis helped Monroe take them to a safe house and into the basement. Within minutes the weaker of the two was confessing and begging for forgiveness. He took the first bullet in the forehead. The second, more defiant one wet himself just before Monroe shot him as well.

"Good. Now get the word out, quietly. It seems every so often an example needs to be made," Damone said.

"Our not-so-friendly Muslim brothers, the Imam especially, have been enriching themselves more than we knew," Damone told his trusted lieutenants.

"That's not a surprise, boss," Lewis said.

"No, it's not," Damone agreed. He held up his cup for Monroe to fill it and thanked him.

"The problem is, there isn't much I can do about it right now," Damone said.

"I was thinking," Lewis said. "Maybe we could quietly work with Saadaq to find out where the money is going. The old thief has to be putting it somewhere."

"He can't spend it all on American whores," Monroe added.

Damone smiled at Monroe's comment and said, "From what we hear, he's trying."

Damone sat quietly for a moment sipping his coffee. He looked at Lewis and said, "Get together with Saadaq. See what he thinks. There are other more important interests at stake. But be discreet. Do it right away. Today. When I get back, I'll want to know if it is feasible. Can we find out where the money is without him knowing about it?"

"I don't mean to question you, but I think both me and Monroe should go to Chicago with you," Lewis said.

"Thank you for your concern, my friend. I'll be fine. I'll be with Jeron. It's only a couple of days. We'll be back Thursday morning."

"Yes, sir."

"Go see Jimmy Jones. I've decided to meet with the Italian. Thursday afternoon. Here, downstairs in the conference room. Maybe he can make up for some of the lost revenue."

Carvelli's personal phone was ringing. He automatically reached inside his coat pocket before remembering where he had left it. He opened the console between the seats, took it out and looked at the caller ID.

"Now what?" he muttered to himself then put the phone to his ear.

"Yeah," he answered it. "What's up?"

"It's Jeff Johnson," the FBI agent said. "We need to get together for an update."

"I just met with you yesterday. I don't have time," Carvelli said.

238

"Today, now. I just got off the phone with Washington and they're breathing down my neck. We can meet at your place. Give me fifteen minutes so I can get something for them to get them off my back."

"Okay," Carvelli agreed. "I'm in my car. I'll be there in ten minutes."

"Great. Thanks, Tony."

Carvelli cut off the call without a reply to Johnson's last comment. Instead, he made a turn while dropping the phone back in the console.

"Yeah, yeah, yeah," he muttered. "'Cause I'm not busy enough."

Still grumbling, he parked the Lincoln on the street in front of his house in South Minneapolis. Johnson and his partner, Tess Richards, were sitting in their car across the street. Before Carvelli had a chance to exit the Lincoln, his business phone rang.

"Yeah," Carvelli answered it.

"Russo?" he heard Jimmy Jones ask.

"Yeah, it's me, Jimmy. What's up?"

By now both of the FBI agents were standing in the street next to Carvelli's window. He looked at them and held up his index finger indicating he wanted them to wait.

"You're getting your wish, white guy," Jimmy Jones said. "The man says he'll meet you Thursday afternoon. One of his guys will get in touch to let you know where and when."

"Thanks, Jimmy. I owe you…" Carvelli started to say then realized no one was on the other end.

"Great timing," Carvelli said as he shook hands with the agents. "Our pal, Jimmy. He says the man wants to meet Thursday afternoon."

Still standing in the street, Johnson asked, "You want backup?"

"Maybe. No offense, but I know a couple of MPD undercover guys who could do it, probably better than two obvious Feebs."

"You know, I really don't like being called that," Johnson said.

"Really?" Tess asked. "I think it's kind of cute. Don't take it so personally."

"Jeff!" Carvelli said with a hand over his heart feigning indignation. "Would I do anything to insult a fellow law enforcement officer from the federal government? It's a term of endearment."

"You are so full of shit, Carvelli," Johnson said, even though he could not suppress a grin.

"I'll get in touch as soon as I can after we meet."

239

"Suggest to him that you're gonna need a laundry service. Washington is specifically looking for that. They are seeing money going out, but they don't know from where or to where," Johnson said.

"Will do. Listen," Carvelli continued. "I was on my way to do something. I gotta go."

"Where were you going to do what?" Tess asked.

"Nothing to do with this. A favor for a friend."

"Be careful," Johnson asked.

While Carvelli was conversing in front of his house with the FBI, Maddy was meeting with retired detective Sherry Bowen. They were in the same Northside restaurant in the same horseshoe booth in the back. With them was Tonya Howard and her friend, Bethany Morris. In between them were three young girls. All three of them looked very nervous.

Maddy sat down in the booth across from Sherry, next to Tonya. With seven people the booth was a lot more crowded than last time.

"Hi, Tonya, Bethany," Maddy said.

"These are the three girls I told you about. No names," Sherry said.

"That's fine," Maddy said. She looked at the nervous girls with a warm smile and said, "I will protect your privacy. Nothing that you tell me will go any farther than here. I promise you."

"I ain't testifying," the girl in the middle emphatically said.

Maddy looked her directly in the eyes and said, "No, you won't. Even if we wanted you to, the judge wouldn't allow it. I'm not going to record anything. I won't even take any notes. Okay?"

The three girls shrugged and nodded.

"Can you tell me what happened with Reverend Ferguson? What he did to you?"

All three looked at Sherry and both Tonya and Bethany encouraged them to tell their story.

One of them started, the one who had declared she would not testify. When she got going, the others seemed to relax and join in. Theirs was the same basic story. They became involved in the church. Came to believe that Ferguson was a good man, the father figure they lacked at home, and were eventually assaulted by him. One of them, the shyest of them, was raped. The other two came close before escaping and running away.

240

"Did you tell anyone? Your mother or an adult friend?" Sherry asked when they had finished.

"No, my momma would've blamed me for it," one of them said while the others just shook their heads.

"Can you get them some help?" Maddy asked.

"Yes, we're working on it."

"God, I'm sorry," Maddy said to the girls. "Let Sherry help you deal with it."

FORTY-THREE

Thursday afternoon and Carvelli parks the Lincoln in the driveway of Jake's Limo Service. It had rained off and on all day, and as luck would have it, a minute ago the skies had opened and it was coming down hard. Carvelli stared out the driver's side window for thirty seconds hoping for a letup. Giving up on it, he jumped out of the car, scrunched his shoulders together, turned up his collar, pulled his head in like a turtle and ran for the door.

Once inside, he looked through the window into Jake's office and saw Jake, Dan Sorenson and Franklin Washington watching him. All three were wearing big grins from seeing him trying to dodge the rain.

Carvelli went into Jake's office and said, "Very funny. What is it with cops? Every one of you has a sick sense of humor when it comes to someone else's discomfort."

"Yeah, like you don't," Sorenson said.

"Hey, they don't call me Mr. Sensitivity for nothing," Carvelli said. Carvelli looked outside through the window behind Jake's desk. It had stopped raining completely.

Carvelli pointed a hand at the window, shook his head and said, "Of course. I ran fifteen feet and got soaked, then a minute later it quits."

"You're trying to cheer us up," Jake said. "Thanks."

"Okay, let's get going," Carvelli said.

"Have you been by the place where we're going?" Sorenson asked.

Franklin was listening with a scowl on his face. Sorenson saw it and asked, "What's wrong?"

"I'm a bit bummed about this," Franklin, an African American, said. "I kind of admired this guy. I bought into it that he had turned his life around and was trying to do good things for the black community. Now I find out he's a drug kingpin scammer."

"You want me to find someone else?" Carvelli asked.

"No." The big man shook his head. "I'll be fine."

"If you want to hang out here, I'll take your place," Jake said.

"No, we're just doing surveillance and watching Tony's back. Besides, I'll blend in better than some white, Polack ex-cop."

"There he goes with that ethnic insensitivity again," Waschke said. "Excuse me while I find a puppy and a safe space."

"Have you been there?" Sorenson asked again.

242

"Yeah, I know it," Franklin said.

"I drove by the place," Carvelli said.

"Okay, as you're facing the building on Plymouth. Looking north, to the left is a small parking lot and next to it is a ball court. The lot is between the building and the court," Sorenson said. "I'll park about a half a block east of the building. You," he continued, looking at Franklin, "park across the street from the ball court.

"They're gonna check you for a wire," Sorenson said to Carvelli.

"I know," Carvelli replied. "I'm not even going armed. Here," he continued as he held out his personal phone to Sorenson, "hold this for me. I'll take my burner phone in, but nothing else. I'll get rid of it later because they will likely put a trace on it or wire it."

"Once you're inside, you're on your own," Sorenson reminded him.

"I'm not worried about it. He's a businessman. If he wanted to get me for some reason, he wouldn't do it there."

"Franklin, Jake, anything?" Sorenson asked.

"No, I think you're right. Nothing's gonna happen inside that building. But if you see him escorted out and put in another car..." Jake said.

"We follow, and I call in the cavalry," Franklin replied.

"Okay," Carvelli said. "Let's go."

Jake was staring at Carvelli and said, "Put those glasses on for a minute."

Carvelli complied and Jake remarked, "It's amazing. Glasses, a different haircut and some putty and you look totally different."

"Not any better, just different," Sorenson said.

"Very funny," Carvelli said. "That reminds me, tell Marge I can't make it tonight."

"I could stay out late if you need me to," Sorenson said.

"I'll tell her you offered," Carvelli answered.

Carvelli drove around a block twice when he was two blocks from his destination, delaying his arrival. After the second time, both Franklin and Sorenson had called to let him know they were ready. A minute later, Carvelli pulled into the parking area and parked facing the ball court.

He checked his watch and saw he was six minutes early. As he was about to get out, he saw a familiar looking white man being escorted out of the door by Monroe to the parking lot. The man was carrying a small, black, nylon bag. While he watched, the two men walked toward a familiar windowless, brown, older E-Series Ford van.

"Well, isn't this interesting," Carvelli quietly said to himself.

Carvelli took out his burner phone and while continuing to watch, found Sorenson's number and dialed it. After the second ring, Sorenson answered.

"What's up?" Sorenson asked.

"There's a brown Ford van about to pull out of the parking lot. I want you to follow him. Give Franklin a call and tell him what you're up to. The driver is a little paranoid so don't let him see you. Stay with him. I'm gonna want to talk to him when I'm done here," Carvelli told him.

"You got it. Call when you're done."

Carvelli removed his burner phone from the inside pocket of his leather coat. He handed it to Lewis while Monroe used the electronic wand to wave for weapons and listening devices. They were on the second floor outside the door to what looked to be a conference room. Satisfied, Lewis handed the phone to Monroe then opened the door for Carvelli. Lewis pulled out the chair at the table to the right of where Damone would sit.

"Please, take a seat," Lewis said. "I'll let him know you're here."

At that moment, the door behind Damone's chair opened and Damone came in.

"Ah, here he is," Lewis said. "Tony Russo, Damone Watson," he continued introducing them.

"It's a pleasure to meet you," Carvelli said. "I've heard, well, a lot of things."

This elicited a hearty laugh from Damone as they sat down at the table. Carvelli did not sit in the seat suggested by Lewis. Instead, he took the one next to it. When he did this Carvelli noticed a very slight annoyed look on Damone's face. Lewis went to the opposite end of the table as Monroe came in and sat down with Lewis.

"I hope you don't mind if I have my trusted friends sit in."

"Not at all, Mr. Watson," Carvelli said.

"Please, Damone. And you don't mind if I call you Tony?"

"Of course not."

"Can I get you something to drink?"

"No, I'm fine," Carvelli answered.

"Good. Well, now that we have the pleasantries out of the way, we can discuss a little business.

"Lewis tells me you would like to move up to the wholesale distribution side of things. Is that right?"

"Well, yes. I could make more. You could make more. More money is always good."

The two of them continued their business dance for almost an hour. They went back and forth negotiating supply amounts, costs, commissions and process. Within the first ten minutes, it was clear to Carvelli that what Damone really wanted was Carvelli's contacts. Once he had those, Carvelli would have a shallow grave. He also knew Damone understood it would take months before he would have those connections. It was Carvelli's plan that Damone Watson would have a permanent cell long before that.

As Carvelli expected, there was no solid deal made at this first meeting. There was agreement on price, cost and Damone's share should he decide to go forward. Supply was always the final question. Could Damone's sources provide the quantities Carvelli said he wanted? It was an amount that would immediately increase Damone's profits by one-third, all with minimal additional overhead or risk.

Carvelli tried to casually get information about Damone's money laundering arrangements with little success. Damone took this as a potential rival finding out his business to someday push him aside. Trust was not an asset in this room just yet.

Damone walked Carvelli to the conference room door and opened it for him. Damone said, "The way I do business, from now on, unless a meeting with the two of us is specifically requested, you will work with Lewis. Unless I decide not to go forward and then you will continue to work for Jimmy Jones. For now," Damone quickly added when Carvelli started to object.

"I can understand you not wanting to continue that arrangement. Be patient. Lewis will show you out."

Ten minutes after leaving Damone's building, Carvelli pulled into the lot of a Best Buy store. Before he went inside, he literally tore his burner phone apart to deposit in the trash receptacle by the door. Ten minutes later he came out with a fully charged, prepaid phone with five hundred minutes on it. He was about to get in his car when he decided to make the three calls he needed to make.

"Hello, Johnson," he heard the first call being answered.

"Agent Johnson, Carvelli calling. I got a new number."

"Which I now have," Johnson said. "Did you meet with him?"

"I did. I think I'm in."

Carvelli quickly gave the FBI agent a short briefing on the meeting.

"So, it's not done, though."

"Not for sure, but I saw his greedy little eyes light up when we discussed volume. He'll go."

"Okay. Anything else?"

"Um," Carvelli said, then paused.

"What?" Johnson asked.

"Nothing yet, but something, maybe,"

"What the hell does that mean, Carvelli?"

"I'll stay in touch. I gotta make another call."

"Damn it, Carvelli!" Johnson yelled into an empty phone.

The second call was to Franklin to give him the new number, let him know the meeting was fine and that he was cut loose for the day.

"Hey, Dan. It's Tony. I got a new number. The old one might be bugged. Did you stay with him?"

"Yeah. He's sitting in a parking lot of a Perkins behind the restaurant. There's an alley in front of him and some houses across from that."

Sorenson gave him his location and Carvelli said he was on the way. It was a thirty-minute drive from the Best Buy to where Sorenson was watching the van. When Carvelli got there, he parked next to Sorenson and removed the putty from around his nose and face.

Carvelli finished cleaning off the disguise from his face and then joined Sorenson.

"Is he still in there?"

"Yeah. Every few minutes I can see the van move as if someone is moving around inside. What do you want to do?"

"I should have called Maddy for this. She's gonna be mad at me for not doing that. But I didn't have time."

"Maddy? Who's in there? Marc with some woman he's bouncing around with?"

246

Carvelli laughed and said, "No, nothing like that. Let's go."

The two men crossed the street and into the restaurant's lot. There were no other cars around the van. The van itself had no windows except the ones for the front seat. Because of that, Carvelli and Sorenson were able to easily sneak up on it.

Carvelli very slowly, very quietly pushed down on the handle of the sliding side door. It was unlocked and when it clicked open, he quickly tossed the door back and jumped in.

The van's owner was sitting in the driver's seat with a pair of expensive headphones on. He felt more than heard the door being opened. By the time he turned around Carvelli was on his knees behind the driver's captain's chair, his face less than six inches from the driver. Seeing a man staring right at him, the driver let out a sharp scream and would have fallen but for the steering wheel.

"Hi, Conrad. How've you been?" Carvelli asked as Conrad Hilton clutched at his chest.

FORTY-FOUR

"Jesus H. Christ, Carvelli! One of these days you're gonna do that and I'm gonna fall over dead!" Conrad said.

By now, Dan Sorenson had climbed into the van and closed the door. He was laughing so hard he missed the portable chair and landed on the floor of the van.

"It's not funny, Sorenson," an annoyed Conrad said.

"Gimme these," Carvelli said as he reached for Conrad's headphones.

"No, no," Conrad said as he tried to push Carvelli's hand away.

"What do you have going here?" Carvelli asked as he wrestled with Conrad for the headphones.

"This is attorney-client privileged information," Conrad said holding onto the headphones.

"Well, in that case, we should all listen in," Carvelli said as he pulled the plug on the headphones connected to Conrad's equipment. Given the volume Conrad had the recorder set to, the interior of the van was immediately filled with very loud noises. The noises could only charitably be described as very passionate.

"So, where's the camera?" Carvelli asked.

"No camera," Conrad sullenly replied.

"Conrad! Where's the camera?"

"No camera. Sound only."

"Who you are working for, the husband or the wife?" Sorenson asked.

"None of your business. That's privileged," Conrad said.

By now, Carvelli had found the volume knob on Conrad's equipment. He turned it down while saying, "We're gonna draw a crowd if we keep that up." Carvelli looked at Conrad and asked, "Husband or wife?"

"I'm working for the husband," he reluctantly answered.

"So that's the wife?" Sorenson asked. "Passionate little devil."

"Don't you wish Marge could stay awake long enough to…" Carvelli started to ask.

"No kidding. What's this guy's name. I need to talk to him. Find out his secret."

"She's a hottie, too," Conrad said. "But I don't think he knows the secret. I think she's um, well, ah, working. And acting."

"She's hooking! Are you serious?" Carvelli asked.

"Pretty sure," Conrad said. "She's doing two or three different guys a day. Believe me, none of 'em are male models. That house across the alley right in front of us. They drive in through the alley and park in the neighbor's driveway."

"Sounds like they're done," Sorenson said.

"So, she's hooking in their house…"

"His house. Had it before they got married," Conrad said.

"His house, during the day while he's at work," Carvelli finished. "She deserves to get popped. What does he do?"

"Sales for some small tech firm. He travels a bit."

"You plan on being out here for another month or so?" Carvelli asked.

"Nope," Conrad said. "Wait here. I'll be right back."

He left them sitting in the van while he walked down the alley to the house next to his target. Conrad used his phone to take several shots of the customer's car, including the license plate.

"I got enough," he said when he climbed back in the van. "Believe it or not, it gets boring sitting here listening to this."

An older man and a much younger woman appeared at the back door. Conrad picked up a DSLR from the passenger seat with a 300mm lens. He took several photos of them while they kissed.

"He must have money, too," Conrad said. "That's a shiny new Benz he has parked next door."

"We need to talk, Conrad," Carvelli said.

"Okay, so talk," Conrad said while he scrolled through the photos he had taken. "See, she is a hottie," Conrad said as he held up the camera for Sorenson to take a look.

"Oh, my," Sorenson said. "Yes, indeed."

He was looking at a photo of her with her robe open wearing nothing underneath.

"Put that away," Carvelli said.

"We're going to Jake's. You follow me, Dan will follow you. Hey! Put it away," he yelled at the two men who were still scrolling through the photos.

"And if I say no," Conrad said.

Carvelli leaned in close across the front seat, looked directly at Conrad and said, "There's money in it for you. We're working on Vivian's dime."

"Hey! Where's my girl? Where's Maddy?"

"Your girl?" Carvelli asked.

"I can have fantasies, too," Conrad said.

"You better hope I don't tell her that," Carvelli said.

"Good point."

The short, three-car caravan pulled up in front of Jake's Limo Service. Carvelli had called ahead, so Jake was expecting them.

"Have a seat, Conrad," Carvelli said.

While Conrad nervously said hello to Jake and sat down in the chair Carvelli indicated, Carvelli's personal phone rang. He took a quick peek at the ID.

"Hang on a second, I have to take this," he told the others.

"What did you come up with?"

"Well, it's kind of interesting," Paul Baker, Carvelli's hacker, replied. "I have six different looks, all similar to a certain degree. I ran them all through various facial recognition programs, including the one used by a certain company near Washington that I won't talk about over the phone. Don't try guessing. Just get over here as soon as possible."

"It's that good?"

"Yeah," Baker replied.

"I'm in a meeting and I'm not sure how long it will last. I'll be there when I can," Carvelli assured him.

Carvelli had his back turned to Conrad. He replaced his phone as he turned to look at him.

"Why am I here?" Conrad asked.

Waschke was seated at his desk, Sorenson next to Conrad on his right. Carvelli pulled up a metal folding chair with a padded seat and sat down in front of Conrad. He brushed an imaginary piece of lint off Conrad's knee while Conrad nervously looked about.

"Am I being kidnapped?" Conrad asked.

"Shut up," Carvelli said. "We're just looking for a little information."

"Why did we have to come here…"

"A little information about you and Damone Watson," Carvelli said.

250

"Who?" Conrad asked, sounding like an owl.

Carvelli narrowed his eyes, frowned and nodded at Sorenson who gave Conrad a light slap on the back of his head.

Waschke, enjoying the show, laughed and said, "I do, occasionally, miss the fun of dealing with some idiot who thinks he knows more than we do."

"Should we try it again?" Carvelli asked.

"Okay," Conrad said rubbing the back of his head.

"That didn't hurt, you weenie," Sorenson said.

"You and Damone Watson, pals are you?" Carvelli asked.

"No, I, ah, just sweep his office every couple of weeks," Conrad said.

When he said it, his eyes gave him away. For a brief instant, they shifted between Carvelli, Waschke and Sorenson. Barely noticeable to the untrained eye, to three experienced detectives, it was the equivalent of an obvious tell to a professional poker player. So much so that Conrad may as well have held up a sign that read: "I'm lying."

The room went silent for a moment and then Carvelli nodded at Sorenson again. The slap was a touch harder this time.

"Oww! Dammit!" Conrad howled, then began rubbing the back of his head. "I just do a little…"

Carvelli held up an index finger in front of Conrad's eyes which shut him up.

"Conrad," Carvelli softly began, "have we ever mistreated you…"

"Yes! Several times."

"Okay. Let me rephrase that. Have we ever mistreated you when you were straight with us?"

"Probably. I just don't remember right now." As he said this, Sorenson raised his left hand as if to slap him again. Conrad winced, put his hands up for protection and ducked.

When he realized Sorenson was not going to slap him again, a thought occurred to him.

"Hey, how do you know I've done work for Damone?"

"What difference does that make? We know," Carvelli said. "I saw you come out of his building earlier. One of his guys was escorting you to your van.

"Conrad," he continued. "I had a meeting with him right after you left. I don't know how I know, but I do know I was being filmed. I was meeting in his conference room on the second floor. He almost insisted

I sit in the first chair to his right. That's the best one for monitoring his guests, isn't it?"

By now Carvelli had leaned forward so much that he was barely an inch from Conrad's, nose.

"Yeah, it is," Conrad whispered.

"Video, audio, both?"

"Both," Conrad said. "The entire second floor, including his private office."

"Does he know his private office is wired for sound and video?" Jake asked.

"Yeah, well, mostly," Conrad said.

"What does that mean: mostly?" Carvelli asked.

Before Conrad could answer, Jake stood up, sat on the edge of his desk, looked down at him and said, "I think I know. You have him wired so when he shuts it off, he only shuts off the part he gets. You have the place set up so that he is always wired, but only you know that."

"And you still get both video and audio when Damone thinks it's shut off," Carvelli said. "You sneaky little devil. How long have you been doing this to customers and how much money have you made blackmailing them?"

"Not a dime, I swear," Conrad said. "And I don't do it to everyone. Only those I feel the need to cover my ass."

By now the bead of sweat that Conrad had around his receding hairline had burst like a dam.

"If he finds out…" a badly shaken Conrad started to say.

"If he finds out this guy will barbeque you. Alive," Waschke replied.

"Where are you keeping this?" Carvelli asked.

"On a private, off-site server. I have it well protected," Conrad said. "No way can I let you guys have access to it."

"How long would it take your guy to hack it?" Sorenson asked Carvelli.

"Couple days."

"Paul's good, but not that good," Conrad said. He had worked with Paul before and knew the man was very capable.

"Okay, three days. But he's not going to because Conrad's going to get us the juiciest stuff."

"Hey, why were you meeting with him?" Conrad finally asked Carvelli.

"Your guy's going down," Carvelli replied. "And you should be thankful we caught up with you before you go down with him."

FORTY-FIVE

"Hey, dude, where's the Camaro?" Paul Baker asked Carvelli.

Paul had been anxiously waiting for him, even going so far as to look out front every few minutes. He saw the Lincoln park in front and was disappointed to see Carvelli was still driving it.

Carvelli came through the front door Paul was holding for him and said, "It's in storage and what have I told you about calling me 'dude'?"

"Sorry, dude," Paul replied.

They went into the first-floor living room where the hacker was set up on a large, wide-screen TV to show Carvelli what he had found. Before taking a seat on the couch, Carvelli looked around with a sour expression on his face.

"You gotta stop living like this," Carvelli said. "I consider you a friend and I'm telling you, this is not healthy."

"You gonna bust my balls over the way I live?"

"Yes! Since I've known you, you've gained, what, eighty pounds?"

"Nah, come on man. I don't know. Maybe thirty, no more than forty," Paul seriously said. "A little, but ya' know."

"Bullshit. At least fifty. And bathe every day. Open some windows. Get a haircut, buy a razor. For God's sake, go outside once in a while!"

"Hey, are you done stepping on my nuts, Mr. Health Freak?"

"Sorry. I didn't mean... I guess...you don't look good and it's not healthy."

"Sit down before you say something that will hurt my feelings."

Carvelli sat down on the couch and Paul took an armchair in front of the coffee table. He picked up a small stack of prints and handed them to Carvelli, who started to look through them.

"This him? This is the homeless guy who was behind Ferguson in the street?"

"Maybe," Paul said. "I think it's pretty close, but I can't be positive."

"Well, the guys went through all of the homeless spots here and over in St. Paul. No one recognized him with the makeup and facial hair," Carvelli said. He had carefully looked through all six prints and was about to put them back in the envelope when Paul stopped him.

"Wait a minute. Take out number six. Number five, too."

Carvelli held them up in the light side-by-side. "They look pretty similar."

"Yeah, watch this."

Paul turned the television on. There was a photo already on it of a much younger man. Carvelli looked at the two photos again and then held them to compare each to the man on the screen.

"He's quite a bit younger," Carvelli said referring to the man on the TV screen.

"He'd be about twenty, twenty-two," Paul said about the younger man on TV.

"Yeah, okay," Carvelli said.

"Now look at this," Paul said. He picked up a print lying face down on the table and handed it to him.

"Jesus, that's him," Carvelli said meaning the younger man on TV was the same person as the print Paul handed him. "Or his twin. How…"

"I took prints five and six and ran them through aging software. I took twenty years off of them and voila, there he was."

Paul pointed at the print Carvelli was still holding, number seven, the younger man, and said, "Print seven is number six with twenty years removed."

"Okay, who is he? Who's the guy on TV?"

"I printed this off for you," Paul said as he handed Carvelli a stapled, multi-page document.

Carvelli scanned the top of the first page and asked, "Is this his military record?"

"Yeah," Paul said.

"So, you got into the Pentagon," Carvelli replied. A statement, not a question.

"Well, um, yeah, I did, but that's not where I found this," Paul said.

Carvelli looked at him with a curious expression.

"I got this, his picture and records from the CIA. In fact, the Pentagon didn't have his records anymore. Take some time to read them and you'll see why," Paul said. "You want a beer?"

Without looking up, Carvelli said, "Yeah, sure, why not?"

Paul was back in less than a minute and handed Carvelli a bottle. It took him a while to get through the almost forty-page report. He sipped his beer and occasionally shook his head in disbelief. When he finished, Carvelli placed the document on the coffee table.

"Do you have that picture, the one of the homeless guy, we got for you?"

"Sure," Paul replied. He reached down to the floor and picked up a file folder. He found the photo and gave it to Carvelli.

Carvelli held it up and compared it to print number six. "Did you take print number six and add the makeup, beard, putty, glasses and hat?"

"I knew you'd ask," Paul said and then handed a new print across the table.

Carvelli laid them all out on the table and looked at them for a moment. "It's him," he quietly said. "This Charles Dudek guy is the homeless guy hanging around Ferguson."

"I think so too and so does the computer," Paul agreed.

"Who the hell is this guy? Why does CIA have his military record but not the Pentagon?" Carvelli asked.

"CIA tried to recruit him when he left the Army," Paul said. "They purged his military record from the Pentagon and tried to bury it.

"He turned them down, walked away and apparently disappeared," Paul said.

"Did you read this stuff about him going into the caves of Tora Bora after nine eleven? By himself to hunt down Osama? The medals this guy has?"

"The psych evaluation," Paul said. "He's a stone cold, sociopathic killer. I could not find a single Charles or Charlie Dudek that was remotely close to this guy. He's likely living off the grid under assumed names. He's smart enough to do that. He could be living anywhere under any name. In fact, he probably is living a quiet, normal life. His neighbors would be shocked if they knew."

"Yeah, if he's been at it since he was discharged. It's been, what, almost, twenty years?" Carvelli said.

"Not quite but getting there," Paul replied.

Carvelli finished his beer and made a call on his personal phone.

"Hey," he said when Marc answered. "What are you doing right now?"

"I'm still in the office going over the jury list. Why?"

"I'll be there in fifteen minutes. I came up with something you need to see."

Maddy finished reading the military record of Charlie Dudek and handed the last page to Connie Mickelson. There were four of them, including Connie, in the conference room. Starting with Marc, while Carvelli patiently waited, they were passing the photos and the report around to each other.

After Maddy finished reading and handed the last few pages to Connie, she said to Marc, "Let me see the photos again, please."

Maddy laid them all out on the table. She carefully looked them over and then picked up number six. This was the print of how Paul thought Charlie would look at his age today. She stared at it for a while, then turned it so Marc and Carvelli—both sitting across the table from her—could see it.

"I've seen this guy. I don't know where or when, but I would swear in court that I have seen him." Maddy said.

"Pretty bland, ordinary-looking face," Marc said.

"Yeah, that's true," Maddy sighed. "But he really looks familiar."

Connie finished reading, then neatly put the pages together. She was sitting next to Maddy across from Carvelli and slid the document over to him.

Connie looked at Marc and in a school girl's voice said, "Mom, Dad, I'd like you to meet Charlie. Charlie's gonna take me to the prom. Then, afterwards, he's gonna suck all of the blood out of my body. Can you imagine this guy showing up at your door?"

After the laughter died down, Carvelli said, "You know what? I'll bet this guy never hurt anybody or anything without reason. He wasn't that freaky kid who liked to pull the wings off of flies just to watch them."

"No, that was you," Marc said.

"We all have our little quirks," Carvelli said. "This guy is a professional's pro. That's why he is able to operate and live under the radar. He's not some psycho. He's likely a sociopath, someone without a conscience. In fact, the army says he has an I.Q. in the one-forties."

Connie said, "That still begs the question: what do we do with this?"

The table went silent while each of them looked for an answer from somebody else.

"I don't know," Marc finally said. "None of this is the least bit admissible."

"What if we could link him with someone else? Someone who wanted Ferguson dead?" Maddy asked.

"Who you got in mind?" Carvelli asked.

"Tony, I'm just throwing it out there," she replied.

"I know. But that's the problem. If this guy is who we think…"

"And that's a mighty big 'if', legally," Connie added.

"He was hired by someone to pull this off. Who?"

"Wait a minute," Marc said. "Let's break this down. We haven't been able to get a whiff of the homeless guy. We've had people out pounding the streets with his picture everywhere."

"We've shown his picture to about every homeless person in the metro area," Carvelli said. "We didn't even find anyone who thought they might've seen him."

"That certainly lends credibility to the theory that this Dudek guy is, in fact, the homeless guy pretty much stalking Ferguson. But I can't identify him as this Dudek guy."

"Why not?" Carvelli asked.

"Lack of foundation," Connie said. "How did we come to that conclusion?"

"Well, your Honor, we have a world-class hacker who got into the CIA computers and…" Marc said. "Even if I were still involved with Margaret, she wouldn't let me get away with that.

"I do have a legitimate way to get the film in that Gabriella gave us to supply us with pictures of the homeless guy. And we have the witnesses, the girls, to testify they saw him. If nothing else, I can plausibly argue that he picked up the gun and ran off."

"Will that be enough?" Maddy asked.

"Is that reasonable doubt? Maybe. But a gun that only Rob saw? I don't know."

Maddy said. "We need to take another run at that reporter, Philo. I think he's holding something back."

"How do you want to do it?" Marc asked.

"We can probably think of something," Maddy replied, then winked at Carvelli.

"Is this something legal? Or shouldn't I ask?" Marc said.

"Almost," Maddy said. "Or, at least, it should be. Better you don't ask."

"Are you going to put Rob on the stand?" Carvelli asked to change the subject.

"No choice," Marc answered. "It's the only way we can get the missing gun into evidence."

"If it's missing, how can Rob testify about it?" Maddy asked.

"He's presumed to be telling the truth," Marc replied, "as are all witnesses. The benefit of the doubt sort of thing. It's then up to the prosecution to cast doubt on his credibility. Unless he gets Rob to admit he's lying about the gun, which he won't, we can use it. The jury can then decide if they believe there was a gun or not. You can bet every witness Steve puts on will testify he or she did not see Ferguson or anyone else with a gun."

"What about their motive? What are they gonna do about that?" Carvelli asked.

"Racism," Marc replied. "They've been investigating Rob for any sign of it. And, they have several cops, or so we've heard, who will testify about locker room talk from the guys who got stuck doing crowd control for this protest. Some of it is pretty graphic and Rob was present. I don't know if any of them will claim Rob engaged in any of that talk. Steve's gonna say Rob hated Ferguson and blamed him for all of the racial trouble. Most of the cops did. They were all getting pretty tired of being screamed at, cursed at, called names and spit on. I haven't talked to Rob about this yet. I've been told who the cops are who are gonna testify to this. I want the jury to see Rob's reaction."

"Well," Carvelli said, stretching out his arms above his head while he sat, "I need to get going. I'm due at Vivian's for dinner and business talk."

"Mind if I tag along?" Maddy asked. "I haven't been there for a while."

"No, not at all. I'm sure she'd love to see you," Carvelli replied.

"Will I be interrupting anything of a romantic nature?"

"No, I think that's pretty much done," Carvelli replied. "We're still good friends."

"Do you mind?" Maddy asked Marc.

"No, go. I'll be here probably until midnight, at least," he replied.

FORTY-SIX

"How's the opioid business?" Maddy asked. She had left her car at Marc's office and was riding with Carvelli.

"Actually, we've taken a ton of it off the street. It's costing Vivian a fortune, but she doesn't care.

"The women on my sales list are gradually being weaned off of the stuff even if they don't realize it. We've switched to capsules, and the capsules are half and half; half oxy and half substitutes like Ibuprofen and Acetaminophen. We got that lab in Chanhassen turning them out. My customers are doing pretty good with them."

"What are you doing with the proceeds?"

"Every dime is accounted for and in a safe at Vivian's. I make a weekly report to Paxton accounting for the money and the product," Carvelli said.

"Who do you have doing the switch from pills to capsules? Can you trust them?"

"Yeah, I got an ex-narco cop in charge. I doubt you know him. Bennie Solo?"

"No, I don't know him," Maddy said.

"Bennie was undercover a little too long, years back. He developed a taste for crack. Now he's a crusader. He owns three rehab places. Our place in Chanhassen is in one of them. He has some other ex-cops working with him on this. Bennie keeps better records than I do and because he has licensed rehab clinics, he can order large amounts of the substitute stuff to put in the capsules. It's used in rehab."

"You should go see her. Spend a weekend with her."

"Who?" Carvelli said.

"Who? Paxton, of course!" Maddy said. "Men are so dense."

"And that's our best quality. How're things with Marc?"

"Good. Really good. I think I've finally met a man who doesn't spend most of the day thinking about himself."

"Stop it. They're not all like that. What happens is women want fireworks to go off. When it does, it's all wonderful and fun. Then the fireworks fade, and women start looking for the flaws. And you always find them because they're always there. Trust me. Marc has them too and I love the guy. He's a good man and a friend. You can trust him. And he's a good father."

"Are you trying to sell him to me?" Maddy said with a big smile. "You don't have to."

She went silent for a minute and stared out the windshield.

"I thought you said you don't know anything about women," Maddy said.

"I don't," Carvelli replied. "I just know you two were together for a long time before you finally realized you love each other."

"That's not true. I knew long before he did. I just wasn't ready to admit it."

"Listen, sweetie, don't go looking for flaws and don't criticize little things that he does. That's the beginning of the end. Believe it or not, you have flaws and annoying little habits, too."

Maddy turned in her seat to face him, slapped him on the shoulder and yelled, "I do not! Name one. I dare you to name just one."

"Your obsession with your hair," Carvelli quickly said. "Not to mention, shoes."

"I'm not obsessed with my hair," she replied. "Much," she added more quietly. "And shoes are a must. Men don't get it."

"No, we sure don't. There isn't a woman I've ever been involved with who doesn't ask my opinion about the shoes they're wearing."

"Vivian?"

"Constantly. She could be wearing pink high-top Converse sneakers for all I care."

The two of them went silent for another couple of minutes. Maddy finally broke the silence.

"I am a little obsessed with my hair," she quietly admitted.

"It's your one concession to vanity. The rest of you is naturally beautiful and you know it. Hair changes," Carvelli said.

Maddy turned again to him and asked, "So, you think Marc knows?"

"Well, yeah, of course, he knows. He's asked me a couple of times how much longer he should put up with it before dumping you."

Maddy's mouth and eyes went wide-open before she said, "Really? He's thinking about breaking up with me?"

Carvelli could not suppress the laugh for more than a second.

"No, he worships you. Stop it. He's never said a thing about your hair or shoes. Although you might want to stop asking him about shoes. Men know nothing about women's shoes. And those that do have boyfriends of their own."

"That's true," Maddy laughed. "Okay, no more shoes and watch the OCD about my hair."

"He loves your hair. It's attached to you," Carvelli leaned over and whispered. "Don't start looking for flaws or things to criticize. Believe me, you'll have a tough time finding somebody where the grass is greener."

"Okay," she said. She turned to him again and sincerely asked, "What do men want?"

"We're easy. Sex on demand and quiet when there's a football game on TV, especially when the Vikings are beating the Packers. Just let him enjoy."

Maddy, the Chicago girl, asked, "Do I have to be quiet when the Bears are beating the Vikings?"

"Since that rarely happens, don't worry about it, but," Carvelli, a Chicago boy, said, "if it ever does happen, feel free to rub it in."

"I'm glad you came!" Vivian let loose at Maddy when she answered her door. They gave each other an affectionate hug.

"Yes, you too, Anthony," Vivian said and gave him a brief kiss.

"Was I looking glum?"

"That's his normal look," Maddy said.

"Oh, not always," Vivian replied raising her eyebrows and smiling. "Come in, please."

"I'm sorry I haven't been around much lately," Maddy said. "Marc's trial is keeping me busy."

"Is it starting on time? Still Monday?" Vivian asked as she led them to the office.

"So far," Maddy replied.

"Come in," Vivian said. "Let's get business taken care first before dinner."

One of the household staff, a man, appeared while they were still in the hallway.

"Hello, Thomas," Carvelli said. "How've you been?"

"Good, sir, thank you," the man answered.

They each gave him a drink order and then went into Vivian's office. A few minutes later they had their beverages and Vivian told Thomas when they would be ready for dinner.

About forty minutes later, Vivian and Carvelli were done wrapping up that week's drug business. Tony gave his share of the proceeds to

Vivian who placed them in a safe inside the office credenza. As she did this, Tony showed Maddy a ledger listing the amount of money Vivian had spent. She was buying up oxy from Damone and storing most of it for disposal. What little they did sell were the ones cut with Ibuprofen to wean Carvelli's customers off of it.

"That's how much of your own money you have spent on this?" an incredulous Maddy asked.

"I lost a favorite niece to this and her boys lost their mother. I don't give a damn about the money. We're getting drugs off the street and we're going to put some bad people in prison."

"'Atta girl," Carvelli said.

"Be careful you don't go with them."

"Everything is being well-documented and kept by Anthony's good friend," here Vivian winked at Maddy, "Paxton O'Rourke. I'm famished, let's eat," Vivian said.

Half-way through dinner, Carvelli's phone rang. Vivian gave him a very disapproving look, but he answered it anyway.

"Hey, kid, what's up?" he asked, avoiding Vivian's glare.

"How busy are you tonight?" Gretchen Stenson asked.

"Why, what do you need?" Carvelli asked.

"I hate to ask…"

"I owe you, don't worry about it," Carvelli replied.

"Okay, I got a date tonight, ten o'clock, and I'm supposed to meet him in the bar of the Frontier Room. You know it?"

"Of course," Carvelli said.

By now, both Maddy and Vivian had stopped eating and were watching and listening to Carvelli.

Carvelli covered the phone with his hand and quietly said, "Gretchen," to the two women.

Vivian immediately, but quietly, asked, "The prostitute?"

Carvelli nodded an affirmation and smiled when he heard Vivian say to Maddy, "This could be good."

"This guy is new," Gretchen continued. "I got introduced to him by a regular I trust, but this guy makes me feel a little creepy. You know what I mean?"

"Sure," Carvelli said.

Vivian leaned to him and mouthed the word 'what' at him with an eager look in her eyes.

Carvelli covered the phone again and quietly said, "Stop it," back to her.

This exchange caused Maddy to start laughing and say to Vivian, "You are so bad. Shame on you!"

Vivian moved away from Carvelli and said to Maddy, "I've never known a prostitute before. At least none that I know of. I've met her. She's terrific. Reminds me a bit of you."

"Thanks," Maddy sarcastically replied.

"Where are you and who are those people in the background?" Gretchen asked.

"I'm having dinner with Vivian and Maddy. You've never met Maddy. Anyway, what do you need?"

"Forget it. I don't want to impose."

"Shut up. I owe you. You want me to come and watch your back?"

"Yeah, would you mind?"

"I'll be there at nine forty-five," Carvelli said.

"He's probably okay and someone I can handle but...."

"I'll be there. It's eight thirty now, I'll make it, no problem."

"Thanks, Tony. I appreciate it." Gretchen said with obvious relief.

"What?" Vivian asked. "I want to go, too. I've never seen a hooker in action."

"What do you think we're gonna do? Watch them go at it through the peephole?"

"You are so bad," Maddy said again, only laughing hysterically this time.

Carvelli quickly told the two women what was going on and what the favor was.

"I still want to go," Vivian said.

"No," Carvelli emphatically said. "The idea is to blend in and be inconspicuous. Half the people there will know who you are. Besides, this is nothing. I'll take Maddy. All we're going to do is watch two people have a drink. Gretchen will know by then if everything is okay. No big deal. Nothing to see."

The Frontier Room is an upscale bar and restaurant in a downtown hotel. The place was humming when Carvelli and Maddy strolled in just after 9:30. They got lucky and found a table in a corner behind some foliage with a good view.

Gretchen arrived at 9:55. At first, she stood in the entryway of the bar area looking for her date. Unable to see him, she took a seat at the bar. Gretchen knew all three bartenders and all four waitresses. Normally, a restaurant in a hotel of this caliber would never permit a hooker to ply her trade here. But Gretchen was always dressed tastefully and never looked the part. Plus, she treated the wait staff very well. While the bartender was getting her beverage, a soda with a twist, her date came in.

Carvelli turned his head to his left just in time to see Gretchen's date come in. It took a couple of seconds for it to register who he was. When it did, Carvelli involuntarily tucked his head in and covered the left side of his face with his hand.

"Don't look," he whispered to Maddy.

"Why? What?"

"Sssh," he said. Carvelli slowly turned his head to see Gretchen and her date arm-in-arm going to a booth.

Gretchen sat on the side facing Carvelli and Maddy. Her date sat with his back to them.

"Okay, you can look," Carvelli said.

Maddy looked and saw Gretchen but could not tell who her date was.

"Who?" she asked.

"It's that reporter. That Philo guy," Carvelli quietly said.

Maddy immediately covered her mouth with her left hand to squelch her laughter.

This caused Carvelli to do the same thing.

"Now what do you want to do?" Maddy asked.

"I don't know. Should I text her? Tell her who he is and that she can kick his ass if she needs to?"

"Why are we hiding? So what if he sees us? How can he tie us to Gretchen? We're just sitting here having a drink," Maddy said.

"True, but it would be better to get out of here," Carvelli said.

"This could be perfect," Maddy said. "You had suggested we might try to use her to find out everything he knows about the Ferguson shooting."

"Yeah," Carvelli replied.

"We both thought he knew more than he was telling."

"Yeah, we did, and he does," Carvelli said. "I'll send a text, then we'll get out of here. She'll be okay. I'll call her tomorrow."

FORTY-SEVEN

"I'm not even sure I want to go back there with you," Arturo Mendoza said to Marc.

"Oh, it'll be alright. Don't be such a wuss. Just nod your head in agreement if she asks you anything," Marc replied.

"That's why I don't want to go back there with you. I don't need to be made an accomplice," Arturo said.

It was 8:10 A.M. on Monday morning, the first week of the trial. The two lawyers were seated at the defense table. Marc had grabbed the closer of the two tables to the jury box.

Marc had called Steve Gondeck at home the previous evening and told him he had some things to discuss in camera this morning. Marc had hung up while Gondeck was still cussing at him.

There were already a dozen or so people either in the reserved section for the media or scattered about the gallery. Gondeck and his very capable second chair, Jennifer Moore, came in. As they passed through the gate, Gondeck asked, "Where's Maddy?"

"She broke up with me, said she never wanted to see me again and was moving back to Chicago."

"What did you do, you idiot?" an incredulous Gondeck seriously asked.

"Unless I miss my guess," Jennifer interrupted, "she's with the police escort bringing the defendant here."

"Oh, yeah, that's right," Marc said. "I forgot she did say she was gonna do that first. One of these days I am calling your wife. I could represent you in the divorce."

"I wouldn't need a lawyer. I'd need an undertaker. So, why are we here so early?" Gondeck asked.

Before Marc could answer, Lois, Judge Tennant's clerk, came through the back door next to the bench.

She took her usual seat and addressed the lawyers.

"Everybody here?"

They all answered affirmatively.

"Uh, where's your client, Mr. Kadella?"

"On the way, your Honor," Marc said and immediately regretted it.

"Call me that again and I will hurt you," she replied.

"Sorry," Marc meekly replied. "I was kidding."

"You want to wait for the defendant?"

"No," Marc replied.

"Okay, go back and you, watch yourself. You're lucky I like you."

As they were going through the back door, Lois quietly said to Marc, "Pissing off the judge's clerk is not the way to start a trial."

"I'll send flowers," Marc told her.

"You better."

"Good morning, everyone. Have a seat," Judge Tennant said to the four lawyers.

"Ready?" she asked the court reporter who nodded his assent. She then read the case name and court file number for the record.

"Note your appearances," she told the lawyers. When they finished, she looked at Marc and said, "Mr. Kadella has some last-minute issues to bring before the court before we begin jury selection. Mr. Kadella."

"Thank you, your Honor," Marc began. "It's no secret that the defendant told the police that he saw the deceased pointing a gun at him. We believe it may have been someone else who was alongside Reverend Ferguson who was holding the gun and pointing it at Officer Dane. We believe we have found the person who did that by photographic evidence."

"What? Why haven't we…" Gondeck started to say.

Judge Tennant held up her left hand to silence him while she said, "Mr. Gondeck, please, let's see what he has."

"We found witnesses who saw a man, a homeless looking man, following Reverend Ferguson. We went to a source with Channel 8, Gabriella Shriqui, who reviewed their film of the first three days of the protests. They found him. He was, in fact, filmed by them. They did not film the protest the fourth day, the day Ferguson was killed, but we have witnesses who saw him on the fourth day."

Marc removed two plastic cases from his coat pocket. He handed one to Jennifer Moore and one to the judge.

"Do they show the mystery gun?" Gondeck asked.

"No," Marc admitted. "But we have reason to believe he is wearing a disguise. His real name is Charles Dudek and he is a professional contract assassin."

"Hold it! What? How…"

267

"I'll take it from here, Mr. Gondeck," the judge said. "Mr. Kadella, I've known you to be a straight, honest lawyer. With that being said, tell me how you came to find this out?"

"Your honor," Marc began, "even if I could, I admit the foundation for admissibility is tenuous at best." He turned his head to look at Gondeck and continued, "Steve, I think I can say you know me well enough to know I am not one to resort to wild histrionics, but I'll tell you something, I believe this is absolutely true. Ferguson was being stalked by a contract killer who induced Rob Dane to pull his gun and shoot Lionel Ferguson."

Tennant looked at Arturo and asked, "Mr. Mendoza, what do you have to say about this?"

"I believe Mr. Kadella, your Honor. I am not privy to how he came to this conclusion, but I believe it. Absolutely."

"Your Honor," Gondeck said.

Tennant held up her hand again to stop him, then said to the court reporter, "Off the record."

"Marc," she began, "I know you well enough to know that you're not lying, at least in the sense that you believe this man is this Dudek character. But I gotta have more than that. At least tell me how you came to this conclusion."

"I can't, Judge. Attorney-client privilege precludes it. It's that simple. Even if I could tell you, it probably wouldn't be good enough."

"Well, I'll hang onto my disk for now and you yours," she told Gondeck.

"How do I know this hasn't been tampered with?" Gondeck asked.

"It has," Marc admitted. "What you have there is a spliced compilation. The original is being held by security at Channel 8."

"If you come up with something or you decide to tell us how you got this, we'll revisit this. Back on the record," Tennant said.

"What are you requesting, Mr. Kadella?"

"That the defense be allowed to present what we believe is exculpatory video evidence that a paid contract killer by the name of Charles Dudek was following Lionel Ferguson and he induced Officer Robert Dane to shoot and kill Reverend Ferguson. He did this by slipping behind the Reverend and reaching around Ferguson's side while pointing a gun at officer Dane."

"Objection. Lack of foundation and extremely speculative," Gondeck said.

"Sustained," Tennant ruled. "The video of this man who may have been behind Reverend Ferguson is inadmissible, lacking foundation. There will be no mention of anyone named Charles Dudek. Anything else?"

"No, your Honor," Marc replied.

"Okay," Tennant continued. "Jury selection. You both received the list of prospective jurors and the questionnaires?"

"Yes, your Honor."

"We have one hundred and fifty veniremen waiting. We will bring them up in groups of fifteen. As you know, for first-degree murder, we must question each of them individually. We'll bring them in, one at a time and leave the remaining ones in a jury room of one of the empty courtrooms down the hall. They will be guarded to keep people away, especially the media.

"I will question them first. I'll ask about hardship, obvious biases, their knowledge of the case through the media. Pay attention to what I ask them and what they answer. I don't want a lot of repetition. If you think you have a bias that I didn't catch, fine. Go ahead and inquire. But don't flog a dead horse either.

"The defense has the mandatory fifteen peremptories and the state has nine. Use them wisely. I will not be inclined to hand out extra ones. Am I clear about this?"

All four lawyers answered in the affirmative.

"Good. Well, let's go pick a jury."

"There is one more thing I wanted to address again," Marc said.

"If it's the camera in the courtroom, forget it. It wasn't my idea. I don't like it either, but it's a done deal," Margaret said.

The local media had brought a motion with Chief Judge Harold Jennrich requesting that a camera feed be allowed. Due to the seriousness of the trial and the public's interest, Jennrich agreed. He also believed it would help keep emotions in check if people could watch and see that the trial was conducted appropriately.

Marc had already argued against it and was overruled. This morning he tried to take one more shot at it.

Stopped dead in his tracks on the camera issue, Marc said, "Okay, then. I guess we can start picking a jury."

"I thought you'd see it my way," Tennant said.

"Do I have a choice?" Marc asked.

"Not anymore," she replied, a veiled reference to their prior relationship, which brought a round of laughter.

Back in the courtroom, they found Rob Dane at the table and Maddy sitting in front of the railing. The gallery was less than half full. Jury selection could be, and usually was, long and boring. Sitting in the front row, directly behind Maddy, were three uniformed Minneapolis police officers. Rob had wanted to fill the gallery with them; Marc and Arturo had decided otherwise.

This was a racially charged blue on black matter with a white cop shooting a respected black minister. A roomful of blue uniforms could easily be construed as an "us against them" event. A little support from the cops would be expected, but too much could be a problem.

Also seated in the front row were Rob's wife, Leah, her father and Rob's father.

"Did she give you any trouble?" Marc asked Rob, referring to Maddy.

"A little, but nothing I couldn't handle," Rob replied.

During trial preparation, Maddy had been around enough for Rob and Leah to get to know. Leah overheard Rob's remark and said, "Yeah, right, Mister Big Talk."

Marc motioned for Maddy to come forward. She rolled her chair up and he whispered to her, "Do me a favor. Go ask Steve if he would like you to sit at his table. Tell him you're mad at me and don't want to sit with me."

"I will not!" she replied.

"Come on. Please. If he says yes, tell him you're calling his wife."

Maddy slyly looked at Gondeck and then said, "Okay."

She strolled over to Gondeck who did not notice her at first as he set up his table. Jennifer did, poked his arm and looked up at her.

"Would it be okay if I sat at your table for the trial? I'm mad at him. He's such a jerk."

Jennifer clamped a hand over her mouth to avoid laughing. Gondeck's face turned red and he leaned forward, looked at Marc and said, "I'll get you for this."

To finish it off, Maddy leaned down and gave Steve a quick smooch on the cheek. Unfortunately, Judge Tennant came through the back door just in time to see the kiss.

When the courtroom attendees had returned to their seats, Tennant looked at Maddy who was now seated behind Marc, trying to hide.

"Good morning, Ms. Rivers," Tennant said with a slight smile. "Nice to see you again. Trying to rattle the prosecution?"

"I am sorry, your Honor. I'm just teasing him a little. Sorry."

"Judging by the color of his face, I'd say you were successful." She then looked at Marc and said, "Mr. Kadella, I assume there will be no more of that."

"I'll try to keep her under control, your Honor," Marc replied.

By this point, Maddy was hiding her face in her hands and the entire courtroom, including the judge, was laughing.

When everyone was settled down, the judge read the case name and number into the record and asked if the parties were ready to begin jury selection. Judge Tennant told the deputy by the door to bring in the first veniremen and the trial was technically underway.

FORTY-EIGHT

The first prospective juror to be called was also the first name on the list. William C. Howell was a fifty-two-year-old retired Marine. He had joined the Corps at the age of 18 and risen through the ranks. Upon his thirtieth anniversary, Howell retired as a Lieutenant Colonel. When Arturo Mendoza, and everyone else involved in the selection, saw his name and profession, Howell was to be listed as an automatic 'no way,' especially by the jury consulting firm they hired.

Marc had the final word and put him as a 'maybe.' The automatic impression of anyone military would be someone who is a strict law and order type. But a man who put himself through college and worked his way up through the ranks must have a solid head on his shoulders. Even with his iron-gray crew cut and ramrod bearing, Marc liked him.

Judge Tennant started the questioning by probing for any bias or preconceived notion of guilt or innocence. Howell came across as honest, intelligent and even quite affable. He admitted to knowing about the case through the media and even admitted it did not look good for the defendant. Why lie about it?

"Do you believe you can set aside any opinions you may have and decide this case based solely on the testimony and evidence presented during the trial?" Tennant asked.

"Yes, your Honor. I can, and I will," he answered.

With that, Tennant passed him to Marc.

Marc stood and walked to about ten feet from the man. He introduced himself and his co-counsel, Arturo, who stood, nodded and smiled. He also introduced Rob Dane, who did the same thing.

"Colonel Howell…" Marc began.

"Objection to the use of the prefix 'Colonel'," Gondeck said.

"He's earned it," Marc quickly snapped back at Gondeck. He knew Tennant would sustain Gondeck, but he did not want to miss an opportunity to stroke the man a little and make Gondeck look petty.

A significant purpose of jury selection by both lawyers is to sell yourself to them. Make them believe you can be trusted, someone you would not mind having as a neighbor. It is normally a little more difficult for the defense. No matter what people may claim, if you are a defendant, serious people such as the police are saying you are guilty of something.

272

A good defense lawyer wants them to believe that if you that nice man of woman is helping the accused, then maybe they won't prejudge.

"We'll use Mr. Howell for our purposes," Judge Tennant said.

"Mr. Howell," Marc continued, "You joined the Corps when you were eighteen and did thirty years?"

"That's right."

"Where did you get your degree?"

"I started in California at a community college, then finished my degree at George Mason in Virginia while serving at Arlington."

Of course, Marc knew all of this from the witness questionnaire. What he was trying to do was build a little rapport and, more importantly, goad Gondeck into objections.

Marc continued with a few more personal questions until finally getting to the main one. He then went over the concepts of innocent until proven guilty, the prosecution's burden of proof and proof beyond a reasonable doubt. Satisfied the man understood each of them, Marc moved on.

"Mr. Howell, can I have your word that if you are selected to be on this jury, you will keep an open mind and wait until you've heard all of the testimony and seen all of the evidence before making a decision?"

"Yes, sir, you have my word."

"I have no objections to this witness, your Honor."

Tennant had already questioned him about the presumption of innocence, the burden of proof and guilt beyond a reasonable doubt. Normally Marc would go over these same subjects again. With the Marine Colonel, Marc sensed that was not necessary, it might offend the man and he would hear it again anyway.

"Mr. Gondeck," Judge Tennant said.

Before he stood up, Gondeck stared at Marc, who ignored him for several seconds. What was running through his head was the question: *What does Kadella know about this guy that I don't? Why is he okay with a law and order Marine on this jury?*

Gondeck only spent ten minutes with the Colonel; mostly to sell himself to the man. Marc had spent very little time on this. This is not the type of person to be swayed by superfluous puffery. Men and women who work their way up through the ranks of the Marine Corp likely do not suffer fools gladly. Gondeck sensed this also and cut his void dire short.

"Acceptable, your Honor," he announced.

"The deputy will take you to be situated before releasing you. You'll be notified when the actual trial will begin.

"You will not discuss this case with anyone or read newspapers or watch TV reports about it. I'm sure you realize that. In fact, don't even tell anyone you're on the jury. Avoid it entirely. Thank you, Mr. Howell.

"We'll take a fifteen-minute break," Tennant announced.

Marc noticed as Howell was being led out of the courtroom, he looked at neither the prosecution or defense table.

"I think you're right about him," Arturo said.

The four of them, Maddy included, had made a circle at the defense table with their chairs.

"Yeah," Marc agreed. "He's smart, cool and tough. He'll keep his word and decide based on the evidence. If we can deliver reasonable doubt to him, no one's gonna talk him out of it. Plus, he's got leadership written all over him. I'm hoping he'll be the foreman."

"On the other hand," Maddy interjected, "they will all look to him. If he doesn't find reasonable doubt, he'll convert any who do with little more than a stern look."

By the end of the first day, they had made one more selection. A sixty-two-year-old black grandmother that Marc had as a low-ranked 'maybe.' Marc wanted to use a peremptory on her, but he had already used two. At this rate, he would be out of them by Wednesday afternoon.

Maddy liked her and reminded Marc about what Ferguson was really like. If they could get any of that in it would not sit well with this woman. Reluctantly, Marc acquiesced. Oddly, as the deputy held the gate for her, she turned and smiled at Maddy.

While Marc, Maddy and Arturo were working on jury selection, Tony Carvelli a/k/a Rossi, was enjoying a latte at the Highland Hills Golf and Tennis Club. It was a beautiful early October day. The tennis courts were full and there were three foursomes lined up on the first tee. October in Minnesota is normally a month to enjoy in lieu of what was not far off.

Carvelli was at an umbrella covered table watching Wendy ply their trade. They were starting to lose money only because there were a number of customers without a serious addiction. With the cutting of the oxy with OTC painkillers, some of the women were losing interest.

"Hey, sailor, new in town?" Carvelli heard a familiar voice say from behind him. Gretchen dropped her bag in an empty chair, then sat next to Tony.

"Sorry about not calling back," she said to him. "Sundays are used for business and I forgot about you.

"What happened Saturday night?" Gretchen asked.

"I told you in the text I sent you," Carvelli said. "We knew your date. Didn't you get it?"

The waiter appeared, and Gretchen ordered a light Margherita.

"Is that what you wrote? Have you ever tried decoding one of your texts? So, you knew him and…?" Gretchen asked.

"I didn't want him to see us hanging around."

"He's kind of a strange character," Gretchen said. "Thank you," she told the waiter. "Put it on his tab." She took a swallow and said, "Not a bad guy or weird or anything. Nothing kinky. He just needs his ego stroked a bit like a lot of guys."

"Oh, baby, oh, baby," Carvelli said. "You're the best ever."

"No," Gretchen laughed. "His work. His job as a reporter. He likes to brag. He told me about the shooting of Lionel Ferguson. Hey, that starts today doesn't it?"

"They're in jury selection as we speak," Carvelli said.

"He said something strange to me. He said he knows something that would blow the case wide open. Well, by that point I'd had enough of his bragging and didn't think much of it," she continued.

By now, Carvelli was pulled up to the table and listening intently. "What did he say? He was the one who got the photo for the paper of Ferguson lying dead in the street. He claims he didn't see anything else. That's what he told the cops and my friends, Kadella and Maddy."

"He backed off a bit when he said that, so I let go. Like I said, I thought he was just puffing out his chest."

"Do you have another date?"

"No, not yet."

"Can you make one? Set up one where we can monitor it? Or maybe you could just ply him with a little booze and get him talking?"

"Maybe. If I don't hear from him in a couple of days, I can call him and tell him I have an opening. You want to make up a discount if I have to give him one?"

Carvelli looked her in the eyes and said, "I thought we were friends."

"It's not my problem what you think."

"You drive a hard bargain."

"I know," she replied.

"Okay, I'll cover it under miscellaneous field expenses."

A half-hour later, Wendy was back at the table with them.

"How'd it go?" Carvelli asked.

"Fine, except several of them are getting mild withdrawal symptoms," Wendy replied.

"Good, we'll keep an eye on it."

The waiter stopped and they each ordered something. When he left, Carvelli decided to tease Gretchen.

"He's got an eye on you," Carvelli said.

"And he's a hottie," Wendy added.

"I have shoes older than him," Gretchen said. "Besides, see those two guys sitting by themselves next to the pool. The two nursing club sodas?"

Carvelli took a casual look and then said, "They're undercover cops from the sheriff's office."

"Is that where they're from? I knew they were cops, but I wasn't sure who they worked for," Gretchen said.

"How did you know they were cops?" Wendy asked. "Shouldn't we get out of here?"

"It's obvious by the way they're acting and no, we should sit tight," Carvelli answered her.

Carvelli had taken out his personal phone, found a number and dialed it.

"Watch them," he said to Gretchen. "See if they follow me."

He got up and walked toward the clubhouse. When the phone call was answered, he did not bother with a greeting.

"Hey, I need you to do something. I need you to call the Hennepin County Sheriff and tell them…"

He explained where he was and why he called.

Carvelli was back at the table in less than two minutes. He quietly asked Gretchen if the two sheriff's investigators had watched.

"No, paid no attention to you at all," Gretchen replied.

A few minutes later, the older of the two men answered his phone. Carvelli watched and smiled when he saw the man talking with the caller.

The exchange was very brief. The call ended. The man looked at his phone, then said something to his partner. Carvelli saw the partner spread his hands and spoke the word 'why.' At that point, they both stood and quickly left.

"Pays to know people," Carvelli said with a grin.

"How did you…"

"I called my FBI pals and asked them to call the sheriff. The sheriff was told they, the Feebs, are running an investigation and told him to get his guys out of here."

"Pretty slick. I'll keep that in mind," Gretchen said.

"Has anyone hassled you?" Carvelli asked Wendy.

"No, everything seems fine," she replied.

After the waiter brought their drinks, they waited another fifteen minutes after the deputies had left, then left themselves. When they got to the parking lot, Wendy got in Carvelli's car and Gretchen left in hers.

Before Carvelli dropped Wendy off, she had given him a small, brown leather satchel with today's proceeds and the leftover inventory.

"How much longer?" Wendy asked. By now Wendy knew what they were really up to.

They were parked in the underground garage of Wendy's luxury townhouse association. Carvelli sat silently thinking for a moment before saying, "Not much longer. I'm not sure why, but I got this cop feeling that something's coming to a head. Why?"

"Now that I'm clean and sober," Wendy replied, "I don't want to do this. These people are friends and friends of friends. If one of them was to OD and die…"

"If it makes you feel any better, the dosages we're giving them probably aren't enough to cause an OD. Unless they start shopping somewhere else."

"I hope you're right."

Carvelli's phone rang and he answered it. "Yeah, Dan, what do you have?"

"You need to get over here ASAP. I just hit pay dirt and I'll tell you, I think Conrad's holding back," Dan Sorenson said.

In the background, Carvelli heard Conrad yell, "No, I'm not!"

"I'll be along in a few minutes."

FORTY-NINE

"So, what do you have?" Carvelli asked Sorenson.

Carvelli, Sorenson, Franklin Washington and Conrad were in Conrad's kitchen. Conrad had a small two-bedroom he had converted into a one bedroom with a large office out of the second bedroom, a few blocks south of Lake and Thirty-Fourth. The four of them were sipping a beer, taking a break.

"A very interesting conversation between the dearly departed Reverend Ferguson and the City's newest community organizer slash choirboy," Sorenson said.

"Damone Watson?" Carvelli asked. "What about?"

"Church contributions," Franklin quickly said with a laugh.

"Yeah, that's it," Sorenson said. "Ferguson is hitting him up for church contributions."

Realizing they were being sarcastic, Carvelli joined. "Yeah. That's nice. How much did the good Rev get out of him?"

"Not much. We're all set up for you to listen in," Sorenson replied.

"Why don't we have video? I know damn well I was being filmed when I was there. That's why he insisted I sit in a particular chair. Then when I didn't, he didn't look pleased," Carvelli said, addressing Conrad.

"I didn't set it up to get the video, just the audio," Conrad said with a suspicious look that Carvelli noticed.

"Except?" Carvelli asked him while staring into his eyes.

"Ah, no, I…"

"Conrad, you're the worst poker player on the planet," Carvelli said.

"Why haven't we invited him to a game with us?" Sorenson asked.

"Okay, okay, I, ah, thought you wanted the stuff in order. Sure, I have some video," Conrad said.

"How much?" Carvelli asked.

"Actually, a lot. A couple hundred hours' worth. But most of it is nothing," he quickly added. "Although there is a lot about him and his drug business. And, ah, other things. Women and such."

"You have his bedroom wired, don't you?" Sorenson asked.

"Yeah," Conrad reluctantly admitted. "And his private apartment, his office and just about anywhere he could meet with people.

"Hey! This guy's a crook. I needed some leverage…"

278

"Do you know what he would do to you if he knew?" Franklin asked. "Boy, you'd end up fish shit in Lake Mille Lacs."

"Let's go listen to what you found," Carvelli said.

All four of them went upstairs to Conrad's workshop. His recording equipment was all set up to play what Carvelli was there to hear.

"Come in, Reverend," they heard a voice, that Conrad identified as Damone, say.

"Thank you for coming. I've wanted an opportunity to meet you since moving to this fair city. You're a legend in the community and-"

"Don't give me your shuck and jive bullshit, boy," they heard a black man's voice interrupt Damone rather abruptly. Conrad identified the voice as Lionel Ferguson.

"I know who and what you are, so what do you say we cut to the chase and get down to business?"

There was a pause of several seconds before they heard Damone calmly reply. "I, ah, I don't understand. I'm not sure what you mean."

"Get him out of here," they heard Ferguson say. A moment later they heard the conference room door open and close as someone left.

"Who?" Carvelli asked.

"Don't know," Conrad replied. "One of Damone's guys. Lewis or Monroe."

After the door closed, Ferguson spoke again. "You're a drug dealer and a gangster."

There was a short pause, then Ferguson spoke again. "Don't bullshit me, boy. You think I was born yesterday?"

"I talked to the two girls; Karenna Hines and her friend, Shelly Cornelius." This was the next thing that Damone said.

"Stop it," Sorenson said to Conrad referring to the playback.

"Who are they?" Carvelli asked.

"You remember the cop shooting of that drugged out gang banger, Mikal Tate?" Sorenson asked.

Carvelli paused for a moment and then remembered. "The guy who beat up his girlfriend, a couple of EMT's got the gun away from one of the patrol guys whose partner then shot and killed him? Yeah, I got it. So, who are the girls?"

"Karenna Hines was the girlfriend Tate beat on a regular basis," Franklin told him. "Shelly Cornelius was a neighbor friend of Karenna's. Ferguson got a hold of them and convinced them there would be money from a lawsuit for them if they just got their story straight. Ferguson dragged them out in front of an angry mob on the steps of City Hall. They lied and changed their story to make it sound like Tate was a model of the community gunned down by racist cops for no reason."

"I remember that. I remember when they found out the two of them couldn't cash in on this because they weren't related to Tate, they went back to their original story and the cops were cleared," Carvelli said.

"That's them," Franklin said. "It really hurts my heart when black hustlers like Ferguson try to exploit black people like that."

"Start it again, Conrad," Sorenson said.

Instead, Carvelli said, "Go back, I want to hear that again, what Damone just said."

"Okay," Conrad agreed.

"I talked to the two girls, Karenna Hines and Shelly Cornelius," they heard Damone say again.

"I know you did. Did you think I wouldn't find out? Do you think I give a fuck?"

"Such language from a man of the cloth," they heard Damone quietly, casually respond. "That collar you wear is a nice prop. I want you to stop this nonsense. You know those two cops are innocent."

"So, what?" Ferguson bellowed. "It makes the point that needs to be made. White cops gunning down young black men is epidemic in this country."

They heard Damone heartily laugh before speaking. "We both know that's not true. No, you're just exploiting a tragedy for your own purposes. How much money have you taken in from contributions? Enough for that new Mercedes?"

"This is absurd coming from a drug-dealing gangster. All right, gangster-boy. You want to shut it down. Why?"

"Because it's not true and what the community needs are good relations with the police."

That statement, coming from Damone, made the three ex-cops look at each other with mildly astonished expressions.

Ferguson was laughing for quite a while before saying, "Not good for the community? Oh shit, boy. That's rich."

There was another pause and they heard Ferguson take two or three deep breaths.

"Okay," Ferguson finally continued. "I want a hundred, no, make that one twenty, every month. I'll get you the bank account information.

Oh, and I'll take that new Mercedes. Make it a nice S-Class Sedan. Black. I'll look good in it."

"Where do you propose I get that kind of money? Even I don't have a car like that."

They heard a chair being pushed away from the table, then Ferguson's voice again.

"If you want to stay in my city and if you want calm in my city, that's the price. And I'll want an answer, the car and the first payment in two days."

They heard the room's door open again and someone come in.

"Thank you for coming by. Have a pleasant day, Reverend. Lewis will show you out."

"Stop it," Carvelli said to Conrad. "Well," he continued, "there it is. Ferguson was eliciting bribes, or more accurately extortion, from Damone Watson.

"But what do we do with this?" Carvelli asked. "Can it be used in court for Rob Danes case?"

"There's more coming up," Sorenson said. "I gotta pee. Let's take a quick break and we'll get to it."

When they resumed, Conrad told Carvelli, "You're going to hear a phone call between Damone and his brother, Jeron. He runs the family business in Chicago."

"Okay."

"But, because Damone is smart, he only talks on burner phones and he gets a new one every day. I can only record Damone's end of the conversation."

"You'll understand what they're talking about," Sorenson said.

"Okay, start it up," Carvelli said.

The next sound they heard was the door opening after Ferguson had been escorted out.

"You know, maybe we can use this trouble the good reverend has created for our purposes," they heard Damone say and then continue. "Monroe, give Jeron a call and get him on the phone for me or have him call me as soon as possible. Do you have a new phone for me?"

"Yes, Boss," they heard Monroe say.

The audio went silent for a few seconds, during which they assumed Monroe gave Damone the new phone.

"You want me to give him that number?" Monroe asked.

"Yes, do that and tell him it's urgent and thank you," Damone said.

"You asked me to remind you about the accountant," they heard Lewis tell Damone.

"Yes, I remember. He'll be here in forty minutes. What does he want?" Damone said.

"He wants to talk to you about supply."

"Okay. Jeron?" Damone said, apparently answering his phone.

Conrad shut off the player for a moment and looked at Carvelli.

"This is where the conversation between Damone and his brother begins."

"Okay," Carvelli acknowledged.

Conrad started the player again.

"Give me a minute," Damone said. "I need to take this in my office. Shut off the recording equipment in there."

They heard Damone get up and leave, then Carvelli said, "Wait a minute. He ordered his guys to shut off the recording equipment where he's going. In his office. Did you get the rest of this?"

"Um, yeah," Conrad said. "They don't know about all of the equipment. I'm the guy who sweeps for it."

"You are playing with a rattlesnake wrapped around your neck," Carvelli said.

"I know. That's why I'm with you guys. I gotta get out."

"Turn it back on," Carvelli said.

"How are things?" Damone asked.

Silence while Jeron replies.

"Your numbers are fine. We knew Chicago would be difficult."

Another break while Jeron spoke.

Damone again. "We knew that when we set out. Keep your eye on the ball. Remember what our goal is and why we are doing this."

"Stop it for a second," Carvelli told Conrad.

"What is he referring to? Our goals and why we are doing this? Any guesses? Conrad, have you heard anything about specific goals or plans?"

"No, uh, uh," Conrad replied.

"Interesting. Usually, that's just money. What else do these guys have in mind? Keep that in mind while we're going through this stuff. Listen for a goal they may have."

"Tony, we need a couple more guys," Sorenson said.

"I know. Go ahead and get them. Okay, Conrad, start it."

"I have a delicate job. I need a professional—not some street thug who's going to spray the streets with bullets. I need a surgeon. Not a fool. Do you know anyone like that?" Damone said.

"You don't know who he is?" Damone asked, after a brief silence.

"He got a positive response," Carvelli excitedly said.

"Wait," Sorenson said.

"And is he good?" Damone asked.

Again, Jeron must have answered affirmatively.

"This sounds exactly like what I need. Find out what you can. How do we get in touch with him? Find out everything you can," Damone replied.

Silence.

"As soon as possible. There is too much trouble and protesting on the streets here."

Silence.

"It's not important for you to know. At least not over the phone. Do what you can to get this man for me."

Silence.

"Good. Call back today."

Conrad shut the player off. The four men had been listening so intently, they all needed a moment to stand up and stretch.

"Let's get a beer," Carvelli said.

"I have a transcript of that for you," Conrad said. "I knew you'd want it."

"Good. You're right, I do."

In the kitchen, each of the men retrieved a bottle of Michelob from the refrigerator, then found a place to stand or sit. Carvelli was in the breakfast nook with Dan Sorenson. The transcript of Conrad's recording was lying on the table top. Franklin and Conrad were leaning against the sink counter.

"There's your pro," Sorenson says.

"Is there more, Conrad? Is there more of Watson talking about him as if he showed up?"

"I don't know, I haven't had time to go through all of it," Conrad said.

"Tell you what," Sorenson said. "Why don't we skip ahead to the day of the event. Listen to everything a few days before, during and after. They are bound to have said something."

"Good idea."

"Now what?" Franklin asked.

"I'll take this transcript to Marc and see what he thinks," Carvelli said.

"There's more," Sorenson said.

"God, I hate this," Franklin said.

"What?" Carvelli asked.

"You know who Jalen Bryant is, the councilman?" Sorenson asked Carvelli.

"Sure. He seems like a good guy. At least for a Democrat," Carvelli said.

"What's that about?" Conrad asked.

"Cops don't vote for Democrats," Sorenson said. "Anyway, we got him on audio soliciting a bribe from Damone."

"Ah, man, are you kidding? I like this guy, Bryant. Hell, he could be a Republican he's so much on the side of cops," Carvelli said. "What happened?"

"Damone's guys stripped him naked looking for a wire. Bryant hit him up for the money, then Damone threw him out. Didn't bite," Franklin said.

"You think Bryant might be the leak in the city council?" Sorenson asked.

"No, I don't think so. Doesn't seem the type. Too acrimonious. Do you think he might've been setting Damone up?" Carvelli asked.

"It doesn't sound right," Franklin agreed. "He's never had one bit of trouble. Now, totally out of the blue, he hits up the number one gangster this side of Chicago for a million bucks? Just doesn't sound right," he repeated.

The kitchen went silent while they thought this over and sipped their beer.

"It's been a long day," Carvelli said. "And I'm not getting any younger."

He stood up, picked up and folded the transcript, put it in his coat pocket and said, "Time to get some sleep. Conrad, make a couple CDs for me of the stuff we listened to tonight. I'll pick them up some time tomorrow."

"Will do," Conrad agreed. "Um, ah, I got a question. I don't mean to sound greedy and I really enjoy working with you guys to shut down a good customer but…"

"I'll get you paid," Carvelli said. "More people," he said to Sorenson.

"I got a couple people, including Sherry Bowen, coming by in the morning," Sorenson said.

"Sherry's a good gal," Franklin said. "I know she can use any extra money she can make. Any work you can throw her way…"

"I'll do it," Carvelli said. "Get her driving for Jake."

"She is," Sorenson said.

"I'll tell Maddy, too. She can use some help from time to time. I'll see you guys tomorrow."

FIFTY

Carvelli stepped off the elevator on the seventeenth floor of the Hennepin County Government Center and turned left. It was a few minutes past 10:00 A.M. Before leaving the house this morning, he had completed, what was for him, a difficult task.

The first thing he had done was to call Paxton O'Rourke in Chicago. He had dialed her personal phone to avoid any monitoring. They talked for at least a half-hour. At first, Carvelli brought her up-to-date on his undercover. That took maybe five minutes. The rest was the two of them chatting like a couple of teenagers.

The difficult task came next. Tony, not the most tech-savvy guy, had to figure out how to scan the transcript into his computer. After fifteen minutes and no luck, he called Paxton back.

Holding back her laughter, she tried to explain to him how to take pictures of the document with his phone and send it that way. While she explained this, an idea came to him.

"Tell you what," he said. "I'm gonna see Maddy in a little while. How about I have her do it."

When Paxton finished laughing, she agreed that would work best.

Carvelli quickly found Courtroom 1745, the one with two sheriff's deputies guarding the door. Fortunately, Carvelli knew both of them. They were both ex-MPD cops now working as county deputies, double-dipping their pensions.

"Well, if it isn't Sam Spade, private eye," one of them said as Carvelli approached.

"Ha, ha, ha," Carvelli replied using an extremely fake laugh. "Whew. That's pretty funny, Johnson. Did you come up with that all by yourself? I always wondered why you didn't go into comedy. Do standup.

"Hey, Stu," Carvelli said to greet the other one who was suppressing a laugh.

"What do you want?" the now annoyed Deputy Johnson asked.

"Ooo. Testy. You can dish it out but not so good at taking it. Relax. I was just tossing it back at you," Carvelli said.

"Okay, fine," Johnson said trying to sound more conciliatory. "What do you want?" he asked again.

"I need to go in," Carvelli said.

"I don't know. I'm not sure the judge wants the interruption," Johnson said.

"Stu, you know who Maddy Rivers is?" Carvelli asked.

"Oh, yeah," Stu replied, wiggling his eyebrows.

"Get her for me, will you please?"

"You bet. I'll be right back."

Less than a minute later, Stu brought Maddy into the hallway.

"What?" she asked.

"I need to see Marc and I'm afraid I've annoyed Deputy Johnson here. He won't let me in," Carvelli said.

"Oh, stop it, Jamie," Maddy said in a flirtatious voice, then lightly slapped him on the shoulder. "Let him in. He's with me."

"You should've said that in the first place," Johnson said.

"I didn't want to ruin your fun."

While Maddy led him up the center aisle toward the gate, Judge Tennant looked at him, smiled and wiggled her fingers at him.

There was a young woman sitting by herself in the jury box. Jennifer Moore was politely asking her questions when she let it slip that she could not sleep for several days following the death of Reverend Ferguson. Up to that point, she had seemed acceptable.

Maddy and Tony took chairs behind Marc when the young woman admitted this. Marc and Arturo both started to rise when Judge Tennant held up a hand to stop them.

"I'm sorry, Ms. Adams. Why couldn't you sleep for several days after the death of Reverend Ferguson?" Tennant asked.

"I was just so upset that someone could do such a horrible thing," she replied.

"Thank you for your candor," Tennant told the prospective juror. "You're excused."

"What? Why? I can be fair…"

"I'm sorry, you're excused. The deputy will show you out."

As the deputy led the dejected woman out, Tennant asked, "Time for a break?"

"Yes, your Honor," both tables replied.

Marc wheeled his chair around to face Carvelli and Maddy. Rob asked one of the deputies to escort him to a restroom. Arturo was due to question the next venireman, so he was preparing for that.

287

"That was close," Marc whispered, referring to the young woman who had been excused by Tennant. "We had her listed somewhere between acceptable and maybe. She would have probably been accepted."

"You think she said it on purpose to get kicked loose?" Carvelli asked.

"I doubt it," Marc said. "Besides, she'll find out it didn't work. They'll take her back to the jury pool and reassign her. So, what's up?"

"Come out in the hall," Carvelli said.

While Arturo stayed at the table, Marc and Maddy followed Carvelli out. There were several people lingering in the hall, so Carvelli went onto the bridge connecting the two sides of the building. He stopped halfway across and handed Marc the copy of the transcript.

With Maddy reading over his shoulder, the two of them read through the recorded conversation. When they finished, Marc gave it back to Carvelli.

"What can we do with it?" Maddy asked.

"At this point, nothing," Marc replied.

"Can't you take it to Steve?" Maddy asked.

"And say what? It's not really proof of anything. We know what it likely means, but what does this have to do with Ferguson's killing? Is this enough for motive? Probably, but we have no way of getting it into evidence."

"But we do know who did this," Carvelli said.

"We think we do," Marc said. "I think we have it but presenting it in court with what we have is barely speculation. We're pointing the finger at someone else for a murder with inadmissible evidence."

"Wait a minute. How did you get this?" Marc asked.

"Conrad," Carvelli said. "Conrad Hilton. Didn't I tell you? He's the guy who set up Damone Watson's recording equipment inside his office and apartment. I got some of the guys going through it now.

"I wasn't looking for your case. I was looking for evidence of the drug business. We came across this by dumb luck. Dan Sorenson heard it and knew it was significant. Now, we're looking for both.

"I told you, I'm working with the Feds on this, didn't I?"

"Yeah, you did. You should give this to Paxton," Marc said.

"Oh, man," Carvelli said as he lightly slapped himself on the forehead. "Thanks for the reminder." He looked at Maddy and said, "I need a favor. Can you use my phone, take a picture of this transcript and email it to her?"

288

"Why can't you?" Maddy asked, knowing the answer was tech deficiency.

"Are you gonna squeeze my shoes or do me a favor?"

"Give it to me," Maddy laughed.

"Use her Gmail address. That's her personal one," Carvelli said.

"I should get back in there," Marc said. "Where are you off to?"

"To see my Feebs and give them what I have," Carvelli replied.

"Is that a good idea?" Marc asked.

"I don't know. I've been kicking the idea around and I'm not sure."

"Hold off for a couple of days. In fact, I'm going to keep this to just us for now. I won't tell Rob or his cop pals or even Arturo. Not until we come up with more to connect it together."

"Could Conrad testify? He's not working for law enforcement," Carvelli asked.

"That might work, but it's still too tenuous. Plus, putting Conrad on a witness stand doesn't fill me with a warm, fuzzy, happy glow."

Maddy came back and handed Carvelli his phone and the transcript.

"It might be fun to watch," Carvelli said. "Thanks," he told Maddy. "I'll see you later."

By noon of the second day, they had finished with the first batch of fifteen potential jurors. They had selected two of that group yesterday, none so far today. Marc had used three peremptories and Steve Gondeck one. Margaret Tennant was being very careful. Of the thirteen excused for cause, she had excused ten of them herself. Apparently, the media and community scrutiny of the trial was bringing out the caution in her.

Following the afternoon break, they started in again. Oddly, after scoring only two of the first fifteen, they accepted three of the next four. Believing they might be on a roll, Judge Tennant pushed them until 6:00 P.M. and they managed to get one more. Six were selected in the first two days of a highly publicized homicide case; a very good start and a happy judge.

Unfortunately, it would be three days, Friday afternoon, before number seven was selected. It would be almost another week before all twelve, plus six alternates were selected, sworn and instructed regarding the media, the public and communication with each other.

A rumor had gotten to them that they were to be sequestered. When Judge Tennant kicked them loose for three days, the relief on their faces was palpable.

"Opening statements Monday morning, nine A.M.," Judge Tennant told the lawyers. "Have a good weekend."

FIFTY-ONE

"She'll be with you in a minute," Lois, Judge Tennant's clerk told the lawyers. All four were standing in the back hallway where the judges' chambers were located. It was Monday morning, the first day of trial and Marc wanted to make one final request.

"You can come in now," Lois said from her desk through the door.

"Go in," she said to Marc. "You know the way," she added with a grin.

"Good morning, your Honor," Marc said as he led the others into her chambers.

"Have a seat," she said. "What's up?"

"Your Honor," Marc began when everyone was seated. "I want to make one more request that Mr. Gondeck not be allowed to use racism as a motive. He has one cop who claims he heard the defendant…"

"And you have a half-dozen who say they didn't hear it," Gondeck said.

"Come on, Steve, we both…"

"Address the court, Mr. Kadella," Tennant said.

"Yes, your Honor. As I was saying, we all know that once that word is spoken, it will hang over this trial like the sword of Damocles. There will be people on that jury who won't wait, won't keep an open mind. Racism. Case closed. Get a rope."

"Marc, the last time we were here on this issue, I weighed it for three days. Believe me, I thought of little else," Tennant said as she leaned on her desk, her hands folded together. "The state has a right to bring this in for motive. It's prejudicial, but it's also probative.

"You're a good lawyer. Don't sell this jury short. You are capable of rebutting it. Do you want to put this on the record again?"

"No, your Honor," Marc said. "But I will object before Officer Schilling testifies. For the record."

"That's fine," Tennant said. "Mr. Gondeck, anything else?"

"Nothing from me, your Honor."

"We ready to go?"

"Yes, your Honor," both sides said.

"You still planning on giving your opening today?" Tennant asked, looking at Marc.

"Yes, your Honor," Marc said.

"Okay, let's have at it."

It was ten o'clock by the time Gondeck began his opening statement.

"Ladies and gentlemen," he began. "My name is Steve Gondeck and my associate is Jennifer Moore. We are lawyers for the people of Minnesota. It is our job to present the evidence against the defendant for the callous murder of a minister, a religious icon in the community, Reverend Lionel Ferguson."

The opening statement is not supposed to be an argument for or against a guilty verdict. That is what the closing argument is for. There had been a pretrial argument about what to call Ferguson. Marc wanted him referred to as the deceased or, at most, Mr. Ferguson. Gondeck wanted him as close to deified as possible, second only to Jesus himself. Tennant ruled they use Reverend Ferguson. But Gondeck referring to him a religious icon of the community is an example of Gondeck going too far. It almost brought Marc out of his seat. He let it go after exchanging looks with the judge.

Gondeck knew he had pushed the envelope a little too far and had gotten away with it. Not wanting to press his luck and be chastised this early in the trial, he scaled it back.

He carefully, completely walked the jury through his case. He told them, in order, what happened, who did it and would be told why. He assured them they would hear from witnesses who would testify to each and every element of the case.

"At the end of the trial, a trial that is not really in dispute, I believe you will find the defendant, Robert Dane, guilty of the crimes charged. There is no doubt, Robert Dane is the one who pulled his service gun and fired three bullets into the heart and lung of Reverend Ferguson that caused his death."

It was only a few minutes past eleven when Gondeck finished. Judge Tennant called the lawyers up to the bench and turned on the white noise device, so they would not be overheard.

"How long, Marc?" she asked.

"Less than his," Marc replied.

"Okay. Let's take a break, then you can do yours and then lunch," Tennant said. She looked at Gondeck and said, "Have your first witness ready at two."

"Yes, your Honor."

Fifteen minutes later, after the break, while the gallery was still filling, Judge Tennant addressed the crowd.

"I understand that this case has generated a lot of attention. Let me be clear about something. I am a very punctual judge. When I say the break will be fifteen minutes, I mean fifteen minutes—not sixteen. From now on, if you are not in your seat at whatever time I say, you will be kept out. I am not waiting for the media or spectators and I will not allow disruptions.

"Mr. Kadella, are you ready to proceed?"

Marc stood and said, "Yes, your Honor."

"You may proceed."

Marc walked out in front of the jury box and began. He started by thanking them and introducing himself, Arturo and Rob Dane. He introduced Rob as Officer Robert Dane of the Minneapolis Police which almost drew an objection. He also introduced Maddy Rivers.

"Seated behind the defense table is our investigator, Madeline Rivers," Marc said while extending his left hand toward her. Maddy stood and when she did, Marc watched the looks on the faces of the male jurors. Several of them smiled and leaned forward.

"Normally, I would not introduce her, but her name will come out during the course of the trial. Also, it's obvious she is sitting there so I thought you should know who she is. To put a face to the name, so to speak."

Maddy sat down and Marc continued.

"Mr. Gondeck is a skilled trial lawyer, as is Ms. Moore. I know they will put on a very well prepared and convincing case.

"Each and every one of you during jury selection gave your word, your solemn oath, to this court, to the people of Minnesota and," here Marc paused for several seconds and looked in the eyes of every juror before continuing, "more importantly," he said, barely above a whisper, "to each and every one of you and to yourselves."

He stepped back, looked them over again and said, "And that oath was to keep an open mind, to wait until all of the witnesses have been heard, the evidence presented and to follow the law as given by the judge before you make a decision."

He paused again, folded his hands together, sighed and said, "Mr. Gondeck is absolutely correct. There is no point in denying it. I'm not going to insult you by trying to con you with some nonsensical claim that some other dude did it.

"Officer Robert Dane, during a street protest in downtown Minneapolis, drew his service sidearm and fired three bullets into the chest of Lionel Ferguson. And, there is no disputing the medical evidence, that is what killed Ferguson.

"Mr. Gondeck told you that he would present you with the motive for why Officer Dane did this. But he didn't tell you what he will claim that motive is. And the reason he didn't tell you?"

"Objection, your Honor. Counsel is speculating as to what the state's case will be…"

"Overruled. If he is telling the jury something that isn't true, I'm sure you will point that out.

"You may continue, Mr. Kadella."

"As I was saying, the reason he didn't tell you is he wants to use it for its shock value. To surprise you with it."

Marc paused and paced a little first, looking at Gondeck, then back to the jury.

"I know what it is and I'm going to just put it out there. You might as well know. He's going to claim that Officer Dane was, as were all of the other police monitoring the protest, getting tired of it. This was the fourth day and they were tired of being screamed at, cursed and spat upon. And Officer Dane's racism boiled over and he decided to kill the man responsible for it.

"There it is," Marc said. "They will claim racism is why he did it. Well, ladies and gentlemen, it simply isn't true. I brought it out so you would know what's coming and to remind you of your oath. Your oath is to wait until you have heard from both sides. Wait until you have heard all of the witnesses, seen all of the evidence, been given the law by the judge.

"If you do that, if you do what you promised, what you said you would do, what you swore a solemn oath to do, you will come back with a verdict of not guilty. I believe that because the defense will present witnesses to refute it, including the defendant, who will tell you what really happened. That's right, ladies and gentlemen, you are going to hear from the defendant and he will tell you what actually happened. Why he shot and killed Lionel Ferguson.

"While we are taking you through this trial keep something else in mind. Officer Dane is a duly licensed police officer and a member of the Minneapolis Police Department. As such, there are times when a police officer is legally justified in using deadly force. You will hear testimony that this was one of those times."

"What do you think?" Marc asked his tablemates while the courtroom was emptying.

"I think you were right to tell them Rob will testify," Maddy said. "No matter what they hear, they will have it in their heads that he is going to take the stand and give his side of it."

"I think that will at least keep most of them from making up their minds. They will want to hear from him," Arturo agreed.

Marc looked at Rob who said, "I'm ready. I'll take the stand today, right now."

"Easy, tiger," Marc said. "Just maintain your cool during the trial."

FIFTY-TWO

"Sergeant Coffey," Gondeck began with the first witness sworn and seated. Sgt. Brent Coffey was one of the first three police officers to reach the scene of the shooting. Being the senior officer, he took charge and tried to secure the area.

Gondeck led him through his early testimony, mostly about himself, his years as a police officer—eighteen—his awards and promotions. Forty-year-old Coffey was a veteran who had testified many times. His answers were a little too practiced, but these were credibility questions. As an eighteen-year veteran, jurors tended to believe him anyway.

"If you secured the crime scene, how did a Star Tribune reporter walk past you to take pictures?"

"That was a lapse, a mistake on my part, and I took responsibility for it. Not to make excuses, but the area was still in a state of bedlam. There were people running everywhere."

"What did you find when you first arrived?"

Coffey explained finding Ferguson lying in the street and Rob Dane about ten feet away holding his pistol skyward. He checked Ferguson for a pulse while one of the other officers called it in to dispatch. Technically, this would be hearsay, but Marc let it go. The next witness was likely the officer who called it in and could testify to it anyway.

"I didn't find a pulse on Reverend Ferguson and he appeared to be dead already. I then took Officer Dane's sidearm. By then, there were a few more officers at the scene.

"Rob, I mean Officer Dane, was saying over and over that Ferguson had a gun. I assigned an officer to stay with him and told the others to search the area for a gun."

"Did you find one? Did anyone find a gun?" Gondeck asked.

"No, not to my knowledge, no."

"How thoroughly did they search?"

Coffey sighed a bit and stole a quick, sympathetic glance at Rob.

"Quite thoroughly, I would say. We, I mean the police officers, searched at least a ten square block area of downtown. By then it could have been anywhere," he blurted out.

"Sergeant," Gondeck politely said, "I understand that you feel sympathy for a fellow officer. But please don't embellish your answers."

For the next ten minutes, he explained to the jury what he did after securing Rob's gun. By then, the EMTs had arrived and the MPD detectives were right behind them. Coffey turned Rob's gun over to the detectives.

Before he finished, Gondeck used this opportunity to get the gun into evidence through Coffey.

"Sergeant Coffey," Marc began after a short break, "do you recognize this man?"

Arturo was handling the laptop to put visuals up on the monitors as soon as Marc finished the question.

"Objection, your Honor," Gondeck stood and said. "Goes beyond the scope of direct."

"May we approach, your Honor?" Marc quickly asked.

She signaled them forward and turned on the white noise machine.

"Judge, all I'm asking is if he has seen this man. I believe he has. Now, if you sustain his objection, I will subpoena this witness and most of the others to come back and do it later. Or, we can go through it now and save everybody the time and trouble."

"Who is he?" Gondeck asked.

"A protester who we believe is central to this case. That's all I can say for now. Before we're through, everyone will know," Marc said.

"And if he doesn't make a connection, I'm sure you'll let the jury know about it," Tennant said to Gondeck. "You want to withdraw the objection or have me overrule it?"

"Overrule it," Gondeck said.

When everyone was back at their tables, Tennant said, "The objection is overruled subject to later connection." A small victory for the prosecution. "You will answer the question, Sergeant."

"Yes, in fact, I have seen him."

"Where?"

"In the protest march. I distinctly remember him because he looked out of place. He looked strange."

"How so?"

"A white, homeless man marching around downtown. He sort of stood out."

"Do you recall how many times you saw him? How many days he was with the marchers?"

"I think he was there every day, but I can't say absolutely. I know I saw him at least a couple of times."

"Where was he when you saw him?"

"I'm not sure what you mean," Coffey replied.

"Isn't it true that he was marching in close proximity to Reverend Ferguson? In fact, right behind him?"

Coffey looked off toward the back door as if thinking. After a brief moment he said, "Now that you mention it, yes, he was."

"Were you on crowd control for all four days of this particular protest?" Marc asked.

"Yes, I was. As a sergeant, I was not assigned a specific location. I roamed around."

"Where were you when the shooting occurred?"

"I was across Sixth about a half a block west, on the other side of Nicollet."

"Did you see the shooting?"

"No, I did not."

"How long have you known Officer Dane?"

"Oh, I don't know. At least six or seven years. Since he was a rookie."

"Have you ever known him to do or say anything of a racist nature?"

This was a very risky question. Marc had no idea how the witness would answer. He hoped to get the reply he wanted and was counting on what his client told him about his own behavior. Something clients lie about all the time.

"No, not that I recall, no."

Gondeck could not let that last question and answer go. He had to at least punch a little hole in it on redirect.

"Sergeant Coffey, explain to us how well you personally know Officer Dane."

Having been over this very thoroughly in their preparation, Gondeck was well aware of the answer.

"I'm not sure what you mean?"

"Well, are you his supervisor?"

"No, not directly."

"Ever been his partner?"

"No."

"Made an arrest with him?"

"I'm sure we've been at crime scenes before…"

"With other officers?"

"Yeah, that would be true."

"Your Honor, he's leading the witness. Objection to this entire testimony."

"Overruled," Tennant said. "The questions are not suggestive of the answers."

"Ever been out for a beer with just him?"

"No, not that I recall."

"Ever been bowling or any other activity?"

"No, I don't think so."

"Sergeant Coffey, do you really know what's in this man's heart concerning racism and his attitude toward African Americans?"

"Well, I've never…um, I guess maybe not," Coffey said with his eyes downcast.

"Mr. Kadella," Judge Tennant said.

Marc asked one question on recross.

"Sergeant Coffey, have you ever personally heard or seen anything said or done by Officer Dane of a racist nature?"

"No," Coffey said emphatically.

The rest of the afternoon was taken up by the other two officers who reached the scene first. Since their participation in events was minimal, the direct examination did not take long. Their testimony was brought in to back up what Sergeant Coffey had said.

Marc's cross was basically the same as Coffey's. The photo of the homeless man was put up and both admitted seeing him. They also admitted they saw him near Ferguson and believed it was every day. Neither had ever seen or heard Rob say or do anything of a racist nature. Although both admitted they did not know him well.

While the courtroom was emptying, Maddy pushed her chair up to Marc.

"I thought you would ask these guys if it was possible the homeless guy picked up the gun and ran off."

"Good catch," he told her. "I decided not to. They were too far away, and anything is possible."

An hour later Damone was in the Tahoe with Lewis and Monroe. They were on their way to a meeting with Imam Sadia and some others. Monroe took a call on his phone and gave the caller the number for today's burner phone. A moment later that phone rang while Damone was holding the phone waiting for the call.

"It's the man in court," Monroe said.

"Yes," Damone answered by saying.

"Nothing unusual happened today," the caller said.

"I know, I was able to watch most of the afternoon session," Damone replied. "This Kadella, he seems to know his business."

"He is solid. He prepares well and has a plan to create reasonable doubt. It remains to be seen if he can pull it off."

"Who is this homeless man? The one he put up on the TV?"

"Don't know yet. I don't know if he has come up with a name for him. I think he would have used it today if he knew."

"Keep me informed," Damone said, then ended the call.

Five minutes after the phone call, Lewis parked in the side driveway of a safe house. They were approximately a mile North of Cedar/Riverside on the fringe of Little Mogadishu.

Waiting in the dark by the back door was Damone's man, Saadaq. Damone and Saadaq greeted each other with the traditional Muslim greeting.

"He's not here. One of his lackey dogs is here with an excuse. I think he knows we are onto his deceit and theft," Saadaq said.

Damone shifted his omnipresent Bible from under his right arm to his left without speaking.

"The recruiter is here," Saadaq said, referring to the man in the gray suit and wrap around Ray Bans. "They have three more recruits and are waiting for your permission."

"Do you know them? These three recruits?"

Saadaq frowned, shrugged and said, "Mere boys. Still teens. Ready to die but nothing to us."

"Not involved in our business?"

"No, Boss," Saadaq said.

"Well, let's at least say hello to our Middle Eastern guest."

The house was a large pre-war that from the outside looked to have fallen on hard times. However, the inside was fully remodeled. Except,

300

it was not remodeled for luxury. It was remodeled for efficiency. Especially the large basement.

Saadaq led the three men downstairs and found five people waiting for them. Two, including the man with the wraparounds, were the jihadi recruiters working America, especially Minneapolis, for fresh meat.

"As-salamu 'alaykum," Damone greeted both of the recruiters.

In turn, they both replied, "Wa'alaykum as-aslam."

The three recruits were sitting against a wall in uncomfortable folding metal chairs. Damone looked at the three young men.

"Are you truly ready to die for Allah?" he asked.

All three jumped up and eagerly replied.

"You are not going to a soft American Boy Scout camp. You will be put through the most difficult training possible. You will be harder than any ten U.S. Marines. Do you understand?"

All three yelled, "Yes!"

"You will be shot like a dog if you fail and there will be no place in Paradise for you. Do you agree?"

Again, "Yes!"

Damone shook the hand of each of them and wished them luck. He gave his blessing to the two recruiters and turned to leave. It was then he saw the Imam's servant at the bottom of the stairs.

Fighting the urge to simply shoot this dog, Damone walked to him and quietly, politely said, "I need to see the Imam himself. Please be so kind as to pass it on to him. Go in peace," he said in English.

FIFTY-THREE

The second day started with a series of witnesses who had been holding the Black Lives Matter banner. Franklin Washington had tried to interview them, but with no luck. There were six in total listed on Gondeck's witness list and none of them cooperated.

The first three took less than an hour to testify. Each of them had the same testimony; not just similar, but exactly the same. It was so obviously memorized that they were almost reading off of the same script.

The only germane point each of them made was the immediate aftermath of the shooting. Each of them testified that the moment they heard the shots they turned and saw Ferguson on the ground and the white cop standing over him. None of them saw a gun; none of them saw a homeless man running away, but they all saw a hateful, angry look on the defendant's face.

Marc barely bothered to cross-examine them. He asked the same two questions.

"Bearing in mind that I can find out if you're telling the truth, did you call the police and volunteer to testify today?"

Each of them reluctantly admitted they did.

"Have you ever volunteered to be a witness for the police before?"

Again, all three reluctantly admitted they had not.

The third one finished and was excused. Judge Tennant called for a short, ten-minute break.

"I'll see counsel in chambers."

Before the lawyers even had a chance to find chairs, Tennant turned on Steve Gondeck.

"Mr. Gondeck," she began, not even trying to hide her annoyance, "how many more of these witnesses do you have?"

These were Jennifer Moore's witnesses so Gondeck took the cowardly way out and looked at her.

"Three, your Honor. They came forward but…"

"Not in my courtroom," Tennant said.

"I prepared them, but we did not see this coming. I know, they looked ridiculous," Moore said.

"They made you look ridiculous," Tennant more calmly replied.

"Jermaine Fontana is in the hall telling the others we won't be calling them," Gondeck said.

"That's too bad," Marc said. "I was looking forward to a few more of them testifying." Jermaine Fontana was a supervising investigator with the county attorney's office. She is also the one who will testify and the one allowed to sit at the rail behind the prosecutor. She's an excellent investigator and it is no coincidence that she is also an African American woman.

The rest of the day was taken up by two technical witnesses. The first was Sergeant Leo Cohn of the Minneapolis Crime Scene Unit. Sgt. Cohn is one of those rare people who, by luck or chance or alignment of the moon, planets and stars, fell into the job he was made for. In reality, it was none of these things. Leo Cohn had secretly grown up wanting to be a crime scene investigator. Along the way, he had earned a master's degree in criminology.

Normally, anyone with that level of interest, education and ability would be with the FBI. Unfortunately, Leo had a flaw. Life had paid a cruel trick on him and left him with a mild stutter that could turn serious on a witness stand, especially under cross-examination. To fight it and overcome it, Leo liked to testify.

Meticulous as ever, despite the insignificance of it for this trial, Leo had made, to scale, a four by six-foot poster board of the crime scene.

Leo spent the entire remaining part of the morning session explaining to the jury where everyone was and what happened. He had a re-creation of the Black Lives Matter banner and protestors who held it. To the best of his ability, he had placed images of all the people within fifty yards of Ferguson's dead body. By the time he finished, everyone in the courtroom had a bird's eye view of the scene.

"How did you come up with this?" Jennifer Moore asked.

"I, I, ah, ah, used, um witness, ah, witness statements and, ah, police reports," Leo managed. It was the very first time since he sat down that he stuttered even a little bit.

"I have nothing further," Moore said.

Knowing he was about to be riddled with rapid-fire questions from the villainous defense lawyer, Leo noticeably stiffened.

"May I approach the state's Exhibit B, your Honor?" Marc asked.

"Yes, you may."

Marc went to the illustration of the scene and pointed at three figures standing together in the street.

"These three figures here, where I'm pointing, they appear to be maybe fifteen to twenty feet from Reverend Ferguson and behind him, would you agree?" Marc asked.

"Yes, that la-looks right," Leo agreed.

"Do you have any knowledge or indication of who they might be?"

"I might, if, um, I could check my notes," Leo answered.

"Please do," Marc said.

Almost a minute passed while Leo looked through his case notes.

"Oh, ha-here it is," he finally said. He looked at the board, then back at his notes and said, "Yes, that ma-must be them.

"I have them la-listed only as, as three teenage ba-black girls," Leo said.

"No names," Marc asked.

"No, I di-did not have their, their names."

"Do you know how you came to know that there were three black girls standing there?"

"Um," Leo said as he checked his notebook, "Detective Dirk Shepherd with the county attorney's office gave me that."

Marc pointed at the area directly behind Ferguson.

"Sergeant, this area here, directly behind Reverend Ferguson, there are no other people between Reverend Ferguson and the three unidentified teenage girls. Would this be according to what the investigators with the prosecution's office gave you?"

"Yes, yes, it is," Leo answered. "But, ah, there, there wa-was a lot of people in there but they did, didn't include them be-because no names. Didn't ID them."

"So, there were people in this area behind Ferguson, but the police didn't find them to identify so you did not include them, is that correct?"

"Yes."

"I have nothing further."

Before the afternoon session began, Tennant called the lawyers into her chambers.

"Something's come up on another case. I need to hear a motion on it today. Who do you have coming up, Steve?"

Gondeck looked at Jennifer Moore who said, "Ballistics report."

"Can you be done in an hour?"

"It's Emerson," Moore said mostly to Gondeck.

"He can be a little too, how shall I put it…?"

"Enamored with the spotlight is the polite way of putting it," Marc said.

"You know him?" Tennant asked.

"Yes, Judge."

"I'll talk to him. Tell him we need him to cut to the chase. We don't need a complete history of lands and grooves," Jennifer said.

"I'll call my other case and tell them three-thirty. That will give me time to read over their pleadings. Okay?"

Apparently, the ballistics expert, Nathan Emerson, got the message. Jennifer Moore spent fifteen to twenty minutes establishing his credentials as a firearms ballistic expert. Emerson took another half-hour explaining how bullets are compared, why they are compared that way and why they are unique to individual firearms. Normally he could stretch this out until everyone in the courtroom was yawning.

Next, Emerson put up photos on the TV monitors. Each of the three bullets was shown next to one fired by Emerson from Rob's gun. Despite having been told to cut it short, Emerson took so long making the comparisons Moore had to cut him off.

"What is your expert conclusion, Detective Emerson?"

"All three bullets, state's Exhibits C, D and E, were fired from state's Exhibit A, Officer Robert Dane's service gun."

"Nothing further," Moore said.

Marc had the bullets taken from Ferguson's body tested by his own expert. Because his guy came to the conclusion they came from Rob's gun, which was not really in dispute, Marc was not going to bother with a cross exam. Why risk alienating the jury?

"Mr. Kadella?"

"No questions, your Honor."

To the layman, the testimony may seem tedious and a waste of time. It's not. The state has to build its case piece by piece and get it all on the record in the event of an appeal. If they failed to connect the bullets by expert testimony with Rob's gun, they would lose. They would have legally failed to show that the bullets that killed Lionel Ferguson came from Rob's gun. Reasonable doubt.

"Why didn't you ask him any questions?" Rob asked Marc.

"Like what? There's no denying you shot the guy. They matched the bullets to your gun. There's no point in trying to deny it. We're trying to show the shooting was justified.

"Look, Rob. They're going to methodically put on their case that you shot Ferguson and that's what killed him. The issue here is: why? They're gonna claim you're a racist who had enough of the protests and decided to kill the cause of all the trouble. We need to make them believe you're not a racist. And, with that, your claim that there was a gun makes sense. Don't worry. This trial starts when we start."

Damone was standing offstage in the auditorium of Patrick Henry High School. He was watching a televised debate between mayoral candidates Jalen Bryant and Betsy Carpenter. In Damone's somewhat biased opinion—Damone was a closet misogynist—Bryant was clearly winning. He was much more knowledgeable about issues as well as solutions. Plus, having been in city government, he was well versed on its workings.

While he watched, he sourly thought, *Carpenter has a huge advantage over him in this city; she is a female.*

Lewis took out his phone and stepped through the crowd to answer the call. Whenever Damone appeared at a public place or event, within minutes, he was surrounded by a small crowd of admirers.

Less than a minute after taking the call, Lewis was whispering in Damone's ear. He was about to get a call on today's burner. By the time Lewis finished warning him, that phone buzzed in Damone's pocket.

Followed by Lewis and Monroe, he walked away listening to the caller.

"Were you able to watch the trial today?" Damone was asked.

"No," Damone replied. "I didn't have time. Anything interesting?"

The caller quickly told him about the Black Lives Matter witnesses.

"Idiots," Damone hissed. "I thought we made it clear it was a script to follow, not to memorize."

"We did," the caller agreed. "I'm sure the prosecutors prepared them, but it didn't help."

"How much damage did they do?" Damone asked.

"Minimal. It looked embarrassing for the prosecution, but that's about all. The judge called it off after the first three."

"Okay, good. Keep me informed," Damone said.

"Will do."

FIFTY-FOUR

The pathologist with the medical examiner's office, an elderly, long-time doctor, Clyde Marston, was first up the next morning. As possibly silly as it may seem to a layman, it is not enough that the deceased was shot three times in the chest. The prosecution must prove, beyond a reasonable doubt, that it was those bullets that caused the victim's death.

Doctor Clyde Marston did not make a good first impression. He looked like, and had looked like for almost a decade, that he was pushing retirement. He was barely five foot eight and at least forty pounds overweight. Combined with a frumpy attitude toward clothing, Marston did not create a professional image. In fact, he looked and, most of the time, acted like the cranky old man who yelled at kids to get off of his lawn.

Underneath the veneer was a solid and very capable professional. He always brought his case notes into court but rarely had to refer to them.

And despite his appearance, he was an excellent witness. More than one case had turned to guilty solely because of his testimony.

Gondeck turned him loose by starting with his credentials. Legally, it must be established that the witness is qualified to be treated as an expert. The good doctor had this part of his testimony memorized because he had given it so much.

His credentials established, Marston spent an hour using a drawing of a man Ferguson's size explaining bullet holes, entry wounds and the height at which they entered the body. With photos of the actual body parts, heart and lungs, he literally explained and showed the jury the damage done by each bullet. Color photos of shot up internal organs should be shown after lunch, not before. Several jurors looked less than thrilled by the sight.

"May I approach, your Honor?"

"Yes, you may," Tennant said.

Gondeck picked up several photos from his table. He carried them and stopped at the evidence table. There he picked up three small plastic bags.

"Doctor, I'm showing you three plastic bags marked State's Exhibits C, D and E. Do you recognize these?"

"Yes."

"How do you recognize them and what are they?"

"I recognize them because they are the bags I placed the bullets in, the bullets I removed from Reverend Ferguson's body. I then initialed each bag and delivered them to the evidence box."

Gondeck took a few minutes to do the same identification process with the photos.

The photos and bullets were admitted into evidence with objection from the defense that the photos were too prejudicial without probative value. Autopsy photos are always a source of contention. The prosecution wants the most gruesome ones possible given to the jury. The defense would allow, if any, crayon drawings by grade school kids of the same thing.

"Doctor Marston," Gondeck asked, getting toward the end, "how was the deceased's general health from what you could determine?"

"Well, he was obviously quite a bit overweight. From what I could see of the lungs, I believe he was probably a cigar smoker. The lungs were otherwise healthy—no sign of cancer or any problems from his cigar smoking.

"The heart was showing signs of fatigue probably caused by his weight, smoking and lack of exercise. On the whole, I would say his health was fair."

"Did he die from natural causes brought on by poor health?"

"No, no heart attack or disease of any kind," Marston answered.

"Doctor Marston, in your professional, expert opinion, what was the cause of death of Reverend Lionel Ferguson?"

Marston paused, rubbed a hand on his chin, then looked at Gondeck with a puzzled expression before turning to the jury. "Well, I'll tell you, it's kind of hard to say."

When he said this, Marc turned to Gondeck to see the look on his face. Grim, would be the best way to describe it. This was Marston's way of pulling Gondeck's chain a little. Get to the big moment and act like he's not sure what killed the victim.

"You see," Marston continued still addressing the jury, "I can't say with one hundred percent certainty…"

He paused and rubbed his chin a couple more times.

"…exactly what killed him."

Marston looked at Gondeck again while Marc and Arturo both put a hand over their mouth to smother laughter and a smile.

Marston apparently decided to avoid giving Gondeck a heart attack and continued.

He looked back at the jury and said, "It could have been any one of the three bullets. From the entry wounds, I believe the first bullet hit the deceased in the heart. The second one also went through the heart and the third through his left lung. It's safe to say the third shot through the lung was not what killed him. It would have eventually, but he died before it had a chance. It was the first one, the first bullet that hit the deceased in the heart, that killed him. If that didn't do it, the second one certainly did."

"So, he died from the gunshots he received in his chest," an annoyed Gondeck said with finality.

Marston put his puzzled look back on his face and said, "Well, yeah. He took three bullets in the chest. What do you think killed him?"

"Nothing further," Gondeck replied.

"Mr. Kadella?" Judge Tennant asked.

"I have no questions, your Honor."

"Very well. You may step down, Doctor. We'll take a fifteen-minute recess."

As Marston walked toward the gate, Gondeck looked at him and quietly asked, "Why do you do that?"

"Just for the fun of it," Marston replied.

Marc expected the next witness would be from the police civilian review board. Instead, Jennifer Moore called Philo Anson to the stand.

The prosecution wanted Philo to testify about the photo in the paper. They were looking to subtly impress upon the jury the impact that photo had on the community. Of course, it was absolutely irrelevant to the issue of guilt beyond a reasonable doubt. But add a little spice by putting it in the jurors' minds that children saw this, well, it couldn't hurt.

To accomplish this, Moore was using Philo's proximity to the shooting as a witness to the act itself. He did not see the shooting, but he saw Rob afterward.

Philo had never testified at a trial before and he was determined to make the most of this one. Moore did a good job of getting him to explain who he was and why he was there.

As part of the preparation of each witness, they are told to look at and speak to the jury. Moore quickly lost control of Philo. One of the first things Philo looked for when he sat down was the camera set up in a back corner of the room. Every time Philo spoke, and it was a lot since he took over his testimony, he was looking directly at the camera.

Philo prattled on about his education, his years at the paper and the articles he had written about the racial unrest. Clearly, he was auditioning, and Moore was able to figure it out.

Marc considered objecting that Philo's answers were nonresponsive, which they certainly were. Instead, Marc let him go. The jury seemed very annoyed with him so why should Marc help the state and put a stop to it?

At one point he even got up without asking the judge and went to the drawing of the scene and pointed out where he was. Maybe fifteen feet ahead of Ferguson.

It took over an hour, but Moore finally got to the point.

"What did you do after the shooting?"

"Well, I'll tell you," Philo began. "My journalism instincts apparently took over. Sure, I ducked down, but I also pulled my phone out to get photos.

"What I saw was bedlam. People were running in all directions, screaming and panic-stricken. I kept my cool. I remember seeing a cop standing in a shooter's stance, his arms extended, holding a gun."

"Did you get a picture of him?"

"Unfortunately, no. I tried to, but there were too many people running around. I couldn't get it."

"Could you identify this police officer?" Moore asked.

"Sure, no problem. It was the defendant, Officer Robert Dane."

"What did you do, then?" Moore asked an open-ended question she quickly regretted.

It took him fifteen minutes to explain how courageously he acted by getting photos of the dead Ferguson.

"How many days did the photos appear in the paper?" Moore asked.

For the sole purpose of aggravating Jennifer more than she already was, Marc objected. "Objection. Assumes facts not in evidence."

"Sustained."

Moore drew a deep breath and asked, "Did the photo appear in the Star Tribune?"

"Yes, it ran three consecutive days starting with the front page, A section, above the fold the next day."

Moore asked for and received permission to approach the witness. She carried with her a copy of that day's A section with the photo of Ferguson on the front page.

She went through the steps of having Philo identify it and then asked that it be submitted into evidence.

"May I see it?" Marc asked.

Jennifer handed it to him, and, after a few seconds, Marc said, "The defense objects to its admission, your Honor. Both the photo and the headline are highly prejudicial and have no probative value."

"I agree," Tennant said. "The newspaper will not be allowed into evidence and there will be no further mention of it."

Tennant looked at the jury and said, "If any of you remember seeing it, you will put it out of your mind. A photo and story in a newspaper are evidence of nothing."

Moore took the paper away from Marc, went back to her seat and passed the witness.

"Do you recognize this man?" Marc asked of the photo on the TV screen.

"Yes," Philo replied. Not waiting for Marc to ask another question, Philo went right to it. "He was marching in the protest every day. He seemed to be having a good time."

"Mr. Anson, please answer only the question I ask," Marc said.

"Oh, yeah, sure. Sorry."

"On the day of the shooting, did you see him before the shooting of Ferguson?"

Philo thought for a moment, then said, "Yes, he was there that day."

"Was he in close proximity to Ferguson?"

"Yes, yes, he was."

"Did you see him after the shooting" Marc asked.

"No, I didn't."

"Your testimony was that you heard the shots, turned around and saw Ferguson on the ground but you did not see this man running away, is that correct?"

"Yes, that's right."

Marc hesitated, thinking he might try to cast some doubt on Philo's story of his journalism heroics. Obviously, Philo did not do the things he claimed, or he would have seen the homeless man running away. Getting him to admit it was not likely.

"I have nothing further, your Honor," he said instead.

Carvelli parked the Lincoln on Chicago Avenue a half a block from the restaurant. He was meeting with the FBI, Jeff Johnson and Tess Richards. The guys going through the recordings that Conrad had made came up with more incriminating evidence. It even included discussions Damone had with Saadaq Khalid. Very detailed discussions about dealings with Imam Sadia and his Somali accomplices. What would really pique the Feds was the Cedar/Riverside State bank and the other various laundry services they used. The numerous small businesses that they were using to wash money.

Carvelli slid into the booth next to Tess across from Johnson. Before he could say a word, his favorite waitress was there.

"Hi, Tony," she said. "What can I get you?"

"Hey, Sherry. You know what? I'll have a soda, a Coke and a cheeseburger and fries.

"You two…" he started to say to Johnson.

"We ordered."

When the young girl left, Carvelli removed two disks in plastic cases from his inside jacket pocket.

"Here it is. At least so far. We have more to get through," Carvelli said. "Dates, times, you name it."

"And your guy, the guy who has this, he's not working for any law enforcement entity at all?"

"Nope. I don't know if this is kosher, but I may as well tell you. He set up the recording system, both audio and video, for our pal, Damone. He's gonna want immunity."

"Tell Conrad that won't be a problem," Johnson said.

"How did you know it was Conrad?" Carvelli asked.

"A good guess. This sounds like him," Johnson replied.

"This is gonna take a few days," Tess said.

"A few days? If the federal government only takes a few days to do something, it would be a land speed record. What about Paxton?"

"We've been talking to her. Things are moving. We'll get coordinated with her end in Chicago and here and hit them at the same time. Does she have this?" Tess asked referring to the disks.

"Yes, she does."

FIFTY-FIVE

"Detective Fontana," Marc began. He was doing the cross-examination of the prosecution's lead investigator.

Gondeck had finally put her on the stand to testify to the investigation. She was very thorough but added little. They did not find a gun, nor did they find anyone who saw a gun. They did not find anyone who saw the shooting. The investigation was basically to find a motive for Rob to have shot Ferguson. She tried to testify about the police officer, Daniel Schilling, who came to them with the racism claim against him. Marc objected that this was hearsay and Tennant sustained their objection.

"You were contacted by a Minneapolis police officer by the name of Daniel Schilling, were you not?" Marc asked.

"Yes, that's true."

"He approached you three days after the death of Lionel Ferguson, isn't that true?"

"Yes, I believe that is correct."

"And he called you, personally?"

"Yes, I believe so."

"Well, did he contact any of the other two investigators who then referred him to you?"

"No."

"Before he called you, how many MPD cops had the three of you, your investigation team, interviewed?"

"I can't remember specifically," she said with a puzzled look.

"More than ten?"

"Yes, at least."

"More than twenty?"

"Maybe."

"Would twenty-five sound about right?"

"Actually, that might be a little high."

"Officer Schilling was not one of the police officers you sought out to interview, was he?"

"No, he was not."

"You didn't interview Officer Schilling before that because, although he was on crowd control duty for the protest march, he was stationed at least a half mile away from Officer Dane. Is that right?"

"Yes, it was."

"Your prior testimony was that, in total, you interviewed over one hundred police officers, most of them after you spoke with Schilling, isn't that correct?"

"Yes, that's right."

"The twenty-five mentioned previously were interviewed before Schilling?"

"Yes, that would be correct."

"All of the others were interviewed because of what Officer Schilling told you, isn't that true?"

"Yes, it is."

"Of those one hundred in total, how many were African Americans?"

"I would need to check my notes."

"Please do," Marc told her.

Fontana had her case notebook on her lap. It took her a minute or so to find it and when she did, she answered, "Twenty-seven."

"Isn't it true that of all of the officers of the Minneapolis Police Department that you interviewed, except for Daniel Schilling, not a single one had anything bad to say about the defendant, Officer Robert Dane?"

"Well, cops will try to…"

"Yes or no," Ms. Fontana.

"Yes, that is true," she replied.

"In fact, not a single one, even the black officers, told you anything that would lead you to believe that Robert Dane is a racist, did they? Yes or no, Ms. Fontana."

"No, they did not," she admitted.

"And you specifically asked every one of them that question, didn't you?"

"Yes, by that point we were looking for it."

"Isn't it true, Ms. Fontana, that Daniel Schilling came to you claiming he had information about Robert Dane that you had not discovered yourself, then after interviewing Schilling, your team interviewed another eighty cops and none of them backed up what Schilling claimed? True or false, Ms. Fontana?"

"Yes, that's true."

"Ms. Fontana, did any of the people you interviewed tell you about a homeless man marching with the protestors every day near Reverend Ferguson?"

"Not to my knowledge, no."

Arturo put up the photo of Charlie Dudek as the homeless man on the TV screens.

"Ms. Fontana, do you recognize the man now being displayed on the court monitors?"

"No, I do not," she answered.

"I have nothing further, your Honor."

Damone, along with Lewis and Monroe, were watching the trial in Damone's office. After the cross-examination of Fontana, the judge adjourned for the day.

"I'm trying to decide if he looks anything like the man I met at Minnehaha Falls," Damone said. "I don't see any resemblance at all. I'll tell you something else, if you saw either of them walking down the street, you wouldn't notice him. A minute later, if you were asked to describe him, you couldn't do it."

"What now?" Rob asked.

The four of them, including Maddy, were in a small conference room attached to the courtroom. This little room, with a round wooden table and four chairs, had become their conference room.

"He must be about done," Arturo said. "Unless he has a surprise, he'll bring in the civilian complaints and Schilling tomorrow."

"Should be about it," Marc agreed.

"Any way to keep the complaints from the jury?" Rob asked.

"We argued about this at our suppression hearing," Marc said. "Margaret doesn't believe they're too damaging. The prosecution is arguing his motive is racism and they have a right to present evidence of it."

"I don't think they are that bad," Arturo said. "He was exonerated in all of them. A couple of them, he was, at most, minimally involved."

"It's a done deal," Marc said. "They're coming in."

"The State calls Cornell Wright, your Honor," Jennifer Moore announced.

Cornell Wright was a member and Deputy Director of the City's Department of Civil Rights. His primary responsibility was overseeing the Police Conduct Oversight Commission. He was also its chairman and the most despised man known to the Minneapolis Police Department. A master's degree from Princeton in diversity studies and a Ph.D. from Howard University certainly qualified him for the position.

Wright was a slender, forty-something, single, black man. Just shy of five-foot-seven inches tall. In Cornell Wright's opinion, he never met a cop who was not guilty of something. Rumor had it that there was no one angrier with the world than him.

Of the seven members of the oversight committee, four were black—two women, two men—two were American Indians, both women, and one white man. None of the others held the same 'guilty until proven innocent' attitude Wright did. He did little to hide it, often saying they were not a court of law. Those rules did not apply.

Jennifer used up the entire morning session getting the loquacious Cornell Wright to go over each complaint. He did so in a calm, rational manner. No one in the courtroom could have known his personal opinion about any of them. He even openly admitted that, in a secret ballot, Officer Robert Dane was exonerated for all of them.

Except Jennifer had used Wright's education, experience and curriculum vitae to skillfully get Judge Tennant to qualify him as an expert. He had never testified before Tennant previously. She had no idea who he was or the bias he brought with him.

"In your professional expert opinion, Dr. Wright, what do you see regarding the racial attitude of the defendant?" Jennifer asked.

"Objection," Marc said. "This question is outrageous and lacks any foundation for it. This witness-"

"Overruled," Judge Tennant said. "The witness can give his opinion and you may cross-examine him on it."

"Given the number of complaints, the clear pattern of racial involvement and the fact that he does not have a single complaint from a white person, he is obviously a closet racist."

"A closet racist," Jennifer said. "Would you explain that, please, Doctor?"

"Certainly. His racism is not overt. It is not out in the open. He doesn't talk like a racist all the time. He doesn't ordinarily use racial epithets. But he never seems to miss an opportunity to use violence against an African American. That's far more dispositive of a racist police officer than the fact he rarely uses the 'N' word."

Jennifer paused for a moment while looking at her witness. She was thinking about possibly more embellishment. Having received what she wanted from him, she had enough sense to stop.

"Nothing further, your Honor."

Following the lunch break, Marc wasted little time with pleasantries.

"Doctor Wright let's talk about the worst of the complaints first," Marc began. "Now, bearing in mind that you are under oath, subject to perjury..."

"I resent that!" Wright indignantly said.

"The witness will refrain from making comments," Tennant said.

"Isn't it true, in the case of Faaruq Noor, the vote to exonerate Officer Dane was six to one?"

"How do you know that? These are secret ballots and..."

"Nonresponsive, your Honor," Marc said.

He was absolutely correct. The committee's votes are supposed to be secret. It took Maddy Rivers two scotch on the rocks and less than half an hour sitting next to him in a bar to get Peter Forester, the only white man on the committee, to spill it all.

"You're under oath and I can bring in witnesses," Marc said.

"Yes, that's true, but I did not find his claim credible. That he only hit Faaruq once."

Marc would have normally cut him off from explaining except he wanted it out there.

"Really. So, you didn't believe the doctor, you didn't believe Sergeant Dave Powell or Officer Diane Logan? That Mr. Noor jumped on top of Officer Dane and, while holding a knife to his face, tried to get his gun. And Officer Dane, in a fight for his life, punched Mr. Noor once and broke his jaw?"

"No, I did not."

"In fact, Doctor, isn't it true that of the other three complaints against Officer Dane, the vote on all of them was six to one, you being the lone vote against him?"

"They all appeared to be good complaints," Wright mildly claimed.

318

"Doctor, isn't it true you almost always, with very few exceptions, vote guilty when the complainant is black and the officer involved is white?"

"I, ah, don't believe that, no."

"I said *almost* always, Doctor Wright, and I am prepared to subpoena witnesses to back it up. So, I will give you a chance to correct your answer. Isn't true you almost always vote guilty when the complainant is black and the police officer is white. Yes or no, Doctor?"

"Maybe, perhaps," he answered, trying to soften it.

Marc sighed and said, "One more time, Doctor. Isn't it true…"

"All right, yes, I suppose but…"

"Isn't it also true you vote to exonerate a black police officer far more than a white one? I'll subpoena the committee's voting records."

"If that is true, it's because black officers deserve more leeway because they are not treated with the same level of respect white officers are."

"Really, and you know this because of your many years of experience riding in a police car?"

"Objection, argumentative," Jennifer said.

"Withdrawn," Marc said.

"Tell me something, Doctor, who has the real race problem? White police officers or you?"

"Objection!" Jennifer yelled.

"Sustained," Margaret ruled just when Wright was indignantly claiming he did not.

"Mr. Kadella, I'm on the verge of fining you or putting you in a cell," Tennant said.

"I have nothing further, your Honor," Marc said.

"Redirect?" Tennant asked Jennifer.

"A moment, your Honor," Jennifer said then conferred with Gondeck. They quickly came to the conclusion that to try to rehabilitate the witness would likely make it worse.

"Your Honor, the State objects to the entire cross-examination as argumentative and defense counsel's use of confidential committee voting information is improper and sets a bad precedent."

"Overruled," Tennant quickly said. "We'll take a short break."

Jennifer Moore also conducted the direct examination of Officer Daniel Schilling, the cop who went to Jermaine Fontana with claims of

Rob Dane's racism. He had little else to offer other than the locker room talk.

"What exactly did Officer Dane say to you?" Jennifer asked.

"Look, you gotta understand, there was a lot of angry talk in the locker room before we went on duty. Everyone was getting tired of the marches and protests. It seemed like we'd been doing them all summer. A lot of people were griping," Schilling said, trying to sound reluctant.

"What did he say?" Jennifer asked again.

"He said, 'I'm sick of this bullshit and I hate that fuckin','" Schilling paused, looked at Tennant and said, "he called him the 'N' word, your Honor, Reverend Ferguson. Then he said, 'I hate all these black assholes. They all sit on their ass on welfare then protest cops who protect them. I'm tired of them screaming, cussing, and spitting at us.'"

"What did you say?"

"I told him he needed to calm down and not take that anger and attitude out on the street—words to that effect.

"He said, 'yeah, you're right' and that was it. I thought that was the end of it."

"Your witness," Moore said.

Arturo had convinced Marc to let him do the cross-examination of this witness. For appearance's sake, a person of color would be better.

"Officer Schilling, how many people were in the locker room with you?"

"I'm not sure. Probably about thirty."

"Would it surprise you if I told you there were fifty-four police officers there?" Arturo asked. This was a number Arturo and Marc picked out of thin air. They actually had no idea how many there were. He was asking Schilling if it would surprise him. He did not state it as a fact.

Schilling squirmed a little knowing where Arturo was going before answering, "No, I guess not."

"And yet you were the only one who heard Officer Dane use racial epithets and hateful speech about Reverend Ferguson, is that what you want this jury to believe?"

"I don't know what anyone else may or may not have heard. I heard what I testified," Schilling smugly said, sat back and looked at the jury.

"Isn't it true there were quite a few of them complaining about the protests?"

"Yes, I guess so."

"They were tired of being screamed at, including yourself?"

"Yes, sure."

"Tired of being cursed, including you?"

"Yeah," he answered more meekly.

"Tired of being spat upon, including you?"

"Yes, of course, wouldn't you?"

"Your Honor," Arturo said.

"Answer the question as put to you, Officer," Tennant told him.

"Isn't it also true that several, if not many officers in the locker room, angry about their treatment by the protestors, were spewing what could be called inappropriate racial statements?"

"Yes, I guess so."

"Including a number of African American officers? You're under oath, Officer."

"Yes, that's true."

"Are you a friend of Officer Dane?"

"Sure," Schilling answered.

"Really? Ever been to his house?"

"No, not that I recall."

"Go out for a beer, just the two of you?"

"No,"

"You barely know the man, but it was you and only you hanging out with him in the locker room and you who he so carelessly, foolishly spoke such vile, racist things to. That's what you want this jury to believe?"

By now, Schilling was starting to look a little pale. He took a deep breath and gathered himself before slowly, carefully answering.

"The jury can believe whatever it wants. I know what I heard him say."

FIFTY-SIX

When Arturo finished his cross of Schilling, the State's case was complete. Gondeck and Moore had crossed all of the t's and dotted all of the i's to get into evidence every element of every charge.

Margaret Tennant had called a recess until Monday morning. An extra day for the defense to prepare.

As the crowded courtroom emptied, Maddy Rivers came in and fought her way through the crowd going upstream toward the gate. When she reached it, Marc looked at her with his eyebrows raised.

"Got him," she said. "I caught up with him in a bar a couple of blocks from here. I saw him leaving the building down on the second floor and followed him."

"Who?" Rob asked.

"Dirk Shepherd," Marc replied. "He's one of the investigators who work for the county attorney."

"He's got quite a mouth on him, too. Called me the 'C' word once, the 'B' word several times."

"Oh, god," Marc said. "Is he okay? Is he in the hospital? You didn't...?"

"No, I just left, although I might go back and have a little chat with the bartender. He thought it was pretty amusing," Maddy replied.

"Don't, please," Marc pleaded. "Just leave it alone."

"What?" Arturo asked.

"Usually, when someone talks to her like that, they find themselves on their back wondering why everything hurts.

"Well, everybody," Marc said as he picked up his briefcase. "First thing Monday morning, we're up."

Carvelli had parked the Lincoln in a lot near the Guthrie Theater downtown. He turned up the collar of his trench coat against the wind that was blowing along the River. Other than the wind, it was a pleasant enough October day. *But why meet outdoors?* he wondered.

Carvelli followed the pathway along the river until he came to a park bench. A lone man was sitting on it, watching the water go over St. Anthony Falls while waiting for Carvelli.

"Where's Tess?" Carvelli asked FBI Agent Jeff Johnson.

322

"Paperwork," Johnson replied.

"What's up?"

"Nice view," Johnson said. "Especially with the leaves changing colors along the river."

"Yeah, it's lovely," the cynical ex-cop in Carvelli answered.

"I'm finding out there's been a lot of things going on, Tony. Almost swirling around us that I didn't know about and neither did you, that the higher-ups, I mean Washington, at the Bureau and DOJ have been less than open about."

"This shocks you, does it?" Carvelli sarcastically asked. "Why should those of us out here, with our ass hanging out, know what's going on?

"What can you tell me, Jeff?"

"Not much, except things are moving fast. Ten days, two weeks at most. There's been a secret Grand Jury impaneled in Washington. Everything from here and Chicago has been fed to it. Indictments are already being issued so, be ready."

"Am I going to be arrested?"

"No, no," Johnson said with assurance. "They know what you've been doing. Um, I sort of broke your trust and told them. Sorry."

"I knew you would. I guess I kind of counted on it," Carvelli said.

Carvelli's personal phone vibrated in his coat pocket. He looked at the ID and saw a text message come through. He read it and put his phone away.

"I gotta go. Anything else?" Carvelli asked.

"Yeah, me too," Johnson answered and stood up. "When the shit hits the fan, it will happen quick. No one wants anything leaking out. I'll keep you in the loop as much as I can."

"What do you need?" Carvelli said into his phone. He was on his way back to the Lincoln calling the person who sent the text.

"Why can't you text? Never mind," Gretchen started to ask.

"I'm too stupid," Carvelli replied.

"At least an honest answer," Gretchen said. "Can you come by? We need to talk about Philo."

"About what?"

"It's getting complicated," Gretchen said.

"Oh, oh. Don't tell me you're falling in love."

Carvelli waited for twenty seconds before saying, "Stop laughing. It's not impossible. I'm in my car. I'll be there in ten minutes."

"Come in," Gretchen said. She had buzzed Carvelli into the building and he had signed in at the security desk. The armed security guard had been informed that Carvelli was coming as a visitor.

Gretchen led him into the sunken living room as he, again, looked around the luxury condo.

"I wish I could afford something like this," he told her.

"You're in the wrong business," she replied. "Have a seat. You want something to drink?"

"A water," Carvelli said. "I'm thirsty."

A minute later Gretchen returned with ice cubes in a stemmed, crystal glass and a bottle of Evian. While Carvelli filled the glass, Gretchen took a seat across from him.

"I saw Philo again last night," she said. "Something is eating at him. Tony, we just went out to dinner. He drank way too much, and I had to put him in a cab."

"He has a drinking problem. That's not news," Carvelli replied.

"No, there's more to it. He starts out with his usual hubris. Then the more he drinks, the more melancholy he becomes. And he'll drift off like he's thinking about something. And I think it has something to do with Marc's trial."

"What?" Carvelli asked, suddenly showing more interest.

"He muttered something about a picture of a homeless guy they asked him about. I asked him, 'what about the homeless guy?' Then he looked at me, shook his head and said, 'Nothing, I was just thinking out loud.'"

"Does he owe you money?"

"I'll take care of that," Gretchen said waving him off.

"When are you seeing him again?"

"I'm not sure. He said he had to go home for a few days for his mother's birthday."

Carvelli thought for a long minute, then said, "He knows something. Or saw something and it's bothering him—something to do with Rob Dane. When he gets back, as soon as you hear from him, give me a call. I need to have a little 'Come to Jesus' chat with him."

"He said he'd be back by Wednesday or Thursday. He told me he would call me for a date," Gretchen said.

"Are you becoming his mother figure? Does he have a little Oedipal complex problem?" Carvelli asked with a salacious grin.

"God, I hope not. I've had that happen before. Hey, how did you come up with the Oedipal complex?"

"The ignorant cop? I've read more than just Playboy and the S.I. swimsuit issue."

"Nice try," Gretchen laughed while Carvelli answered his phone.

"What's up, Dan?"

"We're done," Sorenson replied. "Everything of value is on DVDs and CDs. We came across something a bit interesting."

"Which is?" Carvelli asked.

"Someone has been calling Damone every day with an update of Marc's trial."

"What are they telling him?"

"We're only getting one side of the conversation. Most of it seems to be pretty routine stuff," Sorenson answered.

"He probably has someone in the audience," Carvelli said. "We think he's the guy who hired the homeless guy to set up Rob. Of course he'd want to know what's going on. Makes sense."

"Sure," Sorenson agreed. "Are you coming by to pick up the disks for your pals?"

"Yeah," Carvelli replied.

"Meet me at Jake's. I need to get out of here."

"Don't leave Conrad alone. He needs protection."

"We're moving him this afternoon," Sorenson said.

"I'll see you in a while," Carvelli replied.

On his way to Jake's, something occurred to Carvelli.

"Hey," he said when Sorenson answered his call back. "I just thought of something. On the tapes, because Damone changes phones every day, whoever calls him has to call Lewis first and get the new number."

"Yeah, that's right. So?"

"So, I have Lewis' phone number. If you can get the time that this mystery man in court calls Damone, I can get my guy to track the calls Lewis gets, come up with a phone number and get this guy's name."

"That's why you're a detective," Sorenson replied with a mocking, smart-ass manner.

"And don't you forget it."

"I'll give Conrad a call and have him get on that," Sorenson said.

FIFTY-SEVEN

"The defense calls, Lieutenant Colonel Gabriel Stewart," Marc told the court.

Friday morning, three days ago, the entire office staff, the lawyers, Marc, Maddy and Arturo, had a two-hour debate. Who to call first for the defense? It is well known that people tend to hold in their memory primacy and recency. What this means is that people recall best the first and last things, and witnesses, they have heard.

It was generally believed by the office members that the jury should hear from Rob first. They had been waiting several days to hear from him. Get him up there and let him tell them what happened. It was Barry Cline who argued otherwise.

The last witness the state put on the stand was the cop who adamantly testified about Rob as a racist. The jury had three days to dwell on it—the racist claim needed to be refuted right away.

As the opinions and arguments went around the room, Marc was finally persuaded Barry was right. What convinced him were the opinions of the staff. The non-lawyers, including Maddy, thinking like ordinary people, came around to agree with Barry that the racist claim needed to be refuted right away.

Lt. Colonel Stewart came through the doors and strolled up the center aisle as if he owned the place. He was ramrod straight and a six-foot-three, trim one-ninety. Wearing his dress blues with shoulder straps, five rows of campaign ribbons and his airborne insignia; he was enough to make anyone proud to be an American. He was also a black man.

Marc tossed him a few soft questions to get him started. He asked him about his background, years of service, deployments in combat and current billet.

"Colonel Stewart, how did you come to be here today?"

"I watch the news. I heard about the protests and the shooting of Reverend Ferguson. When I found out it was Rob Dane who was accused of it, my jaw almost hit the floor."

"What did you do next?"

327

"Well, I made sure it was the same Rob Dane I had served with, then I found out who his lawyer was. I contacted you and offered to do whatever I could."

"Why would you go to such trouble?"

"First, because the news was portraying him as some mad racist who murdered Ferguson without cause. This was not the Rob Dane I knew."

"Why do you say that?"

"Because Sergeant Robert Dane, that man sitting next to you, was awarded a Bronze Star with valor for saving my life in Afghanistan."

"Tell the jury how this happened?"

"I was a captain at the time, in command of a company in Kandahar Province. We were on patrol having been told there were Taliban in our area. To make a long story shorter, we were set up and ambushed.

"A Taliban RPG—rocket-propelled grenade—almost hit me. The explosion knocked me down and unconscious. Sergeant Dane helped set up a defensive zone then volunteered to crawl on his belly almost a hundred meters to where I was.

"When he got there, I was coming to but still very groggy. We were taking small arms fire. Rob threw me over his back and carried me back to the rest of the company."

The colonel looked directly at each of the jurors and asked, "Does that sound like something a racist would do?"

Gondeck almost objected to this embellishment but decided it was too late. Best to let it go.

"Colonel," Marc began asking, "how many men were under your command at that time?"

"Two hundred, give or take."

"What does that mean, 'give or take'?"

"We were almost never at full strength. Wounded men were evacuated, there were always some on sick call, things like that."

"Killed?"

"Yes," Stewart quietly said. "I lost seven KIA during that tour."

"How many men were African Americans?"

"There were sixty-seven black soldiers when we first deployed in country. I actually don't like that term, African Americans. It sets people apart and divides us. We are all Americans."

"Thank you for that. Was there racial trouble between the soldiers in your command?"

"A little, I suppose. It's generally not like that in the military. The military is a great equalizer, especially in combat."

"Did you ever know Rob Dane to be involved in any of it?"

"No, of course not."

"How did you get here today?"

"I paid my own way to come here. I would have gone anywhere to do this."

"Your witness."

"Colonel Stewart, how long has it been since you saw or talked to the defendant?" Gondeck asked.

"Since he separated, I suppose. I'd say seven or eight years."

"Isn't it true, Colonel, you have no idea what the defendant's attitude toward black people is today, do you, sir?"

"I'd be very surprised…"

"Please, Colonel, yes or no?"

"No, I don't," he agreed.

"People can change in that time, can't they?"

"Yes, I suppose so."

"In fact, if the Robert Dane you knew had to stand on watch for several days while crowds of angry black people marched passed him yelling at him, cursing him, even spitting on him, isn't it safe to say that Robert Dane could get fed up with it?"

"No," Stewart emphatically said.

"No? How can you be so sure?"

"Because he was a disciplined soldier who knew how to follow orders."

"That's right," Gondeck agreed. "The Robert Dane you knew was, and I emphasize the word 'was', a disciplined soldier eight years ago. But you can't possibly say he is the same today, can you?"

"I believe he is."

"Nonresponsive, your Honor," Gondeck said.

"Answer the question, Colonel, yes or no," Tennant told him.

"No, I can't positively say that," Stewart said almost in a whisper.

"Isn't it also true, Colonel, you were not out there on that street with the defendant dealing with the protestors, were you?"

"No, I was not."

"I have nothing further, your Honor," Gondeck said.

"Redirect, Mr. Kadella?"

"No, your Honor."

"We will take fifteen minutes. You may step down, Colonel Stewart."

Stewart stopped at Marc's table while the courtroom emptied.

"Sorry, Rob," Stewart said.

"No, thank you, Colonel," Rob said, then saluted the man. After Stewart returned the salute, he turned to Marc.

"You were fine. You answered honestly, and I thank you for coming. I think I know what just happened," Marc said. "Do you need a ride? What time is your flight?"

"One fifteen," he replied. "I would be delighted if Miss Rivers could act as my driver one more time."

"My pleasure," Maddy said.

When they were gone, Marc turned to Rob and Arturo.

"He just about gave us an argument against both first and second-degree," Arturo said, referring to Gondeck's cross.

"Yeah, we could convince the jury that he snapped. But that's not what happened. He's gonna give us a plea deal for manslaughter," Marc said.

"No way, I won't..."

"No one's asking you to. But, as your lawyer, I suggest you keep an open mind. We'll see," Marc told him.

For the next day and a half, Marc presented a parade of character witnesses. Every cop who had ever spent any significant amount of time with Rob was put on the stand. And every one of them testified the same way: they had never heard Rob utter a single word or do a single act that could be construed as racist. Saving the best for last, Marc put Sergeant Dave Powell, a black man, on the stand. Powell was the first policeman, along with his partner Diane Logan, to the Cedar/Riverside mini-riot that resulted in Rob's first civilian complaint.

Powell testified about how well he knew Rob and about his performance at the conflict.

"What caused this altercation?" Marc asked.

"What caused it, and what continues to cause this on an almost daily basis, is something the media never reports. Somali men of all ages are extremely racist and bigoted. They especially hate African Americans and are quite racist toward them," Powell said.

Judge Tennant looked at Gondeck for an objection and when she did not get one, she stepped in.

"There will be no more of that, Sergeant Powell. In fact, strike it from the record as without foundation. The jury will disregard the last statement by the witness."

"Yes, your Honor."

"Tell the jury your thoughts when the defendant arrived," Marc said.

"I was relieved. I know officer Dane to be a cool and competent cop who would be of help if anything got out of hand.

"At first, his presence helped settle things down. Then, all hell broke loose. Faaruq Noor sucker punched Rob, got him down, was trying to stab him and get his gun. If he had gotten it, he could have killed several people. We're lucky he did not."

"Based on your experience, would you characterize Rob Dane as a racist?"

"No."

"Ever heard him say or do anything to make you think he was?"

"No."

"Your witness."

It took Jennifer Moore less than two minutes to establish that Powell was not in the locker room before the shooting. He had no idea what was said there. Also, he was not on crowd control and could not know what the other officers were thinking, putting up with or how they were being treated.

While the crowd was leaving for the day, Gondeck walked the three or four steps to the defense table.

"Let's talk," he said to Marc.

"Sure," Marc replied. *Here it comes*, Marc thought.

While a deputy stayed with Rob, the four lawyers went into the conference room adjoining the courtroom.

"What are we going to talk about?" Marc asked as innocently as possible while they all took seats around the small table.

"We're finding out things about the dearly departed Reverend Ferguson," Gondeck started off saying.

"Like what?"

"This isn't the time or place," Gondeck said. "Let's just say no one will put him up for sainthood. Plus, the cops out there did have to take a lot of abuse…"

"Get to it, Steve. What are you offering?"

"Third-degree. We'll request the minimum from the guidelines, one hundred and twenty-eight months. He'll do two-thirds, be out in seven years.

"You didn't charge third-degree," Arturo said.

"Oh, I think the judge will let us amend for a plea," Gondeck said.

"What do you think?" Gondeck asked Marc. "Will you recommend it?"

"Since my client insists this was a righteous shooting, well, I'll tell him about it because I have to, but I'm not sure I can recommend it. I'll let you know."

"Cut the recommended time down to seventy-two months, then maybe," Arturo said.

Marc looked at his co-counsel and was appalled. Never counter without your client's consent.

"I'll run it by my boss," Gondeck said.

When Gondeck and Moore left, Rob was brought in. Marc told him the offer without Arturo's mistake. Rob rejected it out of hand. After he was taken home, Marc had a chat with Arturo.

"Lawyers do things differently, but I never make a counteroffer without talking to my client. Or at least having a good idea what he thinks," Marc said.

"Sorry, I just thought…"

"It's okay. I'll tell you this, too: Steve Gondeck is his own boss. If he wants to, he can pretty much accept any deal, especially for sentencing. He could have offered to reduce it further. If he wanted it, he would have jumped on it. He doesn't need Felicia's permission.

"Besides, he already told her what he was going to offer. If she didn't like the final sentence, he can always blame a sentencing departure on the judge. Just so you know."

FIFTY-EIGHT

"What's the matter, baby?" Gretchen purred into Philo's ear.

Philo was laying naked on his stomach on a bath towel in bed in the Hyatt on Fourth and Seventh in downtown Minneapolis. Gretchen was dressed in black lace undergarments. For a woman in her forties, she pulled it off with style. In fact, most twenty-somethings would wish they could do it as well as her, feminism notwithstanding.

During dinner, Gretchen could see that whatever had been bothering him was getting worse. He barely touched his meal and drank more than usual. She even chastised him about his drinking—something she would normally never do to a client. Gretchen knew better than to point out their flaws. She was not their wife, mom or counselor.

Gretchen was straddling Philo, giving him a rubdown with a scented body lotion. She had been at it for about five minutes and Philo was barely responding. Something was wrong.

Gretchen rubbed the cinnamon scented oil on her hands. She started just above his waist and worked her way along his spine to his shoulders and neck. When she got there, she leaned in again and whispered, "Tell Momma your troubles."

"How's the trial going?" Philo asked.

"What trial, baby?" she asked trying to be coy.

"The cop who shot the fat, black minister," Philo replied.

Gretchen continued her massaging as she said, "Oh, I don't know. I haven't been following it."

"How can you miss it? It's on the news and in the papers every day," Philo turned his head and angrily said.

"Sorry! I have better things to do than follow a trial in the news," Gretchen replied, acting annoyed, thinking she should play along.

"Sorry," Philo whispered. "I didn't mean, well, you know…"

Gretchen poured more oil on her hands and went back to work. After a sufficient pause, while sitting up, she stopped.

"It's time you tell me what's bothering you, Philo. It has something to do with this trial and it's been bothering you for a while now. What is it?"

Gretchen climbed off of him and the bed. She picked up a damp hand towel and wiped her hands clean. She sat down at the room's table, retrieved a cigarette from her purse and lit it.

"This is a smoke-free hotel," Philo said. "May I have one?"

Gretchen gave him hers and lit another for herself. They silently smoked for almost a minute while Philo was thinking.

He got up and put on a bathrobe. Finding his phone in his coat, he went back to the bed and sat on the edge right next to Gretchen.

They both put their cigarettes in a plastic glass with water. Philo was scrolling through his phone while Gretchen waited.

"This is what's been bothering me," he said. He held the phone out to her so she could see what it was.

Gretchen looked closely at it for a moment, then said, "What is it? I'm not sure what I'm looking at."

Using an index finger, Philo explained what it was.

"This is the fat Reverend Ferguson. The large, black man with the angry look on his face," Philo said.

"It looks like he's holding a gun and pointing it at something," Gretchen said.

"Or someone," Philo said. "But he's not. Look closely, that's not his arm. You can see Ferguson's right arm here," he pointed out to her. "Underneath the gun."

"Yes, I see that. You're right. It is below the gun. Then whose..."

"Watch," Philo said. "If I zoom in, look over Ferguson's right shoulder, right behind his neck. What do you see?"

Gretchen took a close look and asked, "Is that the top of a baseball cap?"

"Yes, it is," Philo said. "The cop who shot Ferguson has claimed all along that Ferguson pointed a gun at him. Ferguson didn't point the gun at him. Someone else did. He snuck up behind Ferguson, reached around him with the gun and caused the cop to pull out his gun and shoot believing it was Ferguson who had the gun."

"Who did this?"

"There was a homeless guy marching in the protest. Nobody paid much attention to him. He looked like some homeless guy that you wouldn't look at twice. I saw him a lot and I'm not sure I could identify him. I know he had on a battered, old Twins cap. It has to be him. I now believe he was checking out the protest march the first three days looking for a cop and the place he might be able to pull this on. He found both."

"You think so?"

"It has to be. Nothing else makes sense," Philo replied. "The question is: why? Who was he working for?"

"You think he was hired? A pro?"

"Would have to be and he would have to be very, very good. Brass balls to pull off a stunt like this," Philo said. "And the photo doesn't lie."

"You have got to go to the cops with this. Or the lawyers, somebody."

"I know," Philo heavily sighed. "I'm scared I'll get in trouble for withholding evidence. I'm not sure what to do."

"I know someone—an ex-cop. He'll know what to do. And I think he'll know how to protect you," Gretchen said.

"Really? Who? That would be great. How…"

"Email that photo to me. In fact, email all of them you have," Gretchen said.

"I only have that one of what happened. Then, a few shots of Ferguson lying in the street and some of the crowd before the shooting," Philo said.

"Whatever. Send them," she said and gave him her email address.

While Philo sent the photos, Gretchen made a call.

"Come on, answer your damn phone," she said while it rang in her ear. After the sixth ring, Carvelli's personal phone went to voice mail.

"Hey, it's Gretchen. Call me the instant you get this no matter what time it is. We need to talk. I have something important for you."

When she finished the call, Philo started getting dressed.

"Don't worry. I'll pay you. Put it on my card," Philo said. "I haven't felt this good in weeks."

Gretchen was checking her phone to make sure she received the photos. Satisfied, she looked across the room at Philo.

"Why didn't you come forward before this?" she asked.

"The honest answer?"

"That would be good," Gretchen said.

"I thought I might be able to make some money with this. Or make some kind of a big splash news wise revealing it at the last minute or something."

Gretchen stopped getting dressed, looked at him and scolded him, "A man's life is on the line!"

"I know, I'm sorry, I already feel like an asshole," Philo pitifully replied.

Gretchen finished dressing, then calmly said, "Hey, forget it. What's done is done. Let's see if we can't fix it.

"The guy I called will call me back as soon as he gets the message. It could be any minute or maybe not until morning. Keep yourself available," she said and then paused.

"I will, I promise. Call me as soon as he gets back to you. In fact, just to be on the safe side, I'm staying here tonight."

"Good idea. I'll call you right away."

When Gretchen called him, Carvelli was in a late-night meeting with FBI agents Johnson and Tess Richards. Paxton O'Rourke was on the phone from Chicago. Washington had listened to and viewed the latest batch of recordings from Damone's headquarters. Without revealing why, Washington had reason to believe that Damone Watson was a serious flight risk. The timetable for throwing a net over everything was being moved up. At most, one week, if not sooner. Of course, recently it had become the highest priority.

"Hey, it's about time," Gretchen said into her phone. "I've been calling all morning."

"Yeah, well, it was a late night and sorry, but I didn't check my messages before I got up."

"Tony, it's ten o'clock in the morning. Get your ass moving."

"What's so important?"

"Philo spilled it last night. Tony, I have a photo of the gun that was being pointed at Rob Dane when he shot Ferguson."

"Are you serious? He had a picture of it? How clear? How..."

"It's good. Now, get moving. I'll call him back and we'll meet at his condo."

"I'll be at your place in twenty minutes..."

"Shower first," Gretchen said.

"...wait for me downstairs."

Precisely twenty-two minutes later Carvelli, driving his Camaro, pulled up to the front door of Gretchen's building.

"Hi," she said as she closed the passenger door. "Your hair's still wet so you must have showered."

"I even shaved," he replied.

He was weaving his way through traffic while Gretchen checked to make sure her seatbelt worked.

"You talked to him?"

"He'll be at his place when we get there," she replied.

"Email those photos to me," he said, then gave her his email address.

He took his wallet from an inside coat pocket and gave it to her.

"There's a card in there from a lawyer…"

"Marc?"

"Yeah. His email address is on there. Send him the photos, too. Then call and tell Sandy or Carolyn, whoever answers, that you're with me and you sent photos to Marc. Ask her if she can make sure he got them."

Carvelli's phone rang a couple of minutes later. He checked the ID, then answered it.

"What did you come up with?' Carvelli asked.

"The phone is in the name of an Angela Emmett," Paul Baker, Carvelli's hacker, said.

"You run a check on her?"

"Yeah and I don't get it," Paul replied. "As far as I can tell, she's a thirty-seven-year-old mother of three, married, lives in Chaska and has no criminal record of any kind. Even traffic tickets."

"Husband?"

"Michael Emmett, age thirty-eight. Manages a Target and he makes a good living. No criminal history. Not exactly criminal types."

"Not too helpful," Carvelli said. "Let me think about it. I have to go."

"Okay, let me know if you want me to do anything more."

FIFTY-NINE

"Detective Shepherd," Marc said in preparation of asking his next witness a question.

Shepherd was one of the investigators who worked for the county attorney's office. Because Marc called him as a witness, he was not allowed to use leading questions to get his testimony. Except, Shepherd was obviously hostile. He put up resistance even while Marc tried to elicit his background information. By the time he finished with this line of questioning, Judge Tennant had allowed him to treat Shepherd as a hostile witness. This allowed Marc to switch to leading questions.

Before finishing the question he had started, Marc walked over to the large illustrated drawing of the shooting site. He pointed a finger at the three unidentified girls behind Ferguson.

"Detective Shepherd," he said again, "isn't it true you questioned these three people, earlier identified as three black teenage girls?"

"I don't recall. I can't remember everyone I talked to off the top of my head," the uncooperative investigator said.

"Let's refresh your memory. Would you believe me if I told you Sergeant Leo Cohn of the crime scene unit testified that he produced State's Exhibit B, the drawing of the crime scene?"

"Yes, I guess so."

"Would you believe he also testified he made Exhibit B from information obtained by the investigation team, including you?"

"Yes," Shepherd said and squirmed in his seat.

"And he testified that it was you who identified these three figures on Exhibit B as three, black, teenage girls?"

"Yes, I remember now."

"In fact, they came to your office, didn't they?"

"Yes, now that you mention it, I recall that they did."

"You spent twenty years with the Duluth police and now three years with the Hennepin County attorney's office. Would you consider yourself an experienced investigator?"

"Yes, I would."

"I'm guessing you've probably investigated hundreds of crimes, haven't you?"

"Yes, sure."

"Do you have your case notes with you?"

"Yes, I always bring them when I testify."

"Good," Marc said, still standing before Exhibit B. "Would you check your case notes and find your notes concerning these three girls."

Shepherd knew exactly who Marc meant and found them very quickly. He was not sure what the lawyer was up to, but his cop sense knew it was not good.

"Okay, I found it," Shepherd said.

"Good. Read to the court what you wrote down after talking to these three girls."

Shepherd read off the date, time and place of the interview, which was his office.

He continued, "Interviewed three, black, teenage girls who claimed they were in the protest march fifteen to twenty feet behind and to the right of Ferguson. Waste of my time. They saw nothing."

"And? Is that it?" Marc asked.

"They didn't see anything. They had nothing to add to the investigation."

"You didn't even include their names in your case notes?"

Shepherd, now sweating a bit at his forehead, checked his notes again then said, "I'm sure I have them but…"

"You didn't bother to write them down or give them to Sergeant Cohn, did you?"

"They had nothing to add," Shepherd indignantly said.

At that moment, Marc looked at Arturo who put the homeless man's photo on the TV monitors.

"Do you recognize this man, the one showing on the courtroom monitors?"

"No, I've never seen him."

"We have had police officers testify that he was one of the marchers in the protest. He was seen every day close to Reverend Ferguson," Marc said preparing his question. When he said this, despite his best efforts at maintaining a poker face, Shepherd's eyes widened, and his face tightened.

"Those three girls you interviewed, they told you about him, didn't they?"

"If it's not in my notes, they must not have told me," Shepherd indignantly said.

"Detective, I have those three girls waiting in the hallway, would you like to change your answer?"

"Okay, I don't recall being told about him, no."

"Obviously, you spent no time looking for him or trying to determine who he was. Is that fair to say?"

"Um, yes," Shepherd agreed.

"No one else in the investigation did either, did they?"

"Not that I am aware of, no."

Marc walked slowly back to his chair and sat down. He looked at Shepherd and said, "One more question, Detective. Isn't it true that once you knew that Ferguson was shot dead by a police officer and you were handed racism as a motive, the investigation was over as far as you were concerned?"

"There was nothing left to investigate."

"I have nothing further, your Honor."

"Mr. Gondeck?" Tennant asked.

"One moment, your Honor," Gondeck said.

The two prosecutors and Jermaine Fontana conferred for a moment. Unintelligible whispers, shaking heads and an angry look from Fontana resulted. Finally, Gondeck shut it down. Having determined there was not much they could do to fix it, Gondeck passed. Unless Kadella could come up with something connecting the missing homeless man to the shooting, Gondeck could easily dismiss his involvement during closing argument.

The remainder of the morning session was taken up by the three teenage girls. Arturo took all three because he was the one who prepared them.

Their testimony could have come from triplets. All three of the girls, having never been in a courtroom before, were visibly nervous in the beginning. That did not last long. Once they got going, Arturo had a hard time controlling them.

The first one up was more or less the ringleader, Tonya Howard. By the time Arturo got her talking about the protests, she was on a roll. In fact, she probably came up with the best line of the trial. When asked why she and her friends had attended, she readily admitted they were mostly interested in meeting boys.

"Ms. Howard," Arturo began after the homeless man's photo appeared on the monitors, "do you recognize the man on the courtroom monitors?"

"Oh, yes. Absolutely. That's the strange white man who was there every day. He just seemed to be, I don't know, hanging around. But it's funny 'cause he looked like a homeless man, but he wasn't panhandling. We never once saw him asking anyone for money."

"Were you looking at him or Reverend Ferguson when the shots were fired?"

"Ah, no, no we wasn't."

"Do you remember what you were looking at?"

"Well, we were, you know, checking out some boys we saw on the Mall. On Nicollet."

Once the laughter died down Arturo asked, "What did you do after you heard the shots?"

"At first, we couldn't tell where they came from. Then I saw Reverend Ferguson on the ground and him running away. Which seemed odd."

"By 'him' do you mean the homeless man on the TV monitor?"

"Yeah, yeah, him. He was running away from Ferguson. It was strange because he looked old and like he couldn't walk fast. But when he ran away, he was running fast. Like he was a lot younger and in better shape than he looked."

"Objection, the witness is not a physical fitness expert," Gondeck said.

"Overruled. She can make a layman's observation," Tennant ruled.

"Did you see the defendant?"

"Yes, I did. He was standing over Ferguson with his gun pointing up."

"Did you see the shooting itself?"

"No. We heard the shots, then saw a lot of people running around. It was scary."

"Other than the gun the police officer was holding; did you personally see any other guns?"

"No, nuh uh. Except those from other police officers."

"After the shooting, what did you do?"

"We ran, like everybody else."

"When did you call the police to talk to them?"

"It was a couple of days later. I slipped up and told my mom we were there. She didn't know we went to the protest."

"Was she upset with you?"

"Oh, yeah. She told my dad and he made me call the police."

"Did you talk to an investigator?"

"Yeah. My dad drove us down and we all had to tell this older, bald man everything we knew."

"Did you tell him about the homeless man?"

"Sure. We told him he should find him because he was closest to Ferguson and he must have seen what happened."

"Did you tell him you saw the homeless man running away?"

"Your Honor," Gondeck stood and said, interrupting Arturo. "We've heard a lot about this so-called homeless man without any relevance. Next, we'll be hearing about shadows on the grassy knoll."

Marc stood to respond and said, "He doesn't want the jury to hear any more about the sloppy job his crack team of investigators did."

"That's enough, Mr. Kadella. Come up here," she said gesturing with her hands.

"You have two more out there, her friends?" Tennant asked.

"Yes, your Honor," Arturo replied.

"Are either of them going to give us any surprises?" she asked.

"Like the magical, mysterious, disappearing gun," Gondeck said.

"Knock it off, counselor," Tennant told him.

"No, their testimony is essentially the same," Arturo replied.

"The jury needs to hear that one of their investigators was told by three separate witnesses that a material witness was out there and that they did nothing to find him," Marc interjected.

"Steve, Jennifer?" Tennant asked.

"I think we've heard enough," Gondeck said.

"I tend to agree, but this is a homicide case. Get to the salient points, Mr. Mendoza," Tennant said.

"Yes, your Honor."

When they started again, Tonya admitted she could not remember the question, so the court reporter read it back to her.

"Oh, yes, we told him about the homeless man running away. Did he say we didn't? If he said that he's lying," Tonya indignantly embellished her answer for which the judge lightly chastised her.

Gondeck passed on cross-examination, as he did with the other two girls. Their testimony was essentially the same, made mostly to cast doubt on the investigation. By the time Mendoza finished with the third one, it was time for the lunch break.

"Hey," Maddy said to Marc while reading a message on her phone.

"What?"

"I got a text from Tony. Here, read it."

Marc took her phone and read: "Don't leave. We are on the way with vital info. Wait for us."

"Who is 'us' and what vital info do they have?" Marc rhetorically asked.

"And who wrote the text? That's from Tony's phone, but the message is too clear for him to have written," Maddy replied.

"What's up?" Arturo asked.

Marc showed him the text then gave Maddy her phone.

"Ask them for an ETA? Tell them we'll meet across the street at Peterson's. I'm starving."

Gretchen showed Carvelli the reply message from Maddy and agreed to meet them at Peterson's. His phone rang and Gretchen answered it.

"Yeah, he's right here," she said. "Sorenson."

"What's up, Dan? I'm in a bit of a hurry."

"Our mystery caller told Damone about a plea deal offered by the prosecution. Third-degree? Do you know about that?"

"No, I don't."

"Who would? That wouldn't be generally known unless he accepted it and Damone's pal said he didn't"

"I don't know. I'll ask Marc about it. Did the call come from the same phone?"

"Yeah, it did."

SIXTY

Marc and Maddy were seated in a large, horseshoe-shaped booth. It was barely five minutes before they saw Carvelli come in. Marc waved to them and as they walked toward them, Maddy quietly asked, "Why are Gretchen and Philo with him?"

Before Marc could reply they were at the booth.

Without sitting down, Carvelli asked, "Have you ordered?"

"No," Marc replied.

"Slide over," Carvelli said, then sat down next to Marc. Gretchen and Philo sat opposite them.

"Check this out," Carvelli said, then looked around the restaurant while holding his phone in front of Marc's face.

"Why am I looking at the background picture on your phone?"

"What?" a confused Carvelli asked.

He looked at his phone and the picture of the gun was gone.

"Damn," Carvelli said. "Here, find the photo for me," he said handing his phone to Gretchen.

By now Gretchen had already retrieved her phone from her purse, found the photo and said, "Use mine. It's better quality anyway."

Carvelli reached for it and Gretchen pulled it back.

"Not you, you'll probably break it. Here," she said and handed the phone to Maddy. "I swear we need to send you to tech school before you break something," Gretchen told Carvelli.

"Too late," Maddy quietly said. She was holding Gretchen's phone so she and Marc could both see it.

"What am I looking at?" Marc asked. "Is that what I think it is?"

"What do you think it is?" Carvelli asked.

"It looks like Ferguson pointing a gun at someone," Marc said, trying to control his excitement.

"It looks like that," Maddy said. "But that's not Ferguson's arm. Look closer,"

"You're right, then who…"

"Zoom in on Ferguson's right shoulder," Gretchen told Maddy. She slid around the seat and was right next to Maddy. "Here," Gretchen said, pointing at the spot.

Maddy zoomed into that spot until they could clearly see the top of Dudek's baseball cap.

"That's our homeless guy," Marc said. "My god, he did it. He sneaked up behind Ferguson, reached around him and pointed a gun at Rob."

"Just like you guessed," Maddy said.

"I did, didn't I?" Marc bragged. "I'm a genius."

"You got a lucky guess," Maddy said. "The date and time stamp are right. This is the shooting."

She looked up across the table at Philo with a grim face and said, "And where the hell has this been? And don't tell me you just found it."

Philo, his face beet red, did not say a word. By now, Marc had his phone out and dialed a number from his log.

"Hey, Lois, it's Marc. Is she in?"

"She's eating a salad. Why?"

"I need to speak to her right now. It's critical," Marc said.

"Hang on."

A few seconds later, Marc heard a very familiar voice.

"Marc, what do you need?"

"I apologize for interrupting your lunch, Margaret. We have to meet in chambers. Now."

"Why, what have you come up with?"

"The end of this trial. I'll call Steve Gondeck and we'll be there in ten minutes if that's okay."

"Yeah, this salad sucks anyway. I need a steak and baked potato. I'll call upstairs and get Steve and Jennifer myself. Where are you?"

"Peterson's," Marc said.

"Aw, man! A Peterson's burger. I'd kill for one."

"I'll bring you one."

"No, don't. Get back here."

Marc ended the call and turned his head to his right. He found Maddy with her right elbow on the table and her chin in her right hand. She was staring at him within inches of his nose with a very serious look on her face.

After a few seconds, Marc said, "What?"

She continued to silently stare, then finally said, "So, you still have her phone number on speed dial, I see."

"What? Wait, what? It's not...okay. I'll remove it."

Still looking at him exactly the same way, Maddy said, "You are so easy to rattle and it's so much fun."

By now the entire table was laughing.

"You got me, okay? Let's go."

Gondeck and Jennifer Moore came through the guarded courtroom door together. Marc and the gang were already waiting for him. Marc had spoken to one of the deputies who promised to have Rob brought back.

"What's so important you had to ruin my lunch?" Gondeck asked.

"You could stand to skip lunch once in a while anyway," Marc said.

"That's not nice," Maddy said.

"She kind of likes portly," Carvelli added.

Gondeck straightened up, looked at Maddy and said, "I am portly."

When the laughter died down, Lois came out to get them.

"Do you want to wait for your client?" she asked.

"No, let's go," Marc said. He looked at Maddy. "Keep him here," he said referring to Philo. "Break a leg if you have to."

"Oooo," Maddy said, "you know how to charm a girl."

"Where's Arturo and your client?" Margaret asked as the three lawyers took seats.

"Arturo's at his office. I called him. He's on the way and one of your deputies is rounding up Rob."

"Okay, what?" Margaret asked.

Marc took Gretchen's phone from his coat pocket and brought up the photo on the screen. He stood up, stepped behind the desk to lean over the judge and held it for her.

"You'll want to come look at this," Marc said to the prosecutors.

Margaret put on her cheaters while Gondeck and Moore joined her.

"Is that what it looks like?" the judge asked.

"Oh, no, you don't," Gondeck practically sputtered with anger. "You're not bringing in some phony, photo-shopped picture of Ferguson with a gun."

"Thank you for the ruling, Judge Gondeck," Tennant wryly said. "Or, maybe I'll decide what comes in."

"This is..." Gondeck started to say.

"This is a photo taken by one Philo Anson of the Star Tribune at the time and place of the shooting of Reverend Ferguson," Marc said. "Note the date and time stamp," Marc said pointing.

"Let me zoom in..." Marc began to say and reached for the phone.

Margaret slapped his hand and said, "As I recall, you're not real good at this. What is this on his right shoulder?" she almost whispered as she used the zoom to get a close-up.

"Looks like the top of a man's head wearing a baseball cap," she said. Tennant sat back, took off the glasses, looked up at Marc and asked, "Your mysterious, missing, homeless man?"

"Yes, if you look closely you can tell that is not Ferguson's hand holding the gun. In fact, his right arm is pinned against his side. The whole thing happened so fast it took everyone by surprise."

"Please, sit down," Tennant said.

When they were seated, she asked Marc, "What are you proposing?"

"Dismissal with prejudice right now."

Before Gondeck said anything, Tennant held up a hand to stop him. "I'm not going to do that, at least not yet.

"All right, let's think this through," she continued.

"Judge, we cannot even be certain it is the same place where the shooting occurred," Gondeck said.

"I'll get to your concerns, Steve. Assume the police had found the gun. Officer Dane would have been put on administrative duty pending an investigation. The question is: would they have found this to be a righteous shooting?"

"Of course," Marc quickly said.

"Steve? Jennifer?"

"Be honest," Marc said.

"Probably," Gondeck admitted.

"Let me see it again, please," Jennifer asked. After carefully examining the photo, she placed it back on Tennant's desk.

"I've handled these cases," Jennifer began. "Assuming it is a genuine photo, I believe he would have been exonerated.

"He's on crowd control and all of a sudden there's an angry looking man staring right at him. He looks to be pointing a gun at him. Robert Dane has less than one second to decide what to do. Pull his gun or get shot.

"He's an Army Ranger with loads of training and combat experience. He's a veteran cop. Officer Dane will pull his sidearm and shoot center mass every time. That's what we've trained him to do. Hell, that's what we pay him to do."

"Three times?" Tennant asks.

"Three times, in my opinion, and I believe the review board would agree, is not excessive. Four or five, maybe, six, probably. Three, no, he's okay," Jennifer answered.

"I'm glad I brought you along," Gondeck sulkily said.

"Steve, we're supposed to be looking for justice here. Not a conviction to notch the scoreboard," Tennant said.

"I resent that, Margaret. You know me better than that."

"Yes, I do. That's why I said it," she replied.

"Is Mr. Anson here?" Tennant asked.

"Yes, Judge. He's in the courtroom being watched by Maddy," Marc said.

"Fetch him, please."

When Marc and Philo returned, Tennant's court reporter was setting up his equipment.

"This is going on the record," Tennant told them.

Margaret reminded Philo that he was still under oath and had Marc question him. It barely took ten minutes for Philo to testify that he took the picture, along with many others, and had withheld it until today. He also swore it was not doctored in any way and was taken at the exact same time and place of Reverend Ferguson's death.

Gondeck did a short cross, trying to cast Philo in a bad light by hoping to cash in on the photo. He was not successful, especially when he tried to get Philo to say it was altered. Philo stood his ground on that issue.

Philo was excused and told to wait in the courtroom.

"How long to get it over to the BCA lab and have it authenticated?" Tennant asked.

"Since we're in mid-trial, they'll give it a priority. Especially if I show the lab geeks a little leg," Jennifer said, then winked at the judge.

"Take Maddy with you," Tennant said.

"No kidding," Jennifer said. "For her, they'll deliver it this afternoon. For me, sometime tomorrow. I'll take it myself. Where is Philo's phone? The original?"

"Gretchen has it," Marc said. "One of the...."

"That is Gretchen Stenson," Jennifer said. "I thought it was her."

"Oh, oh," Marc quietly said to himself.

"And who is Gretchen Stenson?" Tennant asked.

"She's a friend of Tony's," Marc quickly said.

348

"She's a high-class, expensive call girl, Judge," Jennifer said.

"A friend of Tony's?" Tennant asked.

"He's had a long and, well, colorful career," Marc said.

"He certainly has," Tennant laughed.

"Okay, get Philo's phone, get it to the BCA and see what they say. I'm going to send the jury home. I'll have them back day after tomorrow; Friday morning. We'll either keep going or dismiss it."

"Judge," Gondeck said, "even if the photo is authentic it is still a question for the jury."

"I'll think about it."

When they got back into the courtroom, Arturo was just arriving. Marc took him aside and filled him in on what he had missed.

SIXTY-ONE

Judge Tennant had been notified of the result regarding the photo of Ferguson and the gun. It was genuine and not doctored in any way. Marc Kadella also received an email with the lab test report.

The meeting in Judge Tennant's office took place at 3:00 P.M. Along with the four lawyers, Felicia Jones, the county attorney, and MPD Chief Marvin Brown were also present.

"Thank you for coming," Tennant started off. Instead of being seated at her desk, she was leaning on the front of it without her robes.

"First of all, and I don't mean to insult anyone, whatever is said in this room stays in this room. This is a settlement conference and nothing said here can be allowed to get to the jury. Also, I want everyone to speak freely.

"Marc, why don't you tell everyone the defense side, so we're all on the same page."

"Sure. Thanks, Judge."

Marc stood and said, "You're all aware that my client, the defendant Officer Robert Dane, has been charged with several counts of homicide for the death of Lionel Ferguson. The fact that Officer Dane, while on duty, shot Ferguson has never been in dispute.

"Rob has maintained all along that a gun was pointed at him and he believed it was Ferguson who was doing it.

"He reacted like any trained, licensed law enforcement officer would do. He pulled his sidearm and fired three shots, center mass, into Ferguson and killed him.

"The gun he swore he saw was never found. Now we know why. We have photographic proof, authenticated by the BCA lab of the State of Minnesota, that a gun was pointed at Officer Dane. But it does appear it was not Ferguson who was pointing it. Have you seen the photo?" he asked, looking at Chief Brown and Felicia Jones. Both answered affirmatively.

"From the photo, it appears a man was hiding behind Ferguson, who was a very large man. This man reached around Ferguson, pinned Ferguson's arm down and pointed the gun at Officer Dane, probably for only a second or two, causing Officer Dane to react the way he did. We can only guess that this man's motive was to induce Rob Dane into shooting Ferguson. Otherwise, the man had multiple opportunities to do it himself."

"Thanks, Marc," Tennant said. "That pretty much sums it up. We're here to decide what to do. As I see it, there are three options. One, the prosecution can ask the court to dismiss the charges, which I would grant. Two, I could dismiss the charges on my own in the interest of justice. Finally, we can proceed with the trial and let the jury decide.

"Chief Brown, let me ask you. Knowing what we know now, having seen the photo, do you believe this was a good shooting?"

"Yes, I have no doubt the review board would have ruled it to be so," Brown replied.

"Felicia?" Tennant asked the county attorney.

"I'm not going to undercut my lawyers, Margaret. I have to trust their judgment and have their backs. Steve's call."

"Mr. Gondeck?"

Before he could answer, Marc interrupted him. "Why don't we put him on the stand? Let Philo testify about the photo. Steve can object and cross him if he wants to. If you are satisfied, afterwards, you can move for dismissal or I will."

"Mr. Gondeck?"

Gondeck looked at his boss who silently nodded her head.

"I didn't get to sleep last night until I realized sending him to prison for this would be a gross miscarriage. Although I do like Marc's idea, let's make a record of it and be open about why we're doing it," Gondeck said.

"The city is not going to like it at all," Chief Brown said. "The race hustlers will raise hell that another unarmed black man was gunned down by a white cop and the system let him get away with it. I don't care, but I can see it coming."

"I'm not sending an innocent man to prison just to placate those who would incite a mob," Tennant said. "We'll do it tomorrow, Marc's way. Can you get him in here?"

"I'll send Maddy after him if I have to," Marc said.

Tennant laughed and then said, "Anything else?"

"I'll contact the mayor and…" Felica Jones started to say.

"Don't tell him what's going on until it's done. Otherwise, it will be in tomorrow morning's paper," Chief Brown said.

"Okay, I'll make an appointment to see him personally at ten o'clock tomorrow morning. I'll tell him and then we can set up a press conference for later. Does anybody else want to be there?"

When no one spoke up, she added, "Thought not. Cowards."

They all laughed, then Marc said he would. Gondeck did also along with Chief Brown, Jennifer Moore and Arturo Mendoza.

"Strength in numbers. Okay, I'll let all of you know when the press conference will be and where. Probably across the street on the third floor."

When Marc and Arturo exited the elevator on the Second Floor Atrium, Marc made two calls. The first was to a very anxiously awaiting Rob Dane. Of course, Marc had shown him a photo of Ferguson and the gun and told him about today's meeting. Rob almost melted with relief and gratitude while on the phone. When the call ended, he was sobbing uncontrollably. He managed to collect himself to tell Leah followed by more tears and hugs.

The next call was to Maddy. She was babysitting Philo at his townhouse. They would meet back at Marc's office.

On the way back to his office, Marc called Carvelli with the news. Carvelli told Marc he had serious news as well and would meet at Marc's office.

Despite leaving together, by the time Marc parked his car, Arturo was in the lot waiting for him. A moment later, Maddy drove in with Philo.

"You understand what's expected of you? No misunderstanding?" Marc asked.

"Yeah, I got it," a chastised Philo said. "The testimony, that won't be a big deal."

"I'll walk you through it just like we practiced it. All you have to do is tell the truth. You do know how to tell the truth. I mean, I know you work for a newspaper but not all of the stories are completely made up, are they?"

"Very funny," Philo replied. "This other thing, I'll have to meet-"

Maddy came through the conference room door and stopped him in mid-sentence. She had been using Marc's office to make some phone calls.

"Okay, it's all set. Half an hour," Maddy said.

"I should stop at home and get a recorder," Philo replied.

"I have one in my car, you can use it," Maddy said.

"Okay, then let's go," Philo said.

There was a ruckus out in the work area at that moment. Carvelli, who loved to make an entrance here, had arrived and stirred things up. In a good way.

Carvelli came into the conference room while Maddy and Philo were getting ready to leave.

"Philo, we're going to put you up in a hotel tonight. I want to be sure you show up," Marc told him.

"I'm not a child. I'll show up."

"And you're getting a sitter…"

"Maddy or Gretchen," Philo said.

"Ms. Rivers is going to be busy tonight. She has plans," Marc said.

"I do?" she asked.

"Yeah," Marc said nodding his head back and forth with an expectant look on his face. "You know…"

The light went on and she said, "Oh, yeah, that's right, I do. Sorry, Philo."

"Can you get Sorenson or one of the guys?"

"Sure," Carvelli replied. He looked at Maddy and said, "Call me when you're done with whatever you're doing."

When Maddy closed the door behind her, Carvelli said, "It's happening Sunday morning, six A.M."

"Get them back in here," Marc said. "I have an idea."

Carvelli went out and brought Maddy and Philo back into the conference room.

"You want another big scoop?" Marc asked Philo.

"Sure, always. What do you have?"

"Can you keep your mouth shut? Keep it to yourself for a couple of days?" Carvelli asked.

"Because you're finally cooperating and saving an innocent man's ass, we'll toss this to you," Marc said. He looked at Carvelli and added, "He doesn't need all of the details, yet."

"Okay. There's a huge federal task force drug bust coming down. It covers Chicago, Minneapolis and the entire Upper Midwest. Over a hundred warrants. That's all you get for now. I'll be around Sunday morning. You'll get it first. There will be a press conference, Monday."

"All right! I'll get together with you on Sunday."

"Maybe we'll get some clients," Arturo said to Marc.

"You might. I won't take these guys," Marc said.

"Who are they?"

"Miniature cartel was working out of here and connected to a gang in Chicago," Carvelli said.

SIXTY-TWO

"The defense recalls, Philo Anson, your Honor."

At the in-chambers settlement the previous afternoon, everyone was sworn to secrecy. None of the attendees violated that promise. Despite that, as if the walls had ears, a rumor swept through the building. Something big was up in the trial of Rob Dane. Every seat was full, another hundred people were milling about in the hall, and a couple thousand were downstairs.

Philo, having arrived under armed guard, was seated in the front row. He walked up to the witness stand, was reminded by Tennant that he was still under oath and then took the stand. Having spent almost an hour preparing Philo the previous evening, they were as ready as they ever would be.

Not wanting to waste any time, Marc asked, "Let's get right to it, shall we, Mr. Anson?"

"Sure," he replied, happy to be back in the spotlight.

A photograph came up on the TV monitors of Lionel Ferguson. There was a stirring in the courtroom. The hand with a gun in it at Ferguson's side was clearly visible.

"Mr. Anson, on the screen is a photograph marked for identification as Defense Exhibit Four. Do you recognize it?"

"Yes, it is a photo I took with my phone."

"Explain to the jury what it is."

"It is a photo of Reverend Ferguson taken at the time of the shooting. There is an arm pointing a gun at someone-"

"Objection! Speculation, foundation, the witness cannot know from the photo, who the gun is pointed at," Gondeck stood and interrupted.

"I'll overrule subject to connection."

"Who is he pointing the gun at?"

"Officer Robert Dane."

"How do you know that?"

"By the date and time stamp on the photo and I saw Officer Dane standing at that exact place on the sidewalk after the shooting. It is the precise time and location where Reverend Ferguson was shot."

"How did you manage to get this picture?"

"I was holding my phone up. I did that quite a lot during the protest and was taking a lot of pictures. I even videotaped sometimes. Basically, I just got lucky."

"Is it Ferguson holding the gun?"

"No. If you look closely, you can see that Ferguson's right arm is pinned to his side by the arm holding the gun. And behind Ferguson's right shoulder is what appears to be the top of a baseball cap."

"Did you see the man with the gun run away?"

"No, I was looking at Officer Dane. He was crouched in a shooter's stance less than ten feet from Ferguson's body. There was, literally, smoke coming from his gun barrel."

"Was Officer Dane standing where the gun in Defense Exhibit Four, the photo of Reverend Ferguson with a gun at his side, had been pointed?"

"Exactly," Philo replied.

"Where have you been? Why have you waited until now to come forward?"

"I was acting as a journalist and to be honest, a very selfish one. It was eating at me until I could no longer take it. So, I had a friend contact you."

"Nothing further, your Honor."

Steve Gondeck was tempted to go after him and eviscerate Philo for his behavior. Because the dismissal was planned, he decided to let it go. Marc had created sufficient grounds on the record for the dismissal, a CYA exercise.

"I have no questions, your Honor," Gondeck said.

Then Gondeck stood and said, "At this time, your Honor, because sufficient evidence has been submitted showing the shooting death of Lionel Ferguson was justified by Officer Dane, the state moves to dismiss all charges."

Even though the calendar still read October, normally a very pleasant month in Minnesota, the authorities got lucky. During the previous night, a nasty storm system had arrived. The temperature dropped to the low thirties, the wind increased and a mix of rain and snow made for an ugly day. Because of this, the news of the dismissal brought nothing onto the streets in protest. Even outraged protestors have their limits.

The Friday afternoon press conference at the Mayor's office was heavily attended. The media, all of the locals and at least a dozen national news sources were in attendance. In addition, almost twenty community leaders, including black and white ones, were invited and in attendance.

The press conference lasted from 2:00 until almost 4:00. On the podium were the usual suspects of politicians and police. Each, in turn, stepped to the microphones to take questions. Even Marc. He was mostly tossed softballs concerning his client and how Rob was doing.

Felicia Jones, despite her youth and relative inexperience, was the one who came across best. She spent over forty-five minutes being grilled almost unmercifully. In their never-ending quest to prove their liberal credentials, the cable, national and local media demanded to know how Rob Dane could be let off. He had admittedly shot and killed an upstanding member of a minority. As they always see it, the media must serve and protect all minorities from the injustices of the system.

Felicia handled each question, calmly, rationally and stood by her––she took the hit––decision to dismiss the case.

"All right," she looked over the crowd and said, "I'll say this one more time. The death of Lionel Ferguson was a tragedy. You could even call it an accident. But Officer Dane no doubt responded to a gun being pointed at him justifiably. That's all." She then turned and walked away.

Saturday at 6:00 A.M., Maddy's eyes popped open and she was wide awake. It was as if there was a clock in her head telling her it was time. Less than a minute later, while still lying in bed, she heard a very light plop sound coming from the front door.

After two or three minutes in the bathroom, Maddy was in the kitchen and poured herself a cup of coffee. Wearing only a large, men's white T-shirt and boxer shorts, she retrieved the paper. While walking into the living room, she admired the screaming headline at the top of page one:

Ferguson Accused of Pedophilia

The byline was Philo Anson.

For the next twenty minutes Maddy sat cross-legged on the couch reading the story. As a reward for finally coming forward and testifying, Marc had decided to give Philo the scoop on Ferguson's behavior.

Two nights ago, Maddy called Sherry Bowen. Sherry had rounded up a half dozen girls willing to tell their stories of rape and molestation at the hands of Lionel Ferguson. Even Philo, as cynical as anyone, was almost moved to tears by what they told him.

The night before his day in court, Philo was up until 2:00 A.M. He wrote two stories. The first was the facts about Ferguson, his use of his church and authority over young, vulnerable girls. The second, a sidebar about the damage these girls had suffered. Of course, none of their names were used.

It had been Marc's decision to do it in the hope that it would tamp down any sentiment people might feel. At least try to cool the resentment many would have from another white cop getting away with shooting an unarmed black man.

"How is it?" Marc asked, standing in the kitchen entryway sipping a cup. "We look like twins," he noted, taking in their identical dress.

"It's not good for the dearly departed Rev Ferguson," Maddy replied.

Marc sat down next to her and she gave him a kiss. Maddy then asked, "What about this guy, this guy we think is someone named Charles Dudek?"

"I don't know," Marc said. "We told the cops what we know. It's not really our problem and I don't advise that we go looking for him. He's very good at what he does. Oddly, I'd like to meet him. I'll bet he's an interesting guy."

"You'd like to meet a sociopathic hitman? An assassin?"

"Well, yeah, um, you know. Him on one side of the plexiglass and me on the other," Marc said. "Hey, I've had clients that I wouldn't want my daughter bringing home. Some of them you've met. Remember?"

"True enough. But this guy might be a bridge too far."

"So, this is what it's like at five o'clock in the morning after you've been sleeping and then get up," Carvelli said to Jeff Johnson.

"Here, Tony," Tess Richards said, handing him a cup of black, freshly brewed from Dunkin' Donuts.

"Oh, thanks, Tess. You're a life saver."

"There are some donuts over by that Suburban," she said pointing to an SUV.

"No, thanks," Carvelli replied. "So, what's the game plan?"

The three of them, along with another sixteen agents, were one of four law enforcement teams gathered this morning. This one was in a strip mall parking lot a few blocks from North Minneapolis. Thanks to Carvelli's infiltration of Damone Watson's organization and Conrad's wiretaps, there were over sixty arrest warrants to serve. And another fifty in Chicago this morning.

Jeff Johnson said, "Of the people here, there are four teams. The targets are under surveillance and all are reporting no activity.

"You get to tag along when we hit Damone. He's been under surveillance for a couple of days. He was last seen arriving back at his building yesterday afternoon. He has not gone out again."

"Okay," Carvelli said. "Let's go wake my pal Damone."

There was a set of indoor stairs as a way into the back of Damone's building. The plan was for every team to hit their target precisely at six A.M. This would make sure no one could get on the phone and start warning people. With about a minute to go, one of the SWAT guys with Johnson was going to hit the back door with a battering ram. As he swung it back, Carvelli stepped in.

"Wait a minute. Do you want to wake the whole neighborhood? There are more guns in this area than an NRA convention," he quietly said as he stooped in front of the door.

"Give me a little light," he said. Tess shined a flashlight on the lock while Carvelli worked with a couple of burglars' picks.

"As a law enforcement officer, you should be ashamed that you even know how to do that," Johnson said.

"That's what my mother used to say to me about a lot of things," Carvelli replied. The lock clicked and Carvelli opened it.

There were eight of them in total—four for the second floor, and four, led by Johnson with Carvelli behind, to go up to the third-floor apartment. Having been given an excellent drawing by Conrad, they knew exactly where to go.

Fifteen minutes later, Carvelli was sitting in Damone's expensively furnished living room. Johnson came in and joined him.

"Gone," Carvelli said.

"Looks like," Johnson said.

"I thought you had this place under surveillance."

"We did. Hell, there're a hundred ways to beat that if you know about it."

"You think he was tipped off?"

"Probably. Otherwise, where is he?"

Johnson's radio beeped from the second-floor team.

"Find anything?"

"Really? I'll be right down," Johnson replied when he was told what was on the second floor.

A minute later, while Tess finished the third-floor search, Johnson and Carvelli were standing over the bodies of two large, black men.

"Hello, Lewis, you're looking well. Except, of course, for that third eye you have in your forehead."

"You know them?"

"Lewis Freeh and Monroe Ervin," Carvelli said. "Damone's two main guys."

"What do you think?"

"I think Damone got a tip and knew the party was over. He's in the wind. Probably on a beach somewhere."

"Sooner or later, we will find his ass," an angry Jeff Johnson said.

By noon every warrant had been served with four notable exceptions.

Damone, of course, and his brother, Jeron, were missing as was a Somali man by the name of Saadaq Khalid. He had been identified as Damone's liaison with the Somalis.

The fourth unserved warrant was for Imam Abdallah Sadia. At six o'clock the Imam was already up and at prayer. When he heard the door crash from the battering ram, he immediately knew what it was. Barely a minute later, two of the agents kicked open his locked bedroom door. The Imam was staring at them with a pistol in his mouth. Before either man could respond, the Imam pulled the trigger.

While everyone else at FBI headquarters in Minneapolis was slapping each other on the back, Carvelli took a phone call.

"What's up?" he asked his hacker friend, Paul Baker.

"Hey, dude, I'm seeing a big bust on a TV. Congrats."

"What have I told you about calling me dude," Carvelli said.

"Yeah, yeah, whatever. Listen, Tony, I ah, made a mistake."

"I want that in writing," Carvelli said.

"No, seriously. When I ran that phone number for you, well, I should have checked for family members. I think the caller is a relative. In fact, I'm positive. It's gotta be her brother."

"Jesus, you're kidding me," Carvelli quietly said after Paul gave him the name. He thanked him then hung up.

A minute later he found Jeff Johnson and pulled him away from the celebration.

"Hey, did either Lewis or Monroe have a phone on him?"

"Yeah, they both did," Johnson replied.

"What's the time of death for them?"

"Don't know yet. Has to be after two and before five or six Saturday afternoon, by the rigor and how cold they were."

"You got a tech guy around here who can check both of those phones for incoming calls yesterday afternoon?"

"Well, hell, I can do that. Why?"

"I may be able to tell you who gave Damone the heads up we were coming."

"Let's go. I know right where the phones are."

Johnson drove his government car with Carvelli in the passenger seat. Tess had begged off, preferring to stay in the office. Johnson parked on the street in front of the small bungalow. Both men sat quietly staring at the house.

"I hate this," Carvelli said. "He seems like a good guy."

"Well, let's go get him," Johnson said.

When they reached the front door, Carvelli rang the bell while Johnson prepared his phone.

When the door opened, the man looked at the two of them with a startled expression.

"Hey, Tony, what's up?"

"We need to talk to you, Arturo. Can we come in?"

At that moment, Johnson having pushed the send button on his phone, Arturo's phone began to ring.

"Ah, yeah, sure. Let me get my phone."

They stepped into the foyer as Arturo answered his phone.

"Hello."

"Arturo Mendoza?"

"Yeah, who's this?"

Johnson pushed the end button as he and Carvelli entered the living room.

"My name is Agent Johnson with the FBI, Mr. Mendoza. You are under arrest for impeding a federal investigation and obstruction of justice and likely other crimes that we'll think up later."

Arturo turned to face them as Johnson started to say, "You have the night to remain silent…"

SIXTY-THREE

"Excuse me, sir," the flight attendant quietly said while lightly shaking the passenger's shoulder.

"Yes, what is it?" the man answered. He had been sleeping but fortunately he was a light sleeper. He normally woke up almost instantly.

"We're making our final approach. The captain has put on the seatbelt sign," she replied while locking in the man's tray table.

"Of course, thank you. How much longer?" he asked while buckling up.

"About twenty minutes."

While the woman walked off to other duties for her business class passengers, Damone Watson leaned his head back on the seat headrest. He had been on the move since the phone call he received four days ago on Saturday afternoon.

Saadaq Khalid had called with the news that the FBI was about to arrest Damone, his brother Jeron and a least one hundred others. Damone and Saadaq had known since the beginning that eventually this would happen. Because of that, they had an escape plan in place and ready at the drop of a hat.

Saadaq had used his underground contacts to obtain three sets of IDs for each of them. Complete with legitimate passports, U.S. and International driver's licenses, valid credit cards, a car, and cash. For security reasons, neither man knew the other's ultimate route out of the country, but they did know each other's destination. Saadaq had also made the same arrangement for Jeron Watson.

After finishing the call with Saadaq, Damone told Lewis and Monroe to wait in the conference room on the second floor. Damone went up to his apartment to prepare for his departure. He had a "Go Bag" ready with clothing and toiletries to last for several days. He placed the most important item, his laptop, in its bag for carrying. The laptop contained all the business transactions and information for Damone's drug business.

When he finished upstairs and was ready to leave, he had one more duty to perform. He retrieved a .45 caliber semi-auto handgun from his bed stand. He checked it to make sure it was loaded and had one in the chamber. Satisfied, he started downstairs to say goodbye to Lewis and Monroe.

Oddly, on his way down, he was feeling guilt and regret. They were both loyal employees, good men and had become almost friends.

When he entered the conference room the two men were seated at the table. They stood up, and without a word, Damone's hand behind his back came forward. Lewis, from the look on his face, knew immediately his life was over. Monroe seemed more surprised than Lewis and was startled and shocked by what he saw.

Damone fired two quick shots, first to Lewis in his forehead and then Monroe, who was looking at Lewis, was hit in the temple.

Damone stood over them for a minute and said a silent prayer. When he finished, he said, "Goodbye, my friends. I regret this, but I could not take you or let you stay."

Ten minutes later, he slipped out the back door and into the back seat of a dark blue Chevy Impala; a very unnoticeable car.

Saadaq drove away and three blocks later pulled into a church parking lot next to his identical Chevy.

"Did you take care of him?"

"Yes, the fire department should be there by now," Saadaq replied. He was referring to the accountant. It was Saadaq's job to kill him and burn him and his office/home completely to erase any evidence.

The two men faced each other and Damone said, "If we don't see each other in a few days, we will meet again in paradise."

They embraced, then Saadaq said, "In-sha Allah."

"In-sha Allah," Damone replied.

Damone drove to Houston where, the next morning, he used a credit card for a flight to Belize. For the next three days, he moved around the Caribbean until he ended up in Marseilles, France. It was from Marseilles that the flight he was now on had originated. This was supposed to be the next to last leg of his journey. The rest of his trip would be made by car.

The Air France A380's wheels gently bumped onto the tarmac. The crew threw on the big jet's brakes pushing Danone slightly forward in his seat. He turned and looked past the empty seat to his right and watched as the airliner slowed.

"This is your Captain," he heard a man's voice come over the intercom and say, "welcoming you to Beirut. We're a few minutes ahead of schedule which is always good news. As you can see, it is a partly cloudy day with a very pleasant temperature of twenty-six degrees celsius, seventy-eight Fahrenheit. We will be at the gate in just a few minutes. Thank you for flying Air France and enjoy the rest of your day."

For the first time since his release from prison, Damone felt truly free and at home. He could now stop pretending. He hated America and everything it was and stood for. America truly was the enemy, the Great Satan. But for American power, Israel would be long gone, the Jews would all be dead, and Islam would be marching toward Allah's goal of world domination.

While in prison, Damone had not found Christ and Christianity. In fact, just the opposite. He had become a radicalized Muslim.

Having been taken under the wing of an undercover, radicalized Muslim by the American name of Terry Schofield, Damone had seen the light. America, with its freedom, liberty and the corruption that came with it, was indeed, the great oppressor.

Damone's talent for crime and drug dealing had been put to good use. He was assigned to sell poison to the Americans and funnel the money to radical, political groups in the Middle East. According to his go-between contact, Saadaq Khalid, Damone was very successful.

Having retrieved his large piece of luggage—too big to carry on—Damone left the airport's security area. He saw the door where he was to meet Jeron and Saadaq and went toward it. His heart leaped a bit when he saw his younger brother waving to him and his friend and ally, Saadaq, waiting with Jeron.

When he reached them, they joyfully greeted each other with traditional Muslim greetings. Jeron then took Damone's bag and followed Saadaq out to the car. Waiting by the curb was a slightly battered Land Rover with a serious looking Lebanese man leaning against it.

In Arabic, Saadaq said to the man, "Let's get on the road before it starts getting dark."

Fifteen minutes into the ride, Damone asked for water. Saadaq was riding in the front passenger seat and Jeron was in back with Damone.

Saadaq silently handed Damone an open liter of a local brand of bottled water.

Damone drank almost half of it then gave it to Jeron. He, in turn, drank almost two hundred milliliters of what remained.

"Thirsty?" Saadaq asked smiling.

"Yes," Damone said smiling back. He leaned forward and slapped Saadaq on the shoulder and almost yelled, "It is so good to have us all here."

"Allah qad 'aradaha," Saadaq replied. "Allah has willed it," he then said in English for Jeron.

The car went quiet and ten minutes later both Damone and Jeron were sound asleep.

Saadaq turned around and tried to shake both men awake without success. He looked through the back window and saw another Land Rover following them.

"They're out. Pull over up here," Saadaq said in English.

"How long will they sleep?" the driver asked.

"Not long enough. We have to be certain they cannot know where we are going."

They turned right onto a very narrow, dirt-covered, street and stopped. The Land Rover following them pulled up behind them and also stopped.

Three men exited the second car and the Watson brothers were each given a shot to keep them out. Black hoods were placed over their heads and they were laid out in the back of the SUV. A light blanket was thrown over them and the two cars were back on the road within two minutes.

At two o'clock in the morning, the two Land Rovers arrived at their destination. Of course, Saadaq had phoned ahead, so they were expected.

They turned onto a dusty, narrow dirt road behind a row of nondescript two-story buildings. They were in a midsize village of no significance. Waiting inside for them was Saadaq's real boss.

A garage door was opened behind one of the buildings and the two cars drove in. Several men were there, and they gently carried Saadaq's cargo down a flight of stairs and into a room set up for them.

"How much longer?" the old man asked in English.

"A few minutes, at most," he was told.

"Kill the lights except theirs and wake them," the old man ordered.

Immediately, the room went dark except for two recessed lights directly above Damone and Jeron. The man who was ordered to wake them, a doctor, went to them. They were seated on uncomfortable armchairs in the center of the room in a bright circle of light, one light directed down from recessed lights installed in the ceiling directly above each of them. They were also secured at the wrists and ankles to the chairs' arms and legs with heavy duty, Velcro straps.

The doctor removed the black hood from Damone first. When he did this, Damone's head rolled slightly and he moaned. The doctor held a small vial of ammonia-based smelling salts under his nose. He kept it there for a few seconds and then Damone's head snapped back and his eyes opened. While Damone sat quietly trying to orient himself, the doctor repeated the procedure on Jeron.

"Thank you, Doctor. You may leave us," the old man said.

"I'll wait outside."

"You won't be needed."

"I'll wait anyway," the doctor said.

The old man chuckled and said, "As you wish."

It took several minutes for the fog to dissipate from their heads. While waiting for this, the old man waited silently in the dark.

"I heard you speak and in English," Damone finally said. "Who are you and where are we?"

Another overhead light came on illuminating the old man. He was sitting at a small, government issued, gray metal desk. The man was in his fifties but looked to be seventy. He was portly and bald except for a gray fringe around the back of his head. He also had the friendly look and twinkling eyes of a favorite grandpa. In his case, looks were very deceiving.

The old man stood and stepped to the front of the desk. He wore a pair of brown docksiders, no socks and a disheveled white shirt with khakis. He sat on the front of the desk, one foot on the floor, one off.

"Who are you? I demand to know," Damone arrogantly asked to mask his fear.

"Yes, I suppose we can now tell you some things.

"First, my name is Chaim Ben Segal. I hold the rank of colonel in the Israeli Defense Forces. I am currently on assignment to the Israeli Institute for Intelligence. What you know as Mossad. Let me be the first to welcome you to Israel where you two gentlemen are now our guests. Permanently, I might add, which means as long as you are useful to us."

367

While the old man quietly spoke explaining who he was, Damone's face took on the look of a terrified puppy.

"I, I don't understand," Jeron said. "Who is he and why are we here? We were on our way to Syria."

"You took a detour. Relax," the old man continued, "you're not in any danger. You may not believe me, but we really don't torture people. Your friends do. We don't."

"Where are we?" Damone quietly asked.

"A small town near Tel Aviv. Thank you for going to the trouble of disappearing from the Earth. Now, no one knows what happened to you."

"There is one, and he is very loyal," Damone confidently said.

"Ah, yes, Saadaq Khalid," the old man replied.

Two more lights came on above two men sitting along the back wall behind and to the right of the old man. It was not the sight of Saadaq that made Damone swallow his breath. It was the man seated next to him.

"Allow me to introduce you to the two gentlemen you thought you knew. Saadaq Khalid is actually Captain David Lavi. The man next to him in the gray Italian wool suit, white silk shirt and wrap around Ray Bans, known to you as 'the recruiter', is known to us as Major Elon Dayan."

The remaining lights in the room came on and showed two more people in attendance, a man and a woman.

"The gentleman to my left is Michael Fuller and the lady is his boss, Sharon Cartwright. They both work for an agency of the U.S. Government whose headquarters are located in Langley, Virginia.

"You see, gentlemen," he continued turning to Damone and Jeron, "you have been working for us since the day you left prison.

"We used you to find sources of funding for certain radical groups opposed to our existence. It isn't only your money we traced. We used that to find many more such conduits to these terror groups.

"Although," the old man said picking up a piece of paper from the desk, "your operation—you were very good, very organized—netted us one hundred eighty-four million, six hundred and thirty-four thousand US dollars and change. The government of Israel thanks you for your generous contribution to its continued existence. In fact, the total we have diverted from your cause to ours is close to four hundred million dollars and we have cut off several sources of funding for terrorism."

"You are far worse than we are," a now viciously angry Damone practically spat at him. "You let us sell tons of addictive, deadly drugs to your own people for this!"

"Yes, that was a very difficult, even immoral decision, we had to make," the woman from the CIA admitted. "Right now, thanks to your record keeping…"

"The accountant is not dead," Saadaq/David said. "I lied about that. The FBI has all of your records."

"Wait," Damone said. "How did you know to call me? To warn me? You did not have connections with the police…"

"We gave him a bit of a heads up," the woman from the CIA said. "We have sources and, well, we wanted you here, not in Washington.

"Anyway," the woman continued. "The US Government is going to quietly contact every one of your former customers and pay for their rehab and compensate them."

"You'll never be able to keep that quiet," Damone said.

"Perhaps," Cartwright replied. "But you'd be surprised what enough money, a non-disclosure agreement and the threat of a prison sentence will accomplish. We've done it before."

Elon Dayan removed the sunglasses then stood up, walked to a table and poured himself a glass of water. "The young men who we recruited for jihad are all in excellent health. They are being held, quite comfortably, not far from here. When the time is right, they will be sent back to America where they can convince the Americans they are no longer radicalized or face prison."

"What we have done may seem wrong or even immoral. But, at least for now, we have broken the back of a significant amount of financing for terrorism," Colonel Ben Segal said.

Michael Fuller, the other CIA agent, said, "The innocent people who have been hurt, and we know there have been, can be helped and made whole. You should know, not a single person was sold opioids through you who wasn't getting them before. We realize that makes no difference, but at least now they have a chance to get clean."

"You gentleman will remain our guests for as long as we say," Ben Segal said.

"And if we refuse to cooperate?" Damone arrogantly asked.

"Then it will be my pleasure to handcuff and gag you. Then drop you off into a certain neighborhood I know of in Damascus with a sign around your neck. It will read: 'Israeli collaborator.' And you can take your chances," Saadaq replied.

Epilogue

As the media came out with more and more stories about Lionel Ferguson, the anger over the dismissal of charges against Rob Dane quickly dissipated. No one wanted the embarrassment of being linked to a pedophile, serial rapist and greedy hustler linked to the sale of drugs.

An odd thing happened concerning the news of the indictments. For a couple of days, the bust of Damone Watson's empire was a very hot item. By the Wednesday following the Sunday morning raids, it was as if it never happened. Philo got his inside scoop from Carvelli and wrote up his articles expecting a Pulitzer nomination. Instead, according to what he would tell Carvelli, most of the story was spiked. The cause, again according to Philo, was their concern about Somali involvement. Since immigrants in general and Muslims in particular, having been declared a protected class by liberals, this story needed to die. On top of that, within days, the U.S. Government was throwing a blackout over everything.

With the fall from grace of Damone, the Minneapolis political class went into a furious spin mode. By the end of the week, no one in city government had ever heard of Damone Watson.

On the first Tuesday of November, the usual slate of Democrat suspects were elected or re-elected to run the city. Unfortunately, Jalen Bryant was defeated by the grossly inexperienced Betsy Carpenter. She was able to hang Damone's support around Jalen's neck. If that was not enough, local TV was filled with ads depicting Jalen as a friend of the police in Minneapolis. Since the local media themselves were the ones who did this, no one tried to explain how Bryant could be both tied to Damone and the police.

The U.S. attorneys in Minneapolis and Chicago would, eventually, rack up a 98% conviction rate of those indicted. Of course, most of that gaudy number came from plea agreements. A significant number of the lesser players were allowed to plead to one or two minor felonies. Usually in exchange for testimony against their boss.

Carvelli's "boss," Jimmy Jones, was not one of the lucky ones. He was forced to trial and convicted of more than twenty federal felonies.

Being a four-time loser, Jimmy finally hit the jackpot: he was sentenced to life plus forty. The extra forty was a specific request by the prosecution.

When Jimmy was arrested, he was in the process of getting at the machine gun he kept under his work table. He was lucky he was not shot dead on the spot. In order to ensure that a future grossly inexperienced president would not foolishly pardon him as a nonviolent, urban entrepreneur drug dealer, the machine gun charge was not dropped in exchange for a plea. The idea that gang bangers and drug dealers were not violent shocked most police and prosecutors. Gun charges were no longer being treated as a throwaway charge for a plea.

Bennie Solo, Carvelli's ex-cop, rehab clinic operator friend, saw a significant increase in business. Carvelli and Wendy Merrill sought out every one of their customers. For those who could not pay or use family funds, Vivian Donahue would pay for their rehab. In just a few months, Bennie had almost all of them free of opioids.

Arturo Mendoza, Damone's pipeline of information, got lucky. Once the time of death for Lewis and Monroe was established, Arturo was cleared of obstruction of justice for warning Damone. His phone call, recorded on Lewis' phone that Saturday, came at least an hour after Lewis was dead. Damone was already gone.

As for his other problems stemming from taking money from Damone, Arturo agreed to surrender his license to practice law permanently. The authorities agreed, with Marc's approval, that this was punishment enough.

Ten days after the raids, having gone over their entire inventory of drugs and the money, Carvelli called Jeff Johnson. He told Johnson he was ready to come in and hand over everything all accounted for that was done undercover.

He met Johnson at FBI headquarters North of Minneapolis. Johnson helped carry the drugs and money to be surrendered up to a conference room. It was supposedly all set for this and would only require a few signatures.

Instead, when they walked in, Carvelli was read his rights and told he could not leave. An apoplectic Jeff Johnson about exploded at the deception. It seems there was a new assistant U.S. Attorney brought in from Washington specifically to handle this case who had squelched Carvelli's deal.

Within a half an hour, Marc was there representing Carvelli. At one point, the new assistant U.S. Attorney, an arrogant, twenty-eight-year-old hotshot with Washington political connections, threatened to arrest Marc as a co-conspirator. Everyone else involved on the government's side sat sheepishly, keeping quiet to protect their careers. On his way to the meeting, Marc had the good sense to make a phone call to someone.

Shortly after 4:00 P.M., a serious looking, fifty-something woman opened the door. The local U.S. Attorney and an elegant looking woman strolled in followed by the fifty-something woman who was holding the door open. One look at the woman made the hotshot prosecutor almost melt.

"Yes, Mrs. Hanson," he said addressing Charlene Hanson, a Deputy Attorney General of the United States, the one who held the door for the others. "What can I do for you?"

"I flew out here today to find out just what the hell you are up to," she replied. "We received a phone call this morning from the woman who came in with me," she said, nodding at the elegant older lady, "who told the attorney general that you had gone back on a deal we had made with a close, personal friend of hers. Now I find out that is true. Do you want to explain why you decided, on your own, why the DOJ does not have to keep its word to people who are instrumental in helping us close out a significant investigation?"

The young lawyer stood opposite across the table from his superior from Washington and sensibly kept quiet.

By now, the other woman who came in was sitting next to Marc. Vivian Donahue had made a couple of calls after Marc called her.

Hanson looked at Carvelli and said, "Mr. Carvelli, you're free to go. Your record of this fiasco will be cleaned up.

"As for you," she continued turning back to the red-faced young man, "on the flight here, I made a personnel decision. It is my understanding that an Assistant U.S. Attorney slot is opening in Anchorage. Get your bags packed. When we make a deal, we keep it. Do you understand?"

"Yes, ma'am."

"Hey, happy Thanksgiving," Carvelli said to Jeff Johnson as he sat next to him on a bar stool.

"Well, look what the cat dragged in," Bonnie, the woman behind the bar in Artie's, said to Carvelli.

"Hello, lover, how's my girl?" Carvelli replied reaching over the bar to take her hand, pull her forward and give her a kiss.

"My day is perfect, now," she replied. "What can I get you?"

"I'll just have a bottle of Miller," Carvelli said. "And put it on the government's tab," he added pointing at Johnson.

"Let's get a booth," Johnson said.

"Okay, here's the latest and I thought you had a right to know. I have a couple of good friends, contacts, with a certain agency in Langley. The word from them is our dearly departed friend, Damone, and his charming brother are guests of a friendly, Middle Eastern democracy."

Carvelli leaned forward and quietly, incredulously asked, "The Israelis have them?"

"It would seem," Johnson said and tipped his beer to his mouth.

Carvelli rubbed a hand across his mouth and chin while staring across the table. He took a drink, set the bottle down on the table and said, "What the hell is going on?"

"My guy, and I believe him, tells me this whole thing was a CIA and Israeli operation from the beginning. They had Damone wired and an insider on him from the moment he walked out of prison. They knew everything."

"You mean the CIA and Israelis set up a drug cartel to sell opioids to American citizens? If this gets out..."

"There will be hell to pay. But it worked. They found and shut down a huge funding source for Islamic terrorists. And the government is already in the process of quietly cleaning up the mess," Johnson said.

"And you guys weren't in on it?"

"Nope. The FBI and DOJ knew nothing about it. They were fed just enough from the CIA through Homeland Security to keep us investigating for them until they were ready to pull the plug. You know why?"

"Because they no longer trust you," Carvelli said.

"That's right. After the way the last president, his White House, the two AG's and the FBI higher-ups corrupted the FBI, IRS, DOJ and probably NSA, no one in law enforcement or the Intel community can trust us. It will take years to fix the damage the Chicago Democratic Mafia did."

"Holy shit," Carvelli slowly, quietly said. "Keep your head down. The shit could still hit the fan over this."

"Don't I know it."

Carvelli was still thinking about his conversation with Johnson when he got home. He parked the Camaro in the garage then took the narrow sidewalk along the side of the house to the front door. After getting his mail, he used his key to unlock the front door and went in.

The kitchen light was on providing enough light to see. He thought that was a little odd since he did not remember leaving it on.

Carvelli dropped the mail on the wrought iron, glass-topped coffee table in the living room. He took off his leather coat and tossed it on the couch. He took one step toward the kitchen when his entire body went into uncontrollable convulsions. Carvelli's knees buckled and he dropped face down on the carpeted, living room floor.

Despite the excruciating pain, he knew exactly what had happened. And he also knew who did it.

"You'll be okay," Carvelli heard a voice above him say. "Give it a few minutes." He then felt his gun being removed from his holster and heard it being placed on the coffee table.

A hood was roughly placed over his head and a drawstring was used to pull it tight. Then he felt a handcuff snap shut on his left wrist. Carvelli then heard it being attached to the metal grilling on the coffee table.

"Relax, Tony. It's okay if I call you Tony, isn't it?"

Carvelli was still unable to reply, so the voice continued.

"To quote the immortal Virgil Sollozzo from the Godfather: 'What are you worried about? If I wanted to kill you, you'd be dead already.'"

The room went silent for two minutes while Carvelli recovered from the 10,000-volt Taser shot.

When he was able to speak, he said, "Do I have the pleasure of meeting Charles Dudek?"

"Yes, you do. I must admit, Tony, I'm impressed you guys figured it out. Am I getting careless or are you that smart?"

"I know smart people. In fact, it was Marc who figured it out. You should have given him the pleasure of meeting you like this."

Charlie laughed, then said, "I'll keep that in mind. Maybe next time. I'm not sure I'd want to run into his new girlfriend, though."

"Yeah," Carvelli replied. "She can be a problem."

"Listen, I only have a few minutes and I don't want to make a big deal out of this. This is the only warning you'll get.

"Stay away from me. Don't come looking for me. Don't even try to find out who or where I am. There are people in the government who think I should clean this up and I think you're smart enough to know what that means. Relax, I made it clear to them you are not to be bothered. They won't bother you because they will get my wrath."

"I guess I'm supposed to thank you for that," Carvelli said.

"No need. My pleasure. You don't know it, but our paths have crossed before. I like you guys. Especially Maddy. I have a bit of a thing for her. In fact, I'm her guardian angel. I must admit, she and Marc make a nice couple."

"They'll be thrilled to hear that."

Charlie had another good laugh, then said, "Please, heed my warning. I mean none of you any harm."

"No one ever had any intention of coming after you, Charlie, trust me. You scare the hell out of a lot of people, especially me."

"Good. Just so we agree."

Charlie stood up and said, "I have to go. The key for the handcuffs is laying in the middle of your dining room floor. Your rather empty dining room. You need more furniture."

"Thanks for the interior decorating tip," Carvelli said.

Charlie laughed again, then continued. "You'll have to drag or carry the table with you to get the key. Give it a couple minutes and I'll be gone. Take care, Tony, and say hello to everyone. Wish them a Happy Thanksgiving."

Thank you for your patronage. I hope you enjoyed Exquisite Justice.

Dennis Carstens

Email me at: dcarstens514@gmail.com

Also Available on Amazon
Previous Marc Kadella Legal Mystery Courtroom Dramas

The Key to Justice

Desperate Justice

Media Justice

Certain Justice

Personal Justice

Delayed Justice

Political Justice

Insider Justice

Made in the USA
Lexington, KY
19 January 2019